# ECSTASY

## Also by Mary Sharratt

*Summit Avenue*

*The Real Minerva*

*The Vanishing Point*

*Bitch Lit* (coeditor)

*Daughters of the Witching Hill*

*Illuminations*

*The Dark Lady's Mask*

# ECSTASY

## A NOVEL

||||||||||||||||||||||||||||||||||||||||||||

# Mary Sharratt

*Houghton Mifflin Harcourt*

BOSTON    NEW YORK

2018

hmhco.com

*Library of Congress Cataloging-in-Publication Data*
Names: Sharratt, Mary, 1964- author.
Title: Ecstasy : a novel / Mary Sharratt.
Description: Boston : Houghton Mifflin Harcourt, 2018.
Identifiers: LCCN 2017045483 (print) | LCCN 2017051670 (ebook) | ISBN
9780544800922 (ebook) | ISBN 9780544800892 (hardcover)
Subjects: LCSH: Mahler, Alma, 1879-1964 – Fiction. | Mahler, Gustav,
1860-1911 – Fiction. | Composers' spouses – Fiction. | Composers – Fiction. |
Vienna (Austria) – Fiction. | BISAC: FICTION / Historical. | FICTION /
Literary. | GSAFD: Biographical fiction. | Historical fiction.
Classification: LCC PS3569.H3449 (ebook) | LCC PS3569.H3449 E29 2018 (print)
| DDC 813/.54--dc23
LC record available at https://lccn.loc.gov/2017045483

Book design by Chloe Foster

Printed in the United States of America
DOC 10 9 8 7 6 5 4 3 2 1

For Joske, who loves the music of both Mahlers

*I have two souls: I know it.*

*And am I a liar? When he looks at me so happily, what a profound feeling of ecstasy. Is that a lie, too? No, no. I must cast out my other soul. The one which has so far ruled must be banished. I must strive to become a real person, let everything <u>happen to me of its own accord.</u>*

—Alma Maria Schindler's diary, January 16, 1902,
translated by Antony Beaumont

# PRELUDE

||||||||||||||||||||

## January 1899
## THERESIANUMGASSE
## VIENNA'S FOURTH DISTRICT

Nineteen years old, Alma Maria Schindler longed body and soul for an awakening. In the family parlor, redolent with the perfume of hothouse lilies, she sat at her piano and composed a new song.

*"Ich wandle unter Blumen und blühe selber mit,"* she sang, as she played. *I wandered among flowers and blossomed with them.*

The lyrics were from a poem by Heinrich Heine, but the music was entirely her own. Closing her eyes, Alma let the song play itself, as though it were a living creature she had birthed and let loose in the world. Whether her music was any good or not, she had no idea, but it shimmered with passion poured straight from her heart. Painters, like her late father, the great Emil Schindler, revealed the innermost workings of their souls with brushstrokes, bold or delicate. The piano was her canvas, her notes the play of light and dark, color and texture.

"*My* art," Alma whispered, and then jumped to see her sister, Gretl, one year younger, watching from the open doorway.

Still in her dressing gown although it was two in the afternoon, Gretl seemed to be nursing another headache. But instead of scolding Alma for making such a racket, she sat in the armchair beside the piano and asked her to play the song once more.

"It's uncanny," Gretl said, when Alma had finished. She gazed down at the book of lyric verse opened to the Heine piece Alma had chosen. "You always find a poem that expresses what's inside you. Anyone who hears this song will know you as well as I. It's that intimate."

Her sister's face was as pale as the lilies in their vase, and her dark eyes were fixed on Alma with a solemn scrutiny that unnerved her.

Alma searched for a lighthearted reply. "That explains why my lieder are so introspective! No jolly, thigh-slapping folk songs for me then."

To her relief, Gretl's mood seemed to lift and they laughed together.

"Just imagine," Gretl said, thumbing through the red-leather-bound Baedeker travel guide on the side table. "Another seven weeks and we're off to Italy! I can hardly wait to leave this dreary snow behind." At that, she went off to dress.

Alma played her song again, adding subtle variations to the theme. Joy seized her, a buoyancy that blossomed inside her. Losing herself in the labyrinth of sound, she allowed her yearnings to soar. *If only I were a somebody.* Oh, to compose an opera, a truly great one—something no woman had ever done. She would call her opera *Ver Sacrum,* sacred spring, after the journal of the Secession art movement. Her stepfather, Carl Moll, was the Secession's vice president. His paintings lined the parlor walls along with those of his colleagues and friends. Gustav Klimt. Max Klinger. Fernand Khnopff. Koloman Moser's exquisitely framed letterpress print spelled out the Secession's motto.

*To every age its art.*
*To every art its freedom.*

*Freedom,* Alma exulted. Her stepfather's circle was the vanguard, the cutting edge. They had defied the rigid conventions of the academy to create their own unique styles. After this break from tradition, the arts could never be the same again. As hidebound and conservative as Austria might be, with its emperor who seemed to live forever through every scandal and revolution, Vienna was a bubbling font of artistic innovation. *Ver sacrum, indeed!* Not only were there avant-garde painters and architects, reform dress that liberated women's bodies from crippling corsets, and new writers such as Hugo von Hofmannsthal, but there were also young composers. With her entire being, Alma longed to leave her mark among these blazing new talents. Oh, to compose symphonies and operas that truly expressed the spirit of this modern age! How she longed for the vision and strength to see her dreams reach fruition.

*Help me, divine power,* she prayed, she who had disavowed all formal religion. *Guide me. See me through. May I suffer no hindrance in the battle against my weakness. My femininity.*

Suite 1

# LIEBESTOD

# 1

||||||||||||||||||||||||||||

## May 1899
## VENICE

*ere is where my awakening shall occur,* Alma told herself. In magical Venice, in the spring of the year and the spring of her life. Never mind that it was pouring rain and fog hung as thickly as wool.

In the hotel salon, she played piano, accompanying her mother who sang lieder to entertain their fellow tourists sheltering from the miserable weather. How beautiful was her mother's soprano, how flawless her diction. Mama had been an opera singer before she married Alma's father, now almost seven years dead.

At the song's close came a burst of applause. Alma beamed at her audience. Sitting among the English and German tourists were Gretl; their step-father, Carl; and his colleague Gustav Klimt, who seemed to regard Alma with amused speculation. For Easter, Herr Klimt had given her a silly card of a shepherdess encircled by adoring sheep sporting gentlemen's hats—Alma kept it tucked in her journal.

*He is so handsome,* she thought, heat rising in her face. With his powerful body, his curly hair and beard, he reminded her of the figures on ancient Greek vases. If Gustav Klimt had even the faintest clue how infatuated she was, she would die. Thirty-seven years old, the most celebrated painter in all Vienna, he could marry a countess just by snapping his fingers.

Nonetheless, Alma made herself stare right back at him to prove she wasn't some giddy girl he could disarm with a smile.

Her stepfather was so fond of Klimt, he had all but begged him to join them on their journey through Italy even though Klimt swore that he hated foreign travel and was terrible with languages. As a painter, Carl was no-where near as brilliant as Klimt—or Emil Schindler, whose protégé Carl had been. *Klimt and Papa are giants,* Alma told herself. But Carl was a lesser talent who hung on to the coattails of the great in hope that some of their glory might rub off on him. It wasn't that her stepfather was a bad man, but Alma often wondered why Mama seemed to worship him.

Alma set her sights higher. Nothing less than a man of brilliance would do for her, a truly modern man who understood her need to continue composing even after she was married. She wasn't one, like her sister, to settle for the very first suitor. Gretl was engaged to the tedious Wilhelm Legler, a painter of almost numbing mediocrity. No, Alma vowed to wait for the right man, the one whose love would help her unfold to her highest purpose.

Rising from the piano bench, Alma was gathering up her music scores when an elderly English lady approached her.

"Fräulein, you played so beautifully, like a concert pianist," she said. "Tell me, who was the composer?"

"I am," Alma replied. She lowered her eyes.

"My daughter composed all eight lieder we performed," Mama added, with warmth and pride.

The English lady seemed most impressed. She grasped Alma's hands. "Keep on composing, won't you, dear? Show the men that we women can achieve something."

Alma found herself flushing and speechless, seized with both a bottomless joy and an ambition that left her breathless. Many a girl showed talent and promise only to give it up for marriage, as Mama had done when she was only twenty-one and pregnant—out of wedlock!—with Alma. But wasn't a new age dawning, all the rules for art, music, and society changing at once?

As the English lady and her companions took their leave, Gretl an-nounced that she was dying for a game of whist, so Mama and Carl sat down with her at the card table. But Alma could think of no pastime more deadening to the intellect and spirit. Mumbling her excuses, she carried her music scores upstairs to the room that she and Gretl were sharing.

Closing the door behind her, Alma sank into an armchair and buried herself in Flaubert's *Madame Bovary,* which Mama considered unseemly for a young girl. But Mama had long given up trying to control what Alma read. *You're so stubborn,* her mother was always saying. *So boneheaded.*

Yet truth be told, Alma was rapidly losing patience with Emma Bovary. She found the character incomprehensible. Her madness, her degrading love affairs, her endless lying to herself and others—was this woman flighty, cowardly, or simply coarse and common?

Tossing the book aside, Alma opened the French doors and stepped out on the balcony to breathe in the fresh, cool air now that the rain had finally let up. The canal below was gray with a shimmer of yellow as the sun broke through gaps in the fog. Gray was her favorite color, the way it so seamlessly merged with other hues. An artist's daughter, she observed how every raindrop on the balcony rail became a gleaming pearl. The crumbling palazzos across the canal seemed almost rosy. Everything flickered and glowed in dreamy gray light.

Hearing a noise in the room, Alma left the balcony and stepped inside.

"Gretl?" she called. She had left the door unlocked since her sister was always forgetting her key.

Instead, she found Gustav Klimt standing in the middle of her room. Her heart began to pound even as she told herself that he must be looking for Carl and had wandered in here by mistake.

"Alma," he said. "Are you on your own?"

"Why, yes," she said, without thinking. "The others are—"

Before she could finish her sentence, Klimt crossed the room in two huge strides. A gasp caught in her throat as he pulled her body against his, kissing her with vehemence and heat, his lips firm and insistent, his beard bristling against her chin. Her first kiss.

What magic was this? It was as though her hidden longing had summoned him straight into her embrace. Time seemed to drop away, everything

5

before or after this single moment diminishing into nothingness as the ecstasy surged inside her, crashing like a wave inside her heart.

Klimt cupped her face to his. "I could see all the passion locked inside you while you were playing the piano. The time has come to set it free."

She trembled just to gaze into his gray-green eyes.

"Love me," he whispered, running his fingers around her lips.

She tenderly caressed his hair, feeling the thick, springy curls twining around her fingertips. She kissed him with a hunger that left her aching. The soft quivering in her belly and knees was countered by a shooting heat, a rising energy that made her want to dance. But instead of losing herself in her frenzy, she made herself slow down, kissing him with deliberation, savoring each nuance of his lips against hers, her chest against his, their lungs swelling in unison as if sharing the same breath. All the dusty descriptions of love scenes she had read in *Madame Bovary* and elsewhere seemed meaningless now. *This* was what passion, what awakening, truly was.

When Klimt asked if he could take out her hairpins, Alma nodded, moved beyond speech. He pulled them out one by one until her brown hair fell over her shoulders like a cloak. As if in holy awe, Klimt drew back and stared.

"How I long to paint you."

He positioned her before the full-length mirror. His arm around her waist, he stood behind her, looking over her shoulder. When their eyes met in the mirror, he commanded her to look at herself, as though he, the artist, were revealing her own image to her for the very first time. Alma squirmed but couldn't take her eyes off the mirror, for this was as exciting as it was uncomfortable.

*This is what men see when they look at me.* Tall, she stood shoulder to shoulder with Klimt. Her face was flushed with yearning, her blue eyes huge, blinking rapidly.

"You are so ripe and voluptuous," he said, drawing her attention to her waving tresses flowing over her breasts. His hands traced the curve of her hips. Swinging her around to face him again, he stroked her hair.

"Alma," he said. "My little wife."

*Oh, to marry Klimt.*

A sweet ache bloomed inside her as they kissed, his tongue flicking between her teeth. Then she jolted at the sound of Mama's and Carl's voices in the adjoining room. Before Alma could think what to say or do, Klimt vanished, leaving her shaking and alone with her undone hair.

Moments later, Gretl sauntered in and looked at Alma as though she'd caught her sleepwalking.

"What, so dishabille in the afternoon?" her sister cried. "Did you catch the swamp fever? Mama says we must get ready and meet downstairs in a quarter of an hour. With any luck, Herr Klimt will come sightseeing with us."

"What's ailing you, Alma?" Mama asked, as they ambled across the Piazza San Marco. "There's such a high color in your face. You look feverish."

"Maybe it's something I ate," Alma managed, her heart beating hard and fast.

To think her mother could tell with just one glance that she was forever changed. She didn't feel feverish as much as electrified. The fog had cleared and the blue sky opened into infinity. All around her Italian voices lilted like minuets. Ah, the gorgeous chaos of this square with its accordion players and acrobats and boisterous families and whispering lovers. This sense of utter freedom and levity was something Alma could have never experienced back in Vienna, where every single aspect of existence was so regimented, where even the parks were walled and gated, and it was forbidden to sit on the grass. Possessed by a whimsical abandon, she could barely keep herself from skipping and leaping like the laughing children racing one another across the cobblestones.

"Perhaps we better go back if Alma's not well," Mama said to Carl. "She should lie down and rest."

"Nonsense," said Carl, in his usual hearty fashion. "Fresh air and exercise will do her a world of good."

Klimt trailed behind Alma, the heat of his very presence warming her back. Her lips felt swollen, inflamed from his kisses. *Alma, my little wife.* Mama said it was time he was married. Alma's heart soared—was *this* why Klimt had allowed Carl to entice him on this trip even though he despised travel—because he wanted to court her? Perhaps Mama and Carl were even encouraging him—why wouldn't they want to see her married to the president of the Secession movement? As his wife, Alma would compose operas as magnificent as his paintings.

Klimt fell into pace with Alma and took her arm. "Do you feel out of sorts, my dear?"

Alma offered him a secret smile and nodded.

"I am as well," he said under his breath. "You know, there's only one cure."

"What's that?" she heard herself ask, reveling in the strength of his muscled arm.

"Complete physical union," he whispered.

If he hadn't been supporting her, she would have tripped over her skirts and tumbled face-first. She and Klimt pressed on, disturbing a flock of pigeons that took to flight in a flutter of countless wings, gray feathers stroking soft spring air.

Then Carl claimed Klimt's attention, and Alma burst forward on her own, past Mama and Gretl, into the great doors of Saint Mark's Basilica. Trying to master the storm of sensation exploding inside her, she threw back her head to take in the ancient mosaics filling every cupola. Never had she seen so much gold or magnificence—but even that was not enough to put Klimt out of her mind.

"This is more beautiful than Saint Peter's in Rome," Alma said, when Mama finally caught up with her. She hoped to at least sound like her usual self.

A few weeks ago, her family had attended Easter High Mass at Saint Peter's, an experience that Alma viewed as the greatest ecclesiastical swindle of all time — so much empty pomp. After studying the works of Nietzsche, she considered religion a ludicrous throwback from an authoritarian past, irrelevant in this modern world of science and progress. It was up to every intelligent man and woman to make their own moral choices rather than slavishly obeying priests. Yet this basilica moved her to spiritual contemplation.

She lifted her face to the Dome of the Holy Spirit, where dove's blood streamed down to anoint the heads of saints, filling them with Pentecostal fire. *This mosaic is a revelation,* she thought, *of what is unfolding inside me.* Her soul ignited with sacred love and reverence merging with the profane carnal flame that flickered inside her. When two souls met in love, how could it not be holy? *Complete physical union.* Alma's hammering pulse sent her head swimming. *Oh, to live, to truly live.*

When Mama and Gretl wandered off, Alma found herself entranced with the mosaics of the life of Saint Mark over the high altar. She swallowed a cry when Klimt appeared beside her, as if stepping out of thin air.

"I want to paint you dripping in pure gold leaf," he said, taking her hand. "Like a saint in ecstasy."

His face was so close to hers, she wondered if he would kiss her right there in the basilica.

"You vixen," he said, kissing her, his tongue parting her lips. "You know I can't resist you when you look at me like that."

This time, after a furtive look around, she kissed him back before drawing away, which only made him step closer.

"No one can say we didn't stand together at the altar," he whispered.

As they exchanged smiles, laughter rose inside her. *To be loved by Gustav Klimt.*

"Come," he said, squeezing her hand. "Time to join the others."

Carl decided they would take refreshment at Caffè Florian, where they shared two bottles of Asti Spumante between the five of them. Then they headed back to the hotel for dinner. Alma, her arm linked with Klimt's, brought up the rear, close enough to Mama and Carl to appear completely respectable. Her secret tingled inside her like champagne bubbles bursting on her tongue.

In the soft May twilight, they all stopped on a bridge to view the arch of the Ponte dei Sospiri, the Bridge of Sighs. Gretl, meanwhile, complained of a terrible headache and charged forward, giving Mama and Carl no choice but to follow. Alma prepared to walk on as well, but Klimt stood as if rooted and wouldn't release her hand. She shivered at the touch of his fingers digging into the high collar of her shirtwaist. When he leaned her back against the stone parapet, she felt her neckline tighten, constricting her throat. She had no clue how to respond, and now the others had disappeared around a corner. His gray-green eyes appeared to her as an ocean of desire as his fingers traced the tender hollow between her collarbones, the delicate flesh covering her breastbone. *In Vienna, he would have never dared take such liberties,* she thought. But here in Venice, anything could happen. Every rule and even time dissolved in the briny waters of the lapping lagoon.

"Alma!" Her mother was calling from somewhere beyond a flower cart.

Klimt let go of Alma's collar only to pinch her arm and kiss her lips.

"Silly girl," he said. "If I'd wanted to, I could have laid my hands on your heart."

She flushed when she understood that what he meant by heart was actually her breasts. Then, fighting to regain her composure, she found herself staring not into Klimt's eyes but Mama's. Her mother's mouth was a pale tight line. Behind Mama, Carl looked at Alma and then at Klimt in utter incomprehension. Gretl shook her head at Alma as if to tell her what a fool she was.

"Alma," Mama said crisply. "Why don't you walk on Carl's arm? *I* shall walk with Herr Klimt."

When her mother was angry, her northern German accent grew more pronounced. Mama hailed from Hamburg. Her father was a failed brewer, so Mama had been forced to make do and earn her own living as an opera singer when she was a girl. Now her mother resembled an avenging Valkyrie. Even Klimt seemed to cower in the face of Mama's rage.

"How could you be so naïve, a bright girl like you?" Mama demanded.

Alma and her mother were alone in the room her mother shared with Carl. Through the thin walls, Alma could hear Gretl pacing in the adjoining room—her sister would hear every word. As for Carl, he would be off somewhere with Klimt, trying to smooth things over. Carl, the eternal sycophant, torn between family honor and his horror of alienating his most important colleague. But Mama was clearly not conflicted in the least. All artistic gradations of gray were lost to her mother, who seemed to view the world in stark black-and-white.

"Gustav Klimt is a womanizer." Mama gripped Alma's shoulders as though to make those words sink in. "He has no business toying with you. I hope you didn't encourage him."

Alma burned and wept, still in the thrall of Klimt's kiss, of his fingers that had played her breastbone as if it were a flute. How could Mama be such a hypocrite? Had she herself not fallen in love with a great artist, Emil Schindler, and surrendered body and soul to him before they were married? That was how her mother had conceived her, for God's sake. There were darker rumors —namely that Mama had an affair with Papa's friend, the artist Julius Victor Berger, and that Gretl, christened Margarethe Julia, was that man's child.

How Alma yearned for her dead father. He had given her Goethe's *Faust* to read when she was only eight, as if acknowledging her as a prodigy, his equal. If Papa was still alive, her life would be so different. They would probably still be living in Schloss Plankenberg, that run-down rented castle fifty miles west of Vienna where they had lived like true bohemians, far removed from Carl's world of social climbing and bourgeois pretensions. She imagined Papa giving her and Klimt his blessing.

"Herr Klimt and I are in love," Alma heard herself declare in tremulous defiance.

"Don't be so stupid," Mama said, her words as stinging as a slap on the cheek. "The man has syphilis! He always has at least three love affairs running at the same time. Why do you think I never let you visit his studio? Because it's no better than a brothel with his naked models prancing around. *Two* of those poor girls are pregnant by him. The man is obsessively in love with his *sister-in-law.*"

*Klimt is a bohemian freethinker,* Alma told herself, *and no doubt he's had love affairs, but surely he can't be as debauched as Mama claims.* Her mother made him sound like a scoundrel from a penny dreadful. Would Carl have invited Klimt to join them on their travels if the man was truly so fiendish?

"He called me his little wife," Alma said, desperate to sound reasonable despite the tears running down her face. "You yourself said it was high time he married."

"Marry someone rich and experienced perhaps, but not an innocent girl like you." Mama sighed. "Did you know he's already supporting his mother and sister, and his sisters-in-law and his niece? Insanity runs in his family! His mother and sister are mentally unbalanced. One day he'll go mad himself. Just look in his eyes, Alma. There's something crazy about him."

Alma was beginning to feel half-crazed herself as Mama's disclosures pierced her like flaming arrows. The illustrious Gustav Klimt was merely a degenerate seducer? But that kiss! How could she ever forget his kiss that had transformed her in one shuddering gasp from a girl into a woman who had tasted the ecstasy of desire?

Both she and Mama spun around as Carl strode in, stinking of cigar smoke.

"Klimt has agreed to return to Vienna tomorrow," her stepfather announced, rubbing his hands as though washing them of any unpleasantness. He faced Alma squarely. "In the morning, you'll shake his hand civilly and bid him farewell. He assured me this was just a dalliance, quite regrettable, of course. He apologized profusely and promised to leave you alone."

"A *dalliance?*" Alma thought her shame would set her entire body on fire, immolating her on the spot.

"I told you as much," Mama said in a tired voice, as though her tirade had exhausted her.

"Why must you take it all so seriously?" Carl asked, as Alma collapsed sobbing on her mother's bed. "Weren't you just being a flirt?"

At some stage everyone must die a secret death. Her face raw from weeping, Alma lay awake in the bed she was sharing with Gretl, who snored away, lulled into deepest sleep by the laudanum their house doctor prescribed for her headaches. Klimt's betrayal, his casual dismissal of what had unfolded between them, plunged Alma into a hell of self-loathing. Smug little demons, as relentless as the mosquitoes whining in her ears, parroted her mother's exhortations: *How could you be so naïve?* Her first kiss, the first time she'd ever truly fallen in love—must it end like this?

Worst of all was the conundrum of the desire Klimt had awakened in her that was coupled with the gaping canyon of her own ignorance. It was as though he had led her to the very threshold of that forbidden paradise, let her taste a single drop of that most exquisite nectar, then slammed the door in her face and left her there. An overwrought and humiliated virgin.

Any young man of her age and class would have unburdened himself in the brothels by now, but because she was a girl from a prominent family, she was expected to carry her frustration to her marriage bed. Marriage now seemed as nebulous and distant as the Pleiades.

Back in Vienna there had been the young artists and intellectuals who frequented her stepfather's salon, those young men who flattered her and vied for her attention across the linen-draped table. But not one of them had dazzled her to her very core the way Klimt had. None had presumed to kiss her. The flirting, the pleasantries, had all seemed a game to her, like dancing with different partners at a ball, everything refreshingly light and frivolous without the pressure of having to choose one and forsake all the others.

But Mama said it was time Alma learned to be sensible and pick one young man from that glittering circle. *Listen, Alma, you're at the height of your beauty. You're in demand. Make up your mind! But try not to intimidate them,*

13

*my dear. You can be so bold and opinionated.* Perhaps if she was less ambitious about her music or learned to conceal it the way Gretl hid her sketchbook to better fawn over Wilhelm Legler's lugubrious oil paintings. But how, Alma wondered, was she to make the right choice of a suitor when she knew so little about the physical realities of love?

She seethed with a lust that shook her to her fingertips. *There's only one cure,* Klimt had told her. If he appeared by her bedside, she would let him do whatever he wanted even in the face of her anguish and his duplicity. She would run her tongue over his salty flesh, bite him, devour him, make him hers. But she must go unsated. As for touching herself, that was too appalling to even consider. Such acts were the province of the insane and morally depraved—and those who didn't share a bed with their sister.

If only she could cool her scalded fingers on smooth ivory piano keys. She was tempted to creep down to the parlor and pound out the entire score of Wagner's opera *Tristan und Isolde* even if she woke up every soul in the hotel. Let her leave Klimt as sleepless and churned up as she was. She imagined playing the "Liebestod" theme until she was utterly spent. The sole way out of this wretchedness was to channel all her longing into what she *could* control, her own music.

Her thoughts wandered back to her recital that afternoon before Klimt's kiss and her undoing. The English lady's cornflower eyes meeting hers as though this stranger were a kindly godmother or even a prophetess. *Keep on composing, won't you, dear? Show the men we women can achieve something.* Let her show Klimt that she had a gift that no man could take from her.

# 2

||||||||||||||||||||||||||

**N**obody in the world is more spoiled than Gustav Klimt. Alma thought she would choke on the hypocrisy of it all. At Carl's behest, she, Mama, and Gretl went to the Rialto market to buy Klimt farewell presents. Then her family treated Klimt to a heavy lunch. Her head muddled from Asti Spumante, Alma sat at the far end of the table from Klimt and hardly glanced up from the plate of octopus risotto she couldn't bring herself to eat. Then, after the bitter, scalding espresso she made herself swallow in one gulp, her family saw Klimt off to the train station.

Her face rigid from the effort of not letting him see her cry, she and Gretl surrendered their offerings of wine and cheese, chocolates and pastilles, bread rolls and the thick, greasy sausage Alma hoped he would gag on. Aware of Mama and Carl's eyes on her, Alma shook Klimt's hand. Her fingers quivered in his too-tight grip as he gazed into her eyes soulfully, as though their abrupt parting devastated him. Could he truly be so two-faced?

"Keep a place in your heart for me, Alma," he whispered. "Just a tiny one."

Did he think he could string her along with promises he could never keep? Did he think so little of her, as though she had no pride at all?

"This has to stop," she said, drawing her spine upright. *Remember, you stand as tall as he.*

"Yes," he said, twisting his face as though she had struck him. "It was stillborn."

With a curt nod, she stepped away from him and stood with her family while watching him board the train.

When the locomotive departed in a belch of black smoke, Carl clapped her shoulder, nearly knocking her sideways. "Well done, Alma. Tonight we'll toast your prudence and good sense!"

Parasol clenched in her fist, Alma marched along the lido where listless waves smacked the sandy shore. Ahead of her, Gretl and Carl shared some joke and laughed as though all was well in the world. Mama walked close beside her, as if not trusting her enough to let her out of her sight. Alma poured her entire effort into appearing stoical. If she shed a single tear, she feared Mama would start off on her again. *He doesn't really love you, Alma. Don't deceive yourself!*

Up and down the beach, Italian families took pleasure in their Sunday promenade, the little girls decked out in their white dresses and lacy veils, having celebrated their first communion. It still wasn't warm enough for proper swimming—only a few intrepid souls braved the water, their heads bobbing like jetsam. *The sea is so vast,* Alma thought, *and human beings are so terribly small and ineffectual. Why do we even create?* What would become of her energy, her dreams, her passions—would they just wither away as she learned to be *sensible?*

A young Venetian lady strummed a mandolin and sang in an achingly beautiful voice. Although Alma didn't understand the lyrics, the mournful melody touched her deepest pain, and she thought she might break down for all the world to see. She had been kissed and then told it meant absolutely nothing. She had been awakened only to be brusquely commanded to go back to sleep. She was of no consequence. Just a naïve, easily led girl.

"Alma, there's something I must tell you," Mama said.

She braced herself for yet another lecture, but what Mama said next made the horizon dip and fall.

"I'm expecting a baby in August," her mother said, as matter-of-factly as if telling her they would board the eight-thirty express train to Trieste in the morning.

A baby in August—it was already May. Alma's birthday was in August. Her new sibling would be twenty years younger than she was—it seemed absurd. *How is it possible that I was too dim to even notice?* Alma's eyes passed surreptitiously over her mother's stoutish figure. Mama had always been thick around the waist and corseted herself accordingly, but it was true she seemed a little more cumbersome now, especially in the way she walked.

"Why didn't you say anything earlier?" Alma asked, her temples pounding.

Mama's eyes drifted off over the Adriatic. "I was pregnant twice last year, but I lost those babies. I wanted to make sure this wouldn't be a miscarriage before I said anything."

How unnerving it was to be confronted with this window into Mama's private female travails. To think an unborn baby was something you could simply lose. Alma imagined a phantom infant flying off into the ether, borne on angel wings like a macabre cherub. Once more she felt throttled by her own ignorance. *When will I ever stop feeling like a backward child?*

"Gretl already knows," Mama said, twisting the blade.

How long had Gretl been holding this knowledge over her head, Alma wondered wretchedly.

"Your sister saw me getting sick one morning," her mother explained, "while you were playing the piano."

So it was her music that had kept her ignorant. Alma asked herself, with a guilty start, if this was such a bad thing.

"But Mama, you're forty," she blurted out.

"Forty-one," her mother said irritably. "Even women as ancient as I can have babies, you know."

"But it's dangerous."

The tears Alma had been holding back all day fell freely. To lose a would-be lover was one thing, but to lose her *mother?* The older the woman, the riskier the birth. She was seized with hatred for Carl for doing this to Mama. Surely her mother shouldn't have to endure childbirth at her age. *But, you fool, that's what men do. Men make love to women, who have their babies.* Alma was forced to admit that she didn't care for babies at all. She realized she wanted the impossible — to love the way a man would love, with no fear of betraying her own body in the process.

Alma enclosed her mother in a tight embrace, as if that could keep her safe.

"I shall have a quiet summer," Mama said, hugging her back. "While you and Gretl go to the mountains, I shall stay behind in Vienna and rest."

"What's all this?" Carl's booming voice made Alma grit her teeth. "Is that girl in hysterics again? Let your poor mother breathe."

Shaking in anger, Alma couldn't even look him in the eye.

"I was telling Alma about the baby," Mama said brightly, taking her husband's arm.

Gretl rolled her eyes. "Alma with her head in the clouds. Always the last to know."

# 3

‖‖‖‖‖‖‖‖‖‖‖‖‖‖‖‖‖‖‖

Back home once more, Alma played piano. Steeped in concentration, she gave herself wholly to the prelude and "Liebestod" from Wagner's *Tristan und Isolde* while her music teacher, Adele Radnitzky-Mandlick, looked on. Alma had been studying with her since the age of twelve. They had become so close, she called her Frau Adele. How Alma reveled in this deep immersion in music, her consolation and refuge. The one still point amid her turmoil as she struggled to forget Klimt and reconcile herself to the changes in her family. Mama had commandeered Alma's bedroom for the new nursery, thus obliging Alma to move into Gretl's room. It would be only a temporary inconvenience, Mama had argued, seeing as Gretl would be married next September. Still, this meant that Alma and her sister would be cooped up together for more than a year as their home seemed to shrink around them.

"Absolutely sublime," Frau Adele said, when Alma had finished. "I don't think I've ever heard a more nuanced interpretation."

Frau Adele, her guardian angel. Her teacher was an elegant woman in her thirties who earned her living as a musical mentor of promising young women. Her recitals showcasing her protégées were famous. Some months ago, Alma had performed in the neo-Renaissance concert hall in the Palais Ehrbar and received resounding applause and praise. The *Neue Freie Presse* had declared her brilliant, a rare talent.

"I'm both sad and delighted to inform you that I have nothing left to teach you." Frau Adele's smile indicated that this was the greatest honor any of her students could bestow on her. "You have reached the point where you're ready to take it a step further."

Alma leaned forward, her heart trilling in hope.

"You're now ready to study with my teacher," Frau Adele said. "Dr. Julius Epstein at the Vienna Conservatory."

Alma leapt off the piano bench and breathlessly hugged her teacher.

"Go get your parents, my dear," Frau Adele said. "We must talk it through with them."

Her head swimming with euphoria, Alma dashed off to find Mama. Her shoes clattered on the polished wooden floor. Mama would scold her for making scuff marks. Their family had lived in this house for four years, but it still didn't feel like home to Alma—it seemed too sterile and new, built by Julius Mayreder to Carl's specifications and decorated to Carl's tastes. His Japanese and Chinese porcelain cluttered the cabinets designed by Koloman Moser. *All so curated and self-conscious,* Alma thought. The residence of an aspiring patrician.

Alma found her mother in the sewing room, the one place besides Alma and Gretl's room that remained free from her stepfather's aesthetics.

"Mama!" She pulled her mother up from her wicker chair so abruptly that her knitting tumbled from her hands. "Frau Adele says I'm ready for the conservatory!" Alma had every expectation of her mother's blessing. Mama herself had studied voice there. "Come, she wants to speak to you."

Grabbing Mama's hand, Alma tried to rush her back to the parlor, but pregnancy made her mother's progress cumbersome and slow.

"I'll go talk to her," Mama said, pulling her hand free. "You fetch Carl."

Alma felt her stomach drop. "Why?" Why did her stepfather have to butt his head into everything, even her dream of becoming a great composer?

"You know very well *why,*" Mama said. "He controls the purse strings."

With a sigh, Alma stalked off down the stairs, out the back door, and down the gravel path to her stepfather's studio in the back garden. Its huge windows ran nearly the entire length and breadth of the walls. Alma's resentment bubbled like witch's brew. *Gretl and I must share a room because he impregnated our mother. But he gets an entire freestanding building to himself.* His studio was as big as a laborer's cottage. And there he worked on his canvases, pretending to be a great painter while, in fact, he earned most of his money dealing in other people's art. The vice president of the Secession.

Try as she might, Alma couldn't take him seriously as a father figure. He was four years younger than Mama. Only eighteen years older than Alma was. But she arranged her face in an expression of stepdaughterly affection as she knocked on his studio door and stepped inside. Smiling as sweetly as she could, she took his arm and coaxed him away from his unfinished still life.

Cilli, the maid, served coffee and apricot streusel while Frau Adele stated her case to Mama and Carl. Alma perched on her chair, her sweating hands clasped in hope.

"Alma's nineteen, the perfect age to begin a serious course of study," her teacher said. "As it stands, she's a very talented amateur. But she has the potential to become a professional. With her virtuosity, she belongs in the concert hall."

*I'll study with Dr. Epstein! I'll write symphonies and operas!* Alma saw her future beckon like a glimmering castle on the horizon.

"I'm sorry to say our finances are tight at the moment." Carl lifted his palms in apology. "You must understand, Frau Radnitzky, we have another child on the way and Gretl's wedding to pay for. It's not as though Alma will have to support herself with her music. A girl as pretty as my stepdaughter will be married in a few years."

A white-hot rage climbed up Alma's throat. Ignoring Carl, she appealed to Mama. "*You* went to the conservatory!"

"I received a stipendium," Mama said quietly. "And in those days, I *did* have to earn my living at the opera. Life is so much easier for you, my dear, thanks to Carl looking after us all."

Alma reeled from her mother's betrayal.

"Besides," Mama said. "You told me you didn't like performing on stage and being on display."

"But to not even have a chance," Alma said, trying her best not to cry. "What about Ilse Conrat? She's studying sculpture in Brussels. *Her* parents—"

"Are rich," Mama said. "We, alas, need to think about economy." She reached forward to pat Alma's arm. "Of course, you'll still continue your composition lessons with Josef Labor. There's nothing wrong with being a talented amateur, Alma. We're so proud of your accomplishments, aren't we, Carl?"

Alma blinked back her tears and looked at Frau Adele. Her teacher appeared disappointed but resigned, as though this was not the first such exchange she had witnessed.

"Keep on playing like a virtuosa," Frau Adele said when Alma saw her to the door. "And do keep up your lessons with Herr Labor. You owe it to yourself, Alma Maria Schindler. You have a gift."

Alma shook her teacher's hand and kissed her cheek. After saying goodbye and closing the door, she thundered up the stairs in a flood of tears. In truth, she had expected no better of Carl, but how could her own mother so abruptly dismiss her dreams of being anything more than a dilettante?

Mama planted herself at the top of the stairs. When Alma tried to dash past her, her mother took her arms and tried to hug her. "I'm so sorry, dear. But you don't want to be like those Conrat girls. You know what people say about them." Not only was Ilse an aspiring sculptor, but her younger sister, Erica, intended to study at the university. "Bluestockings aren't taken seriously as women—they're too mannish." Mama dropped her voice and reddened. "The third sex."

Pulling away from her mother, Alma ran into her and Gretl's room—blessedly, her sister was out. She hurled herself on her bed. As hard as she tried to banish her mother's words, the curse of becoming one of the third sex terrified her. Alma had to admit she was both fascinated and intimidated by the Conrat sisters. They put their femininity to the side to pursue years of lonely, dusty striving, yet they'd be lucky to receive even a portion of the regard heaped on men who walked the same path. And so they would doom themselves, Mama seemed to imply. Despised as the monstrous third sex, they would exile themselves from the comforts other women enjoyed. Namely love, marriage, and motherhood. And yet the thought of having to marry a man like Carl made Alma want to claw off her own skin.

*Where on this earth do I belong?* Mama was right in one thing, Alma was forced to admit—she didn't enjoy performing in public. She hated the savage competitiveness among Frau Adele's other students, and she would not be content with a career of merely interpreting other people's music. No, music for Alma was something deeply intimate. Her essence. Her soul. More than anything, she dreamed of transforming her innermost emotions into cathedrals of sound.

*I won't be bullied away from my music or my dreams. I shall persevere.* If one door was now closed to her, another remained open. Alma would devote her entire being to writing her own music.

The very next day Alma set to work composing a fantasia arranged around the leitmotif that kept surfacing in her diary: *Loneliness is my destiny, for I feed off my own thoughts.*

Meanwhile, Gretl, with an obsession bordering on mania, sat in the corner copying recipes into a book. Only a year ago her sister would have filled that selfsame book with her sketches. Was this what it meant to be a grown woman—abandoning any pretense of making anything of yourself just so you could serve your husband the perfect plate of *Tafelspitz*? But at least Gretl was moving forward in life instead of being left behind like Alma. *Now that Mama and Carl are starting a new family, it's time for us to move on,* Gretl had said smartly—Gretl, who seemed only to look to her future when she would be married.

Not for the first time Alma wished she were a young man who could take his share of the family money and go his own way. The problem was there wasn't much in the way of family money. Emil Schindler's only fault was that he'd had no head for finance. He hadn't even managed to write a will. After he died, everything had gone to Mama, and now everything of Mama's belonged to Carl. *Gretl and I are reduced to living off of Carl Moll's charity, with nothing to call our own.*

"Alma, those chords are so strident." Gretl looked up from her recipes. Dark circles shadowed her sister's eyes. "You're giving me a headache. Can you play something more cheerful? Mozart would be nice."

Exasperated, Alma rose from the piano. The parlor's claustrophobic walls closed in as if to smother her.

# 4

||||||||||||||||||||||||||||||

Sometimes Alma felt as though she had two separate selves. On the evening of Berta Zuckerkandl's party, when she glided into her hostess's salon in her white crepe-de-chine gown, Alma became another person. The lonely, cerebral girl brimming with self-doubt was left behind and a vibrant young lady took her place. This Alma sparkled in her confidence that she could win every heart in that room.

Men danced around her, moths drawn to her flame, and she breathed in their attention as if it were oxygen. Koloman Moser hailed her. The architects Joseph Maria Olbrich and Josef Hoffmann, who had designed the brand-new Secession Museum, enveloped her in a flurry of pleasantries. The Belgian painter Fernand Khnopff kissed her cheeks, and the smolderingly handsome diplomat Alfred Rappaport kissed her hand. If only Klimt was here to witness her triumph.

Each man was like a different door she might open, through which she might enter into a whole new world. What future life would be most enchanting—to follow Khnopff back to Brussels or go against Carl's wishes and marry Rappaport, a Jew, and be a diplomat's wife whose home was the great world itself?

Alma turned to Joseph Maria Olbrich, that dear earnest fellow, who had just accepted a lucrative new post in Darmstadt, Germany. "Of course, I shall miss all my friends in Vienna," he said, taking her hand. "But more than anything, I shall miss you, Alma."

He gazed at her with such devotion. Unlike Klimt, this was a man she could trust, as solid and honest as an oak tree. Mama's voice seemed to trumpet in her head. *All he needs is a little nudge and he'll ask you to marry him! Don't miss your chance.* But did she really want to live in Darmstadt, in the most industrial region in Germany, with its countless factories spewing smoke into the air?

Her thoughts were diverted when Fernand Khnopff appeared at her elbow and trotted out a poem in his native French about Viviane, the enchantress in the Forest of Brocéliande. He asked her to set it to music for him.

"The Viviane in the poem is actually *you,* Fräulein," Khnopff said. "For you are the most bewitching flirt I ever met."

"Nonsense!" she cried. "If I so much as smile at a man, he has the nerve to call me a coquette." Alma pretended to be offended when, in fact, she was exulting. How delicious to be the one they all wanted. But while she claimed center stage, she couldn't help noticing how Gretl and Wilhelm seemed happy to just sit together, hardly leaving each other's side.

"Come play for us, my dear." Berta Zuckerkandl drew Alma to the grand piano.

Electricity shot through Alma as soon as her fingers touched the ivory. At moments like these, her two selves were united at last—Alma, who dreamed of being a composer, and Alma, the belle of the ball. Suddenly, she was whole.

She played Wagner's "Liebestod." When Alma finished to euphoric applause, Berta Zuckerkandl took her hand and raised her to her feet. Frau Zuckerkandl looked every inch the New Woman in her reform dress—a flowing uncorseted gown of cherry-red Japanese silk covered in floral embroideries over which she wore a trailing open kimono. The effect was at once exotic and breathtakingly modern. She wasn't just a society lady, after all, but a professional journalist and art critic—you were nobody in Viennese artistic circles until Berta Zuckerkandl noticed you. Her intelligent gray eyes were riveted on Alma.

"Let's raise our glasses to Alma Maria Schindler," Frau Zuckerkandl said, "who has turned the rest of us poor women emerald with envy. Not only is she the most beautiful girl in Vienna, and that's quite bad enough, she's also a brilliant pianist. That's infuriating. But on top of it all, she composes! That makes you sick." Her eyes full of warmth and good humor, Frau Zuckerkandl kissed Alma's cheek and handed her a glass of champagne.

A hired pianist took over and the dancing began. Olbrich was the first to claim Alma, his eyes so soft and tender, and she trembled in the certainty that this evening would end with his proposal. Even though Mama and Carl would consider him a prize catch, she had to admit she felt no passion for him, nothing to set her pulse racing. Just a quiet affection. Was that enough? Perhaps she misunderstood what love was meant to be. Looking over at Gretl and Wilhelm, she witnessed their contentment, their enviable peace. But no fireworks, no frisson.

Alma took a break from the dancing to listen to one of Berta Zuckerkandl's delectable gossipy tales.

"Only last week Auguste Rodin visited Vienna on his way back from Prague," she began. Frau Zuckerkandl was intimately familiar with the Parisian art world. Her sister was married to Paul Clemenceau, the younger brother of the great French statesman Georges Clemenceau. "And who should show Monsieur Rodin the sights but our own Gustav Klimt?"

The mere mention of Klimt's name was enough to make Alma drop her eyes to contemplate the parquet floor. As for Rodin, she understood he was notorious for his sculpture of nude lovers sharing a kiss — she had seen a photograph of this piece in *Ver Sacrum*. *It's not just about a kiss,* she had overheard Klimt telling Carl. *It's about sex itself.* The thought was enough to make her tremble, bringing back the memory of how close she had come to succumbing to Klimt in Venice.

"It being a fine day," Frau Zuckerkandl continued, "Klimt took Rodin to a café in the Prater Garden. Accompanying the two gentlemen were two of Klimt's models — slim red-haired vamps, whom Rodin found most enthralling."

*So Mama was right after all — Klimt is a womanizer.* Frau Zuckerkandl's story almost made him sound like a pimp. Alma felt a sickening lurch.

"Utterly enchanted by it all, Rodin leaned forward, and said to Klimt, 'I've never before experienced such an ambience—your unforgettable templelike Secession Museum filled with startling modern art, and now this garden, these women, this music. What's the reason for it all?'" With a complicit smile, Frau Zuckerkandl paused to look around at her circle of listeners before continuing. "Klimt answered with only one word. 'Austria.'"

At that, everyone lifted their glasses with a rousing cheer, washing Alma of all her gloom. *Austria,* she thought. Not the stolid and regimented homeland she loathed, so far behind the rest of the world. Not the rigidly conservative empire that had opened its universities to women only four years ago. Not Austria, but the new Vienna rising from this fountain of modern art, music, and writing.

No, she wasn't tempted to follow Olbrich to Darmstadt. Instead, she danced with one man after the next. For one night, let her live, surrendering to the elation, the laughter, and the champagne. Of just being present in this room where, apart from Klimt, the finest artists and minds of Vienna were gathered, and she was a part of the sheer effervescence of it all. Here she belonged. She was nineteen and beautiful. She still had time.

# 5

||||||||||||||||||||||||

A lma alighted from the streetcar and marched through the crowded narrow streets of the old city center inside the Ringstrasse. Under her arm, she carried her leather folder of compositions. After weeks of practice and preparation, her next lesson with her composition teacher, Josef Labor, had finally arrived.

Squaring her shoulders, Alma entered the ornate arched doorway on Rosengasse and climbed the stairs to Herr Labor's apartment. It would have been absolutely taboo for her to visit any other man without a chaperone. But Labor was blind and Mama trusted him implicitly — it was she who had chosen him as Alma's teacher. Alma suspected that her mother had selected him for his very blindness. His appraisal of Alma's work was based on its merit alone, not swayed by her looks.

Herr Labor had left the door unlocked for her. His apartment was shabby and dim, with faded wallpaper and mismatched old furniture. It smelled of coffee and stale, used-up air. Alma wondered when his housekeeper had last opened the windows to give the rooms a good airing. But Herr Labor himself was tidy and dapper, with his wavy gray hair and fastidiously groomed moustache. He stood up to shake her hand before sinking back into his chair.

With a nervous flutter in her stomach, Alma arranged her scores on his piano. Sweating in concentration, she played all eight of her completed songs and then held her breath while she awaited his verdict. Herr Labor couldn't read her scores but could only listen to her work and critique it verbally.

"A most respectable accomplishment," he said. "For a girl."

A gall of bitter disappointment rose inside her gorge.

"Herr Labor," Alma said, after an awkward silence. "I would very much like to learn counterpoint."

Counterpoint, she reasoned, was part of the fundamental knowledge she needed to make any real progress.

"My girl, you're not ready for it," Labor said. "A little knowledge can be a dangerous thing, you know."

She was grateful that her teacher couldn't see her tears. Struggling to master herself, she pitched her voice low to sound calm. "But I'd rather be crushed under the weight of knowledge than go on living in ignorance."

Still, Labor demurred, albeit very politely, as though he sincerely believed he was acting in her best interest, cossetting what he dismissed as her slender talent.


After the lesson, Alma sat on the streetcar and stared strickenly at her music scores. Perhaps she lacked seriousness and application. Apart from her music lessons, she'd had little in the way of formal schooling. Mama had educated her and Gretl when they were children, even taught them French. But from the age of thirteen onward, Alma had insisted on educating herself. On choosing her own books and forming her own opinions.

Yet Alma was beginning to regret her haphazard education, which seemed to cast her in the role of the eternal dilettante. *Women will never be emancipated,* she thought, *until they receive the same education as men.* Where did this leave her?

Perhaps if she, like her mother when she was young, had been forced by economic necessity to earn a living with her music, she might actually achieve something. If she never went to another party and chained herself to the piano night and day, would she succeed in proving to Labor how seriously she wanted to be a composer? Or should she give up the struggle, get married, and have children like every other woman. Her gut seized at the memory of Joseph Olbrich's longing eyes—what if she had squandered her chances with a perfectly decent man for nothing?

· · ·

Alma arrived home to find Berta Zuckerkandl's surprise invitation to join her at the Court Opera's premiere of *Tristan und Isolde* the following night. It was Alma's favorite, and she dressed with care, wearing a flowing silvery evening gown that reminded her of an archaic Greek maiden dancing in the moonlight.

"My husband couldn't come since he has some dreary function to attend," Frau Zuckerkandl said, when Alma joined her in her coach. "Besides, it's good for me to spend time with bright young people like you."

Alma smiled, warmed by the light of Frau Zuckerkandl's goodwill. With her nimbus of thick black hair and her diamond *collier,* this lady was the epitome of elegance, as different from her own mother as a woman could be. How Alma yearned to permanently inhabit Berta Zuckerkandl's rarefied world of salons, exhibitions, and operagoing.

Such were the thoughts that buzzed through her head when they entered the neo-Renaissance foyer of the opera house and walked up the grand marble stairway to the Zuckerkandls' private balcony. Nestling in the red velvet seat, Alma trusted that the sheer majesty of *Tristan und Isolde* would soon sweep away her woes. Even the sound of the orchestra tuning their instruments sent her shivering in anticipation.

She glanced through the program. The strapping heldentenor Erik Schmedes was singing Tristan, which left Alma weak in the knees, ready to fall in love with him on stage. The celebrated soprano Anna von Mildenburg was playing Isolde. But Berta Zuckerkandl seemed more intrigued with the conductor Gustav Mahler, a man she counted as her friend.

"Mark my words, he's the one we must watch," Frau Zuckerkandl said, viewing him through her opera glasses as he ascended the podium to rapturous applause. "Have you heard his Second Symphony?"

Alma shook her head. Though she wasn't familiar with Mahler as a composer, she held him in absolute awe for the way he had revolutionized the Court Opera since becoming its director two years ago. Unlike his predecessors, he staged the operas as though they were plays, demanding that his singers *act* instead of just reeling off their arias. He even used the electric lights for dramatic effect, all in homage to Wagner's original intention of the opera being a *Gesamtkunstwerk,* a total work of art on the grandest scale.

"Did you know he asked Anna von Mildenburg to marry him?" Frau Zuckerkandl whispered. "And can you believe she turned him down because she didn't want to give up her career?" She seemed equally astonished and admiring of the soprano's decision.

*If Mama had been that committed to her opera singing, I would never have been born,* Alma reflected, trying to imagine the glamourous and independent life her mother might have lived. She gazed through her opera glasses at Herr Direktor Mahler taking his bows. In his black suit and tails, he was whip thin and athletic in appearance, his dark hair unruly and wild. He radiated intensity, reminding her of an ascetic who lived in a mountain cave and survived on water and air.

Sweeping round, he faced the orchestra. Lifting their instruments, the musicians began the prelude, the notes shimmering and turbulent in an incessant ebb and flow. Wielding his baton as if it were a sword, Mahler was calm one moment, frenetic the next. A luminous aura seemed to emanate from him, transporting him, his orchestra, and his entire audience to a realm of utter transcendence. Music was the new religion — that was what everyone in educated circles was saying.

The swelling chords seized Alma, possessed her, washing her in their tides, saturating her in their pathos and bliss. She found herself in tears, shaking with the desire to write an opera even half as sublime as this. *Oh, Wagner, you Dionysus, you god of eternal ecstasy.*

After the curtains parted and Anna von Mildenburg's first aria soared falcon high, and even after Erik Schmedes strode the deck of the swaying ship rigged up on stage, his muscled arms and calves bared, Alma's eyes kept returning to the conductor, the very epicenter of this hurricane of sound. If Wagner was a god, Gustav Mahler was his high priest.

# 6

|||||||||||||||||||||||||||||

"O f course, you shouldn't marry for the mere sake of bourgeois conven-
tion," Max Burckhard told Alma, as they bicycled side by side along
Lake Hallstatt at the foot of the Dachstein Alps. "What an utter waste that
would be. Remember this, my dear—you are a free soul."

Alma's heart lifted as her legs pumped the pedals uphill past the on-
ion-domed church and farmers scything hay. How she loved cycling. She
wished she could just race on and on, becoming one with the wind sweeping
down from the snowy mountain peaks.

"In fact, you don't have to marry at all," Burckhard said, with a candor
that put a wobble in her handlebars. "I never did. At least not yet."

As his moist gaze lingered on her, she flustered and glanced away, directing her vision to the fishing boats swaying on the ruffled blue lake. Fascinating conversationalist though he was, Max Burckhard didn't interest her as a
man—he was older than her mother, for God's sake.

*That doesn't mean you don't interest him as a woman,* Mama would have
retorted, she who suspected every adult male who came within a barge pole's
length of Alma to have ulterior motives. But Mama was far away in Vienna,
and Alma was most respectably chaperoned, with Gretl and Wilhelm cycling
just behind her, and Wilhelm's parents and Carl bringing up the rear. They
were cycling toward Hallstatt on the southern end of the lake, where they
planned to share a meal before heading back to their rented summer house
near Bad Goisern.

Poor pregnant Mama had stayed behind in Vienna to have her baby
while the rest of them vacationed in the mountains. At least Mama's own

mother was coming down from Hamburg to look after her and the baby when it arrived.

Alma hoped and prayed that Mama would be all right, that the birth wouldn't damage her health. Try as she might, she could still not get over her shock that her mother would be giving birth to a brand-new infant just as she and Gretl had reached the age to marry and have children of their own. She felt guilty about leaving her mother at such a vulnerable time, yet Mama had insisted she needed her peace and privacy. It was as though her grown daughters and even her husband had become an unwelcome presence as the unborn baby devoured her entire existence. It frightened Alma to think of Mama trapped within those walls, as if her pregnancy had transformed her into an unmovable piece of furniture.

And so Alma directed her entire attention on Max Burckhard. Even with the bother of his unwelcome overtures, she found him fascinating. The former director of the Burgtheater, Burckhard had introduced Vienna to the plays of Henrik Ibsen. He was the first man since Alma's late father to take an interest in her mind. For Christmas, he'd given her two huge laundry hampers full of books—all classics in the finest editions. It was he who had introduced her to the works of Nietzsche.

Alma secretly regarded Burckhard as a Nietzschean superman. Possessed of enormous physical vitality, he cycled, hiked, and rowed with the vigor of a man half his age. He was utterly true to himself. While she and her family summered in a geranium-bedecked chalet along the Traun River like so many other tourists, Burckhard had acquired a mountain hut far above the valley where he lived in splendid isolation, with only deer and chamois for company. Though her family frequently set her nerves on edge, Alma shivered at the thought of such solitude. Of existing all by herself with no one but herself to answer to.

As Burckhard fell silent, Alma overhead Gretl's conversation with Wilhelm.

"I want to have four children," Gretl said. "Four is the perfect number.

Two boys and two girls." Her sister's voice sounded unnaturally bright, as though she were a bad actress delivering her lines.

Sometimes her sister seemed so opaque, as though she concealed an entire universe of secrets in the depths of her slender, recipe-copying self. What was she hiding from them all? Why did Gretl get all those headaches—was she merely constitutionally weaker than the rest of them, as their house doctor claimed? Gretl could ride her bicycle as well as anyone else. Alma felt a pang of regret that the two of them were not intimate confidantes like the sisters she read about in novels.

"Death does not exist," Burckhard said abruptly.

*What happened to my father then,* Alma was about to ask him when all thought was swept aside at the sight of the cyclist coming toward them, sunlight glancing off his spectacles and black hair. Could it be, or did she deceive herself?

"Herr Direktor Mahler!" she cried, interrupting Burckhard's discourse on death midsentence.

For it was indeed Gustav Mahler who hailed them and asked directions to Traunkirchen. Accompanying him were two women and a man Alma recognized as Arnold Rosé, first violinist of the Vienna Philharmonic.

In a flurry of deference, everyone jumped off their bicycles. Carl dug out his map and pointed out the way while Alma stole glances at Mahler. She'd never seen him up close before. His high cheekbones, his intelligent brow —this was the face of an artist glowing with exertion and good health. For a man in his late thirties, he appeared almost boyish, with his open, expansive smile. But when he directed that smile at her, having caught her in the act of staring at him, the blood shot to her head. She wanted to creep away, but Carl was now introducing her.

"Are you the Fräulein Schindler who sent me the postcard?" Mahler asked, sounding altogether too amused.

She cringed to recall how before leaving Vienna she had sent him a card begging for his autograph. And here she stood, as sweaty and disheveled as a peasant harvesting potatoes, while her musical idol suavely proceeded to introduce her to his sister Justine and then to Natalie Bauer-Lechner, a violist who performed professionally in an all-female string quartet. Both women seemed to regard Alma pityingly, as though she were the latest soppy, starstruck girl to throw herself in Gustav Mahler's path.

*How utterly humiliating.* If Alma had learned one thing from her debacle with Klimt, it was to worship her idols from a safe distance. Perhaps she should stick to venerating dead men like Wagner.

Eight weeks later, when Alma returned home from the mountains, Mama welcomed her by thrusting a bald, wriggling infant into her arms.

"Your new sister, Maria," Mama said, smiling at the baby and then studying Alma intently, as if to gauge her feelings for her new sibling.

*Maternal sentiment is the measure of femininity,* Alma told herself, as she gazed into those unfocused blue eyes. Women and girls were supposed to *melt* at the sight of a baby. *I must be unnatural—the third sex!* For instead of madonna-like adoration, Alma felt a frantic urge to hand the baby back to Mama before the tiny creature spit up on her. Alma was holding an unwelcome reminder that Carl had copulated with Mama—something too grotesque to even think about.

"Alma!" Mama cried sharply. "Support her head!"

Before Alma could even work out how she was to do this, her mother had snatched the infant from her.

Gretl cooed worshipfully. "Let *me* hold her!"

With the new baby dominating the household, Alma considered herself lucky that she was allowed to play piano—provided that Maria wasn't sleeping, of course.

Alma attempted to compose a sonata. At long last she had persuaded Herr Labor to teach her counterpoint, and she hoped that this, her most ambitious composition thus far, would prove to him that she did, in fact, have talent. She forced herself to concentrate with single-pointed focus, to ignore

Maria bawling in the nursery while Gretl banged around the kitchen — her sister was taking cooking lessons from Cilli. Simply jotting down a few new bars felt like the labor of Sisyphus rolling his boulder up that never-ending mountain. If Alma could even have one day of peace and quiet, she might accomplish so much more.

Sweat pooled under her armpits as Alma played her sonata for Herr Labor, who sat with his gnarled fingers enclosing his blind man's cane of polished walnut. Now was the moment of judgment when he would decree if her hard-won lessons in counterpoint had been worth his while. Her nerves were stretched so thin that she kept striking the wrong notes, and she could feel his impatience as if it were an icy draft.

"Enough!" he cried. "It's stupid of me to teach you! You can't be taken seriously. If that's the best you can do, you better give up."

It was as though the ceiling had come crashing down on her. Alma stared through her tears at the first sonata she had ever dared to write. She imagined Labor ripping it in half and flinging it out the window.

"If you must compose," he said, "stick to your lieder."

A blackness engulfed her heart. Any shred of dignity or purpose she'd ever had was laid to waste.

# 7

A dreary autumn darkened into the coldest winter in three years, the streets treacherous with ice. Nevertheless, the Austrian mail arrived as punctually as ever. Alma's heart gave a little leap to see a postcard from Joseph Maria Olbrich. Now that he was Darmstadt's most celebrated young architect, his joy seemed to radiate from his very handwriting as he announced his engagement to a beautiful actress.

*I'm happy for him. I truly am,* Alma tried to tell herself, though this felt like yet another blow. She tried not to reveal any emotion as Gretl read the postcard and cackled in what sounded like pure schadenfreude.

"Well, you missed that train, Alma! Imagine, *you* could have been his fiancée picking out the furniture for his new house."

Not dignifying her sister with a reply, Alma retreated to the piano and played the overture of Wagner's *Götterdämmerung.* Yes, she'd had her chance with Olbrich. Yes, he would have offered her a way out of these stifling walls, the dead end her life had become.

After the last note of the overture, she reached for her own music. Despite Labor's command to restrict herself to lieder, she began to compose a rhapsody, this being the one defiance left to her. Alma played and played until she had muscle cramps in both hands. Then she sprang up and yanked open the window. Leaning out into the frigid air, she willed the bitter wind to blast away her ennui and self-doubt.

"Are you trying to kill the baby?" Mama came storming up behind her and slammed the window shut before charging back to the nursery, where Maria was howling.

Mama's patience with Alma seemed to dwindle by the day.

Leaving Gretl to her cooking lessons and Mama to her squalling infant, Alma swathed herself in her warmest clothes and burst out the door. The cold stung her face. It hurt just to breathe. The street sweeper's beard was frozen and rimed in frost. But at least the bite in the air made her feel alive. Trying her best to embody the confidence and sophistication of a modern, independent woman, Alma took the tram to the Musikverein, where she joined the crowd queuing up for the afternoon concert. Her stomach seized at the sight of Herr Labor ahead of her in line. But he was oblivious to her presence, and she decided not to call out to him.

Still reeling from the shame of her last lesson back in November, Alma was debating whether or not to continue studying with him. It wasn't as though she had formally quit her instruction as much as she lacked the courage to knock on his door and schedule a new lesson. Enduring his critiques felt like being whipped by a cat-o'-nine-tails, and yet abandoning her lessons altogether might sound the death knell of her ambitions. *How do you think you would have coped at the conservatory if you can't handle Labor's criticism?* By giving up, she would prove to all the world that she, Alma Maria Schindler, was only a pretentious bourgeois girl with no actual talent. She should stick to playing Schubert to amuse Carl's dinner guests.

Ticket in hand, Alma tried her best to banish Labor from her thoughts and focus instead on the conviviality of this Golden Hall with its gilded ceiling and caryatids of carved oak. This was her cathedral, her sanctum sanctorum, this splendid concert hall that boasted the best acoustics in all the empire.

She perused the program. The Vienna Philharmonic and the Singverein's choir of three hundred voices were performing Bruckner's Mass in D Minor, as well as the premiere of a brand-new piece called Frühlingsbegräbnis by the twenty-eight-year-old composer Alexander von Zemlinsky. Zemlinsky himself was conducting.

When the young man made his way to the podium, he struck her as comical, almost a caricature, with his chinless head and bulging eyes. But the instant he started conducting, he held her and the entire auditorium in the palm of his hand. To achieve such mastery so young! Her chest ached with her own frustration, her shame at Labor's thinking she wasn't good enough.

Zemlinsky conducted Bruckner with the utmost competence, but it was his own work, performed after the intermission, that had her perched on the edge of her seat, her heart pounding in awe. Frühlingsbegräbnis, the Burial of Spring, was a cantata for orchestra, choir, and solo soprano and baritone set to an allegorical poem by Paul Heyse. Though dedicated to the memory of Brahms, the piece, with its stirring horns and woodwinds, seemed more reminiscent of Wagner. Alma drank down the music as if it were vintage champagne. It seemed at once whimsical and breathtakingly innovative. During the dramatic finale, she completely forgot herself.

"Bravo!" she cried, her program flying as she leapt to her feet and cheered with gusto until she realized that she was the only one offering a standing ovation while the rest of the audience delivered a spatter of lukewarm applause. Making a spectacle of herself in a city where it was the greatest faux pas to clap out of turn.

From his podium, Zemlinsky stared at her, his face as red as hers must be. A young lady in the first row—Zemlinsky's sister, his sweetheart?—turned around to throw Alma a glacial stare. Even Labor glanced in her direction, as if recognizing her voice.

Chastened, Alma sank back into her seat and ducked her face inside her boa. But she couldn't stop smiling no matter how much of a spectacle she'd made of herself. Zemlinsky's music was the purest elixir, raising her spirits all the way to the ornate ceiling. How could she not abandon decorum in the face of such genius?

• • •

A cloud of mirth enveloped Alma when she stepped back out into the cold and headed to the tram stop in the gathering darkness. The icy cobbles underfoot were so slick that she had to take tiny, careful steps. Farther down the street, she saw a man take a spill, his hat and familiar walnut cane spinning out of his grasp. Too proud to shout for help, Labor kept struggling to stand only to fall again.

"Herr Labor!" she shouted, rushing toward him as quickly as she could without falling on the ice herself.

Alma took his cane in one hand and his arm in the other, and pulled him to his feet. How had she never noticed how slight he was, how thin and frail?

"It's me, Alma Schindler," she added, though he seemed to know exactly who she was.

"Bless you, child," he said, when she handed him his hat and cane. His voice was gruff, as though he was trying to hide his embarrassment. "I'll be fine now."

"We're going the same way, are we not?" Alma kept a firm grasp on his arm lest he fall again. "We can walk to the tram together."

It amazed her that she could be so congenial to this man who kept shattering her dreams. *If that's the best you can do, you better give up.* But even Labor at his gloomiest couldn't dampen her high spirits after hearing Zemlinsky's music. Or so she told herself.

"Alexander von Zemlinsky is truly first-rate," she told Labor. "Weren't you impressed by Frühlingsbegräbnis?"

"I'll grant that it showed some originality," her teacher said, "although it lacked both melody and unity."

"But he's only twenty-eight!" Alma could simply not quell her enthusiasm. "One day he'll be as revered as Wagner. A talent that brilliant can't go unnoticed."

"Fräulein Schindler, I think it can and often does. *Most* genius in this world goes unrecognized, unacknowledged. Buried and forgotten."

"But then it *dies*," she said, with a nauseated pitch in her stomach, as though it were her own music that Labor had harpooned yet again. Was he implying that she should abandon hope?

"Maybe it does die," Labor said, with an underlying melancholy.

Was he so harsh to her, Alma wondered, because his own compositions had been mocked and derided, his own dreams dashed to pieces? What if he was simply too jaded to fairly appraise her work? To think he couldn't even summon up the least excitement for someone as gifted as Zemlinsky. *Find a new teacher!* Resolve filled her. *Now or never. You have no more time to lose.*

Several days later, at Berta Zuckerkandl's soiree, Alma learned what she could of Alexander von Zemlinsky from her hostess's store of facts and gossip. His grandfather hailed from Hungary. The aristocratic *von* added to his surname was an ornamental flourish of his father's invention—none of them were descended from nobility. His family was Jewish, educated, and poor. Zemlinsky lived at home with his parents and sister, whom he supported with his income as kapellmeister of the Carlstheater and with what he earned as a freelance conductor.

"He also teaches composition," Frau Zuckerkandl said. "Arnold Schoenberg is taking counterpoint lessons from him."

*Counterpoint lessons!* Alma could not keep herself from smiling. It was as if the Muses themselves had brought Zemlinsky to her attention.

"But I saved the best morsel for last," Frau Zuckerkandl said. "His opera, *Es war einmal,* is premiering at the Court Opera in two weeks. Mahler himself is conducting."

Golden sparks of light seemed to fly through the air like confetti. Alma wanted to grab Frau Zuckerkandl's bejeweled hands and polka across the room with her. *I was right about Zemlinsky!* And if she had been right in believing in him, perhaps she wasn't crazy to have a little faith in herself.

"May I go to the opera with you for the premiere, Frau Zuckerkandl?" she asked, imagining herself viewing Zemlinsky's triumph from the Zuckerkandl's private balcony.

"I'm so sorry, Alma. I already invited Helene Gottlieb and her parents, and I fear the performance is sold out. But there will be other performances. If you want to meet Herr Zemlinsky himself" — Frau Zuckerkandl smiled deliciously, as though she could see the hopes that danced inside Alma's head — "he's invited to the Conrats' party at the end of the month. As are you, dear Alma."

The Conrats' fete was held in honor of their daughter Ilse visiting from Brussels, where she was studying sculpture with the renowned Charles van der Stappen. This was to be the party of the season, with the most influential people in all Vienna in attendance. Accordingly, Alma made sure to wear her brand-new gown of sea-green silk with accents of midnight-blue velvet. She fastened a *collier* of moonstones around her throat.

The Conrats lived in lordly style in the Walfischgasse, in the very heart of Vienna, only a short stroll from the Court Opera and the Musikverein. After the servants ushered Alma and her family through the colossal double doors, she wandered through the four palatial reception rooms that swarmed with people, each lady more elegant than the next. She wondered how she would even find Zemlinsky amid this crush of bodies.

"Alma!" Erica Conrat embraced her and kissed her cheeks. "Come see Ilse."

Her friend led her to the throng of admirers gathered around Ilse, who stood beaming beside her marble bust of Johannes Brahms. The sculpture portrayed the late composer as a benevolent patriarch with a long flowing beard. Brahms, who had died two years ago, had been a close family friend.

"Ilse, congratulations!" Alma cried. "It's a masterpiece."

She tried to mask her monumental envy of her friend's success, her body of work that was literally carved in stone. No one could dispute her artistry or dedication. Ilse seemed years beyond Alma in maturity and sophistication even though she was a few months younger.

"Alma, you look like a vision tonight," Ilse said, hugging her. "One day I must sculpt you!"

43

But Ilse's attention was soon diverted when the director of the Vienna Academy of Fine Arts came to shake her hand. The man wanted to commission Ilse to sculpt a Brahms memorial for the Vienna Central Cemetery! They all toasted Ilse's success with Heidsieck champagne. Alma smiled until her face hurt. Why did Ilse's accomplishments make her feel so small?

Meanwhile, Erica confided to Alma about her dreams of attending university. "Since they won't admit women to the School of Medicine, I've applied to study art history. If they accept me, I'll be the only woman studying for a degree in the entire department."

"But won't that be lonely?" Alma asked her. "Won't you feel odd and singled out?"

"At least I might find a husband who respects my mind," her friend said shyly. Though not yet seventeen, Erica sounded as though she had her life firmly mapped out.

Alma reflected how brave Erica was. The Conrat sisters were boldly striding into their futures, venturing where none of their sex had previously trod. Wasn't that what she herself aspired to with her composing? But she felt none of their unwavering determination, only a chorus of doubts. If only she possessed a fraction of their fortitude, that long-term vision to turn her dreams into reality.

When Erica excused herself to greet other guests, Alma wandered through the crowd, scanning the faces to see if Zemlinsky had arrived. Instead, she chanced to overhear the utterances of young Otto Weininger. "It's all very well to make such a to-do of a flat-chested, frizzy-haired sculptress," he said. "She's too plain to find a husband. This entire New Woman business only serves to benefit mannish spinsters like her."

Alma burned to hear him mocking Ilse—in her own home, at her own party!

"There's not a single female in the history of thought," Weininger went on, "not even the most masculine, who can honestly be compared to a man of fifth- or sixth-rate genius."

The contempt in his voice raised her flesh. *Do men really hate us that*

44

*much?* She sickened to see his cronies circled around him nodding in agreement.

Mama's voice then echoed in her head. *The third sex!* For all Ilse's achievements, she would only be lampooned and belittled.

"Alma!" Gretl appeared and took her hand. "Come look at Herr Hoffmann's plans for the new house!"

Grateful for this reprieve, Alma followed her sister to the far corner where Josef Hoffmann had unrolled his architectural diagrams of the two semi-detached villas he intended to build on the Hohe Warte, a still mostly rural plateau on the northern outskirts of Vienna. In response to Mama's complaints that their house in the Theresianumgasse was too small for the five of them, Carl had commissioned Hoffmann to design a new family home. Carl's friends from the Secession then decided that they, too, required roomier residences. So Hoffmann was building an entire artists' colony — the Secession's most ambitious *Gesamtkunstwerk* yet.

"We'll lay the foundations this spring," Hoffmann said. "By autumn 1901, the villas should be finished."

"Just think, girls," Mama said to Alma and Gretl. "You'll each have your own room again."

"But, Mama, I'll never live there," Gretl said. "By the time the house is finished, I'll be married." Her voice cracked, as though she found this deeply upsetting.

Alma thought she saw the glint of a tear in Gretl's eye — so unlike her sister. She was about to ask her what the matter was when Berta Zuckerkandl made her grand entrance, her arm linked with Alexander von Zemlinsky's. Up close, he didn't appear any less chinless or goggle-eyed than he had in the concert hall, and it astonished Alma to see that he stood no taller than Gretl.

"And this is Fräulein Alma Maria Schindler." Frau Zuckerkandl smiled beatifically. "She's a great lover of music and a composer herself, aren't you, my dear? And a great admirer of *your* music, Herr Zemlinsky. She attended the premiere of your Frühlingsbegräbnis."

45

"I distinctly remember," Zemlinsky said, as blunt as he was short. "You were the enraptured fan who gave me the one-woman standing ovation."

He had such a direct way of looking at her. Alma found herself flushing to the roots of her hair. But the mere sight of him was enough to wipe her mind clean of Otto Weininger's hateful talk.

"Now if you'll both excuse me," Frau Zuckerkandl murmured with a wink to Alma. "I *must* congratulate our dear Ilse on her magnificent sculpture."

"Standing ovations are terribly old-fashioned," Zemlinsky told Alma. "Don't you know that modern souls are meant to view the world with cynical disdain?"

Alma gathered a strong sense of an underlying cynicism in his nature. But there had to be more to him than that if he composed such dazzling music.

"Just imagine," she said, adopting a light and breezy tone, "I'm so old-fashioned, I haven't seen your new opera yet."

"Then you better hurry, Fräulein. I don't know how much longer it will be in the repertoire."

"I hear you're teaching counterpoint to Arnold Schoenberg," she said, just to remind him that she was an aspiring composer, not just a silly girl who made a fool of herself at concerts.

He shrugged. "The man is a bank clerk who wants to be a great composer *and* he's in love with my sister. What can I do?"

"Was it your sister sitting in the first row at the concert?" Alma smiled at him boldly. "She didn't seem to care much for my display of enthusiasm."

Now it was Zemlinsky's turn to blush. Alma noted, with some satisfaction, that the tips of his sizeable ears were glowing red.

"No," he said in a small voice, as though all sarcasm and cleverness had deserted him. "That was my acquaintance, Melanie Guttmann."

*Acquaintance?* Alma felt like snorting. Sweetheart, more like. Changing the subject, she asked if Zemlinsky was pleased that the star soprano Selma Kurz and tenor Erik Schmedes were singing in his opera.

"Kurz is flawless," he said. "But Schmedes seems half-asleep. Perhaps a heartthrob like him feels it too lowering to be in my obscure little opera when he could be off chasing skirts."

Schmedes's adulterous affairs were the scandal of Vienna. Alma joined Zemlinsky in denouncing the tenor. "He'll ruin his career, as well as his reputation, if he carries on like that."

Even as they conversed, other men were trying to catch Alma's attention and draw her away from Zemlinsky.

"Excuse me," she told them coolly. "I'm speaking to Herr Zemlinsky."

She watched how the young composer blushed, how his eyes softened, as if in spite of himself, to receive this audience with her now that he could see how sought-after and desirable she was. At moments like this, she felt like a queen, full of quiet power. At ease in her own skin.

"My feet are killing me," she said. "I don't suppose there's a place where we could sit."

"Over here, Fräulein."

A shiver of delight ran through her as Zemlinsky took her arm and guided her to an empty loveseat. His face was bright red, as if he was all too aware of the other men's envy. She smiled to herself when he sat beside her, their knees almost touching.

"It appears you're very popular, Fräulein," he said archly, as though taking refuge in his cynicism.

Alma laughed dismissively, as if such notions of flirtation and conquest were beneath her. But the air between them seemed to vibrate. She could not stop smiling.

Zemlinsky started in on the critics' reception of Frühlingsbegräbnis. "Do you know what that old crank Josef Labor wrote about it in the *Neues Wiener Tagblatt*?"

"That it's lacking in melody and overall unity?" Alma studied Zemlinsky's face as he reddened yet again. "Oh, don't listen to him. His generation simply can't keep up with the pioneering young composers. He's been quite savage to my work as well, you know."

47

Zemlinsky grinned and leaned closer. "I tell you what, Fräulein. If we can think of one person with whom neither of us has a grudge, we can toast their honor."

"Gustav Mahler!" Alma cried, raising her glass, for it was Mahler who had selected Zemlinsky's work for the Court Opera.

"To Gustav Mahler," Zemlinsky echoed. His eyes never left her face. "What do you think of Wagner then?"

"The greatest genius who ever lived!" She didn't care if she was gushing.

"And your favorite work of Wagner's?" he asked.

She wondered if this was a test to see if her tastes were sophisticated enough for his. "*Tristan und Isolde.*"

She half expected some sarcastic retort that this was just the kind of opera he expected a girl like her to swoon over, but instead a delight shone on his face, transforming him. His eyes warmly aglow, he became truly handsome.

"Fräulein Schindler," he said, clinking his glass to hers. "We understand each other."

"You must come to call at my home," she said, her heart pounding in her throat. "I'm looking for someone to teach me counterpoint. What about Monday in two weeks," she suggested, not wanting to sound too desperate or eager. "Say eleven?"

He nodded. "I'll reserve the date for you, Fräulein. And you must send me your musical scores. I'd like to see your compositions."

Alma felt as though she were floating to heaven on a magic carpet. Not leaving the sofa, they discussed Wagner's genius until she jumped in shock at Mama tapping her shoulder.

"Alma, it's past midnight. Come, it's time to say good-bye."


In the morning, Alma sent off her compositions to Zemlinsky. Walking back from the post office, she reflected how the young man had cut through her staleness like a mountain wind. Was it her admiration of his music coupled with his interest in her scores that explained the rapport that had blossomed between them? She had spent hours with him, ignoring everyone else in those rooms full of artists and architects, raconteurs and wits. And Zemlinsky had seemed quite pleased to spend his time with her.

So what was stirring inside her? Was it simply the dream of finding a teacher who truly believed in her, or was it something even deeper? Just the thought of him made her skin tingle. A warmth kindled inside her, a joy that threatened to spill over into laughter as she marched down the crowded street.

# 8

||||||||||||||||||||||||

A lma spent the following days racking her brain to think how she would tell Mama she would be taking lessons from Alexander von Zemlinsky. Would Mama put her foot down? Alma didn't even have her own money to pay for the lessons, never mind the fact that she would turn twenty-one this August—the age when other young women of her class would be coming into their portion. *Why* hadn't Papa thought of this in his will? Alma had to stoop to begging the money off Carl, claiming she needed a new pair of gloves.

But on the Monday of their scheduled lesson, to Alma's great good fortune, Mama took Gretl shopping in preparation for her wedding. Though the nuptials were not until September, six months away, the arrangements for this hallowed event swallowed every spare hour of Gretl's and Mama's time. Alma cheerily waved them off. Zemlinsky arrived punctually at eleven.

With a flourish, Alma took his hat and coat and ushered him into the parlor, where her scores were neatly arranged on the piano. After summoning Cilli to bring their guest coffee and a plate of *Vanillekipferl,* crescent-shaped cookies sprinkled in vanilla sugar, Alma seated herself at the piano.

"Tell me, Herr Zemlinsky, did you have any time at all to look at my scores?" She strove to sound dispassionate and professional.

He nodded. "I'm extremely impressed with your lieder. You have a gift."

A warm rush flooded her cheeks. She struggled not to weep all over him in gratitude. Throwing back her shoulders, she proceeded to play and sing her song, "Ich wandle unter Blumen" that the English lady in Venice had so warmly lauded. When she finished, she froze, her old dread seizing her as she awaited his appraisal.

"Fräulein Schindler," he said. "You have talent, to be sure, but little ability. You're full of ideas, but you need to apply yourself." Any air of budding infatuation she had seen in him at the Conrats' party was gone, replaced by an air of brusque competence.

"That's what I'm doing now," she said, championing herself in a way she would have never dared with Labor.

Doggedly, she began to play her song "Laue Sommernacht."

One turn of phrase gave him pause. "That's so good, I wish I'd written it myself."

Alma quivered to hear such praise from a true composer. But before she could even exhale, he returned to his criticisms.

"You're the worst interpreter of your own music, Fräulein. Your playing is too nervous, too fidgety. You lack technique."

She gazed straight into his eyes. "Show me what I must do."

A flush spread through her when he got up from his chair and sat beside her on the piano bench, something Labor would have never done. Alma shifted her seat to accommodate him.

"Watch and listen," he said, before proceeding to play her song more masterfully than she had ever heard it.

His virtuosity made her piece sound good enough to be performed at the Tonkünstlerverein.

"You need lessons in harmony," he went on, as he paged through her scores. "And notation. One thing, though. If you want to be my student, you mustn't contemplate publishing any of your songs for quite some time."

She took a deep breath, almost wanting to pinch herself to prove that this was really happening. Zemlinsky wasn't indulging her or belittling her or even flirting with her. He was taking her seriously, as though she were one of his male students. This, her first lesson with him, was like a thermal bath — invigorating and soothing at the same time. His kindness and encouragement buoyed her up while his incisive critique kept her on her toes.

"To start, I want you to concentrate purely on technique," he said. "Using Beethoven piano sonatas as an example" — he pulled the sheet music out of his briefcase — "I want you to write short movements based on the expositions."

"Herr Zemlinsky," she said solemnly. "I will do this with joy."

They both turned at the sound of Mama and Gretl clattering up the stairs. Alma heard Cilli mutter that a young man had come to give a piano lesson. Straightaway, Mama bustled into the parlor. Alma had left the door wide open as proof of the utter respectability of this enterprise. Zemlinsky was already on his feet, inclining his head in deference to her mother. He appeared every inch the well-mannered gentleman.

"Mama," Alma said, rising from the piano bench. She smiled as innocently as she could in this, her moment of truth. "Let me introduce you to my new composition teacher, Alexander von Zemlinsky." Never mind that Mama had already been introduced to him at the Conrats' party.

"Good day to you, Frau Moll," Zemlinsky said, shaking her hand.

Mama appeared far too flummoxed to be anything but gracious. She could hardly risk being unfriendly to a rising star like Zemlinsky. If she snubbed him, all Viennese society would declare that Carl Moll's wife was a philistine. Mama even managed to ask him if he would stay to drink more coffee, but he declined, having to leave for a rehearsal at the Carlstheater.

After he departed, Mama didn't berate Alma for inviting a young man into their home without her permission. Instead, she looked at her daughter imploringly. "Will you go talk to your sister? She's completely out of sorts."

Alma found her sister slumped on the edge of her bed. Her face was deathly pale. Scattered at her feet lay the many parcels she and Mama had brought back from their shopping trip.

Feeling bumbling and awkward, Alma sat beside her. If only she had a clue what to say. Normally, Gretl was impenetrable, rarely revealing her emotions, but now she began to weep uncontrollably, as Alma had not seen her do since she was a little girl. What, Alma wondered, did her sister have to be upset about? Her life was progressing exactly as a young woman's should.

"What is it?" Alma tried to take Gretl's hand, but she couldn't—her sister's fingers bunched into a hard fist.

It took some minutes before Gretl could speak coherently. "Wilhelm

52

wants us to live in Germany. He's just heard he has a place at the Stuttgart academy."

Alma was frankly baffled why Gretl should find this so disturbing. Many a young Austrian left to seek his fortune in Germany. "Is that so bad? He'll surely make more money there, and Stuttgart's not too far away."

Alma took her handkerchief and attempted to dry Gretl's tears.

"He wants me to convert." Gretl stared off into space with fixed, glittering eyes. "Become a Lutheran."

"Mama's Lutheran," Alma pointed out. "Will you even miss not being Catholic? It's not like we're convent-raised girls who say the Hail Mary every time we sneeze," she added, trying to coax a laugh out of Gretl.

They hardly set foot in church anyway, so what difference did it make? As far as Alma had observed, Wilhelm wasn't very religious either. He was probably asking Gretl to convert just to placate his parents and pastor.

"I can't go through this alone." Gretl began to sob helplessly once more. Turning away, she groped beneath her pillow and pulled out a book, which she handed to Alma—a manual on the Lutheran faith. "Will you convert with me?" Gretl asked, sounding so miserable that Alma felt her heart tear even as she struggled not to laugh at the absurdity of it all.

*I've forsworn religion, but Gretl is asking me to become a Lutheran—without reason or conviction—because of her fiancé, a man I don't particularly like.* And yet, if Alma agreed to this bizarre proposal, Mama would be indebted to her and perhaps not make such a fuss about her future lessons with Zemlinsky.

"All right," she told Gretl. "If it makes you happy."

Her sister flung her arms around her, her tears soaking into Alma's shirtwaist. She clung to her with a desperation that terrified Alma. *My poor sister is falling to pieces.*

"You don't have to do this, you know," Alma said, stroking Gretl's hair.

Her sister pulled away and wept even harder. "But he made it a condition of our marriage!"

Alma held Gretl by the shoulders and swallowed before saying the unsayable. "I mean the wedding. It's not too late to call it off if it makes you so unhappy. You're only nineteen, and there are other men apart from Wilhelm Legler, you know."

Gretl stared in horror, as though Alma had run her through with a butcher's knife. "What? Not get *married?*"

Crying fresh tears, Gretl reached for one of the parcels at her feet and opened it, revealing a lacy bridal veil that she spread out reverently across both their laps.


Alma threw herself into her music. Never had she worked harder or progressed so quickly. If she couldn't study at the conservatory, this was the next best thing. If she persevered with Zemlinsky, she had no doubt that he would transform her from a dilettante into a professional. In the light of his attention, she flourished. Her three-part counterpoint was getting better, and he was pleased with her variations on the Beethoven piano sonatas.

They also saw each other outside of their lessons, as they attended many of the same soirees and concerts. After Alma and Erica Conrat went to see Zemlinsky's opera, *Es war einmal,* he sent Alma a postcard of Selma Kurz singing the role of his princess. He signed it, *To Fräulein Alma Maria Schindler, with all my affection.* Alma's heart brimmed to read those words, and she decided to surprise him with a gift in return.

On a May morning, Alma sat at her escritoire with her most recent photograph. It depicted her as a self-possessed young woman in a lacy, high-collared dress, her hair pinned up elegantly. Her face was in profile, gazing not at the camera but into her dreams of the future. Alma dipped her pen nib into the pot of violet-scented ink and began to write across the bottom of the picture.

*To Herr Alexander von Zemlinsky in heartfelt friendship.*


*What a debt I owe Zemlinsky.* His mentorship lent her the courage she had previously lacked—the sheer willpower to shut out the world and give herself over to composing. Because he believed in her, she would indeed prevail.

54

His faith sent her soaring. How she longed to impress him, to win his admiration on all levels. Working against the clock, she succeeded in writing two new songs for their upcoming lesson. One was set to a poem by Rainer Maria Rilke, the other to a poem by Richard Dehmel. She had surpassed all her previous efforts, for these weren't ordinary lieder but part song, part recitation, part chorale. She had allowed herself the freedom to be truly inventive, to come up with her own unique form.

Sitting at the piano, she played "Lobgesang," based on the Dehmel text.

"Love is like the sea," she sang. "Wave on wave, up and down, wave after wave, surging as one."

The night before her lesson, she was too excited to sleep, her heart drumming away in happy anticipation. Awakening early, she practiced her new compositions, ignoring Gretl's moans of protest and Mama's annoyance that she might disturb the baby. Dashing out to the garden, Alma picked a voluptuous bouquet of peonies to adorn the table beside the chair where Zemlinsky would sit. She nagged Cilli to bake fresh *Vanillekipferl*.

When Zemlinsky failed to arrive punctually, Alma didn't fret at first. After all, he was coming from the other end of Vienna, from the Obere Weissgerberstrasse near the Danube Canal. While the smell of baking *Vanillekipferl* filled the house, she told herself to be patient. She waited and waited, her fingers going clammy as she played her warm-up exercises. Mama and Gretl took little Maria out to the garden. Their laughter wafting through the open windows peeved Alma to no end. The morning post arrived with no message from Zemlinsky, and then the clock struck noon, the hour their lesson was to have ended.

*He didn't come. He sent no word.* Alma buried her smarting face in the peony blossoms. She didn't know whether to weep in disappointment or fume at his fecklessness. Her stream of thoughts was interrupted by Gretl coming in and nibbling one the *Vanillekipferl* intended for Zemlinsky.

"All that moping just for a canceled lesson!" her sister chided, sidling up to Alma on the piano bench. "Have you forgotten that Aunt Mie's collecting us to go cycling this afternoon?"

Alma numbly retreated to their room to button on her high boots and change into her cycling costume, with its crisp white shirt, black tie, and the skirt far shorter than would be seemly for any other activity. She pinned on her straw boater.

Alma and Gretl piled into Aunt Mie's carriage while the driver strapped their bicycles to the running boards. Grimly determined to put Zemlinsky out of her mind, Alma whistled Viennese carnival waltzes. *Never let the world see you sad.*

Though no blood relation, Aunt Mie was a dear family friend and far closer to Alma and Gretl than their real maternal aunts, who lived in faraway Hamburg. She expounded on the beauties of spring as they cycled down the broad avenue running through the heart of the Prater, the sprawling oasis of parkland tucked between the Danube Canal and the Danube River. Their way was shaded by chestnut trees with flowering candles of pink and white. They glided past the Wurstelprater, the amusement park with its Ferris wheel erected only three years ago in celebration of Emperor Franz Joseph's golden jubilee. Alma lifted her eyes to watch the passengers conveyed up to the very top where they might enjoy a sweeping panorama of Vienna, the Danube, and the hills and forests beyond. But just as they reached those giddy heights, the wheel's motion brought them back down to the noisy chaos of the fairground where simple folk crammed their way into the freak show tents to see bearded ladies and the Living Torso — a man with no arms or legs.

*And so it is with me.* Alma reflected upon the dizzy peaks and troughs of her emotions. *For all my ecstasies and agonies, I'm only going around in the same circle over and over again. If only I could find a sense of inner sovereignty.*

She practiced smiling beatifically while they cycled past a replica Ashanti village and the market stalls selling gingerbread hearts. *Serenity,* she told herself while laughing at Aunt Mie's jokes. She tried to find solace in the soothing rhythm of her feet pumping the pedals. She resolved to be a New Woman, completely independent and self-contained.

But she jerked out of her reverie when she heard Aunt Mie's raised voice. "Gretl, what are you doing?"

Alma came to an abrupt halt to see her sister, in her pristine lavender cycling costume, sailing straight into a ditch. Leaving her bicycle on the path, Alma ran to help Aunt Mie tug Gretl out of the mud. In the process, the two of them became nearly as filthy as Gretl, who was now covered from crown to toe in muck, her hat a battered mess. But they were thankful that Gretl had not suffered as much as a bruise from the whole misadventure.

"How could you be so careless?" Aunt Mie asked, trying to wipe Gretl's face clean with her decorously embroidered linen handkerchief.

Gretl only laughed hysterically until Alma nearly wanted to slap her for making such a mockery of their concern. What troubled Alma most was that Gretl hadn't appeared to lose control of her bicycle. It was almost as though her sister had done this deliberately just to get a rise out of Aunt Mie. But surely that couldn't be—those were the antics of a naughty child, not her cool, collected sister.

"Stop making a fuss," Gretl said, sounding once more like her sober self. "I'm fine."

When they returned from their cycling jaunt, Alma found Zemlinsky's letter on the hallway table. It had arrived with the late post. Her heart pitched in sadness as she read his message.

> *My dear Fräulein Schindler,*
> *Please accept my heartfelt apologies for not showing up for your lesson today. My father is seriously ill.*
> *With all good wishes, Alexander von Zemlinsky*

# 9

||||||||||||||||||||||||

T en days later, Alma laid her bouquet of roses and delphiniums on her father's grave in the Vienna Central Cemetery.

Emil Jakob Schindler

1842–1892

Mama and Gretl stood with their eyes closed, their hands clasped in prayer. What was the point of praying, Alma wondered. Did Mama and Gretl truly believe their prayers would make any difference to a departed man?

Alma had loved Papa as much as anyone. His death, just before she turned thirteen years old, had been the most shattering experience of her life. Her family had been visiting Mama's relatives in northern Germany and touring the island of Sylt in the North Sea. Papa had set up his easel on the beach and shared with Alma his delight in the quality of the long summer sunlight that far north, so different than in Austria. Never before had Alma realized that each place and season had its own unique light. It was as though Papa had given her a pair of magical spectacles that allowed her to see the world with brand-new vision. A week later, her father, a hale and hearty man in his prime, was dead of appendicitis. The loss of him had left a permanent scar that would never heal. That was why it seemed such a mockery to make obeisance to a carved stone slab. Alma felt far closer to Papa's spirit, his *essence*, when contemplating the light in his paintings.

Though the anniversary of Papa's death was not until August, they would be away then, and thus Mama had herded them out here to pay their respects to his grave before the family left for their summer vacation. Mama attempted to light the votive candle in its red glass jar, but she kept burning her fingers and dropping the match until Alma lit the candle for her. At last the ghastly rite was complete.

Leaving the cemetery, the three of them headed toward their waiting carriage.

"Since we've hired the cab anyway, could we not take a spin through Prater Park?" Gretl asked Mama. "It's so lovely today."

Only a stone's throw from the graveyard walls, people sat at tables beneath the swaying chestnut trees and sipped coffee while reveling in the beauty and warmth of this June afternoon. A Gypsy played a wildly romantic folk song on his fiddle while elegantly dressed passersby showered coins into his upturned hat, the clement weather making them especially generous. Even the usually dour-faced women selling memorial bouquets at the cemetery gates were laughing and humming along to the Gypsy's music. Yes, a drive through Prater Park would be glorious.

Except Alma had something else in mind.

"Before we go to the Prater," she said, "could I just drop off my music scores at Herr Zemlinsky's apartment in the Obere Weissgerberstrasse?"

She patted the satchel containing her lieder.

"You could have mailed them," Mama pointed out. But since it was on their way to the Prater, she couldn't gracefully refuse.

*Of course, I could have mailed them,* Alma thought, as they set off, the carriage driver whistling a jaunty tune as his two dark bay horses trotted briskly over the cobblestones. But that would have defeated her true purpose, namely to see Zemlinsky one last time before she and her family departed for the mountains. They wouldn't be back in Vienna until late September.

Yet she reflected how uncomfortably morbid it was to come directly from Vienna Central Cemetery to the apartment where Zemlinsky's father lay so ill. Though she prided herself on being utterly modern and free from superstition, she couldn't help worrying that she might bring bad luck with her, along with the traces of graveyard dirt on her shoes. The elder Herr Zemlinsky, she had learned, suffered from kidney stones, an agonizing malady. He had been ailing for some time, which explained why young Zemlinsky was obliged to support his entire household. Perhaps it was in poor taste for her to visit at all, even to drop off her music.

Alma's heart squeezed into a frightened ball as she rang the Zemlinskys' bell. Mama stood behind her like a sentinel while Gretl waited for them in the cab.

A vaguely familiar-looking young woman answered the door and seemed to regard Alma warily. With a vicious stab in the belly, Alma recognized her as the girl who had turned to glare at her for giving Zemlinsky a standing ovation at the Musikverein concert back in January. Melanie Guttmann, Zemlinsky had said her name was. The girl he'd claimed was his "acquaintance" stood swathed in a huge apron, as though she were his wife, his perfect little hausfrau. For all Alma knew, she was his fiancée. Then again, why should that bother her? *Zemlinsky is nothing more than a teacher.* But that postcard he'd given her! *To Fräulein Alma Maria Schindler, with all my affection.* To think she'd given him her photograph.

Alma sucked in her breath and took a step backward, accidently treading on her mother's toe. "Good day to you, Fräulein." She hated herself for feeling like a child as she clutched her music scores with her mother looming behind her. "I wished to deliver these lieder to Herr Zemlinsky." She bit her lip. "The younger Herr Zemlinsky. I hope his father is recovering."

Too late she thought that she should have brought flowers for the sick man, but surely it would have been deeply disrespectful to come calling with a bouquet purchased at the graveyard.

Melanie Guttmann's lips trembled. "We sat up all night around his bed. He died today, may he rest in peace."

Alma's heart tore. "I'm so, so sorry!"

Helplessly, she looked at her mother, who offered her condolences, and back at Fräulein Guttmann.

"My music scores," Alma said lamely.

"I'll show you into his study." Fräulein Guttmann spoke with quiet dignity. "You can leave them on Alex's desk."

"He's not home?" Alma swallowed back her disappointment.

"No," said Melanie Guttmann, looking Alma in the eye. "Alex has gone to fetch the rabbi."

Alma felt completely out of her depth, as though she were trapped in a dream where everything appeared unreal and yet hyperreal at the same time, the colors twice as bright and the shadows twice as dark as in the waking world. What a fool she was, imposing herself on this household deep in mourning, and all because she had longed to catch at least a glimpse of Zemlinsky before her family left for the summer.

Of course, Alma had known from the beginning that Zemlinsky was Jewish. But like the Conrats, like Berta Zuckerkandl, and Melanie Guttmann herself, he was so assimilated that it had been easy for Alma to gloss over the fact. Until today when Fräulein Guttmann had pointedly spelled it out to her right in front of Mama, as if to say, *Leave him alone. You have no business chasing him.*

While Mama stayed behind in the doorway, Alma followed Fräulein Guttmann down the hallway with its heavy oak furniture and family photographs; through the parlor, where the menorah took pride of place on the sideboard; and finally through a set of double doors into the music room with its piano and desk. The faded wallpaper was covered in paintings and sketches that looked like the work of friends and family rather than that of established artists. There was a drawing of Brahms, a photogravure of Wagner, and even a bust of Zemlinsky himself, possibly the work of his student, Arnold Schoenberg, an amateur artist as well as an aspiring composer. Alma thought to herself that this was the room of a true bohemian, radiating unbelievable poetry. But before she could take comfort in this, a young woman she hadn't noticed until now shot up from an armchair. Was it Zemlinsky's sister, Alma wondered. Without a word, the girl rushed out of the room as though not wanting a stranger to witness her anguish — hammering home the fact that Alma didn't belong here.

*No, it's Melanie Guttmann, not you, who sat up all night while Zemlinsky's father lay dying. Melanie Guttmann who calls Zemlinsky by his first name and*

*seems to be running the household, allowing his mother and sister to give them-*
*selves wholly over to their grief.*

Fräulein Guttmann took Alma's scores from her, along with Alma's cheery note of greeting that now made her want to cringe, and set them on Zemlinsky's desk.

Alma was about to murmur her thanks and shrink toward the door when she noticed her own photograph, framed in silver and placed at the very center of the desk beside Zemlinsky's own stack of neatly penned sheet music.

# 10

||||||||||||||||||||||||||||

I n the Lutheran parish church in Bad Ischl, the emperor's most beloved
resort town, which was nestled at the foot of the Salzkammergut Mountains, Gretl marched down the aisle on Carl's arm. Alma's eyes misted with
tears, for Gretl was more beautiful than she had ever seen her in her sweeping veil of Venetian lace, her brow crowned in a circlet of white roses and
baby's breath. Most captivating of all was the radiance on her sister's face as
she looked at her bridegroom.

Following her sister's gaze, Alma choked to see that it was not Wilhelm
Legler awaiting Gretl at the altar but Gustav Klimt, his eyes blazing with
desire. Blushing prettily, Gretl gave him her hand.

Alma longed to bolt out of the church, but she was sandwiched between
Mama and Aunt Mie, trapped in that narrow oaken pew. She tried to close
her eyes, to look away to spare herself, but it was impossible. The unfolding
scene was branded on her retinas, each nuance as vivid and sharply focused
as cinematographic pictures. Klimt's muscular embrace engulfed her slender
sister in her virginal gown. With a savage insistence, he kissed her before the
stuttering pastor could even make them say their vows. To Alma's horror,
Klimt was taking complete possession of Gretl, as he had once tried to do
with Alma with that stolen kiss in Venice, that kiss Alma had thought would
stretch into eternity.

Before the scandalized wedding guests, Klimt began undressing Gretl,
who surrendered to him with cooing sighs, throwing back her head so he
could kiss her throat. Soon the wedding gown and her filmy white undergarments lay in a heap around her sister's trembling ankles. Only the lacy

bridal veil was left to cover Gretl's flushed and naked body as Klimt laid her gently on the floor, about to consummate their marriage then and there. Except now it was Alma who lay in his embrace, completely at his mercy, completely open to him, without shame, her pounding heart drowning out the church bells. A sweet dampness spread between her thighs.

Alma gasped and floundered as Gretl shook her awake.

"Really, Alma, you were moaning like someone was murdering you! I think you drank too much punch last night."

Still in thrall of her dream, Alma was too ashamed to look at her sister. Instead, she attempted to bring herself back to the waking world by focusing on the red gingham curtains and the ibex head staring down imperiously from the pine-paneled wall. This was their room in the rented summerhouse on the Traun River. The date on the calendar pinned beside her bed was September 1, 1900. Gretl's wedding—to *Wilhelm,* not to Klimt!—was still five days away.

Alma did indeed have a thumping hangover from her twenty-first birth-day party the previous night. She had muddled recollections of some impassioned debate with Max Burckhard. *Don't commit yourself to any one person,* the forty-six-year-old bachelor had admonished her. *Every potential mate is a prison.* Drawing on Nietzsche's philosophy of the individual, Burckhard had been arguing, as always, in favor of free love. And she, having already imbibed too much rum-laced punch, had countered, *Don't you know that another person can also be a paradise?* Had she really said that? Then that *filthy* dream about Klimt! As it so happened, she knew Klimt was summering only a short distance away, on Lake Attersee, in his sinful love nest with his sister-in-law, Emilie Flöge.

Burying her head in the pillow, Alma willed herself to sink into the oblivion of dreamless sleep, but Gretl yanked the prickly feather quilt off her and attempted to hoist her out of bed. "You must get dressed, or we'll be late for the pastor."

"Pastor?" Alma cupped her palm to her splitting forehead.

"Our conversion ceremony!" As jumpy as a frightened rabbit, Gretl opened the wardrobe, garishly painted with folkloric motifs, and pulled out Alma's most severe shirtwaist and a somber gray skirt. "You promised. Remember?"

Lurching down the narrow pine stairs, Alma dragged herself into the kitchen and poured herself a cup of coffee from the enamel pot Cilli had left on the woodstove. Sipping the bitter, scalding liquid, she glanced through the *Neues Wiener Tagblatt,* which reported that a record heat wave had sparked off an alarming number of suicides—and this in a city that already claimed the highest suicide rate on the globe. Perhaps the new nerve doctors like Sigmund Freud could explain what it was about Vienna that made people drown themselves in the Danube Canal or swallow poison or shoot themselves in the head. She wondered what the likes of Dr. Freud would make of *her* after her depraved dream.

Out in the garden, Carl was sketching while Mama chased toddling little Maria, whose rapid growth reminded Alma all too starkly of the stasis in her own life. She was now twenty-one, not even engaged, and had nothing to show for herself but a handful of songs.

"Goodness, *Mädele,* you slept so late, the morning mail's already arrived," Cilli groused in her thick dialect, as she bustled into the kitchen and handed Alma a letter from Zemlinsky.

Just when she'd given up on hearing from him! In her excitement, Alma spilled coffee on her pristine blouse. Shutting her ears to Gretl's pleas to hurry, Alma tore open the envelope, finding a card wishing her a happy birthday and a letter on black-bordered mourning stationery. This was the first communication she'd had with him since he canceled their last lesson back in May.

*When I received your lieder,* he wrote, *I was, as you can imagine, in a dreadful state.* Then followed a most detailed critique of her two songs. Before Alma could finish reading, Gretl hauled her off, stained blouse and all, down the narrow lanes of villas and hotels past the farmwives in their dirndls selling bunches of alpine herbs to the summer tourists. Finally, they reached the little neo-Gothic Lutheran church, an anomaly in this deeply Catholic province where one could scarcely walk one hundred paces without passing a wayside chapel or a carved Madonna.

The momentous event of Gretl and Alma's conversion consisted of the two of them kneeling in the otherwise empty church while the pastor mumbled prayers with his back to them. Alma restrained herself out of fear of upsetting Gretl, whose nerves appeared to be stretched ever thinner as her wedding day approached. Was her sister having second thoughts about Wilhelm, Alma wondered. Or was she apprehensive about the physical side of marriage, of what would unfold on her wedding night? Alma's dream about Klimt kept intruding on her thoughts, of Klimt making love to her on that cold marble floor only a few feet from where she and Gretl knelt.

The only way to drive such indecency from her mind was by thinking of Zemlinsky. Then again, her thoughts had dwelled on Zemlinsky that entire summer, not only while attempting to compose a cycle of three songs based on Rilke poems but even as she tried to divert herself with the usual vacation pastimes. During alpine hikes, she couldn't help but daydream about his holding her arm as she ventured up a particularly steep incline. Sadly, the fact remained that Zemlinsky was beyond her grasp, still deep in mourning for his father, whose death had left the full weight of responsibility for the family on his shoulders. He was surely destined to put off marriage for a good few years, and when he did marry, it would be to Melanie Guttmann. Any friendship he shared with Alma must be subordinated to this reality. Then why couldn't she get him out of her mind?

Later that afternoon, Wilhelm called by. Leaving him and Gretl on the terrace overlooking the Traun River, Alma shut herself up in the stuffy little parlor where she read and reread Alex's letter. His analysis of her compositions was sweeter to her than the most ardent love poetry. The *attention* he gave her music made her feel so alive. Only he could discern the potential locked inside her that still needed guidance and mentorship before it could unfold. *Don't you know that another person can also be a paradise?*

Sitting at the battered upright piano, she threw herself into implementing the corrections he suggested. Then Gretl's shrieking made Alma's hands freeze on the keys.

Dashing out to the terrace, she found Gretl and Wilhelm tearing into each other like two rabid dogs.

"So we can only move back to Vienna when you're established?" Gretl's lips were drawn back from her teeth, as though she might literally snap at Wilhelm. Her eyes were glassy and hard. "Only have a family when you're *established*? When the hell is that going to happen? Goddamn it all!"

"Enough of your hysterics," Wilhelm said. "You're carrying on like a spoiled brat who always wants her own way."

"*Me* spoiled?" Gretl's fury distorted her face. Her eyes squeezed into slits. "Fine words coming from a German-loving mama's boy—"

Before she could finish her tirade, Mama and Carl barged in and pulled the sparing couple apart.

"It's just wedding nerves, my boy," Carl said to Wilhelm, with strained joviality as he escorted him out the garden gate. "Women, eh? Don't take it to heart."

Mama yanked Gretl inside, out of view of the gawking tourists loitering in the lane. The whole scene left Alma dazed. Never had she seen Gretl like this, spewing such curses and so jarringly out of control. Mama and Gretl were in the parlor with the door closed, but their voices were raised to such a pitch that Alma heard every word.

"I won't marry him! It's a mistake."

"Gretl, I'm ashamed of you. You're ruining this for everyone. Tomorrow you'll apologize to poor Wilhelm and pray that he forgives you."

Unable to endure another word, Alma retreated to the most secluded part of the garden, where she flung herself on the grass and listened to the rushing river and the distant chime of cowbells. How could Mama be so heartless, pressuring Gretl to go through with this marriage after Gretl had so brutally revealed her misgivings? Alma's heart split in anguish for her sister. *If this is marriage, I want no part of it.*

• • •

Later, when Alma tiptoed up to their room, she found Gretl crying in bed.

"Hush, sweetheart," she whispered, taking Gretl in her arms. She wished she could simply hug the hurt out of her.

"I'm losing everything." Gretl clung to Alma as if she would never let her go. "My home, my country, *you,* my friends in Vienna."

"You'll never lose me," Alma said. Though, in truth, if her sister lived in Stuttgart, they probably couldn't expect to see each other more than once or twice a year. "Don't listen to Mama," she told her sister fiercely. "If you don't love him, don't marry him. We'll be spinsters together."

Gretl shook her head. "That's all very well for you. You have your music. Without a husband, I'm nothing. There'll be nothing left of me."

"That's not true! Your sketching—"

"A few girlish drawings? Oh, Alma, don't patronize me. Besides," she added with a trembling smile, "I want to have children."

How could her sister come so undone? Alma hardly dared to leave her side. They pushed their beds together and held hands while Gretl cried herself to sleep. Alma had notions of kidnapping her sister and spiriting her off to Paris where they would live like bohemians.

But all proceeded according to Mama's orders. Meek and docile once again, Gretl begged Wilhelm's pardon. On September 5, she married him. After the wedding, the bridal couple and their guests strolled along the esplanade overlooking the Traun River, and then they all dined at Hotel Elisabeth, named in honor of the late empress. Alma was relieved to see that Wilhelm seemed gentler and more attentive to her sister than ever before, as if he was all too aware of her emotional frailty. Gretl, in turn, seemed to rally in the light of his kindness. She appeared sweet and calm, as if the raging, cursing woman on the terrace had been a different person.

Alma and her family accompanied the bridal couple to the station, where the newlyweds would catch the train to Salzburg, their honeymoon destination. While Mama, Carl, and Wilhelm's parents were busy congratulating the bridegroom, Gretl took Alma aside to say her good-byes. Clad in her going-away dress of palest blue silk adorned with ribbons and lace, Gretl looked so beautiful and yet so wistful. Alma's heart tore at the way her sister stared at her and kept touching her cheeks and chin.

"I'm trying to memorize your features so I remember what you look like," Gretl said. "Your eyes. Your mouth."

"Sweetheart, you're only going to Stuttgart, not the North Pole." Alma embraced her. "We'll write to each other every week. Now enjoy your honeymoon. I hope you and Wilhelm are very happy." But her voice rang hollow at the sight of her sister's strained face, her rapidly blinking eyes.

"I can't believe I went through with it." Gretl twisted her wedding band round and round her finger, then picked up the slim valise she insisted on carrying herself, not entrusting it to Wilhelm or the porters. "Do you want to know something, Alma? Last winter I was so miserable I bought a pistol."

Gretl spoke in a matter-of-fact manner, not lowering her voice, while Alma found herself looking around nervously, wondering if anyone had overheard. Wilhelm, Mama, and Carl continued laughing and chatting pleasantly.

"One morning I sat for hours on the Albrechtsrampe," Gretl said, referring to the rampartlike structure, a remnant of Vienna's old defensive wall that had been torn down to make the Ringstrasse. "I had the pistol in my purse, and my mind was filled with the most horrible doubts."

A shiver ran through Alma when she thought of her sister all by herself with a loaded weapon in the busy heart of Vienna, surrounded by uncaring strangers. The Albrechtsrampe lay directly in front of the Albertina, the imperial apartments. What a place to contemplate self-murder! She shuddered when she remembered the many stories of similar suicides cluttering the pages of the *Neues Wiener Tagblatt*. And where was she when Gretl had been in the grip of such desperation? Moping over her piano, struggling to learn counterpoint?

"Why didn't you tell me?" Alma asked. Then she remembered when Gretl bicycled into the ditch that spring, willing herself to take the fall. The signs had been there, right in front of her.

"Oh, Alma, don't make such a fuss," Gretl said carelessly. "I'm a coward, aren't I? Too scared to pull the trigger. Too scared to call off the wedding."

Her sister no longer looked distressed, but seemed gripped by an eerie calm that froze Alma to her core. Before she could think of what to say, the train rumbled in, sputtering smoke and steam that left Alma's eyes burning.

Gretl took Alma's face in her hands. "I have that pistol in my valise," she said, smiling as if to reassure Alma that she would be fine, that the pistol was the talisman that emboldened her to sally forth into the as yet unchartered territory of her marriage. "And you know what? It's loaded."

Alma's stomach heaved. She thought she might retch. Gretl released her, picked up her valise, linked arms with her new husband, and boarded the train. To see her gaily waving at them through the window, anyone would think Gretl was a truly joyful young bride.

Alma clenched her hands. What should she do with these awful revelations? Tell Mama about the pistol? Send a telegram to warn Wilhelm? But it wasn't against the law for a woman to carry a loaded pistol if she claimed it was for self-defense. Yet if Alma did nothing, she would never forgive herself if Gretl shot herself or her husband. On the other hand, Gretl had assured her that she was too scared to pull the trigger. What could Alma do that wouldn't be a fundamental betrayal of her sister?

Only one thing remained certain—Gretl was deeply disturbed, and Alma hadn't had even the vaguest premonition. No, even after witnessing Gretl cursing out Wilhelm, Alma had been as oblivious of her sister's affliction as she'd been about her mother's pregnancy the previous year. Gretl herself said it best: *Alma with her head in the clouds, always the last to know!* How could it be that she was so ignorant of what was going on in her own family? Did this prove that she was completely narcissistic and self-absorbed? And if her sister was so troubled, did that mean that it ran in the family, that they were all somehow tainted?

Alma found she was crying openly, not caring if she made a spectacle of herself. Then Mama was there, holding her close and weeping herself, as if regretting her brusque treatment of Gretl.

"I'm worried about Gretl," Alma said brokenly. "She . . . she seems . . . she told me she had a loaded pist—"

Mama cut her off before she could finish saying the word. "Your sister has a nerve disorder. Wilhelm knows. He's promised to look after her. We should all be very grateful that she has such an understanding husband."

*Wilhelm* knew about her sister's debility before she did? Only now did she understand why Mama had been so keen to prevent Gretl from backing out of the marriage—Mama wanted Gretl safely married off while she was still young and pretty, before her malady became too obvious. But where did Wilhelm stand in all this? What did he stand to gain besides an unstable young wife? Carl, Alma reflected, must have pulled quite a few strings to get such a young man a position at the Stuttgart Academy of Fine Arts. To think her own family could be so slippery, so underhanded. And yet perhaps they truly meant the best for her sister. Maybe Mama and Carl sincerely believed that Wilhelm's love could heal Gretl.

# 11

||||||||||||||||||||||||

Upon the family's return to Vienna, Gretl's absence seemed to haunt their house. Hairline cracks appeared in the ceilings and walls. The shadows in the corners appeared darker and more ominous. Without her sister, the bedroom they had once shared seemed like a vast, lonely chasm. Sometimes Alma awakened at night, her heart hammering, certain she had heard Gretl weeping in the next bed, though, of course, no one was there.

If Gretl was mad, Alma wondered if she would be next. What if the family curse of insanity explained her unholy lusts, her wicked dreams, her aversion to babies, and her unfeminine strivings to be a somebody, a composer? Had Papa been mad, too, she wondered. Did that explain why he lived inside his art, hid himself away from the world, and never seemed to manage their finances? Or was Mama mad, and did that explain her rumored affair with Julius Berger, Gretl's likely father?

Alma took refuge in her music, playing and composing with a new reck-lessness, a looseness she had never before allowed herself. If she indeed had this sword hanging over her, she might as well live the most passionate life possible, holding nothing back. After all, what did she have to lose? Let her show the world what she could do. A beautiful song, a masterpiece for cho-rus and orchestra.

Resuming her lessons with Zemlinsky, Alma felt her music flower. Not only that—their friendship unfolded like an exquisitely painted Chinese fan. Zemlinsky suggested they attend matinee concerts together, for this, too, was part of Alma's musical education.

Mama might not have approved of these tête-à-tête rendezvous, but she and little Maria were away in Stuttgart visiting Gretl, who was unwell. Although Alma, too, was anxious about her sister, Mama had not invited her along, indicating that she and Gretl would be discussing the intimacies and intricacies of married life to which only wives were privy.

To ease their loneliness in Mama's absence, Carl invited guests to dinner night after night—not only old friends such as Max Burckhard but also Carl's latest hanger-on, the devoted Felix Muhr. Muhr, Alma learned, had recently come into a great deal of money, and she suspected Carl lived in hope that the young architect would commission some paintings.

With her mother away, Alma acted as hostess to Carl's friends, a thing she resented in the beginning. But when Carl brought up the best bottles from the cellar, she found herself warming to the task, intoxicated by both the wine and the spirited discussions of art and modernity. After dinner, she performed her compositions to much toasting and praise. She couldn't quell her effervescence, her bubbly laughter, her desire to be the center of attention. *You will never be this young or adored again.*

She had to admit that Muhr became fascinating as she got to know him better. He told her of his travels through Persia and Mesopotamia while she listened in awe, transported to dusty mountain villages and lost ancient cities. Without Mama hovering over her shoulder and whispering about marriage, Alma let her heart be at rest. Why couldn't she simply be friends with a man without agenda or design?

Seemingly grateful to Alma for playing the gracious lady of the house, Carl became her ally for once and uttered nary a murmur of disapproval about her afternoon concerts with Zemlinsky. And thus Alma resolved to make the most of this interlude of freedom and independence however fleeting it might prove to be.

Feeling utterly sophisticated, Alma slid into her seat beside Zemlinsky in the Golden Hall of the Musikverein for the Vienna Philharmonic's Sunday noon concert—the Vienna premiere of Gustav Mahler's Symphony no. 1 in D Major, conducted by the composer himself.

As the first notes pierced the expectant silence, Alma remembered Wagner's admonition that one shouldn't listen to music with just one's ears but with one's entire being. The symphony sent a tremor through the very floorboards, thrumming into the soles of her shoes. Her body vibrated like a tuning fork — every nerve, every muscle. The music made her sweat and shake, for she'd never heard its like, the one-hundred-strong orchestra playing in a bewildering jumble of styles that encompassed everything from cuckoo calls, simple folk tunes, the children's song "Frère Jacques," and an outlandishly distorted funeral march, all climaxing in the fourth movement full of crashing, violent chords that finally gave way to a note of triumphalism that seemed to undermine everything that preceded it. The symphony both exhilarated her and annoyed her. It confounded her, for she had no clue what to make of it. Mahler's music seemed to be galloping into the new century at such a pace that she feared she might be left behind.

Glancing sideways at Zemlinsky, Alma saw that his mouth was wide open, as though he was just as perplexed as she.

In the intermission, they didn't go out to foyer with the rest of the audience but remained seated side by side. It seemed they were both in a state of shock.

"What did you make of it?" Alma asked him.

"To be honest, I can't say." Zemlinsky rubbed his face. "There's no question that Mahler's a genius, but it's so overpowering. The way he juxtaposes the pastoral with the tragicomic, the ironic and the grotesque, the way he builds up a theme only to tear it to shreds — is it deeply cynical or ultimately transcendent? All I know is that his music makes mine seem juvenile."

Zemlinsky sat with his head bowed in an air of utter dejection, as though he were a medieval knight who had been beaten in the joust by an older, more experienced opponent.

Alma paused, digesting his words. "I think *you're* the better composer," she said fervently.

For a moment, he seemed too stunned to speak. Then he shook his head and regarded her with wounded disbelief, as if she were mocking him.

"Don't flatter me, Fräulein," he said gruffly.

"Herr Zemlinsky, it's my honest opinion. I love your music more than Gustav Mahler's. And you're still young. What might you be capable of when you're his age?"

"Alma Schindler," he said, his face bright red. "I've never met a girl who speaks her mind the way you do."

But his eyes softened, and she found herself staring at him until she had to look away. Her skin began to throb with an almost physical pain. With a shocked sense of clarity, she recognized that her excitement sprang from the sheer sensual anxiety of sitting beside Zemlinsky. Her skin crackled with the longing to touch him, for him to touch her. She imagined tugging off her glove and taking his hand, imagined his leg brushing up against hers. Where would *that* lead, she wondered, breaking into a sweat and fanning herself with the program. If only they could drop all pretense and surrender to the desire they both knew was there but were too well brought up to do anything about. She would simply have to learn to channel her stifled taboo desires into her music.

# 12

||||||||||||||||||||||||||

The winter of 1900 and 1901 proved the most prolific time Alma had ever known. She composed a piano trio and a violin sonata as well as sonatas, adagios, and rondos for solo piano. And lieder! A new song, "Ekstase," drawn from Bierbaum's poem of pure spiritual ecstasy, shimmered with her every yearning.

> *You are the sun, my god, and I am with you.*
> *I see myself ascending into paradise.*
> *Your light surges within me like a chorale.*

Zemlinsky was delighted when Alma played and sang "Ekstase" for him.

"Such a pity you weren't born a boy," he said. "As a girl, you'll experience countless setbacks."

"I *want* to make my mark," she told him fiercely.

Oh, to sense the heights. To be a mountain. To be great and expansive, bursting with potentiality. *To let myself go, just once.*

At the end of February, Mama returned from Stuttgart looking pale and haggard. When Alma asked her about Gretl, her mother offered only the most oblique replies.

"Your sister just needs time to settle into her new life," Mama said, fussing over little Maria's hair ribbons. "Meanwhile, she's taking the waters. There's a lovely sanatorium, Bad Cannstatt, on the outskirts of Stuttgart. The second biggest thermal spa in Europe after the baths in Budapest—just imagine!"

Why all this subterfuge? How it rankled Alma that both Mama and Gretl appeared to deem her unfit to know what was really going on. *Just because I'm not married, they think me an idiot.* Gretl's letters revealed absolutely nothing but were filled with banal ramblings about Wilhelm's work at the academy.

Alma's anxiety hung like a smoky cloud inside her brain, keeping her awake at night. In the midnight stillness, she heard Mama and Carl talking.

"She hasn't yet been given sexual fulfillment," Alma heard her mother say. "Wilhelm only goes so far and no further. He told Gretl it was because he didn't want children."

Alma threw her quilt over her face in despair. So Gretl had gone through with the marriage despite her misgivings, and all for what — to be left a virgin and shunted off to a sanatorium when her unhappiness became too much of an inconvenience to her husband? *If I get my hands on Gretl's pistol, I'll shoot Wilhelm myself.* Her sister's debacle proved the ultimate disillusionment — even marriage wasn't a guarantee of being initiated into the mysteries of sex.

Alma thought that Mama's return might signal the end of Muhr's being their constant dinner guest. But he still appeared at their table at least twice a week. Mama seemed especially charmed by him and thought nothing of leaving him and Alma alone in the parlor while she put Maria to bed and Carl went out to smoke his cigar.

One night in March, Alma played her latest composition for Muhr — a song set to Rilke's poem "Bei dir ist es traut." She knew that Muhr loved Rilke's poetry. While he sat in the chair she had come to think of as Zemlinsky's, she played and sang.

*All is peaceful wherever you are.*
*Tender clocks beat as in days of old,*
*Telling me sweet things, but not too loudly.*

*Somewhere a gate opens, outside into a blooming garden.*
*Evening listens at the windowpanes.*
*Let us stay silent—no one knows we are here.*

As the last note reverberated, Alma sat with her eyes closed, her head bent over the keys. She wondered what Zemlinsky would make of this song. *Oh, please let him be pleased by it.* Muhr remained uncharacteristically silent— perhaps because it wasn't good at all. A sense of defeat washed through her.

"Alma," Muhr said, in a strangled voice.

She twisted on her piano bench to see him kneeling. The glimmer from the gaslights shone on his monocle and brilliantined hair.

"Herr Muhr, are you all right?" she asked in alarm, wondering what he was doing on the floor. Had he suffered from an attack? A stroke? He gaped at her with a half-open mouth, as though struck dumb. But she was even more aghast when he began to speak.

"Alma Maria, we've become fast friends, have we not? We talk of everything together, from Rilke to Persian miniatures. Will you marry me, my darling?"

Thunderstruck, she could only stare at him. Then, piece by piece, it all fell together. The dinner invitations, Mama and Carl conspiring to leave her and Muhr alone together. Carl and her mother wanted her married off, and Felix Muhr was their handpicked choice. At thirty, he was just the right age. He was rich and revered Carl as a genius. He owned a villa in Baden on the outskirts of Vienna, he was reasonably handsome, and he wasn't Jewish. The perfect candidate in all things but one—Alma didn't feel anything for him, not as a *man,* even though she had cherished their budding friendship.

"Perhaps you hesitate," Muhr said, "because of your musical aspirations. Of course, I would want you to continue composing."

Alma imagined Mama, Carl, and Cilli eavesdropping, holding their breath while they awaited her reply. Would it not be beneficial to all parties? Of the two of them, Alma had the stronger personality, and Muhr seemed mild mannered enough to keep his word and let her have her own way. Surely, she could do worse.

*But what about love?* If she married him for money and convenience, wouldn't she die inside? Alma shuddered to think of giving her body to a man for whom she felt not a drop of passion. Then again, it chilled her to imagine never giving her body to *anyone*. Never maturing, never fulfilled. The entire conundrum was simply too awful.

Muhr awkwardly clambered to his feet. His monocle slipped and he adjusted it. "My dearest Alma, you don't have to give me your answer straightaway. Think it over for as long as you wish. Perhaps I should ask again in six months, which shall give us a chance to become even better acquainted."

Alma's throat constricted. In six months she would turn twenty-two. How much longer could she remain unwed before she became ridiculous — the dried-up spinster nobody wanted?

"Of course, it's your decision alone," Mama said later, after Muhr had gone home. "But think long and hard before you refuse as good a man as Felix Muhr."

Alma attempted to wash away her confusion in a cascade of piano chords, playing "Liebestod," the music she always turned to for comfort. She released her entire soul into the pathos of those notes. And she counted the hours to her next lesson. How deeply she had come to rely on Zemlinsky.

Unfortunately, Zemlinsky had the habit of canceling their lessons at the last minute if he had important rehearsals. Nor was he reliably punctual. Three days after Muhr's proposal, Zemlinsky arrived so late that Alma had given up on him and had washed her hair in preparation for that evening's party at the Taussigs. Carl was immured in his studio, and Mama, Maria, and Cilli were out, leaving Alma to open the door in exasperation, her damp hair hanging loose and unbound while she waited for it to dry.

"You're more than two hours late," she informed Zemlinsky. "At six, the Taussigs are sending their carriage for me. I should really turn you away."

Zemlinsky bridled, clearly not expecting that kind of reception. "My tram broke down!"

"Your tram, Herr Zemlinsky, is *always* breaking down." She folded her arms in front of her.

Not wanting to answer the door in her dressing gown, Alma had hastily thrown on her one article of reform dress, a loose gown of linen with embroidered accents—a birthday present from Aunt Mie. The unfortunate garment reminded Alma of a pretentiously bourgeois attempt at a shepherd's smock, and it didn't flatter her in the least. She felt like an enormous billowing sail.

"I'll have you know that I walked all the way from the Ringstrasse," Zemlinsky said, his voice rising along with the color in his face. "And now you want to turn me away? Do you really need three hours to dress for a party?"

"What business is it of yours how long it takes me to get dressed?"

Alma had to wait until Cilli and Mama were back just to get into her evening gown with all the tiny buttons up the back, and she also wanted Mama to help arrange her hair.

"Fräulein Schindler, if you want to be my student, you either compose or you carry on as a socialite. One or the other. You can't do both. I suggest you stick to what you do best and go to your parties."

Alma glared at him, angry enough to spit. How dare he turn up so late and then talk to her like that, as if *he* never went to parties or caroused in coffeehouses past midnight? A thousand ripostes rippled on her tongue. But she didn't dignify his remark with a reply, choosing instead to lead him into the parlor in icy silence. Since he was here, she might as well have her lesson, or part of it, seeing as she couldn't start dressing until the others were back.

Flicking her damp, loose hair behind her shoulders, she sat at the piano and began to play her newly composed adagio. Not the Rilke song. It would have devastated her to hear him rip apart her Rilke, considering the foul temper he was in. Her eyes on her score, she played her adagio with as much verve as she could muster, not even glancing his way until she had finished.

His eyes were as soft as velvet. "That's one of your best pieces yet. It truly expresses your character."

"How so?" she asked tepidly.

"Your unpredictability," he said. "Your sudden changes in mood."

"*My* unpredictability?"

Appearing to ignore her jibe, he sat beside her on the piano bench and began to play her score with such sensitivity that she could scarcely believe it was her own work she heard.

"So mercurial and bewitching," he said, when he had finished. "Just like you."

She closed her eyes and let his praise course through her. Then she swallowed hard. "Felix Muhr asked me to marry him," she blurted, flushing with shame even though she had no reason to.

Zemlinsky blinked, his face gone white. "I'd advise you to accept. Isn't that what you want? What everyone expects of you?"

Alma looked at him in disbelief, her eyes filling with the tears she could no longer hold back. "To give myself to a man I don't love? Do you really think so little of me?"

He looked so helpless then, his mouth quivering.

As Alma moved to reach for another score, her long, loose hair spilled over the piano bench, one tress flicking like a flame across Zemlinsky's thigh. When their eyes met, he began to shake. Before he could pull away, Alma seized his arms. His face washed red; he kissed her hands, then bent his brow to them. Gently, she rested her head on his, breathing in the scent of his silky brown hair, innocent of pomade. *Let me die here. This is my heaven.*

They drew apart slowly and stared at each other. Clumsily, like two children, they kissed each other's cheeks, and then held each other, his face buried in her hair, her fingers tracing the contours of his shoulder blades through his blue serge suit. Taking his face in her hands, she gazed at him with all the love burning inside her.

"Alex," she said.

He kissed her lips and she kissed him back, no longer the naïve girl Klimt had thought he could lead astray. She was a woman kissing her lover with her full passion, kissing Alex so long and hard that her teeth hurt. He held her so close that she felt his heartbeat as her own.

"Alma," he said. "All winter long I was wrestling with my love for you. I tried so hard to stop loving you, but I couldn't."

Her heart opened, light surging through her breast. *O sweet ecstasy.*

"Now I shall write, compose—everything!—all for you," he murmured, his mouth in her hair. "It's such a joy that you're an artist, too. We'll always have that in common."

# 13

|||||||||||||||||||||||||

"Alma, what a healthy color you have," Aunt Mie remarked, as they cycled through Prater Park on a glorious May afternoon. "Fresh air and exercise give you such a glow."

Having left the Wurstelprater and its amusement park behind, Alma, Mama, and Aunt Mie glided through the wilder reaches, passing water meadows, groves, and the field where the Prater deer grazed. A young stag lifted his head to watch them go past.

"If I didn't know better," Aunt Mie said to Mama, "I'd say your daughter was in love with her piano teacher."

Alma nearly lost her grip on the handlebars.

To her relief, Mama only laughed. "Oh, tosh! Alma just takes her music lessons very seriously, don't you, my dear?"

"I'm making progress on my Rilke song cycle," Alma said brightly, chattering away about the technical aspects of composition until Aunt Mie's eyes glazed over and she changed the subject.

Mama and Aunt Mie then began to discuss their new villas being built on the Hohe Warte. Both their families would be moving there in the autumn after they returned from their summer vacation in the mountains. Alma couldn't express how grateful she was that the excitement of planning the move and decorating the new house seemed to occupy all Mama's time and attention, thus making her oblivious to Alma's love affair with Alex that was taking place right under her mother's nose.

Within earshot of Mama and Cilli, Alex was the model teacher, calling Alma Fräulein Schindler as if nothing had changed. But as soon as they were alone together, they tumbled down that deep well of longing. And so the spring of 1901 progressed. Their courtship unfolded in secret during their lessons and their attending matinee concerts. It wasn't that Alma was ashamed of Alex—quite the contrary—but she knew that Mama and Carl would disapprove and tell her she could never marry a man like him, a poor Jew. She simply refused to allow their small-mindedness to interfere with her and Alex's brand-new love.

On May 15, Alma thought all her dreams had come true at once. Erica Conrat had invited her and Alex to watch the Court Opera's performance of *Tristan und Isolde* from the Conrats' balcony. However, Erica and her mother had come down with colds and could not attend. *Do invite your mother in our place,* Frau Conrat had written in the note that accompanied the tickets.

Alma did no such thing.

And so it transpired, as if ordained by the gods of music, that Alma found herself alone with Alex in the Conrats' private balcony while watching her most beloved opera, that wrenching tale of star-crossed lovers. Anna von Mildenburg and Erik Schmedes sang the arias that Alma knew by heart. Yet, as the music swelled around her, her eyes weren't on the stage but on her lover.

"Even when I'm with you, I long for you," Alex whispered.

In the darkened balcony, surrounded by the stormy ocean of sound, Alex knelt in front of her seat to lift her skirts and stroke her trembling knees in their silk stockings. Alma closed her eyes, her head flung against the velvet backrest, overwhelmed, for now he was kissing the insides of her thighs, the tender skin above her garters. Pulling Alex up to face her, Alma kissed him hard and gave him her tongue. She let him pull her gently down to the floor, out of sight, and let him stroke her all over.

At the climax of the opera, Anna von Mildenburg sang the "Liebestod" aria more beautifully than Alma had ever heard it. Locked in Alex's embrace, Alma surrendered to the absolute sublimity.

*Softly and gently*
*how he smiles,*
*how his eyes*
*fondly open —*
*do you see, friends?*
*Do you not see*
*how he shines*
*ever brighter,*
*star-haloed,*
*rising higher —*
*do you not see?*
*To drown,*
*to founder,*
*unconscious —*
*utmost bliss!*

As those sacred words enveloped her, Alex pressed his body against hers, and Alma felt his groin hardening against her thigh. She had the sensation of something holy. To burn with desire and yet feel so unsullied — surely that happened only once in a lifetime. A powerful, searing rite, something God-given. *A drop of eternity.*

Dreamy and languid, Alma lay in bed the following morning, the taste of Alex's kisses still on her tongue. May sunlight poured through the lace curtains to bathe her closed eyelids in liquid gold as she imagined him touching her every secret part. *He opened me like a book. He is mine. I am his.*

When she finally dressed and padded to the kitchen, she found herself humming a passage of his Frühlingsbegräbnis.

Cilli grumbled about Alma's laziness, rising so late, but nonetheless deigned to brew her fresh coffee, grinding the roasted beans in the coffee mill. Alma savored the taste of sweet butter and Cilli's homemade gooseberry jam on a poppy-seed roll still fresh and warm from the oven. When Mama marched into the kitchen with a letter—had the morning post already arrived?—Alma smiled at her like a simpleton.

"Good morning, Mama," she said, unable to disguise her happiness until she saw the outrage in her mother's red-rimmed eyes.

"Frau Conrat wrote to ask how I enjoyed the opera and she apologized for not being there." Mama flung the letter down on the table. "So you and Herr Zemlinsky were unchaperoned! Frau Conrat sent a ticket for me and you didn't say a word."

Alma tried to sit up straight, to speak to her mother as one grown woman to another. "Herr Zemlinsky and I go to concerts unchaperoned all the time. It's part of my musical education."

"I'll never forgive myself for giving you that liberty, you wretched girl! You were having an affair behind my back. And now you've brought shame on poor Frau Conrat as well. Frau Gottlieb saw you and Zemlinsky embracing like lovers in a cheap French novel."

Alma quailed at the thought of hideous Frau Gottlieb spying on them through her opera glasses.

"But I love Alex!" She banged her fist on the table. This wasn't like the fiasco with Klimt that Mama could try to sweep under the rug. "He loves me. We intend to marry."

"Never!" her mother cried. "I'll never give you my consent."

"I'm twenty-one! I don't need your consent. I'll marry him even without your blessing."

But Alma's bold words belied her powerlessness. Having no income of her own, she was wholly dependent on Mama and Carl.

As though summoned by their raised voices, her stepfather entered the kitchen. "You can't be serious, Alma." He spoke with measured calm while Mama wept. "The boy doesn't have more than two kreutzer to rub together. *You,* of all people, couldn't bear to live on bread and water. Besides, he's a Jew."

"The Conrats are Jewish!" Alma sprang up from the table, knocking over her chair. "You don't mind if I sit in their box at the opera. Or is that because they're rich and they buy your paintings?"

Alma's protests were in vain. Two days later, Mama took her off to the mountains without allowing her to see or speak to Alex before they left Vienna.

"I'm doing this for your own good," Mama said, on the train to Sankt Gilgen. "To keep the two of you from being alone together. This will give you both a chance to cool your heads."

Too angry to speak, Alma turned away from her mother and viewed the blooming meadows and orchards through the haze of her tears.

"I do hope you're not going to fume and rage at me all summer," Mama said. "You know, I've tried to give you the best chances in life. There are girls your age working twelve-hour shifts in factories. Those girls couldn't even dream about counterpoint lessons."

"But I should be left to make my *own* choice of husband," Alma said, with vehemence. "You should leave *me* to choose, judge, and act. You married Papa and *he* was a poor artist."

Mama laughed caustically. "I married him because I *had* to. I was pregnant with you."

Alma flushed and looked around frantically to see if any of the strangers on the train had overheard. It was absolutely shocking to hear Mama speak of such vulgar affairs.

"You don't even understand what poverty is," her mother said. "When I was a child, my entire family had to flee our home because my father's brewery went under and we couldn't pay the rent. My mother had just given birth to her twelfth child and she was raving with puerperal fever. We had to drag her out of her sickbed and carry her out of the house. When I was eleven, I had to work to support my family. First I was a ballet dancer—I made enough with walk-on roles to be the breadwinner."

Alma struggled to imagine her tall, stocky mother as a child ballerina, as nimble as a sprite.

"Later, the ballet company folded," Mama said, "and I worked as a nanny. I had to wash diapers until my hands were raw, and I slept in the cook's room. Then I became a cashier in a bathhouse and finally an opera singer.

"Even after I married, life was a constant struggle. Your father had so many debts. When the bailiffs were threatening to kick down our door, he would just lie on his stomach in bed and try to sleep through it. Carl would run from one usurer to the next and pawn everything he could lay his hands on. Without Carl, we would have starved."

It rattled Alma to hear her mother speak of Papa as a feckless sluggard. Carl had been Papa's most faithful protégé, or so he claimed. But what if his involvement with her mother dated back to those desperate days when Papa was still alive and Alma just a baby? Mama, who so adamantly insisted upon her daughters' purity, was herself far from stainless. Still, it sobered Alma to imagine her parents living in such squalor.

"I have two wishes for you, Alma." Mama adopted a gentler tone. "One: that you don't marry for money without love. Two: that you don't marry for love without money."

"So if Alex could establish himself, you would accept him," Alma said, relieved to discover that Mama objected to him because he was poor, not because he was Jewish.

Mama was silent for a moment, clearly flustered to be outfoxed. "We shall see, my dear. Time will tell."

*I have two wishes for myself,* Alma thought. *First: that I won't have to sacrifice my art for love. Second: that I won't have to sacrifice love for my art.* She wanted both. To give herself completely to a man. To give herself completely to her music.

# 14

||||||||||||||||||||||||

Alma stood at the gate of her family's brand-new villa high above Vienna on the Hohe Warte. She directed her gaze not at the sweeping view of the city below but instead contemplated two flies copulating on the gatepost. How still and unperturbable they were, bathed in golden October light. Now and then a shiver ran through their wings. She gently blew at them, and they flew off lazily and continued their mating a little farther away.

The breath of the world caressed Alma with her memories of Alex. She imagined the flow of his essence, his divine spark, into hers. Catching sight of her lover walking up the street, she cried out in joy. This was her first glimpse of him since that fateful night in May when they had shared such forbidden pleasures against the backdrop of *Tristan und Isolde*. Alma had planned today's rendezvous with the utmost care. Mama, Maria, and Carl were out, and it was Cilli's day off.

"Alex!" she cried, flinging open the gate.

Slightly short of breath from his steep walk up from the tram stop, Alex took her hands. "You live at the end of the universe, Alma Maria Schindler. The princess in her castle on top of the glass mountain."

They gazed at each other before sharing a kiss that broke the dark enchantment of their forced separation. But it wasn't safe to kiss in open view. Kolo Moser next door might see them and report back to Carl.

"Come inside," she murmured, leading him by the hand.

He stopped for a moment to regard the semidetached villa's stark white exterior devoid of ornamental flourishes. "The epitome of modernity," he observed.

"It's built to Carl's taste, not mine," Alma was quick to say. "It reminds me of a sanatorium."

Alma led him into the ostentatiously plain interior with its white walls and blue and white tiled floors. The color pattern was repeated throughout the ground floor rooms. The curtains were white while the woodwork, built-in cabinets, and upholstered furniture were blue. Blue and white Japanese vases occupied the blue windowsills. Even Mama's new coffee service, on display in the glass-fronted cabinet, was blue, white, and pointedly modern with wedge-shaped handles.

"All this blue and white," Alma said, as she took Alex up the stairs. "It makes me want to splash red paint everywhere."

She showed Alex into her room, painted pale green, her personal retreat from Carl's overpowering aesthetics. Tucked beneath the eaves, the space was dominated by a huge bookcase, still empty as she hadn't yet had a chance to unpack her volumes of Nietzsche and Zola. They had only just arrived back from the mountains.

"Look," she said, drawing Alex to the window. "You can see the Vienna Woods."

She trembled at the thrill of being alone with her lover at last. In her room! At first, they perched on the edge of her virginal, lace-draped bed and kissed gently, then hard. Their teeth and tongues fought a fierce battle. They wrestled in silence, Alex resisting her, as if fighting both her and himself. But when she wouldn't let him go, he responded to her embraces like one possessed, coiling himself around her like a spring, clasping her hips so that she slid between his legs, his swollen crotch against her belly. They kissed to the accompaniment of soft exclamations. She sucked on his mouth and drank his saliva. He kissed her until she was completely shattered and could scarcely come to her senses, in thrall of his touch on her most secret parts. How far would they go? *One little nuance more and I shall become a god.* She imagined feeling him inside her, opening her womb to him.

"I'm going crazy, Alma," Alex kept repeating softly. "How are we going to wait until we can marry?"

They both quivered with yearning.

"You're even sweeter than last spring," he said, unable to stop kissing her. "Much more tender."

Tears filled her eyes. "I never imagined I could love anyone like this, Alex."

He buried his face in her loosened hair.

Afterward, they made their way down to the parlor, where Alma sat at the piano and played her summer harvest of compositions. She had even drafted the beginning of her very first attempt at an opera, drawn from Hugo von Hofmannsthal's play *Die Frau im Fenster.*

Some of this is very fine," Alex said, his arms around her waist while her hands danced across the keys. "Your best yet." When she played a passage he particularly liked, he stroked her back, and whispered, "Well done."

He played her new song, "In meines Vaters Garten," so beautifully. Her entire body breathed for him, her every pore. She longed to be his wife, his eternal beloved. *If I don't spend my life with Alex and for Alex, I will be committing a crime against myself.*

How blissfully that October passed, the happiest in Alma's memory. Despite the long tram ride out to the Hohe Warte, Alex visited once or twice a week. When Mama and Carl were present, he was the model of distance and reserve. But in the rare stolen moments when Mama was too distracted with Maria to watch over them, they kissed and caressed until they were aching and breathless.

Alma's heart flamed when Alex presented a copy of his newly published Lieder op. 7, officially dedicated to her, a public declaration of his love. He played and sang "Meeraugen," while gazing at Alma who sat beside him on the piano bench.

*To drown, drown myself*
*in the deep lap of those eyes.*

"You're my muse," Alex told her. "Who knows what I'll go on to write, all for you."

That month, his sister Mathilde married Arnold Schoenberg, so Alex now had only himself and his mother to support.

"Perhaps it might be possible for us to marry sooner," he told Alma. "If only I can make my professional breakthrough."

He had submitted the score of his ballet, *Der Triumph der Zeit*, to Gustav Mahler in hope that the great conductor would stage the piece, as he had staged Alex's opera the previous year. But much to his disappointment, he had never heard a word back from Mahler about his ballet.

If this setback wasn't bad enough, Carl and Mama remained as opposed as ever to Alex as a suitor, dismissing his prospects at every turn. Her courtship with Alex made Alma think of trout battling their way up waterfalls, driven by a deep passion that defied all else, even the force of gravity. How much longer could she and Alex sustain this struggle?

In November a ray of hope came by way of Berta Zuckerkandl's upcoming dinner party in honor of her sister, Sophie Clemenceau, who was visiting from Paris. Both Alma and Alex were invited, and Gustav Mahler as well.

"Here's your chance to speak to Mahler directly in a friendly setting," Alma told Alex. "Maybe he can still be convinced to put on your ballet."

Alex was decidedly less optimistic. "Mahler has strong opinions and makes his own decisions. He's not one to be easily swayed."

As it happened, Alex declined the invitation because he was conducting that evening at the Musikverein. So Alma resolved to use her own powers of persuasion on her lover's behalf.

"I've never seen you more beautiful," Mama said wistfully, as she arranged Alma's hair for the party that evening. "There's a special radiance about you lately."

Alma met her mother's eyes in the mirror and smiled. So even Mama noticed how being in love made her shine as never before, made her skin luminous, her eyes bright and tender. Of course, it helped that she was wearing her new evening gown of lilac satin with a waist of black point d'esprit over a silvery chiffon plissé—only her finest would do for Berta Zuckerkandl's salon.

The Zuckerkandls sent their carriage for Alma, and she traveled the short distance down the steep hill to their villa in Nusswaldgasse in Döbling.

"Thank you for coming, my dear." Berta Zuckerkandl offered her perfumed cheek to Alma's kiss. "You're the only lady guest besides my sister and Mahler's sister Justine. The Herr Direktor hates strangers, but you're so musical, you'll fit right in."

Frau Zuckerkandl was as graceful as a dancer in her reform dress, a striking silk ensemble of flowing stripes and checks that was an art form in itself. Linking arms with Alma, she drew her into the main reception room, where guests lounged on velvet sofas and lacquer-work chairs. A brand-new frieze covered one wall—Alma recognized it immediately as Gustav Klimt's work. She jumped out of her skin at the sight of Klimt himself raising his glass to her and giving her a slow-burning smile. Meanwhile, her hostess introduced her to the small gathering of slightly more than a dozen people, including Max Burckhard.

"Please welcome Alma Maria Schindler, the most beautiful girl in Vienna, daughter of the great artist Emil Schindler, and if that wasn't impressive enough, she's a most accomplished pianist and also a composer!"

Frau Zuckerkandl's choice of words sounded hauntingly familiar to the ones she had spoken when introducing Alma at her salon more than two years ago except now Gustav Mahler was on hand to hear their hostess praising her to high heaven.

Mahler was cordial enough when he shook Alma's hand, but he seemed to take no special notice of her. Alma was secretly relieved that he didn't seem to recall their encounter two summers ago while cycling around Lake Hallstatt. How embarrassing it would have been if she had been fixed in his memory as that red-faced, perspiring girl who had begged him for an autographed postcard.

Unfortunately, Alma found herself too flustered by Klimt's presence to speak to Mahler about Alex's work. Likewise, she could hardly look at Max Burckhard without blushing. She cringed to remember that day in August when she and Burckhard had hiked up the Falkenstein. Mama and Carl had lagged behind, and Alma had felt lovelorn and desperate enough to let Burckhard kiss her. To let him put his *tongue* in her mouth! She shuddered at the memory of his walrus moustache bristling against her nostrils. How would she ever live that down? Burckhard was gallant and gentlemanly, but there was that unmistakable gleam in his eye as though he would never let her forget that kiss for as long as they both lived.

Upon discovering that the seating arrangement placed her directly between Klimt and Burckhard, Alma threw Berta Zuckerkandl a look of helpless supplication. Her hostess only smiled inscrutably before turning her attention to Mahler and his sister on the opposite end of the table. Alma squirmed. She did her best to ignore Klimt, but her icy hauteur seemed only to inflame him all the more.

"You *must* complain to Frau Zuckerkandl for seating you below the salt," Klimt said genially. "Between us two debauched old men."

"Speak for yourself," Burckhard grumbled.

"Alma, I hear you're contemplating marriage," Klimt said. "To that pauper Zemlinsky." He sounded petulant and jealous.

"Zemlinsky is a poor choice indeed," Burckhard said. "You can tell from his physiognomy that he'll suffer ill health and a short life."

Ignoring Burckhard, Klimt leaned close enough for Alma to feel the animal heat rising off his skin. "You're not still vexed at me for Venice, are you? I've never forgotten how lovely you were. You know I would love nothing better than to paint you, but your mother won't let me near you."

"I can hardly blame her," Burckhard said.

"I should have proposed to you two years ago instead of letting Carl chase me away," Klimt continued, gazing at Alma as though he were absolutely besotted.

"Fortunately, I've learned better than to take anything *you* say seriously," she replied.

"Alma," said Burckhard. "I hope you shall play one of your lieder for us after dinner."

"In front of Mahler?" The very thought left Alma petrified. "Surely not."

The servants brought out the first course, a plate of raw broccoli, hardly the sumptuous fare Alma had come to expect at Berta Zuckerkandl's dinner parties.

"Is this the new fashion in cuisine?" she whispered in horror, tentatively poking the broccoli with her fork.

Burckhard burst out laughing. "It's because of Mahler. He's a vegetarian and prefers raw food. He's a teetotaler, too. Look, he's drinking water, not wine."

"I hear it's on account of his hemorrhoids," Klimt said.

"Stop it, both of you!" Alma cried. "That's very disrespectful!"

But bathed in the warmth of their attention, she laughed along with them. The two men were fighting over her, she realized, a ripple of pleasure running up her spine. They were even trying to take the great Gustav Mahler down a peg or two just to impress her. Alma noticed Mahler glancing at their trio, first surreptitiously, then openly. Her and her companions' conversation was by far the most animated at the table even if it wasn't the most refined.

"You should see our new villa, everything blue and white, even the *toilet seat*," Alma gasped, tears of hilarity streaming down her face. "Designed and handcrafted by Kolo Moser! Our toilet is a *Gesamtkunstwerk!*"

All three of them collapsed into helpless laughter.

From the other end of the table came Mahler's voice. "My dear Fräulein Schindler, might the rest of us be allowed to hear your amusing tales?"

After dinner, the guests gathered in the drawing room, where the discussion turned to the theme of the relativity of beauty. Mahler held the floor. Though only five foot three, he seemed larger than life. A frenetic, restless energy crackled through him. His thick blue-black hair and his finely sculpted beardless face made him seem younger than his forty-one years.

"Beauty!" Mahler cried. "The head of Socrates is beautiful."

"In my mind, Alexander von Zemlinsky is beautiful," Alma said, seizing her chance.

Mahler seemed nonplussed. "That's going a bit too far, Fräulein."

"Zemlinsky's famously *ugly*," Burckhard pointed out.

"But his music is exquisite," Alma said, not missing a beat.

"Zemlinsky shows promise, to be sure," Mahler said. "But he's quite restricted as a composer, don't you think?"

Alma flared up to hear her lover so cavalierly dismissed. "Now that we're speaking of Herr Zemlinsky, why don't you stage his ballet, *Der Triumph der Zeit*? You've kept him waiting a year for an answer."

"Because the ballet is worthless! It's unperformable. As a musician, how can you defend such rubbish?" Mahler gazed at her searchingly through his spectacles.

*"Rubbish?"* She was incredulous. "Have you even looked at it properly, Herr Direktor?" Now that she had Mahler's attention, she wasn't going to back down easily. "Perhaps you don't understand it. I'll tell you the whole narrative and explain what it means," Alma said confidently, as Alex had instructed her on the ballet's somewhat baffling symbolism.

Mahler smiled suavely. "I'm all eagerness."

"But first you'll have to explain to me, Herr Direktor, the full meaning of *Die Braut von Korea*," she said scathingly, referring to the production currently being performed at the Court Opera. "So full of kitsch and romantic clichés—it's the most inane ballet I've ever seen."

Instead of taking offense, Mahler laughed, revealing fine white teeth. "Our hostess says you're a composer."

"I study counterpoint with Herr Zemlinsky," Alma said, less sure of herself now. She flushed at how deftly Mahler had turned the conversation away from Alex straight onto her. "He's my greatest inspiration. I think he's the finest young composer in Vienna."

"It's very good of you, Fräulein Schindler, to speak of your teacher with such respect," Mahler said pacifically. "Your loyalty speaks volumes. I'll send for Herr Zemlinsky no later than tomorrow."

A trill of victory sounded inside Alma's heart. She found herself beaming. *Wait till I tell Alex!*

"And you, Fräulein, must bring some of your scores to the opera for me to look at." Mahler smiled at her intently.

Alma realized that the others had drifted away, leaving her and Mahler on their own. It was as though a magic circle enclosed the two of them. In that crowded room, she heard no voice but his. Stunned by his invitation, by his adroit replies to her clumsy petitions, she told him that she would come when she had something good to show him.

"Please don't make me wait too long," he said. "I entreat you to come to the dress rehearsal of *Les contes d'Hoffmann* tomorrow morning. Frau Zuckerkandl and Frau Clemenceau are coming. Please bring your mother as well," he added, as though to convey that his intentions were entirely above reproach. "I would love to meet her."

Alma hesitated. Did she dare surrender her scores, as imperfect as they were, to so distinguished and powerful a man as Mahler? The thought left her both exhilarated and terrified. She found herself mesmerized by this slender man whose genius was a palpable presence, leaving her weak in the knees. His intensity! *This man is made entirely of oxygen. If I stand too close, I might get burned.*

"Yes, I accept," she heard herself say. She told herself that Alex would want her to, that he would be overjoyed for her.

"Where do you live?"

"The Hohe Warte."

"That's not far," Mahler said. "I'll walk you home."

She wondered what her mother would make of her walking up the dark streets on the arm of the great opera director. For a moment, her head filled with spinning points of light. "No, thank you, Herr Direktor. I'll go in Frau Zuckerkandl's carriage."

"Well, at least you'll be at the opera tomorrow morning," he said, his eyes compelling and direct. "For certain?"

"Yes, indeed, Herr Direktor."

"I do hope you enjoyed yourself," Berta Zuckerkandl said, when she kissed Alma farewell before showing her into the carriage. "Tonight you've met your past, your present, and your future." She spoke enigmatically as though she were the Norn spinning Alma's fate.

On the ride home, Alma was racked with misgiving. Had she really made *toilet jokes* at Berta Zuckerkandl's table? She felt like burying her head in shame. What was worse was that she had gone for Alex's sake, to fight his cause, only to flirt with Burckhard and Klimt. And *then* she had unwittingly thrown herself headlong into the blinding spotlight of Mahler's attention. She closed her eyes and tried to summon her lover's face, but she saw Mahler, only Mahler. He was a monolith. *He wants to see my lieder!* Berta Zuckerkandl's mysterious words played inside her head. *Your past. Your present.*

"And my future," Alma whispered, her head pounding in confusion.

Alma arrived home to find Mama waiting up for her with a pot of linden-flower tisane. She dutifully informed her mother of Mahler's invitation to the dress rehearsal of *Les contes d'Hoffmann*.

"You're invited, too," she said, even though she knew her mother had an engagement.

She almost hoped her mother would find some reason to forbid her from going just to take the weight of Mahler's summons off her shoulders. But Mama was beside herself.

"Such an honor, my dear! You can't possibly refuse."

# 15

||||||||||||||||||||||

Alma met Frau Zuckerkandl and Madame Clemenceau before the locked doors of the Court Opera. A frosty November day, the chill from the cobblestones seeped up through the thin soles of Alma's good shoes, but before she could even comment on the cold, Mahler appeared.

"Fräulein Schindler, how good to see you," he said, as he unlocked the doors to usher them inside. "Did I not keep my word? A man is only as good as his word."

Once the four of them were inside, Mahler bolted the doors behind them again. *This is almost like a secret initiation,* Alma thought. She had never seen the vast marble foyer so empty, as though this entire edifice existed for her and her companions alone.

"Make I take your coat, Fräulein Schindler?" Mahler asked, before proceeding to help her out of her black woolen mantle.

But he didn't extend the same courtesy to Frau Zuckerkandl and Madame Clemenceau, who merely shared a smile as though amused by this discrepancy. Mahler, meanwhile, led the way up a hidden staircase. He and the two older women chattered blithely, their words rendered meaningless by the roaring inside Alma's head. *Gustav Mahler is carrying my coat!*

His office was spacious enough to contain a grand piano and a massive mahogany desk. The walls were covered with framed and signed photographs of opera singers, many of them beautiful divas — Anna von Mildenburg, Selma Kurz, and Marie Gutheil-Schoder, to name a few. Their portraits seemed to glow with sophistication and success, holding up a mirror to Alma's self-doubt. *What have I accomplished in my twenty-two years?*

Not knowing what else to do with herself, she stood beside Mahler's piano and turned the pages of the sheet music she found there—a half-finished score by Mahler himself. She recalled how his First Symphony had flummoxed both her and Alex, leaving her lover defeated, his head in his hands. *I'm here for Alex,* she reminded herself. *To champion his career.* Only she felt so tongue-tied. It was rude of her not to join the conversation, but she couldn't think of what to say that wouldn't sound like the gushing of an overawed girl. So many contradictory thoughts and emotions churned inside her. Before Mahler, she felt so small, so insignificant. And those rumors of Mahler seducing his sopranos—how many other young women had he lured to his office? In the corner beside the tiled heating oven was a loveseat. Her hands started shaking.

"Fräulein Schindler," he called out, cutting through her tangled thoughts. "How did you sleep last night?"

She could only laugh in confusion. *What a question!* "Perfectly, Herr Direktor," she lied, hoping to sound lighthearted. "Why wouldn't I?"

He stared straight into her eyes. "I didn't sleep a wink."

Alma raked her brain for some breezy comeback only to find herself gaping at him like a fish.

"Come, Alma, dear." Berta Zuckerkandl took her arm as they walked down together for the rehearsal.

A full dress rehearsal of *Les contes d'Hoffmann* just for the three of them! Alma and her companions sat in the middle of the front row. Madame Clemenceau passed around a small box of candied violets, but Alma shook her head. Eating here seemed too great a sacrilege. The Court Opera was the holiest of cathedrals, and Mahler was the greatest producer she had ever seen. His senses were so acute—he seemed to hear and see every little thing at once. If a singer was out of tune or made an awkward gesture. If the electric lighting was wrong. And his energy! Moving at an allegro furioso, he vaulted tirelessly from his conductor's podium, through the orchestra pit, and up onto the stage before leaping back down again. Under his direction, the orchestra was intoxicatingly lush. Alma perched forward in her seat as the fantastical opera unfolded. The second act was poignant, with the hero falling in love with an automaton. Not until the very end of this vignette did he realize he was enamored of a wind-up doll.

But in the third act, when Marie Gutheil-Schoder appeared as the courtesan Giulietta, the spell was broken. The soprano's skirts were slashed open on the sides all the way up to her waist, affording her tiny audience a shocking glimpse of her sheer pink stockings and silken undergarments. Alma had never seen anything so risqué.

"Ooh, how naughty," Berta Zuckerkandl whispered to her sister, who tittered behind her hand.

Mahler's voice split the air like a thunderclap. "How dare you? This is an abomination! A gross indecency!"

Alma slammed back in her seat and the orchestra came to a crashing halt as Mahler railed at his soprano, his arms whipping in fury. He ordered the stammering lady offstage to get her seams sewn back together. Even after she vanished, he continued shouting over the heads of his orchestra, decrying Gutheil-Schoder's shamelessness. If he was a brilliant director, he was also a stern taskmaster, Alma observed. His singers must admire and fear him in equal measure.

Yet he came to the rail after the dress rehearsal and escorted Alma and her companions to the door again, every bit as kind and solicitous as before. When they said their farewells, he shook Alma's hand with such warmth.

"Remember, Fräulein Schindler, you said you would send me your music. I shall hold you to your word."

What if she sent Mahler her lieder and he hated them, she wondered fitfully. Would she ever dare compose again?

"What was the outcome of your talk with Mahler?" Alma asked Alex the following afternoon while they played a duet on the piano.

"He said he would consider staging another one of my operas." Alex's calf rubbed up against hers as he worked the pedals. "But not my ballet."

"Still, that's a victory," Alma said, hoping to console him. "I put in a good word for you, didn't I? Just as I promised."

As if to mask his disappointment, Alex changed the subject. With a furtive glance at the open doorway where Mama was wont to hover and eavesdrop, he lowered his voice to a whisper. "Come by my apartment Wednesday afternoon. It's so hard to get you alone here."

Mama had become increasingly vigilant regarding Alex's visits.

"I'm forbidden," Alma whispered back. "She says I've stretched her tolerance as far as it will go."

"Surely you could find some excuse to take the tram into the city." Reaching across the keyboard, he touched her hand, causing her to falter and strike a false note while he carried on playing flawlessly. "Say you need to buy a new hat. But come to my place instead. What makes you hesitate? Is it prudery?"

Alma avoided his gaze because she didn't know what to say. In truth, she had begun to think that she and Alex had gone too far too soon. The depths of her own desire frightened her. Each time she plunged into that dark abyss, she thought she would never reach the bottom of it. What if she drowned there? Even now, sitting beside her lover at the piano, she wanted to kiss him, taste him, lie with him. Yet his pestering to get her alone in his apartment was beginning to wear her down. She wished he would leave off that hectoring tone when she had already risked so much for their intimacy. What if they both lost control and she ended up pregnant and disgraced? They should leave *some* final mystery for their wedding night—whenever *that* might be. The way they had been carrying on, she worried they would burn out their passions long before Alex could afford to marry her. Meanwhile, Mama had grown so suspicious, she seemed loath to even leave Alma alone in the house if she could help it.

"Alma!" Mama marched in brandishing a letter. "*This* just arrived —without a return address!" Her mother's voice rang with accusation, as though this piece of anonymous mail was the latest effrontery her daughter had forced upon her long-suffering parent.

Alma shot a desperate glance at Alex, but his confusion seemed to indicate that the missive had nothing to do with him.

After her lesson and before Mama's watchful eyes, Alma opened the envelope to find an unsigned poem written in black ink on thick cream-colored stock with gilded edges. No other message accompanied the verses.

*It happened overnight.*
*I never thought*
*That counterpoint and harmony*
*Would so move my heart again.*

Before Alma could fully comprehend the words on the page, Mama snatched it from her.

"Who sent this?" Mama asked, in a voice like lead. "It doesn't look like Herr Zemlinsky's handwriting."

Mama seemed especially apprehensive after learning that Klimt had attended Berta Zuckerkandl's party, but Klimt was hardly the sort to write a poem about counterpoint and harmony.

"It could only be from Mahler." Alma took the poem from her mother's hand and read it once more.

*I still hear it,* the poem concluded in its final stanza. *A man, his word! / It echoes inside me—a canon of some sort. / I watch the door and wait.* That look he had given her when he said, *I'll hold you to your word.*

Mama burst out laughing. "Oh, Alma, don't flatter yourself. A man like Mahler would hardly write poetry to a girl like you. Someone's playing a prank."

Mumbling an excuse to her mother, Alma grabbed her coat and set off for a walk up and down the steep streets of the Hohe Warte. The spiky outer shells of chestnuts, fallen from the golden-leafed trees, pricked her through her soles. Below, the city glistened in the splendor of mellow autumn light. But Alma could hardly take it in.

Mama could say what she would, but certainty gripped Alma with an unshakable force—the poem was Mahler's. His verses left her as confounded as his First Symphony. *I don't understand this. What does it mean?* Though she could hardly claim to feel for him what she felt for Alex, she could think of nothing and no one else apart from Gustav Mahler. *I will pluck out this poisonous weed and make my heart the exclusive sanctuary for my true love, my Alex.* If only Alex had written that poem.

# 16

||||||||||||||||||||||||||||

Two weeks passed. The trees shook off their remaining leaves, and the first snow drifted down in fat, feathery flakes. The squares of Vienna smelled of roasting almonds. Alex was so busy conducting, he canceled their next lesson, and Alma was too cowardly to visit him at his home. Instead, she struggled to compose while little Maria shrieked and danced around the room.

"You're so pale, Alma," Mama said. "What's possessing you? All you do is play your piano and weep. I hate to see you like this."

Mama took her to see Gluck's *Orfeo ed Euridice.* Mahler was not conducting and it showed — never had Alma been so bored at the Court Opera. Her eyes kept darting up to the director's box where Mahler sat watching the performance.

*What's possessing you?* Alma searched her soul for an answer. *Mahler has cast a spell on me.* She stared at him in his lofty perch while he went on watching the opera as though oblivious to her existence. He was a giant filled with insurmountable power. She strove to put him out of her mind and concentrate on Alex. If only Mama and Carl weren't so dead set against Alex, forbidding an open courtship, everything could be so different. If they approved of him, if Carl was willing to pull strings and help him as he'd done for Gretl's Wilhelm, Alma and Alex would be engaged by now, Alma busy planning their wedding. But as things stood, her future with Alex was beginning to seem impossible. They were star-crossed lovers, all the forces of society and nature set against them. And then Mahler had swept into her life, bringing a sea change in his wake. Did this prove she was fickle? Inconstant?

Just as Alma's self-doubt seemed enough to throttle her, Mahler turned in his seat and finally took note of her, returning her open-mouthed stare. His eyes shone with something that looked like adulation. She blinked back tears as a sense of wonder coursed through her. Alma kept gazing up at him while he smiled down at her, his face appearing wide open and vulnerable, as though he were a boy of her own twenty-two years, not a forty-one-year-old man.

During the intermission, when Alma and her mother wandered out into the foyer, Mahler materialized before them as though conjured out of the marble floor.

"Fräulein Schindler, how enchanting to see you again! Is this your mother?"

Alma had never seen Mama more impressed — she actually blushed when the famous conductor shook her hand. Meanwhile, a throng of inquisitive onlookers began to gawk and murmur.

"Shall we go somewhere a bit more peaceful, Fräulein Schindler, Frau Moll?" Mahler asked. "I shall serve you tea in my office."

Mama squeezed Alma's hand and gave her a giddy smile as Mahler escorted them upstairs. A golden cloud filled Alma's head.

In Mahler's office, Alma sat at the piano and gently turned the pages of his sheet music while he and her mother conversed, Mama laughing and animated and Mahler most charming. A former opera singer, Mama seemed enraptured to have this audience with him.

"You're from Hamburg, Frau Moll?" Mahler asked, before launching into reminiscences of his stint as chief conductor at the Hamburg Stadttheater, where he had conducted Wagner's *Tristan und Isolde* for the very first time.

Alma swung around to hear the name of her most beloved opera.

"You live in the Hohe Warte," Mahler said, glancing from Alma to her mother. "Why, that's my favorite walk."

"Then you must come and call on us, Herr Direktor," said Mama.

Alma was stunned. So her mother was *encouraging* him. Giving him her blessing.

"I certainly shall," said Mahler. "But when? Soon, I hope."

It was his eagerness that overwhelmed Alma and rendered her speechless.

"You name the date, Herr Direktor," said Mama.

Alma swallowed back her breath to see him consult a leather-bound engagement calendar as thick as a Russian novel.

"How about next Saturday," he said, peering at Alma over his spectacle rims.

Her heart banged in her chest. "Herr Direktor, I have a counterpoint lesson that day. With Herr Zemlinsky."

A pained look crossed her mother's face. "Surely that can be rescheduled, dear."

Alma froze to see both Mama and Mahler looking at her, awaiting her response. Now was the time she could take a stand and prove once and for all that her fealty belonged to Alex. But what if she turned away as great a man as Mahler only for Alex to cancel their lesson at the last moment, as he was so prone to do? *A man, his word!*

"Saturday it is," Alma said, her ears ringing.

His smile left her floating several feet above the ground. "I shall look forward to calling on you, Fräulein Schindler. I hope you will finally show me your songs."

"You can *play* your songs for the Herr Direktor," Mama said.

The joy on Mahler's face brought the blood to Alma's cheeks. To see him looking at her like that, anything seemed within the realm of possibility, as though something great and beautiful had entered her life and would remain there forever.

"Herr Direktor," Alma blurted. "One day I would love to try my hand at conducting an orchestra." She immediately wanted to kick herself for making such an outlandish request.

But Mahler appeared to take her seriously. "There's certainly no harm in your coming to a rehearsal and giving it a try. In fact, it would give me great pleasure to see you at the podium."

Alma thought she would swoon as the glory of it all descended on her. A woman conducting the Vienna Philharmonic!

"I hope you would give me your honest verdict," she said earnestly, hoping to sound professional.

His dark eyes seemed bottomless, the skin around them etched with lines of sorrow and joy. "No verdict is ever impartial, Fräulein Schindler."

Mama, seated on the loveseat, seemed to smile to herself.


"How could you do such a thing?" Carl demanded, glaring at Mama over his plate of *Tafelspitz*. "Taking an innocent girl, your own daughter, into a private room with a roué like Mahler? Have you gone mad?"

They sat in the decorous surroundings of Restaurant Hartmann, where Alma and her mother had joined Carl and Max Burckhard for dinner after the opera. Alma winced to see her stepfather making such a scene. He looked positively apoplectic, his face the same color as the red wine in his glass.

Mama sighed. "Really, Carl. The Herr Direktor is a perfect gentleman. He's calling on us next Saturday. Just imagine—Gustav Mahler in our house!"

"You're as naïve and starstruck as your daughter!" Carl threw down his knife and fork with an ugly clatter that caused the waiter to purse his lips in disdain.

Alma opened her mouth to change the subject when Burckhard butted in.

"Mahler's in love with your stepdaughter." Burckhard's disapproval hung in the air like the smell of burned meat. "He's been besotted with her since Berta Zuckerkandl's party. Do you know I walked home with him that night?" Burckhard turned to Alma. "He told me that at first he wanted to dismiss you as a pretty doll, but then he discovered that you had brains and spirit, and he hasn't been able to get you out of his head."

The air rushed through Alma's lungs. To think that one dinner party could change everything.

"What are you going to do if he proposes?" Burckhard asked, while Mama and Carl looked on in silence.

*Propose?* That seemed farfetched. But what *did* she feel for Mahler? Everything was happening so fast, how was she to know her own mind? *It happened overnight,* Mahler's poem proclaimed. And Alma was possessed, transfixed like Leda when Zeus had descended upon her in the form of a swan, enveloping her in his great white wings.

"What would you say if I accepted him?" she asked defiantly, watching Carl squirm.

"Alma!" Max Burckhard cried, causing the diners at the nearby tables to turn their heads. "Remember who you are!"

Burckhard, her friend who had gifted her with *The Collected Works of Nietzsche* and had stuck his tongue in her mouth on a mountaintop several months ago, reached across the table to seize her hand. He looked at her gravely, as though he were a physician fighting to save her from the grip of a life-threatening fever. "It would be a sin for you to marry him. A fine girl like you, of good blood, chaining yourself to an elderly degenerate."

"Herr Mahler is several years younger than *you,* Herr Burckhard," Mama pointed out.

"Mahler's a Jew," Burckhard said, ignoring Mama. "Think of your children, Alma. It would be a crime."

Alma yanked her hand free before turning to her mother. Would Mama now turn on Mahler and shun him the way she and Carl shunned Alex? Because he was a Jew?

But Mama lifted her chin and spoke sternly to Burckhard. "Gustav Mahler is a brilliant and eminent man. How dare you speak of him so crudely? Alma's a grown woman. She can decide for herself whether to accept the Herr Direktor as her suitor."

Alma thought trumpeting angels would swoop down from the restaurant ceiling to hear her mother speak so freely, as though she were as broadminded as Berta Zuckerkandl. Even more astonishingly, Mama spoke as though Mahler's courtship of her was a fait accompli.

Alex was more understanding than Alma had dared hope when she wrote him a letter to reschedule their lesson without telling him why. He arranged to come two days earlier, on Thursday instead of Saturday, as if he could no longer bear to keep himself away from her. But as Alma sat at her piano and attempted to work out the figured basses under her lover's watchful eyes, she was a twitching bundle of nerves. She could hardly look at Alex without feeling an inner stab of remorse even though she hadn't actually done anything to betray him. The few pleasantries she had exchanged with Mahler were hardly a crime.

Alex seemed to sense that something was amiss. When Mama reluctantly stepped out to run an errand, he made no attempt to kiss Alma but only spoke to her earnestly. "You're not yourself. Is something wrong?"

"Counterpoint," she murmured. "I'm still struggling to wrap my head around it. How I wish I could compose as brilliantly as you, Alex."

Her belief in Alex as a composer remained undiminished. She loved his music far more than Mahler's, which bewildered and overwhelmed her as much as Mahler the man did. She remained convinced that Alex would one day establish himself as one of the greatest Austrian composers of their time.

"You're worried about more than counterpoint." Alex frowned. "Is it about us? Alma, if you're having doubts or second thoughts, you have to tell me. Is that why you haven't come round to see me?"

"Oh, Alex." She stared at him, her eyes filling with tears. Mahler was barely acquainted with her, but Alex knew her inside out, from her darkest flaws to her highest aspirations to the depths of her sensual hunger. *He loves me, every note of me.* Yet she was terrified of telling him the truth. Since Mahler had taken her life by storm, she no longer knew what the truth was.

Alex traced her lips with his forefinger. Closing her eyes, Alma leaned forward to kiss him when the jangling doorbell sent a judder up her spine. She and Alex flew apart when Cilli bounded in, her hands clasped to her heart as if she had beheld a vision of all the saints.

"Gustav Mahler is here to see you, Fräulein!" the maid cried in rapture.

Alma leapt to her feet in shock.

"So that's what you were keeping from me." Alex shot her a bruised look.

"I wasn't expecting him today," Alma said lamely. *Today was meant to be for us, Alex.*

But her lover was already packing his briefcase and muttering his curt good-bye. Standing at her piano, Alma listened to the two men exchange the briefest of greetings, and suddenly Mama was back from her errand, showing Mahler into the parlor with great ceremony. He was dressed for walking in a tweed jacket, plus fours, and a red bow tie. He brought with him the smell of fresh air and open spaces.

"I hope you'll forgive me for interrupting your lesson, Fräulein," he said, shaking her hand with a warm grip. "I happened to be walking past and thought you might be in."

Before she could hide her sheet music, he sat at the piano to examine her lieder. It was all she could do not to run out of the room in mortification. Run after Alex and explain herself, or try to.

"How fascinating, Fräulein Schindler. I must send you some of my lieder as well." Setting her scores down, Mahler glanced around at the stark white walls hung with Carl's paintings. "A fine example of the new architecture."

"We only just moved in," Alma said. Her voice sounded stilted and strange. "We're still unpacking."

"Alma, dear, why don't you show the Herr Direktor around the house," Mama said. "Take him up to your room if you like."

"Oh, I would like that very much," said Mahler.

Alma stared at her mother in disbelief. After Carl had made such a fuss over their meeting Mahler in his office, Mama was giving her permission to entertain the man in her *bedroom?* Maybe this was part of her mother's secret plot to make Carl die of a heart attack. The thought made Alma smile in spite of herself as she led the way upstairs with the director of the Vienna Court Opera at her heels. Hauling a basket of firewood, Cilli brought up the rear.

"Green and white," said Mahler, turning in a slow, contemplative circle around Alma's room while Cilli busied herself making a fire in the grate. "Like a forest glade." He peered at an oil painting of a woodland with a stream flowing through it.

"That's by my late father," Alma told him with pride. "Emil Schindler."

Taking a step backward, Mahler nearly tripped over a pile of books on the floor. Her entire library lay scattered in stacks and open boxes, still waiting to be properly arranged in the new bookcase.

"Excuse the mess," Alma said. "If I'd known you were coming, Herr Direktor, I would have tidied things up a bit."

"Ah," he said reverently, crouching with easy grace to stroke her volumes of Goethe and Heine. "We share the same taste in literature."

"My father gave me *Faust* to read when I was only eight," Alma told him.

An unexpected tenderness arose inside her to see him kneeling among her books. His hands, she noted, were beautiful and scrupulously clean, marred only by his bitten-down fingernails.

Flames began to leap and crackle in the hearth. Wiping her hands on her apron, Cilli winked at Alma and excused herself, leaving the door wide open for propriety's sake. But that did not alter the fact that Alma and her greatest living idol were now alone together for the very first time. Her palms began to sweat. She didn't know where to look.

"But this is simply decadent," Mahler said, waving Schopenhauer at her. "And *this*" — he leapt to his feet while brandishing *The Collected Works of Nietzsche* — "should be burned."

Alma watched in horror as he strode toward the fireplace as though truly intent on consigning Nietzsche to the flames.

"You can't burn my book!" She thrust her body between Mahler and the fire. "It's a gift from Max Burckhard!"

"All the more reason!" he cried.

"Herr Direktor Mahler," she said crisply, her hands on her hips. "If your abhorrence of Nietzsche has any justification, you would do better to convince me with a rational argument instead of destroying my property."

His eyebrows shot all the way up his forehead. "Very well, then!" He opened the book and began to read, his voice dripping with contempt. "'The weak and botched shall perish: first principle of *our* charity. And one should help them to it.'" Mahler snapped the book shut and peered at her

112

over his spectacles. "Do you not agree that this is a cold and pitiless philosophy? When a man is weak, you must do him a favor and kick him down? How can an innocent girl like you even sleep in the same room as such a hateful book?"

The two protruding veins on Mahler's temples, zigzagging like lightning bolts, stood out even more prominently when he was in a passion. Cilli could have saved herself the effort of kindling a fire—Mahler himself seemed to be made of pure flame. Everything about him burned and gave off sparks, every single one of his raven-black hairs seemed to stand on end. To think her decorous green and white bedroom walls could contain as elemental a force as Gustav Mahler.

Alma snatched the book from his hand, flung it on her bed, and stared into his eyes. He seized her hands and pulled her close. Then they were kissing, flame feeding upon flame. *We are both so fiery, we shall consume each other.* She tasted his tongue and teeth. His arms wrapped around her, molding her body against his until she felt his muscled flesh beneath his clothes. *My God, under all that tweed, he has the body of an athlete!* She swallowed a cry to feel one particular muscle spring to vigorous life. Abruptly, they sprang apart, both of them panting.

"Herr Direktor Mahler," she said in alarm.

"After kissing me like that you must call me Gustav." His eyes shining and soft, he took her hands once more. "I never expected to fall in love with you like this, so suddenly. I've never felt this way about anyone. You are so intoxicatingly modern. So free-spoken. So uninhibited. Truly, there's no other woman like you."

His praises sent her soaring. The shackles of gravity fell away as he held her in his reverent gaze.

"If you think I rush things," he said softly, "consider my years. Past the age of forty, there seems little point in hesitating when I feel for someone what I feel for you—this kind of passion happens only once in a lifetime. I want to marry you, Alma."

*Surely this is a dream,* she thought. *A beautiful, fantastical dream.* In real life, things never happened this fast—their first kiss and his proposal within an hour of his first visit to her home. Did his intensity prove the measure of his love? Alex had held back for more than a year before their first kiss. *Oh, Alex, what have I done?*

"I think we should go for a walk," Gustav said, as though not trusting himself alone with her in her room for another second.

Hand in hand, they walked down the stairs, where Cilli was busy polishing the bannister. In the hallway below, Mama was arranging hothouse lilies in a blue and white Chinese vase while little Maria played at her feet. As her mother glanced at them, Alma felt herself flush. Gustav's hair was in wild disarray and his bow tie askew, and Alma could only imagine how disheveled she appeared. Yet Mama seemed completely unruffled.

"Herr Direktor," she said pleasantly. "I do hope you'll stay for dinner. We're having chicken paprikash. And Max Burckhard."

"To be honest, Frau Moll, I'm not fond of either one," Gustav said. "But I shall happily accept all the same. May I please use your telephone? I must tell my sister I won't be home for dinner."

"I'm afraid we don't have one," Alma said.

Gustav seemed flabbergasted that this brand-new domicile, designed with such self-conscious modernity, lacked the most essential mode of modern communication.

"There's a telephone in the post office in Döbling," Mama said helpfully.

"I shall walk you there," Alma told him, grateful to have some practical task to relieve her from the awkwardness of standing in front of her mother with Gustav Mahler's kisses still burning on her mouth.

Bundling up against the biting wind, Alma and Gustav set off downhill. Alma could think of nothing to say. She still couldn't get over her astonishment that she was walking unchaperoned at Gustav Mahler's side. *He wants to marry me! I hardly know him!* Likewise, Gustav seemed lost in meditative silence. The only sound was their feet crunching the snow.

Though Mahler was a short man, his stride was so swift that Alma nearly had to sprint to keep up with him. Every other minute, he tripped up on his shoelaces, which kept coming untied. She never thought to see him like this and had to smile.

"Here, allow me," she said, stooping to tie his laces with stout double knots that would not easily come unraveled.

At the post office, she couldn't help but laugh when he confessed he didn't remember his own telephone number. He had to call the opera to get his number before he could phone his sister to tell her he would be out late that evening.

On their hike back up to the Hohe Warte, Alma decided she didn't mind his silence. It gave him the air of a deep thinker, of an artist who spent half his life submerged in his private realm of rumination. The winter twilight was beguiling, the setting sun bathing the snow-covered rooftops and trees in a rosy glow while the church bells rang for vespers. Icicles glittered from the eaves of suburban villas. Everything sparkled in diamond brilliance.

"Before I met you, my life seemed so fixed, so preordained," Gustav said, his breath misting in the cold air. "But then you appeared with all your vivacity. I never met anyone who was so perceptive and so life loving at the same time."

Alma gripped his hands, feeling their warmth through the slippery leather of his gloves.

"But marrying a man like me won't be easy, I'll warn you. I am a creative soul. I am—I *must*—be free."

A sense of suffocation descended on her to hear him speak again of marriage as a foregone conclusion before she had given him her consent. If any lesser man had spoken to her like that, she would have protested in the strongest language.

"I, too, love my freedom," she said pointedly. "It's essential to me. Don't forget that I am an artist's daughter and have always lived among artists. *I* am an artist myself!"

He kissed her and held her arm very close as they continued on their way. "It shall be a spring wedding. Why should we wait longer?" He spoke as though her repartee and their kiss had settled everything. *Perhaps,* she thought, *it had.*

When they reached the house, they crept back up to her room, where they kissed and kissed until Alma thought she would lose herself completely, hot wax in his hands. Not until this day had she experienced the kind of grand passion described in French novels. This was a revolution. With Alex, she had been the seducer, the wooer, but now she understood what it was to be swept away by the sheer power of a man's decisive and unwavering desire for her. Alma and Gustav let go of each other only when they heard her mother sounding the dinner gong.

Mama was graciousness itself, for Gustav Mahler was the most distinguished guest they had ever received at their table. But Carl simmered resentfully, and Burckhard's eyes were frozen in a livid glaze. He had brought a huge bouquet of pink roses for Alma. Mama had set the flowers at the center of the table, where they stood out like an injured appendage in the austere blue and white dining room. As Alma took her seat and unfolded her linen napkin, Burckhard fixed her with a wounded look.

"I thought you were a vegetarian, Herr Direktor," Burckhard said thinly, as Cilli served the chicken paprikash.

"I am," Gustav said, contenting himself with a single bread roll until Cilli brought him a raw vegetable salad.

"How can a grown man survive on rabbit food?" Cilli shook her head.

Alma feared it would be the most uncomfortable dinner of her life, the undercurrent of her and Gustav's ardor and Burckhard's and Carl's bitterness plain for all to see. But Gustav rescued the evening with his wit and charm. Sipping water while the rest of them drank wine, he discussed Schiller, whom he adored, whose plays and poetry provided him with as much sustenance, he declared, as the food on his plate. Alma could barely eat, she was in such awe of this man who was as steeped in literature as he was in music. Even Carl seemed mesmerized, as though hanging on Gustav's every word.

"What do you think of the Russian novelists?" Carl asked him.

"I am a disciple of Dostoyevsky," Gustav replied. "He's a writer of the greatest compassion and humanity. For how can one be happy when a single being on earth suffers?" He let his rhetorical question hang in the air as if to forever silence Burckhard's Nietzschean brutalism.

Gustav then looked across the table and smiled into Alma's eyes until she felt as though the solid flesh of her body were dissolving into a million fluttering butterfly wings. Though she had grown up surrounded by writers, artists, and architects, Gustav possessed the finest mind and the most riveting character of any man she had ever encountered. He was incandescent with genius. Destiny and fate were already binding them together, her youth to his wisdom. *I can no longer live without this man. He alone can give my life meaning.*

After Gustav kissed her good-bye, Alma raced back up to her room to locate her book of Schiller's poetry, which she had hitherto regarded as hideously dull. But Gustav had turned those words to gold, revealing their meaning to her for the first time. She sat up in bed, chanting the poetry under her breath until she was finally calm enough to sleep. *Joy, beautiful divine spark—this kiss to the whole world.*

# 17

*My dear Alex,*

*You haven't written or come to visit because you have deduced eve-rything about Gustav Mahler and me. You've always been able to read my most secret thoughts even from afar. I hope you also know how deeply I have loved you. You fulfilled me completely. Then Mahler came and everything changed.*

*On my knees, I beg your forgiveness for the evil hours I have given you. Some things are beyond our power. Perhaps you have an explana-tion for that, you who know me better than my own self.*

*I shall never forget the joy you've given me, and I hope you shall never forget it either. Dare I ask for your continued friendship, that you visit me once more as my colleague and teacher? Please answer me without reserve. My mother has promised not to read your letters.*

*Most of all, please forgive me. I no longer know myself.*

*Your Alma*

*What wretchedness, what loss.* Alma wept as she sealed the letter. Would Alex even speak to her again? Her world was crumbling into chaos, every-thing collapsing and forming anew.

Gustav visited her every evening after he was finished at the opera. He stayed so late that he missed the last tram and was obliged to walk all the way home to his apartment on the corner of Auenbruggergasse and Rennweg across from Belvedere Castle. But the long trek didn't seem to bother him. He set off whistling like the young wayfarer in his *Lieder eines fahrenden*

Gesellen song cycle he had sent to her. Alma watched from the gate as his slender form receded down the steep lamplit streets.

One evening, when they sat alone at her piano, Gustav told her of his childhood in Bohemia. His late father had run an alcohol distillery. The man was a brute and had made his wife's and children's lives a living hell. Out of fourteen children, only Gustav and three other siblings survived—his sisters, Justine and Emma, and his brother, Alois, who had immigrated to America. Eight siblings died in childhood. As a little girl, Justine had turned death into a game by lying in her cot pretending to be a corpse while a ring of candles burned around her. His sister Leopoldine died of a brain tumor at twenty-six, and most wrenching of all, his beloved brother Otto had committed suicide.

Listening to this litany of hardship made Alma idolize Gustav all the more. What he had been forced to struggle against!

"I've had to stagger on all my life," he told her, "with clods of earth tied to my feet."

The following day, Gustav's score for Das klagende Lied arrived with the post.

> Dearest Almschi,
>     This song is a fairy tale from my youthful days.
>     Your Gustav

The song cycle was drawn from a folk tale about two rival brothers courting a queen. Alma was playing the piece when Carl came in and seated himself in the armchair beside the piano. Abruptly, she lifted her hands from the keys and braced herself for the inevitable lecture—Carl had that paterfamilias look on his face.

"About Gustav Mahler," Carl began. "You're in love with the man and nothing I say or do will put you off. At least it's a relief that it's Mahler, not Zemlinsky."

Alma remained silent, the shame of her betrayal of Alex pressing down on her.

"Mahler isn't exactly the husband I would have wished for you," her stepfather went on. "He's not young, and I have it on very good authority he's in debt."

"He had to support his siblings when his parents died," Alma said, rushing in to champion Gustav. "But now he has only Justine to support. He can afford to marry now—he told me so."

"Just keep in mind," said Carl, "that if he loses his post as opera director his career is finished. He's a man with strong opinions who's forever locking horns with people. He has enemies as well as admirers, not least because he's a Jew."

Alma could have thrown the sheet music in her stepfather's face. "He's the greatest opera director Vienna's ever known! They would be insane to lose him."

More than ever before, Alma lived for the opera. First, she lost herself in the magnificence of *Les contes d' Hoffmann,* which was all the more enchanting for her having seen the dress rehearsal. Marie Gutheil-Schoder, her skirts now decorously stitched together, was flawless. Later that same week, Alma reveled in Mozart's *Die Zauberflöte,* a performance that Gustav had privately dedicated to her. Each time she watched him conduct, she gleaned a deeper understanding of the intricacy of his work. And Gustav turned on his podium to give her his most tender smile. She was so in love, she wanted to shout out her happiness to the world. But their engagement needed to remain secret for the time being. Gustav still had to break the news to Justine, who was possessive of her brother and jealous of female rivals.

When Alma was with Gustav or watching him conduct, it was as if no other man existed. Only when they were apart did her doubts creep in. Now he was off to Berlin and Dresden, where he would conduct his Fourth Symphony.

Alone at her piano, Alma allowed the questions she had shoved to the depths of her consciousness to rise to the surface one by one. Did she truly love him as a man, or had she simply been swept away by the force of his personality? She was so unraveled by it all, she no longer knew what to think or even *how* to think. Did she love Mahler the great conductor and opera director, or Gustav with his bitten fingernails who tripped over his shoelaces and kissed her so greedily? If Carl's forebodings were correct and Gustav lost his position at the Court Opera, would she be just as dazzled by him? He would still remain a genius, the man with thick black hair who knew almost every poem of Schiller's by heart. The man who had raised himself up from nearly nothing, embracing music as his path to transcendence. Who, as a three-year-old boy in Kalischt, Bohemia, had interrupted the cantor in the synagogue by shouting, *That's not music!* Alma thought that if she lived one hundred years she would never meet Gustav Mahler's equal.

Yet he could be so high-handed, condescending to her like a schoolmaster, lecturing her on which books were seemly and which he would like her to burn. Even Mama and Carl didn't presume to control what Alma *read*.

If she married him and bound herself to him for the rest of her life, shouldn't she believe in him unreservedly as a composer? As hard as she tried to understand the scores he sent her, his music left her cold. He surely deserved better from his future wife.

One question plagued her more than any other—would Gustav inspire *her* to compose? Would he support her artistic strivings the way Alex had? The mere thought of Alex opened a chasm in her heart. What if she had made a terrible mistake that could never be undone? She had heard not a word from Alex since sending him her letter of confession. Perhaps he hated her and could never forgive her.

Every day Alma waited for the morning and afternoon mail, for a letter or sign from Gustav to set her anxieties to rest. Dashing out to the front gate one morning when expecting the postman, she saw a familiar figure trudging up the snowy street. The most fragile hope stirred inside her.

"Alex, is that you?" she cried.

"You're looking well, Fräulein." Alex's gaze was guarded, and he addressed her stiffly, with the formal *Sie,* as though an entire glacier divided them.

"Come in, come in," she said, flustered. "It's so cold out here."

In the parlor, Alex sat at the piano while Alma sat in the armchair beside it and watched as her former lover paged through the score of Mahler's Lieder eines fahrenden Gesellen that Alma had been playing all morning in an attempt to better comprehend.

Alex rolled his eyes to the ceiling. "All this studied naïveté and simplicity. Rather disingenuous coming from Mahler, don't you think?"

"He was very young when he wrote it." Alma had spent many hours imagining Gustav as he had been at her age, struggling to compose, to find his own style.

Alex laughed abrasively. "I don't believe he was ever that young. Or that innocent."

"That's a very unkind thing to say." Alma found she couldn't even look at him, only at her hands clasped in her lap.

But Alex turned to her and stared until she looked into his eyes.

"I always knew you'd throw me over for someone with money," he said. "Someone who could keep you in every comfort."

They both blushed to hear Alex slipping back into the familiar *Du* form, as if in spite of himself.

"I don't even blame you for that," he went on. "But for God's sake, Alma, why *him?* A middle-aged man with hemorrhoids! You'll have to fight your way past his sister, who guards him like a rottweiler. She's driven all his other women away."

Alma swayed in her chair to hear Alex speak of Gustav as if he were some failed Lothario. Did Justine's zealousness indeed explain why Gustav had not married earlier?

"I *like* Justine," Alma lied.

She had met Gustav's sister once and was terrified of her. All that Mahlerian intensity poured into a female body and not given any other occupation but keeping house for her brother and guarding his honor. Gustav had brought his sister along on his trip to Berlin and Dresden in an attempt to win her over to the idea of his marrying Alma.

"All his friends are twenty years older than you," Alex said. "They'll look down their noses at you as the child he married."

"I shall still have my own friends," she said hotly. "My own circle."

"You and he both have such strong personalities. He'll never bow down to accommodate you. *You* shall have to make all the compromises." Alex looked at her imploringly, as though trying to reach to her across an abyss. "You're only twenty-two. What about your dreams of becoming a composer? Don't you see, Alma? You're not just betraying me—you're betraying yourself!"

Alex's voice broke, and Alma's eyes blurred with tears. She could think of nothing to say. *Must I be subdued?* Was that what marriage was, a battle of wills with a winner and a loser? Was it not meant to be something divine, an alchemical union of souls that made both husband and wife greater than the sum of their parts?

"It would surely do me no harm," she said, in a small voice, "to study under his tutelage. To be raised to his level."

When Alex took his leave, they shook hands and parted cordially. But there was no getting past his hurt and resignation or her own guilty sense of how her choice had shattered him. She suspected that this would signal the end of their lessons and his visits to her home. With a pang, she thought of *Tristan und Isolde,* the opera that both she and Alex loved above all others. It was as though she were Isolde, and instead of risking everything to run away with Tristan, she had spurned him for King Mark. She had chosen the old king over the young lover. *Liebestod.*

# 18

||||||||||||||||||||||||||

**W**hat about your dreams of becoming a composer? Haunted by Alex's words, Alma set aside Gustav's scores to work on her own lieder. When Gustav returned to Vienna, she would ask him to help her, to teach her. Couldn't a husband also be a mentor? She thought about Robert and Clara Schumann composing side by side.

Gustav's letters, filled with both tenderness and soul-searching, arrived daily.

> *Only one thing troubles me, Almschi: whether a person who is already growing old has the right to such youth and beauty . . . I know I have much to offer, but that is no exchange for the right to be young.*

He implored her to reply by return post and to write *legibly*, for he found her handwriting as difficult to decipher as hieroglyphics.

> *Imagine I'm sitting beside you and you're telling me about your day-to-day life. Every detail!*

Writing her reply, she described her spirited dinner conversation with Max Burckhard about the importance of her individuality and personal potential. How she *must* triumph as an individual soul, one who was devoted to her music.

> *Forgive me for cutting this letter short, dear Gustav, but I must work on my lieder. How magnificent that we're _both_ composers! That I should be your colleague _and_ your wife!*

The following day, Alma went Christmas shopping with her mother. Alma bought a pair of warm fur-lined gloves for Gustav and a pretty bracelet of silver and aquamarine for Gretl while Mama bought a hot water bottle for Cilli, whose circulation was poor and who was forever complaining about her chilblains.

All Vienna seemed to be out and about preparing for the festive season; the squares were crammed with market stalls selling gingerbread, oranges, wooden toys, and brightly painted spinning tops.

After they had finished shopping, Alma and Mama joined Carl at Café Sacher before riding home in an open fiacre, the winter sun beaming down with a brightness that illuminated everything with sharp, crystal clarity. The naked chestnut trees. The businessmen in their top hats tapping their canes in the dirty snow as they strode along. The steam rising off the sweating backs of horses pulling wagons, carriages, and omnibuses.

Alma's heart lurched at the sight of Alex walking down Ringstrasse, his arm linked with that of a young lady she'd never seen before who gazed at him adoringly. Their laughter rose in the frosty air.

"Well, it looks like it didn't take long for Zemlinsky to get over you," her stepfather observed.

"Carl, don't be crass," Mama said. But she seemed unable to hide her relief that she no longer needed to worry about Alma marrying him.

Alma tried to turn her thoughts away from Alex, but she felt half-sick at the loss of him. For she was bereft of not only a lover and a friend but also the finest teacher she'd ever had. *I betrayed him. I destroyed us.* There was no way back. That bridge was gone. She had made her choice and that was Gustav.


When Alma stepped in the door, Cilli came prancing with the thickest envelope Alma had ever seen.

"From Herr Direktor Mahler!" Cilli's face glowed pink with the romance of it all.

Even Carl was impressed with the heft of the missive. "Did he write you a love letter or an entire symphony?"

Alma dashed up to her room to read Gustav's letter in privacy. Flinging herself on her bed, she tore it open, breathless not only from the sprint up the stairs but also from the hope that such a long letter must surely include some analysis of her lieder.

> *My beloved Alma,*
>     *It is with a heavy heart that I set out to write this letter. I know that I must hurt you, but I have no choice.*

Her heart pricked in worry. Whatever could be the matter? He didn't care for her music, was that it? It was true that after the initial interest he had expressed in her scores he had hardly spoken about them. Was it to spare her feelings from his honest appraisal?

As she continued reading that twenty-page letter written on stationery from the Hotel Bellevue in Berlin, every part of her froze. For it was not her music Gustav examined under the glaring spotlight of his scrutiny but her character. In his mind, she was no fully formed individual but an immature girl who lacked any original ideas of her own, who merely parroted the philosophies of those around her or the latest book she had read and only half-digested. How his words stung!

Not only that, he maintained that she had an inflated sense of her own importance as an aspiring composer, which Gustav blamed on men like Burckhard and Zemlinsky who had encouraged her not because she had any actual talent but merely because they were infatuated with her.

> *Because you are beautiful and men are attracted to you, they enjoy paying tribute to you. Would they heap such praise on an ugly girl? My Alma, you have grown vain, your vanity the result of what these men see in you, or would like to see in you . . .*
>     *Almschi, please read my words with care. Our relationship must*

126

*not degenerate into a mere flirt. Before we speak again you must re-*
*nounce everything superficial, all vanity and outward show concerning*
*your individuality and your own work . . .*

*Would it be possible for you to regard <u>my</u> music as <u>your</u> music from*
*now on? As for "your" music, I prefer not to discuss that in detail right*
*now. But how can you imagine both husband and wife being compos-*
*ers? Have you any idea how ridiculous and degrading such a rivalry*
*would become? What would happen if inspiration strikes you—as it*
*did when you broke off your last letter to me—when you're obliged to*
*look after the house for me or to bring me something I need?*

*You must become the person I need if we are to be happy together.*
*My wife and not my colleague.*

Gustav closed by telling her he would send his servant to collect her reply
the following morning—she must have her answer prepared by then.

The pages of his letter fell to the floor. It was as though a cold hand
had wrenched her heart from her breast. What remained was a gaping void.
Nothing left to cling to anymore, not her music or even her sense of self.
Just the promise of his love and their future as man and wife if she agreed to
his demands.

But how could she abandon her music? Could he truly force such an ultimatum on her? *The power is mine! I can refuse!* Just as she had refused to let
him burn *The Collected Works of Nietzsche.* But insisting on her own music
would mean losing him. Their engagement would be over before it had even
been officially announced. She had lost Alex irretrievably. And now she must
lose Gustav, too?

If she married him and carried on composing behind his back, it would
still destroy her creative spirit. It was hard enough to compose without doing
it under the cloak of secrecy without any encouragement or help at all. *He
thinks nothing of my music and everything of his own.* What contempt he had
displayed for her dream of a marriage of two composers who believed in and
supported each other. That kind of partnership would have worked with

Alex. But not with Gustav. Never with Gustav. And it was her own fault for turning Alex away. Then again, what if Gustav was right and Alex had praised her only because he desired her?

*I am so broken, so useless, my talent so slight.* For if her gift was genuine, Gustav surely would have recognized it, would he not? Perhaps he was being cruel to be kind. Sparing her from the humiliation of having the greater world mock her mediocrity and pretensions. All of Herr Labor's criticisms slammed inside her head. *If that's the best you can do, you might as well give up. You can't be taken seriously!*

Alma began to pace, clutching herself and shivering. The fire in her grate had dwindled to ash. *If only I were a somebody, a real person, capable of great things. But I am a nobody.* The weight of Gustav's words bowed her down to the ground. *I am just another bourgeois girl prettily running her fingers up and down the piano keys. I am not remarkable. No Clara Schumann. My ambitions are laughable.* Alma couldn't imagine ever feeling like her old self again, the girl of last summer who was writing her first opera.

She let out a cry as Mama entered the room in a rustle of midnight-blue silk.

"Alma, why aren't you dressed? Have you forgotten about *Siegfried* tonight? My dear, why are you crying?" Her mother looked searchingly into Alma's eyes before bending to pick the twenty pages of Gustav's letter off the floor.

"As fond as I am of Mahler, I would advise you to refuse him," Mama said. "He can't ask you to give up your music. It's monstrous."

The two of them rode in the cab to the opera. They huddled together, bundled against the cold in their winter coats and fur stoles, a rug across their laps to warm their legs. Alma felt a welling up of gratitude to hear that at least her mother believed her talent was real and worth fighting for. Still, she could not stop crying. She was torn in half.

"Don't give him any written reply." Mama squeezed Alma's gloved hand. "Let him come to you—he'll soon be back from his travels. Perhaps he'll even apologize and realize he's been completely unreasonable. Although, I must say, he was very honest about what he expects from a wife—we have to grant him that. If you should agree to marry him under those conditions, at least you'll go into it with your eyes wide open. No naïve illusions about becoming his protégée."

Alma could still not believe how much this hurt, like a hooked arrow sunk deep in her flesh. If only she and Gustav could have discussed this in person, in a conversation that she had a voice in, things could have been so different. No matter what choice she made regarding Gustav and her music, his letter would leave an indelible scar.

At the opera, to Alma's deepest embarrassment, she found that she and her mother were seated in the same row as Felix Muhr, her former suitor—the rich architect with his monocle and brilliantined hair. Noting Alma's swollen red eyes, he beat a path over all the legs and feet to hover at her side.

"My dear Alma, what has happened to leave you looking so miserable?"

"Do you think I'm vain, Herr Muhr?" Alma asked him. "Should I stop composing?"

"Stop when you've been blessed with such a gift?" He shook his head in incomprehension. "Lovely Alma, what vile person has put such ideas in your head?"

*He called me lovely.* Which, in Gustav's view, proved he was only flattering her on account of his own self-serving agenda to win her, to have her. This was absolutely wretched. She could no longer accept a compliment without assuming the worst of the one who offered it. She couldn't bear to look at the adulation on Muhr's face.

"Herr Muhr," Mama said. "You must come to dinner this week! How we've all missed your visits."

Then the curtain opened, and Muhr retreated to his seat. Alma leaned back and watched Erik Schmedes in the role of Siegfried, showing off his bare muscled legs and casting sultry glances at the women in the audience, including her. She should have been in her element, cocooned in her wonder of her beloved Wagner, but all she could think of was how inferior this conductor was to Gustav. The orchestra didn't sound as rich. Even Schmedes didn't seem to be performing at his full power. Gustav's genius had touched her, opened something in her, and now she was unable to get him out of her mind even to experience a moment's peace.

Her thoughts revolved around Gustav's accusation of her being vain. If she indeed was, it wasn't the vanity of the vapid young ladies she met at parties, who could only chatter about their gowns and coiffures, and would faint at the very thought of reading Nietzsche or Schopenhauer. Hadn't she tried her utmost to *make* something of herself? Even if she knew she couldn't hope for a glittering career as a world-class pianist or the first woman conductor of the Vienna Philharmonic, she had until today sincerely believed that if she persevered she would eventually compose works of great beauty. That even if she wasn't the next Wagner or Strauss, she might still create a body of work that would outlive her. *I existed for a reason. I gave something to the world. I mattered.*

And yet, even if her talent was real, talent in itself was not enough. One must be brave enough to seize one's gift and go to battle for it. One had to be a hero like Siegfried, slaying the dragon and then braving the ring of flame to awaken his Brünnhilde. Was she courageous enough to withstand the trial by fire that was Gustav's letter and fight for her music even if that meant losing him forever? Brave enough to set off on her own without Alex, without Gustav, just she and her music, men and their proposals be damned?

But she had to marry someone eventually—she couldn't possibly stomach living as a spinster all her days, never knowing love, that deep awakening of the body. And Mama, she feared, would indeed invite Muhr to dinner. Her mother's hints to Muhr and Alma would grow bolder and bolder. In the kindest way possible, Mama and Carl were pushing her out by degrees. They wanted her respectably married off, the mistress of her own household.

*Be honest with yourself for once, Alma—you're not a hero.* Heroes were men, swaggering and strong, like Erik Schmedes with his sword and piercing tenor. Women, if they wanted to be loved, surrendered themselves in a living

130

sacrifice of devotion, as Brünnhilde did at the climax of *Götterdämmerung,* immolating herself on Siegfried's funeral pyre.

Alma told herself that she would end up serving a man anyway. Would it not be a nobler calling to serve genius instead of mediocrity? How would it be to look back and think, *I could have married Gustav Mahler if only I had been brave enough. Faithful and loving enough.*

In the past three years, she had fallen in love with three men of genius. First Klimt, then Alex, then Gustav. Mama had forcibly separated Alma from Klimt, then she had come between Alma and Alex. Did her mother intend to interfere again? Alma didn't think she could bear it a third time. After this sundering, there would be nothing left of her. She would have to settle for some bland figure like Muhr whom she might like but could never love. The window was closing. At twenty-two years of age, how much longer could she play the carefree socialite before she faded away, a figure of pity, some queer woman like Klimt's beloved Emilie Flöge, a fallen woman and yet a spinster, set apart from the rest of womanhood? The third sex.

*My only hope of distinguishing myself, of doing something truly remarkable, is by marrying a great man and sharing his destiny.* Something inside Alma died at the thought of marrying a Muhr instead of a Mahler.

The next morning Alma sat at her piano and tried with her entire soul to compose. To prove to herself that she had a gift that she couldn't relinquish. Something innate, a part of her that could not be severed. Even Gustav would have to acknowledge that creative spark inside her. But never had she felt emptier or more stupid, her every note more cloying than the last until she wanted to smash her fists on the piano keys and shriek like a maiden in a Greek tragedy. Rend her garments and keen.

For the sake of getting out of the house, Alma offered to run errands for Cilli to the baker and greengrocer down in Döbling. Tearing off down the street with the maid's stout wicker shopping basket on her arm, Alma nearly collided with a stranger who stepped in her path.

"Are you Fräulein Alma Maria Schindler?" he asked her.

This must be Gustav's servant come to collect her reply that she had not been able to write. A wave of white-hot heat cramped in her belly.

"Are you Herr Direktor Mahler's messenger?" She didn't even try to hide her temper. "I have nothing to give you."

The man reached into his greatcoat pocket. "But I have this to give you, Fräulein."

A letter, crisp and thin, with her name in Gustav's handwriting. Her heart beat fast enough to render her woozy. Was it as Mama had predicted? Had he come to his senses? Had he softened, taking this dilemma away from her? To her mortification, she found herself sobbing in front of his messenger, who whipped off his cap as though in deep fear that he had offended her.

"Fräulein, please don't be upset. The Herr Direktor's back in Vienna and has given me his word he shall visit you this evening as soon as he's finished at the opera."

Turning her back on the messenger, Alma ripped open the letter and read it then and there with the stark December sun shining down on the page.

*Never before have I so desired and feared a letter as the one from you*
*that my servant is now on his way to collect. What will you tell me,*
*Alma? It's not what you say that matters most but what you are. Let us*
*put all passion aside and rest in that inner calm and loving certainty*
*to forge the bond that will bind us irrevocably till our last breath. At*
*the very thought of seeing you again, my heart overflows.*
*Your Gustav*

Alma could neither think nor act clearly. Everything began and ended with Gustav. There was no need to wait until evening—Gustav arrived that very afternoon, his eyes gentle and wide.

"Alma, you're in tears." He cradled her head to his chest. "My darling, what have I done? Can you still care for me now that you know how wretchedly honest I am with those I love?"

*The choice is mine,* she reminded herself. *I can refuse him.* She nearly laughed aloud to recall that this was the selfsame advice she had given Gretl when she was so anguished about giving up her country and religion for Wilhelm. What if Alma squared her shoulders and informed Gustav that she could never abandon her music? But she could scarcely find the words to express the torrent of emotion running through her.

"Of course, you're right," she began, "that our relationship mustn't degenerate into a flirt but must be the marriage of two souls in harmony." She took a deep breath before plunging on and speaking her truth. "Does one of us truly have to be subordinate? *Must* I sacrifice my own work to be your wife? Surely our love must be powerful enough to reconcile two opposing viewpoints."

He gazed at her as though her questions drove a blade into his heart. "Almschi, my love, how can you think in terms of subjugation and opposition? If we marry, we exist for each other and hold nothing back. My music *is* yours now. I lay it at your feet."

At that, he sat at her piano and began to play part of a scherzo from his embryonic new symphony.

"I wrote this last summer," he said. "A devil of a movement. I fear no one will understand it. This is the chaos of new worlds being continually reborn."

Alma sat beside him on the piano bench and followed the score while listening to him play. At least the music was a welcome distraction from the turbulence inside her. The scherzo was a peculiar mix of two dances — the Viennese waltz and a rustic country *Ländler.* A juxtaposition of sophistication and folkloric naïveté.

"It's not chaotic," Alma said, a decisive confidence filling her after so much confusion and turmoil. "It's joyous. A celebration of life. It reminds me of being a child in the mountains in summer."

No longer did she feel like the supplicant, the inferior, helpless one. Gustav, her idol, turned to her as if her critique had taken him by storm. He seemed to hang on her every word. With a composure she had not felt in so long, she began to play his piece back to him.

"But the tempo must be slower. You absolutely shouldn't rush. Otherwise it loses its power and seems trivial."

She played on at a stately pace, in a truly Viennese rhythm, imagining herself gliding across the ballroom floor. She lost herself in the scherzo's emotional complexity, its vibrancy.

"Alma," he said, sounding more humbled and respectful than she had ever heard him. "That's brilliant. Absolutely brilliant."

When he looked at her like that, with such ecstasy, she felt caught up in the most sublime spiritual communion with this genius of a man.

"Don't you see, my love?" He kissed her hands. "You *are* my music. I'll write you into my every symphony."

Her knees weakened to hear the love in his voice, his absolute devotion. If she could indeed be his inspiration, an indelible part of his work, and help him shine even brighter, then maybe that would be enough. Maybe that would redeem her sacrifice. With him, she might achieve a greatness incomparable to anything she might realize on her own.

"My muse," he said. "My light."

When he enclosed her in his fierce embrace, she thought that no other man could love her so deeply. That letting this man go would be the greatest mistake she would ever make. Had she ever felt anything so holy? When she held him, she no longer felt his body as something separate or divided from her own essence. They melted into each other.

*It's no longer a question of Gustav's music versus my music. But only of music itself, divine and pure, which cannot be contained or owned by any human being.* Alma promised to give him her all. To live for him and his music, which was also her music.

# 19

|||||||||||||||||||||||||||

Everything happened so fast, reminding Alma of the view from the window of a speeding locomotive. Everything was imbued with feverish, high-pitched intensity.

Two days later, Alma waited in the parlor with Mama and Carl. She wore her prettiest reception gown of ivory tulle, lace, and silk, and she had tea roses pinned in her hair. Cilli had prepared a table full of festive treats —trays of *Zimtsterne,* star-shaped cinnamon cookies; *Stollen* with marzipan and raisins; and chocolate-coated gingerbread. There was tea in the silver samovar and mulled wine heating gently over the copper chafing dish.

Alma tried to soothe her nerves by playing the piano, but her stomach was tight, her ears pricked for the doorbell. Then Gustav arrived, accompanied by a pale and circumspect Justine, who looked around the blue and white parlor as though she found the starkly modernistic furnishings unbearably pretentious.

At thirty-three, Gustav's devoted sister was his mirror image in female form. Alas, the Mahler features were far more becoming on a man than a woman. As lean and spare as her brother, Justine had severely pinned her dark hair back from her angular face. Alma went to greet her, trying her utmost to be warm and hospitable, but whenever Justine looked at her, Alma's nape prickled. She couldn't banish the feeling that her future sister-in-law was sizing her up. Alma wondered if she could ever pass muster. *Gustav could marry the tsar's daughter,* she thought, *and Justine would still think it an unworthy match for her illustrious brother.*

But there was no more time to fret over Justine. Gustav took Alma's hand, and the two of them turned to face Mama and Carl.

"Frau Moll, Herr Moll, I have asked for your daughter's hand in marriage and she has accepted me. Now I humbly ask for your blessing."

Mama smiled, tears in her eyes, and hugged Gustav and kissed his cheeks. Carl pounded his back and promised to share a cigar with him later — despite Gustav's vegetarianism and abstinence from alcohol, he was an avid smoker. Alma shared a hug and kiss with Justine. *You must love her — she's your sister now. Part of who you are, just as Gustav is.*

Cilli poured a cup of tea for Gustav and served mulled wine to everyone else, then Carl led them in toast after toast to the betrothed couple's future happiness. *Officially engaged!* Alma wanted to throw back her head and dance ecstatically like a maenad in a Dionysian rite. Yet she couldn't entirely give herself over to her jubilation for fear of the gods who cannot bear to contemplate pure joy.

"We've already set the date for the wedding," Gustav said, his arm around Alma. "March 9 at Karlskirche."

Years ago, in order to be eligible for his appointment as director of the Vienna Court Opera, Gustav had undergone a perfunctory conversion from Judaism to Catholicism.

"Justine is also getting married, the following day." Gustav proudly took his sister's hand. "To Arnold Rosé, principal violinist of the Vienna Philharmonic."

"How splendid!" Alma cried, kissing Justine's cheek with added enthusiasm. She couldn't express how relieved she was that Justine would also be married and not living with her and Gustav.

"Since I don't need to keep house for my brother anymore, I, too, shall marry at last," Justine said, with a slightly aggrieved air, as though the distinguished Arnold Rosé came a poor second to Gustav.

"We must keep both engagements secret for the time being," Gustav said. "I fear what will happen if the newspapers and gossips get wind of this."

• • •

Despite Gustav's intention to keep their wedding plans sub rosa, someone leaked the news to a reporter. On December 27 their engagement was splashed across the Vienna papers in big bold letters:

DIREKTOR MAHLER ENGAGED!

The press made much of Alma's musical accomplishments, her beauty, her youth, her sparkling wit. The *Fremdenblatt* called her brilliant, which gave her pause for thought, considering what she had renounced to make this engagement possible. Did Viennese society take her talent seriously after all—what if she was throwing away something precious? But in a stroke, her lifelong dream of becoming a somebody had been achieved. Overnight, she had become famous, not through any accomplishment of her own but simply by virtue of being Gustav Mahler's bride-to-be. She received a veritable avalanche of telegrams, letters, cards, and flowers sent by countless well-wishers. Aunt Mie gave her an ostrich feather fan to befit Alma's new status as the grande dame of the Viennese music world.

Alma fluttered her fan when she took her place in the director's box at the Court Opera for the very first time, sitting with Mama and Justine. But instead of settling back into her musical reverie as she watched Gustav conduct Otto Nicolai's *Die lustigen Weiber von Windsor,* she quailed to see that every pair of opera glasses was trained on her, as though her engagement had transformed her into royalty. During the intermission, Anna von Mildenburg came down to congratulate Alma.

"So you are to be our Herr Direktor's wife," she said, with an undertone of envy.

Back in the director's box, Alma tried to ignore the gawkers and concentrate on Gustav's conducting. He seemed so far away from her, lost in that forest of music. The baton danced in his hand as though it were a living thing. At the close of the opera, the crowd applauded more rapturously than Alma had ever heard, some even leaping to their feet to cry bravo, as though as much in celebration of their esteemed Herr Direktor's engagement as the performance. Alma looked on in awe as Gustav was called back to the curtain again and again.

On the afternoon of December 31, 1901, Alma alighted from the cab on the corner of Rennweg and Auenbruggergasse, and gazed up at the handsome Jugendstil apartment building. Above the main entrance was a carving of a woman's enigmatic face, her mouth open, as though in wonder of the new world she saw unfolding before her. With an exquisite frisson of anticipation, Alma entered the foyer and told the concierge that the Mahlers were expecting her. How like a New Woman she felt as she ascended those graceful curving stairs alone until, light-headed and breathless, she reached the fourth floor.

Though Mama had most sternly forbidden her to visit Alex at his home, now that Alma was engaged to be married, any such prohibitions fell away when it concerned calling upon Gustav and Justine. And it just so happened that Justine would be out this afternoon. Smiling to herself deliciously, Alma rang the bell. Gustav tore open the door and pulled her into his arms. They kissed for a long time before they had to come up for air. Then, taking her arm, he gave her a grand tour of the high-ceilinged apartment where they would soon live together as husband and wife.

Five rooms overlooked Belvedere Castle and its formal gardens. There was the parlor, the dining room, Justine's little room, and Gustav's study and bedroom. To the right of the entrance was the maid's room, and at the back of the apartment, overlooking the inner courtyard, lay the kitchen, Justine's sewing room, a storage room, and the bathroom. Alma noted that her future marital residence was meticulously clean, thanks to Justine's ministrations. However, any sense of warmth or ambiance was lacking, something she might fix by hanging a few well-chosen paintings on the walls.

But Alma hadn't paid this visit with decorating foremost on her mind. Gustav showed her into his study with his grand piano, his stacks of scores by him and countless other composers, his shelves of Russian novels and the works of the German romantics, and the sofa where he invited her to sit beside him. They were soon locked in an embrace, kissing and stroking each other until Alma thought her torment would become unbearable. *Why must they wait for a church wedding?* Such old-fashioned thinking seemed ridiculous in this modern age when all the rules were crying out to be written anew.

Through the walls came the racket of the army officer in the next apartment playing his gramophone at full volume—some awful brass military march.

"He does that just to annoy me," Gustav told her. "Especially when I'm playing the piano and trying to compose."

Their jagged breathing soon drowned out the brass music. Slowly, with great deliberation, Gustav took off his waistcoat and then his shirt. Looking deep into her eyes, he guided her hand to his bare chest, holding her palm to his pounding heart. Then he drew her hand down to his swollen groin. The blood roared in Alma's temples. *This is holy, pure. A divine mystery.* His body was *hers.* No one, nothing existed other than Gustav. No other thought. He loosened her hair so that it streamed down, as loose and filmy as a mermaid's, and he buried his face in it. She let him open her blouse and kiss her breasts. Every part of her was his. She let him help her out of her skirt and draw down her drawers, exploring every part of her until she thought she would explode.

Standing up, Gustav let his trousers fall to the floor. Alma caught her breath as he swung himself over her. *This is the moment I become a woman.* That raw carnal hunger that Klimt had awakened in her in Venice nearly three years ago would finally be sated. She closed her eyes, opening herself completely to this miracle of transformation. Then, just as she felt Gustav penetrate her, he lost all strength. He collapsed, his head on her breasts, and wept in shame.

Alma roiled, at wit's end. Those intimate caresses and the promise of what lay beyond had stirred her blood to its boiling point, and now Gustav lay there, limp and humiliated. A force rose inside her, beyond her control, uncoiling like a cobra, rising, undulating. She straddled him and kissed him mercilessly, not letting him go, until he, too, was on fire. And then she yelped at the sharp jolt of pain. In savage victory, she cried out as wave after wave of heat rippled from her loins to her head. *A woman at last.* She thought her passion would be enough to slay them both—this her *Liebestod,* the climax of everything. The *petite mort* she had read about in racy novels. Except it transpired that they were still very much alive. She had never seen Gustav's face glow like that, as though lit from within.

"*Lux,* Alma, my light." Gustav kissed her eyelids, her breasts. "My *Luchs,*" he added playfully, calling her a lynx, a wildcat. "You carried me to sixth heaven. The seventh is still waiting for us."

Five days later, Alma returned to her fiancé's apartment, this time accompanied by Mama, Carl, and Kolo Moser. Justine was hosting a dinner party to introduce Alma to Gustav's friends.

Alex had warned her that Gustav's elite circle would never accept her, but she pushed that dire prophecy out of her mind and attempted to embody a queenly assurance as she strode into the parlor with its assembled guests. Had she not mastered the art of parties, of winning hearts with her conviviality and charm? She was clad in the same lilac evening gown she had worn to Berta Zuckerkandl's soiree back in November when Gustav first fell in love with her. The diamond-edged brooch he'd given her for Christmas glittered at her breast. Their lovemaking had filled her with a lingering radiance. Even now she felt a sinuous grace moving through her limbs as though their embraces had indeed transformed her into a lynx. Something wild and rare.

But Gustav didn't even appear to notice Alma had arrived because he was so completely immersed in conversation with a gray-haired woman in her forties. After a moment, Alma recognized her as the violist Natalie Bauer-Lechner. The woman was staring at Gustav pitifully, like a lovesick dog. Meanwhile, Justine introduced Alma to the others in the room.

Siegfried Lipiner, a poet and translator who worked as a librarian for the Imperial Senate, looked Alma up and down as though she were a heifer up for auction.

"So you're the girl who turned old Gustav's head," Lipiner said. "My dear child, most of us here have known and loved him since before you could walk."

*All his friends are twenty years older than you,* Alex had informed her. Alma shook hands with Lipiner's divorced first wife, Nina, and her husband, Dr. Albert Spiegler; Lipiner's current wife, Clementine; and his reputed mistress, Anna von Mildenburg. Though surrounded by a veritable harem of his women past and present, Lipiner seemed to loathe the idea of sharing his friend Gustav with Alma. His hostility was enough to raise her skin.

Alma nearly dropped her punch glass when she overheard Natalie Bauer-Lechner's plaintive murmurings to Gustav. "I thought you would marry *me*."

Laughing uneasily, Gustav edged away from the violist. Finally, he noticed Alma and kissed her in greeting, then warmly welcomed Mama and Carl. But before Alma could set herself at ease, she overheard Justine's chilly rejoinder to Natalie Bauer-Lechner. "My dear, you know my brother could only marry someone *beautiful*."

For the remainder of the evening, the gray-haired violist glared at Alma in contempt. Waves of animosity seemed to slap Alma from every corner of the room. When she sat at the dining table, she could hardly bring herself to eat. It seemed that her style of hairdressing, her evening gown, her frank way of speaking were all under review, as though this were some ghastly audition she had to pass before Gustav's inner circle would allow her to marry their brilliant friend. They seemed to hold Alma's youth and beauty against her as evidence that their friend was the victim of his own misguided infatuation with an insipid socialite. Her stomach curdling, Alma began to wonder if Justine had arranged this on purpose to undermine her. For this was the last dinner party that Justine would host here before Alma took over as mistress of the house.

Anna von Mildenburg fixed Alma with a tight-lipped smile. "How surprised we all were when we learned of Gustav's betrothal." The diva pouted at him. "Back in Hamburg, I thought he was going to marry me."

Gustav laughed and shook his head as though he had come to expect such teasing from her. Everyone else chuckled along, even Mama, as though to hide her embarrassment. Justine, after fighting for years to keep these women at bay, leaned back in her chair and appeared coolly amused by the fracas. If that wasn't bad enough, Lipiner seemed intent on prying into Alma's lack of formal education.

"I was schooled at home. My father was the great artist Emil Schindler," Alma heard herself say defensively.

"If you're such an expert on art, my girl, do you not agree that Guido Reni is a magnificent painter?" he asked.

"I've never heard of him," Alma said flatly.

"Is your stepdaughter truly so ignorant?" Lipiner asked Carl.

Alma shot a beseeching look at Gustav, but he seemed too engrossed in his discussion with Dr. Spiegler to notice her distress. How dare Lipiner demean her like this, this failed poet and bogus Goethe who hadn't published anything since 1880? In an attempt to reestablish her sovereignty in the art of conversation, Alma changed the subject to literature, hoping that Gustav would join in by quoting Schiller. She mentioned that she was reading Plato's *Symposium*. But this only elicited smug, surmising glances across the table.

"Surely, child, that's far above your head," said Lipiner, with a dryness Alma had never before encountered in any human being.

Like a she-wolf who sensed Alma's weakness, Anna von Mildenburg moved in for the kill. "What do you think of Gustav's music?"

*She's setting me up for the fall.* Alma knew that whatever she said they would ridicule her. And Gustav just sat there not uttering a word in her defense while his friends raked her over the coals. *Did I bring this on myself,* Alma wondered, with a queasy stab in her gut. By giving herself to him so completely, body and soul, before their marriage? By wholly submerging herself in his being? Had he lost all respect for her as a person in her own right? *Liebestod,* indeed.

But she could hardly just sit here and passively endure this. If Gustav's friends were going to burn her at the stake, she might as well have the satisfaction of playing the witch.

"I know very little of his music," Alma said. "But what I do, I don't like."

*Why did I say that?* she asked herself, wanting to clap her hands over her mouth. It was a lie. Gustav had sent her the score for his Fourth Symphony, which had impressed her very much. But at least she managed to make Mildenburg's face turn purple.

"Alma!" Mama cried. "For shame! Did I raise you to be so rude?"

"Evidently," Lipiner said, with some relish.

At least Alma's outburst knocked Gustav out of his complacency. Laughing loudly, he sprang to his feet and escorted Alma away from the table into Justine's little room.

"It's horrid out there," he said, holding her as she fell weeping against him. "Let's stay here for a while, just the two of us."

They sat kissing and holding each other on his sister's bed while in the next room Alma could still hear his friends muttering about her disgrace.

Alma was filled with the foreboding that Gustav's friends were united in their aversion to her. That they would conspire to convince him that his marriage to her would be an utter disaster. Alone in her room, she wept and wailed, resigning herself.

Yet two days after the party, Gustav called in, as loving as ever, with the score for his Fourth Symphony arranged for piano.

"Perhaps you'll come to love my music," he said gently, "if we play it together."

And so they played through the entire symphony, their four hands up and down the keyboard. Her virtuosity at the piano, at least, was something that his friends could not dispute. Alma and Gustav played in perfect accord, both his music and his tenderness moving her close to tears. Although his friends hated her and had tried to sway him, Gustav had stayed the course, faithfully hers.

When they were together, Alma felt serene and content in the warmth of Gustav's admiration, which allowed her to be the woman he wanted her to be. Earnest and self-improving. His awestruck beloved who held nothing back. But when they were apart, a second self surfaced, selfish and outspoken. This self only desired to be free.

*I have two souls,* she told herself. But which was her true soul, her fundamental essence? The self-sacrificing fiancée or the shrew who insulted Gustav's music in front of his friends? When she saw the love and happiness on his face when he stepped through the door with his sheet music or a book he wanted her to read, the most profound elation gripped her. Was that a lie? *No, no, no.* That false self, that vacillating, capricious self, must be banished. Drive a stake through her heart and bury her in a lead coffin lest she rise again and again.

And so the inner war raged on inside Alma until the middle of February when she discovered it was too late to back out of this marriage even if every part of her was screaming for release.

Scrambling out of bed one morning, she clung to the blue and white toilet, and spewed until only blood and saliva came out. Afterward, she was so weak, she collapsed on the tile floor and wept in helpless fury that in the eleventh hour the choice had been taken from her. She had only herself to blame. So much for being a courageous New Woman! She was just an idiot who had to rush into marriage because she was pregnant. When she finally had the strength to pull herself upright, she saw her mother in the doorway.

"Oh, you poor, foolish girl," Mama said, taking Alma in her arms, rocking her back and forth. "Don't despair, my dear. The wedding's only a few weeks away. You won't be showing yet. You'll still look beautiful."

Alma's wedding was no elaborate affair like Gretl's. No orange blossoms or lacy bridal veil for her. Gustav hated big ostentatious weddings. He fooled the press by announcing that the nuptials would take place in the evening. Instead, the ceremony was held early in the morning before journalists and gawkers could gather.

Alma, Mama, Carl, Justine, and Arnold Rosé all arrived by cab. But Gustav insisted on walking to the church despite the torrential rain. His galoshes squelched on the Karlskirche's marble floor as he marched up the aisle to where Alma and the others awaited him. Their party of six had that monumental church to themselves.

Battling both morning sickness and the beginnings of a cold, Alma witnessed everything through the shimmer of her rising fever. Amid that baroque splendor, in this church designed to give a foretaste of the magnificence of heaven, she and her bridegroom exchanged their eternal vows. Above them soared the huge oval dome with its frescoes of angels and clouds, and at the very top hovered the dove of the Holy Spirit. *You carried me to sixth heaven. The seventh is still waiting for us.* Before them, high over the main altar, the Hebrew name of God blazed amid a transcendent, upward-pointing triangle emanating golden rays.

During the rite, Gustav tripped over a hassock, which made everyone laugh. Even the priest smiled.

*"Urlicht,"* Gustav whispered to Alma, with a backward glance at the altar before they walked out of the church arm in arm, husband and wife. "I always envisioned God as the light at the beginning of time."

Her bridegroom looked so gallant, so loving, so filled with hope. *To be worthy, truly worthy of his love.*


The following day, after Justine and Arnold Rosé's wedding, Alma and her new husband boarded the train to Saint Petersburg, where Gustav would be conducting works of Mozart, Wagner, Beethoven, and Tchaikovsky. As the train pulled out of Vienna, Alma took comfort in the fact that she and Gustav were alone at last, beginning their new life together. She no longer needed to conceal her pregnancy under the cloak of shame.

"It's a pity I'll be so busy with my work," Gustav told her, holding her close in the privacy of their sleeper carriage with its mahogany paneling and lacy curtains, its pull-down bed with the thick eiderdown quilt. "But let's make this a proper honeymoon."

He drew her into his embrace.

An unutterable tenderness seized her. *I love him with my entire being. I made the right choice. Of course I did.* Alma vowed she would make it her life mission to serve his genius. To move every stone from his path. To live for him alone.

Suite 2

# ADAGIETTO

# 20

||||||||||||||||||||||||||||

In the April twilight, Alma climbed the steps of that hallowed temple of modern art, the Secession Museum, just across Karlsplatz from the church where she and Gustav had married a little more than a month ago.

After the cold of Saint Petersburg, Alma was grateful to be back in Vienna in this most hopeful time of year. Great urns of Easter lilies and daffodils flanked the museum entrance. The foyer throbbed with cultured souls, all gathered for the 14th Secessionist Exhibition. Before Alma could even make her way to the garderobe to relieve herself of her hat and coat, family and friends thronged to greet her. Mama, Carl, Aunt Mie, Berta Zuckerkandl, and the Conrat sisters. Ilse was looking more elegant than Alma had ever seen her, in a sweeping white gown, her hair piled as high as a queen's. She had returned from Brussels for this event where her work would be showcased along with the finest avant-garde sculpture in the empire. Caught up in the electric thrum of excitement, Alma congratulated her and kissed her cheeks before hugging Erica.

Laughing and vivacious, Alma was her most charming self. It was the same as before her marriage, yet entirely different. A confusing tumult sounded in her heart when Klimt came to kiss her fondly.

"Dear Alma," he said. "Marriage becomes you. You look absolutely radiant." He spoke with a profound respect, as though her wedded state placed her high above the reach of his lecherous designs. "I have a surprise in the exhibition hall just for you."

Before Alma could ask him what it was, Klimt smiled mysteriously and slipped off to greet the Bloch-Bauers.

To her old friends, she was still Alma, but she could not quite get used to the novelty of being addressed as Frau Direktor, as the sculptor Max Klinger now did, the star of tonight's exhibition.

"Frau Direktor," he said breathlessly. "I can't tell you how honored I am that your husband has so graciously agreed to perform for us."

Alma smiled and dipped her head. Gustav was to be an integral part of this evening's festivities, his presence intended to transform this musically themed sculpture installation into a total work of art.

When it was time for everyone to file into the main exhibition hall, Max Klinger took Alma's arm. Gustav and his ensemble of six trombones stood at attention beside the bulwark of Klinger's colossal new sculpture that was still shrouded beneath a dust sheet. Twenty-one other new sculptures, including work by Ilse Conrat, were arranged around Klinger's piece to form a constellation of stone and bronze. Running the length of the left wall, Klimt's brand-new frieze created a spectacular backdrop, glittering with gold leaf.

A hush fell over the crowd. Carl, with an air of great ceremony, unveiled Klinger's new masterpiece, a huge statue of Beethoven enthroned with an eagle at his feet. This was a truly grandiose work, crafted from marble, bronze, alabaster, amber, ivory, mosaic, and gold leaf.

Her heart in her throat, Alma looked to her husband, who smiled and held her gaze for one long incandescent moment before turning to his ensemble. His baton whipped like a willow in the wind, and his arrangement of the "Ode to Joy" chorus from Beethoven's Ninth Symphony filled the room. Originally, Carl had wanted a full orchestra and choir, but owing to space constraints, Gustav had instead decided for the radical simplicity of these six trombones. The music rang as stark as granite, moving Max Klinger to tears.

As the triumphant notes swelled, Alma viewed Klimt's *Beethoven Frieze*. The yearnings, depicted as sinuous young women, floated off on a quest for meaning and grace. But the hostile forces of madness, disease, and depravity stood in their way, taking the form of a giant ape with a serpent's tale surrounded by lascivious nude women. Farther along, Beethoven appeared in golden armor, an avenging knight to battle the powers of darkness in order to redeem humanity. On closer inspection, Klimt's Beethoven revealed itself to be a portrait of her husband, Alma realized with startled wonder. So this was the surprise Klimt had alluded to. She recognized Gustav's angular profile, his dark hair and sculpted face, his slim body.

The yearnings, persevering on their pilgrimage, found their deliverance through poetry and music. Finally, they were subsumed in the rapture of the kiss of absolute union, depicted as a naked couple locked in an eternal embrace. Around them a choir of angels sang the "Ode to Joy" chorus that Gustav's ensemble now played.

This divine alchemy of music and art swept Alma away. Gustav was the great magician, the most revered person in that room packed with artists and intelligentsia. He knew no borders, none. Everything merged in sublime beauty. Gustav Mahler, Beethoven's true heir, the artist-savior and champion of modern art and music. He, the epicenter of this brave new order. And she, his bride, four months pregnant with his child. She with her clipped wings, her own music sacrificed to his.

Alma felt a hot wash of pain to see Ilse stand smiling beside her sculpture *Wet Hair* while a journalist photographed her. The life-size plaster-cast statue had won a gold medal in Munich the previous year. The female figure was bent forward, holding her long wet hair in one hand and reaching for a towel with the other. Though the figure was nude, there was none of the eroticism of Klimt's or Rodin's work—this was not an image intended to arouse male desire but an exquisitely crafted sculpture of a woman performing an everyday act, her eyes lost in contemplation. Alma was astounded by the technical brilliance. How had Ilse managed to make that wet hair look so lifelike? Ilse was receiving so many commissions, she could support herself with her art.

Erica, meanwhile, looked on in sisterly pride. She held hands with her adoring beau, Hans Tietze, her fellow university student. No one had pressured Ilse to marry. No one had forced Erica to choose between love and pursuing her dreams.

• • •

Mistress of a spacious apartment so close to the heart of Vienna, Alma thought she should have been the happiest woman alive. The music room windows were open to receive the sweet May air. Across the way, she could see Belvedere Castle and its manicured lawns.

Taking her seat at Gustav's piano, Alma's fingers caressed the keys, itching to play, to lose herself in music as she had always done. How marvelous it would be to compose, to even have regular lessons again. But she had made her pact with Gustav. Then again, he was away at the opera. He wouldn't even know. The shiver of the forbidden rippled through her when she opened the heavy accordion-pleated folder where she kept her scores hidden away. Her lieder and sonatas. But when she tried to play her song "Bei dir ist es traut," her fingers froze on the keys.

Gustav would know she had broken her promise. He would read it at once from the distraction on her face. He could tell when she was elsewhere, lost in reverie. Straying from her absolute dedication to him felt like a sin as grave as adultery. He was as demanding a taskmaster with her as he was with his musicians, accepting nothing less than her utmost effort.

In the hallway, the telephone rang, a shrill shattering of the stillness. Alma nearly twisted her ankle to pick it up on the fifth ring. Gustav's assistant at the opera informed her that her husband was on his way home for the midday meal.

"Resi!" Alma shouted, rushing into the kitchen. "Hurry with the soup."

As if to spite them both, the maid was still sullenly chopping celery.

"*Meine Güte,* all these cursed vegetables!" Resi grumbled, a look of martyrdom on her face, as they surveyed the cutting board of sliced carrots and onions. "You know, Fräulein Justine was so conscientious, she insisted on making the Herr Direktor's vegetarian cuisine herself. She would trust no one else! What do *I* know of such things? I have to chop up an entire garden just to make soup!"

After years of serving Justine, Resi seemed especially resentful of having to take orders from Alma, the young usurper. Too exasperated to argue, Alma began flinging the vegetables the maid had already managed to chop into the simmering pot of vegetable stock. It was true that they would taste better if they were first browned in butter before going into the broth, but there was simply no time. It took Gustav less than fifteen minutes to march home from the opera. When he reached the street-level entrance of their building, he'd ring the bell downstairs to alert Alma that he had arrived. By the time he had climbed the four flights of stairs to their apartment, he expected to find his hot soup waiting for him on the table.

"Are there fresh rolls?" Alma asked Resi. "Butter? Honey and fruit?"

"Yes," Resi sputtered. "I had to run to the market and drag my basket up all those stairs. My knees are murdering me. Why can't we get our groceries delivered? Fräulein Justine used to let us get everything delivered."

"You know we must economize, Resi."

Alma wondered how she had been saddled with the most unbiddable maid in Vienna. Back at Mama and Carl's house, Cilli managed to do both the cooking and shopping without complaint. Perhaps Alma's rudest awakening after the wedding was discovering how badly Justine had managed her brother's finances. Carl had been right—despite Gustav's princely salary, he was deep in debt to the tune of 50,000 gold crowns. Alma reckoned it would take at least five years of austerity to pay it off. She was beginning to feel grateful for her husband's spartan diet.

Before Alma could stop her, Resi threw what Alma judged to be far too much salt in the soup.

"Not even chicken broth or a ham hock to add flavor," the maid lamented. "You won't even let me add cream."

"My husband detests creamy soups. You know that, Resi."

"One day that man's crazy diet will kill him," the maid muttered darkly.

Her heart banging in urgency, Alma raced the clock to set the table and fill the water glasses. She folded the linen napkins and arranged the vase of lilacs just so. Her husband kept to a rigid schedule, rising early when she was still too racked with morning sickness to lift her head from the pillow. He worked on his music, hammering on the piano, before he sprinted off to the opera at nine. After the midday meal, he insisted on a long walk for the both of them owing to his conviction that exercise was imperative for healthy digestion. They hiked either four times around Belvedere Park or else once around the entire circuit of the Ringstrasse. Then they took their *Jause,* a light repast, at five before he returned to the opera. When he was conducting, he expected to see her in the director's box. If he wasn't directing, he still expected Alma to arrive at the opera on foot at the end of the evening and walk him home. After their late supper, they might have some precious time together to talk or play four-hand piano before they both collapsed exhausted into bed.

Gustav could tolerate no disruption in his routine even to accommodate her pregnancy or their newlywed status. There were to be no surprise guests, no parties, and no salongoing unless he scheduled it. As his wife, Alma now had to safeguard his peace and privacy just as Justine had in the past. In this vein, Alma had taken to sleeping in Justine's old room so her bouts of nausea wouldn't disturb his rest. Being pregnant was so all-consuming, she could barely manage living according to Gustav's regime and could only wonder how much harder it would be once the baby was actually there, demanding all her attention.

She jumped to hear her husband ring the bell downstairs.

"Resi, be quick with that soup!" Alma shouted, before opening their apartment door, a thing Gustav insisted on, to save him the trouble of fumbling for his key.

No sooner than the maid had delivered the soup to the table, Gustav marched in like a conquering hero, a healthy color in his face. Banging doors open and shut, he sprinted to the washroom to clean his hands and face before returning to kiss Alma and take his seat at the table.

"Almschi, you look so pale," he remarked. "You need to spend more time outdoors."

Thanks to Resi's sabotage, the soup was both undercooked and oversalted. Gustav shook his head in dismay.

"Almschi, perhaps you should study Justi's cookbooks. I'm sure they have much to teach you."

Alma smiled thinly. Her sister-in-law, as her final dig before departing her brother's household to begin her new life as Arnold Rosé's wife, had most pointedly left behind her cookbooks for Alma's edification. Then again, not even Alma's own mother would feel much sympathy for her plight. Hadn't Mama warned her that one day Alma would come to regret her utter dearth of domestic skills? Gretl, after all, had done the proper thing and taken cooking lessons before marriage, studying recipes with the same zeal as Alma had once studied counterpoint. A sense of loss flooded Alma again, a grief she tried to swallow down like the god-awful soup. Now that she and Gustav were married, the wild romance of their courtship seemed well and truly over. He was no longer the ardent lover who had sworn he couldn't live without her but a schoolmaster sternly shaping her into the wife he expected her to be.

"Please, Almschi, no white rolls next time. You know I eat only whole-grain bread."

Not able to stomach the soup, Alma nibbled on a poppy-seed roll her husband wouldn't touch. Gustav, meanwhile, spoke excitedly about their upcoming trip to Crefeld, Germany, where he had been invited to direct his Third Symphony.

"I know it's only a provincial town, but just imagine, Almschi. My Third will be performed in its entirety for the very first time!"

When he looked at her like that, on fire with enthusiasm, so much love in his eyes, her resentment and misgiving melted away.

"What a triumph for you, Gustl." Alma reached across the table to take his hand. "For *us*."

Perhaps a change of scene was all it would take to make everything sweet again. *Deliver me, o gods of music, from the hell of housekeeping.* For a few blessed weeks, Alma would be spared from having to wrangle with Resi. There would be parties and receptions, and Alma could be her convivial old self, laughing and charming her way into the hearts of Gustav's hosts. But what would she wear? By June, she would be six months pregnant. As for buying new clothes, finances were tight, but the thought of squeezing herself into last year's summer apparel was a daunting one. She might have to swallow her pride and beg Mama to lend her some of her reform dresses that were loose enough to accommodate her swelling body.

*Mama, is it normal to feel this lonely as a wife?* The question Alma didn't dare speak aloud clung to her tongue like the taste of bitter medicine. Perhaps she could confide in Gretl, but she had Gretl's fragile nerves to consider. At least her sister seemed happier in her marriage these days. She had written Alma an exultant letter announcing that she, too, was pregnant with her first child. Mama was over the moon.

"This year I'll be a grandmother twice over," Mama said.

In the garden at the Hohe Warte, Alma and her mother sat in the grass with little Maria, who was nearly three years old. The pudgy, dark-haired child was busy building a fortress of painted wooden blocks. If her little half sister had been a boy, she and Mama would be joking that the child had a future as an architect. *But, poor Maria, you're just a girl. Even if you grow up among artists, you'll only get married and have babies.*

The men sat only yards away, but they were in a separate sphere, discussing the symbiosis of art and music. The painter Alfred Roller, Carl's colleague from the Secession, was embarking on a collaboration with Gustav to design stage sets for the Court Opera's production of *Tristan und Isolde* this coming winter. Alma watched with yearning as Herr Roller showed his sketches to her husband. How she longed to wriggle away from her little half sister to join the men's discussion. Carl and Kolo Moser were also gathered there, all four men engaged in a spirited conversation. But now that Alma was an expectant mother, everyone, including Gustav and Mama, seemed to think it crucial that she at least make an appearance of doting on little Maria. Besides, even if Alma had brazenly elbowed her way to the table, there wasn't a free chair for her to occupy. She could only observe as the men lionized her husband.

Both Mama and Carl had come to worship Gustav. During Alma's visits to what had once been her home, she had come to feel like the odd one out, with her mother and stepfather falling over themselves to make Gustav welcome. Cilli loved to spoil him with special vegetarian dishes that made the food coming out of Alma's kitchen taste like pig slop. From the open kitchen windows, Alma caught the aroma of vegetable strudel baking in the oven.

"I must go in to help Cilli," Mama said. "You'll watch Maria, won't you, dear?" With a covert glance at the men, Mama lowered her voice. "Cilli's copied some recipes for you. Poor Gustav looks like he's lost weight since the wedding. You have to try harder in the kitchen, darling, even if it means firing that awful Resi and getting someone else. Your sister, for all her travails, still manages to serve her husband a decent meal."

At that, Mama disappeared inside the French doors and left Alma in charge of Maria. With dogged insistence, the three-year-old stacked her castle walls higher and higher until the entire edifice collapsed around her. Alma tried to help the child rebuild, but Maria slapped at Alma's hands in frustration.

"Mama!" Maria wailed, only then seeming to notice that she had been left alone with Alma.

Shrieking in alarm, the child charged in the direction of the open French doors only to trip over her own blocks before Alma could catch her. Falling headfirst, her half sister banged her head and began to scream in earnest. Alma took the child in her arms and frantically tried to soothe her. But Maria only howled inconsolably for her mother.

Mama stormed out, her hands on her hips. "Alma, can't I leave you alone with your sister for one minute?"

Gustav, who prized his peace and quiet, came to gently take Maria from Alma's arms. "Such a powerful set of lungs," he said indulgently. "Maria Moll, I think you'll be an opera diva one day."

The child stopped screaming to gaze at him in astonishment as he crooned a lullaby, bouncing her in his arms until Maria was grinning. With a fit of giggles, she attempted to yank off his spectacles. Gustav seemed so natural with children. He'd had much more practice with his large family of younger siblings. After his parents' deaths he had stood in as a father figure for them.

157

"Maria," he said, in his Bohemian-accented German, not rolling the *r*. "If Almschi and I have a little girl, we shall also name her Maria. After my mother."

Although Alma supposed that she should be grateful to Gustav for rescuing her from her half sister's tantrum, she found she was furious beyond words that he had already named their unborn child without so much as asking her opinion.

Mama thanked Gustav profusely before shaking her head at Alma. "Thank goodness *one* of you is good with children."

Alma smarted, aware that Carl, Alfred Roller, and Kolo Moser were staring at her in horror, as if her ineptitude with a toddler proved that she was a monstrosity. Now that her complete incompetence as a woman in all areas apart from the bedroom and the ballroom had been firmly established, she wanted to cover her face and hide. Read Nietzsche and pound out *Götterdämmerung* on what had once been her piano.

As if fearful that Alma might make matters even worse by saying something ungracious, Mama loudly summoned her to help give Maria her bath. "You should know how to bathe a child, seeing as you're having one."

Alma, her mother, and Maria passed through the parlor, where Carl's latest paintings were on display. Since Alma had left home, her stepfather's art had undergone a radical transformation. A large tender portrait showed Mama and Maria at the breakfast table, their every gesture radiating domestic bliss. Now that Alma had moved out, it seemed that their beautiful modern home was an oasis of tranquility. *No wonder they couldn't wait to see the last of me.*

# 21

⁙⁙⁙⁙⁙⁙⁙⁙⁙⁙⁙⁙⁙⁙⁙⁙⁙⁙⁙⁙⁙

At the end of May, in the midst of a record-breaking heat wave, Alma and Gustav made the long train journey to Crefeld, an industrial city of 100,000 souls on the banks of the Rhine just north of Düsseldorf. The city appeared as a dusty jumble of neoclassical buildings, textile factories, workers' tenements, and brand-new villas where the factory owners resided. Since Crefeld possessed little in the way of inns, she and Gustav were invited to stay in one such industrialist's oppressively overfurnished home. Their wealthy host offered up his own master bedroom to the famous guest conductor and his wife.

Crefeld struck Alma as backward and hopelessly provincial. She and Gustav could hardly step out of their host's front gate to go for a walk without being trailed by a gang of loudmouthed youths heckling Alma for her reform dress, the only clothing she could bear in this miserable heat.

"Hey, lady, why are you wearing a flour sack?"

The pimply yokels also taunted Gustav on account of his eccentric gait, his nervously twitching leg, his habit of carrying his hat instead of wearing it. Even when they returned to their host's home, the boys loitered outside, loudly mocking Gustav's and Alma's foreign accents.

Though Gustav was accustomed to drawing crowds of curious onlookers wherever he went, this puerile taunting seemed to wear him down. As a man who relied on his routine and privacy, he appeared completely out of his element. Alma managed to persuade him to give up their punishing walks in the heat and instead hire a carriage to take them into the countryside, where they might leave their tormentors behind and find some peace and a cooling breeze.

"Perhaps coming here was a mistake," Gustav said, mopping his sweaty brow as their carriage rattled along a rutted road through the vineyards skirting the Rhine. "I'd hoped to finally earn some applause and even some money for my own work. But these people probably won't like my symphony, let alone understand it."

"Nonsense," Alma said, taking his hand. "You're admired as a conductor everywhere, but now you have a chance to prove that you're a great composer. Have courage, Gustl."

Alma attended every rehearsal without fail, following the score and taking notes.

Her husband's Third Symphony was his most ambitious to date, a work of staggering scope, a behemoth, running more than an hour and forty minutes in length, which explained why it had never before been performed in its entirety. It demanded the combined forces of a full orchestra, a contralto soloist, a women's choir, and a boys' choir. Gustav had confided that the Third was his attempt to explore the creative life force in a symphony that embraced every aspect of nature and human experience. Dark and light, comedy and tragedy, decay and resurgence all comingled. It was certainly a challenging piece to perform. Alma observed the perspiring musicians and singers struggling to come to grips with the music. They had just nine days to prepare for the concert. By force of necessity, the rehearsals ran hours over the official time until Gustav and his ensemble were utterly depleted.

"Almschi, what did you think?" he asked her anxiously, as though he trusted her discerning ear more than any other. He was worried that the concert would be a monumental failure.

"The contralto's voice is darkly beautiful, just what you want," she told him. "But the horns in the first movement sounded mawkish. I think they should be more crisply articulated. And be careful not to let the pace drag, especially in the final movement."

Alma felt closest to Gustav when he turned to her like this, addressing her as his partner in music as well as marriage. His soul's harbor. When it was just the two of them with no family or false friends to interfere or cast judgment on her.

"All in all, it's beginning to sound splendid," she said. "This will be the turning point of your career. I'm sure of it."

"In Crefeld, of all places!" He laughed. "I miss home. Don't you?"

She lowered her eyes and held her tongue. She did not, in fact, miss their frenetic regime in Vienna.

"At least I thought I was homesick," he said, staring into her eyes. "Except now I realize my home isn't a dwelling place or a city or a country. But another human being. *You*, Almschi. You are my home."

A light blazed inside her, her heart beating like the wings of a thousand white doves.

The concert day was upon them, the world premiere of the first full performance of Gustav's Third Symphony. Justine and Arnold Rosé had traveled up from Vienna. Even Richard Strauss had come, the most influential living German composer, hailed as the greatest thing since Wagner. Strauss was a strapping giant of a man who towered over Gustav when he shook his hand. Alma understood it to be a huge victory that such a celebrity had deigned to come all the way to Crefeld to hear her husband's symphony. But what if Strauss hated it and let everyone know? Gustav's future as a composer hinged on this performance.

In that packed and sweltering concert hall, Alma was so absorbed in the music, she forgot about the smell and press of the other sweating bodies around her, about her puffy ankles and aching back. The first movement, opening with the grandeur of eight horns playing in unison, sent tingles running through her. This movement alone lasted forty minutes, as long as an entire Beethoven symphony. Originally, Gustav had conceived it as a tone poem with the title "What the Stony Mountains Tell Me." Those sonorous horns told the tale of emergent life struggling to break free of dense, inanimate matter until, at the climax, the orchestra erupted into swelling sound, igniting new tension. This symphony was its own universe with exploding volcanoes creating new landmasses. Life evolved, taking on increasingly complex forms. Although Alma had spent more than a week listening to the rehearsals, the music took her breath away, as though she were hearing it for the first time.

At the end of the first movement, Richard Strauss stood up, and cried, "Bravo!" Leading the applause, Strauss marched up to the conductor's podium to offer Gustav his official benediction.

Everything that happened afterward seemed like one magnificent crescendo after another. With each movement, the audience seemed more deeply stirred. Alma watched their spellbound faces as the solo contralto sang "O Mensch! Gib Acht!," a poem taken from Nietzsche's *Also sprach Zarathustra.* In his younger days, Gustav had admired Nietzsche as much as she did. *The world is deep,* the poem declared, *and deep are its sufferings, yet joy runs deeper still, and all joy yearns for eternity.*

After this solemn declaration of the human longing for transcendence, the women's and boys' choirs broke into a joyful chorus. The women sang of angels while the boys chanted the tones of ringing bells. Then, in the sixth movement, after the adagio finale, the entire audience leapt from their seats and surged in a frenzy to the stage. Alma laughed and cried at once to see them moved to the heights of ecstasy, just as she was, by this symphonic celebration of love and life. The fickle Richard Strauss sauntered out before the final note, but it no longer mattered. The audience was now as convinced as Alma was of Gustav Mahler's genius.

Alma was profoundly and irrevocably in love with Gustav's music, her previous reservations swept aside. Catching sight of Gustav's incredulous face when he turned around on his podium to bow to his audience, she felt a rush of pure passion and then the first stirrings of their unborn child, that kick of life inside her. This, her husband's vindication as a composer and the part she had played in it, bound them together as soul mates far more pro-foundly than the formal wedding vows they had exchanged in Karlskirche.

"Almschi, you were right," he whispered to her later, back in their guest room where they held each other, both of them trembling with wonder at what had transpired that night. "This is the turning point."

# 22

||||||||||||||||||||||||||

A fter the triumph of Crefeld, Alma and Gustav traveled directly to his summerhouse in Maiernigg on Lake Wörthersee near Klagenfurt. Alma thought it would be paradise, just the two of them. The Wörthersee was famous throughout Austria, a sparkling, glacier-fed lake with water that was pure enough to drink. Yet it was also the warmest body of water in the Alps, making it ideal for swimming.

Their villa was enchantingly situated, complete with its own dock and boathouse. On closer inspection, Alma discovered that the house, built for Gustav by a well-intentioned neighbor and still not paid for, was clumsily constructed, with hideous wooden fretwork over all the kitchen cupboards that attracted cobwebs and dust. Though it might have been a fine retreat for a bachelor and his unmarried sister, it seemed far less suitable for newlyweds expecting their first child. Thanks to the philistine floor plan, Alma and her husband were obliged to sleep on separate floors, she in Justine's old room sandwiched between the parlor and the guest room. Gustav slept two stories above her, at the top of the house, where he had his bedroom with its own balcony, his study, and his private bathroom.

Alma could not quite suppress her disappointment regarding their sleeping arrangements. Now that her morning sickness had abated, she had looked forward to their holiday as a time of renewed intimacy and thought they might at least have adjoining rooms. But Gustav insisted that he needed his privacy in order to work. Alma suspected that her mother had taken him aside and warned him that lovemaking during pregnancy could harm their baby—not that he had ever thought to ask Alma her opinions on the subject. *To be honest, Gustl, I would much prefer a bit of gentle lovemaking to those grueling walks you drag me on!* But to keep the peace, she held her tongue.

A steep ten-minute hike uphill from the villa led to Gustav's private composing hut, a stone cabin with windows on three sides. It housed a piano and his complete works of Goethe and Kant. Surrounded by dense forest, the composing hut afforded no view of the lake below, but Gustav adored it, for he could work in peace with the windows wide open and breathe the pristine air, tangy with the aroma of pine.

He had brought sketches of his new Fifth Symphony with him—two completed movements with the rest still in gestational stages. Since his summer vacation was the only time he could make real headway composing, he adhered to an even stricter schedule than in Vienna. He arose at six and rang for the maid. On Mama's advice, Alma had dismissed Resi and hired Elise, a young cousin of Cilli's who could not have been harder working. Elise prepared Gustav's breakfast—freshly roasted and ground coffee, milk, bread, butter, and a different jam each morning—which the poor girl then lugged up to his composing hut, taking a separate and more tortuous route than Gustav himself lest he meet her on the way and be jolted out of his creative reverie. After leaving the breakfast tray in his hut, Elise scurried back down before Gustav could catch sight of her.

Gustav worked until noon, then came down to swim in the lake or go boating with Alma before they shared their midday meal. In the afternoon, they went for three- or four-hour hikes, never mind that Alma was approaching her third trimester.

"You are *young!*" Gustav told her, squeezing her hand in encouragement as he guided her up a nearly perpendicular slope. "Healthy exercise will do you and the baby no harm. Oh, Almschi, the world is so beautiful. Together we shall ascend to the very heights!"

When Alma was ready to weep from exhaustion and throw herself on the ground in defeat, Gustav held her tenderly and whispered in her ear how very much he loved her until she summoned the strength to march on with him, up and up to the stony path. These private moments with her husband were so precious, Alma managed to convince herself that pushing herself beyond the limits of her endurance was holy and good. That it was all worth it just to see him smile at her as though she were his sun and moon, his *lux*.

They clambered over fences and squeezed through hedges, avoiding the well-trodden trails. Instead, they sought out deer tracks and less traveled ways until they reached a lonely farmstead where milkmaids busied themselves making cheese while their cows and goats grazed in a high meadow, lush with lady's mantle and harebells. For a few kreutzer, Gustav bought cups of fresh buttermilk that he and Alma sipped while sitting on a rustic bench beside the water trough, a hollowed-out log through which spring water streamed. Holding hands, they contemplated the view. Far below, the Wörthersee shone like a sapphire in the green velvet hills against a backdrop of diamond-bright Alps. Bees droned in the warm sunlight. Cowbells chimed amid the higher-pitched counterpoint of goats' bells.

"Almschi, perhaps I should include *cowbells* in my new symphony! What could be more pastoral?" Gustav dug his notebook out of his pocket and jotted this down.

He wore his oldest clothes to ensure their privacy and his anonymity, for nothing irked him more than when strangers presumed to strike up conversations with him. Nothing and no one was permitted to disturb his creative trance. As they made their way back down the steep green slopes, a fit of inspiration seized him. Alma sat at the edge of a wild meadow full of midnight-blue monkshood while Gustav scribbled frantically in his notebook.

"A new theme for my new symphony," he told her excitedly, when he closed his notebook. "An adagietto, Almschi, to preserve our idyll for eternity."

Taking his hand as they carefully picked their way down the track, Alma reflected on how their life together this summer was stripped of all dross, almost inhuman in its purity. No thoughts of fame or worldly glory seemed to enter her husband's head. Instead, he lived inside his music, fairly sprinting downhill, and once they had returned to the villa, he retreated to his composing hut to get some more work done while Alma set the table and Elise prepared supper. It was Alma's task to keep the household running smoothly and discourage inopportune guests so Gustav didn't need to worry about anything besides his own work.

Sometimes, for all Alma's love for Gustav, it was hard not to feel abandoned by him.

One morning while her husband was holed up in his composing hut, she sat at the piano in the villa. Her hands shook as they hovered above the keys. Even if she could no longer compose, it would be such a solace to play through the score of *Siegfried* like she used to. Only that was impossible —she mustn't disturb her husband. Sounds carried farther than one might think. Even now she could hear Gustav's piano echoing down from the forest along with the birdsong and breeze.

Biting her lip, she sought to play as quietly as she could, her foot clamped down on the soft pedal, but her every note seemed as jarringly loud as rocket fire. She finally gave up, her stomach knotted in misery when she imagined Gustav's reproach of her. Then, before she could stop herself, her hands edged to her forbidden folder of music scores. *My music!* A hollow rattling filled her skull as she glanced through the etudes, rondos, and song cycles she had composed under Alex's tutelage. To think that just last summer she had been composing the beginnings of an opera! She seized the score.

*I won't play it,* she told herself. With painstaking care, she merely fingered the keys without pressing down or making the slightest sound, chord after chord, bar after bar. Wasn't this similar to what Beethoven had been forced to do after he lost his hearing? He composed his Ninth Symphony when he was stone-deaf! Studying her own composition, she felt such an upsurge of desire, the frantic urge to create. Then her vision blurred and her own musical notation lost all meaning, as though it were a senseless jumble of hieroglyphics.

She was possessed by the most piteous yearning for a friend who esteemed her. Who could help her find herself again. For she was a woman who had lost herself. Once she had composed sonatas. Now she was no more than a hausfrau. It was as though someone had savagely grabbed her arm and dragged her away from herself. With all her soul, she longed to return to where she used to be, only now she was without direction. She could no longer find the bridge back to the other side.

The past eight months, dating from when she first encountered Gustav at Bertha Zuckerkandl's dinner party in November, floated past her in mockery. That long winter in which she hardly composed while waiting breathlessly for Gustav's visits and letters. Then she had surrendered her body to him. And now this mindlessly hectic existence, enslaved to her husband's regime. All her self-contemplation must be abandoned and sacrificed to him. To his career, his genius, his glory.

Not to mention the loss of her friends. Her eyes filled when she realized how much she missed Alex. And the Conrat sisters. Even Max Burckhard, who could at least make her laugh if nothing else. And what had she gained in return? A husband who seemed incapable of even imagining the grief that racked her. He was simply too absorbed in his work.

Then again, how dare she complain? Here she was, in a villa on Lake Wörthersee, married to a man whose career was beginning to soar like a meteor. Her suffering was his bliss — how could she refuse a great man like him? Compared to Gustav Mahler, she was a woman of negligible talent. A mere footnote to his brilliance.

After hiding her music folder in her wardrobe, Alma climbed the three flights of stairs to Gustav's study, his lofty perch that rose above all mundane concerns. On his desk, she discovered a thick leather-bound book containing the complete philosophical works of Spinoza. As she turned the pages, words and sentences leapt out at her. *Immanence. Panentheism. The cosmic animating life force interpenetrates and irradiates every particle of the universe and extends timelessly and spacelessly beyond it, containing every conceivable and inconceivable thing.*

Sinking into Gustav's desk chair, Alma's desolation weighed on her. Why had he kept this book to himself instead of sharing it with her, letting her read passages aloud to him after dinner to spark a true intellectual discussion instead of small talk? But, no, he had hoarded it for himself. Perhaps, like his cursed friend Siegfried Lipiner, Gustav thought Spinoza's philosophy to be far above her head. She, who as an unmarried girl had read Schopenhauer, Goethe, and Ibsen.

Hours later, Gustav came bounding down from his hut, his face lit up, suffused in inspiration. He was still brimming with his work that was his sacred vocation, dearer to him than any outer distraction.

"Almschi!" he cried, holding her by her thickening waist and swirling her in a circle. "You've given me such tranquility and peace! I've never worked so well in my life." A slight frown creased his lips. "Except I did hear you on the piano earlier. Perhaps you could play in the evenings after I've finished composing."

Despite his admonition, he glowed in contentment. But she crumpled in his arms and wept inconsolably.

"Almschi, why on earth are you crying?" he asked, sounding both confused and perturbed.

"Why did you never tell me what you thought of my songs?" she demanded, taking an unsteady gulp of air. "Did you even take a proper look at them before forbidding me to compose? You seemed so interested in my music when we first met."

She fought back the urge to hammer her fists against his chest and scream in his face. *I miss my music so much, I'm dying inside. My soul shrivels a little more each day.* Never before in her life had she cried as much as she did now. *Infantile.* Did her ingratitude prove that Gustav's friends were right and that she was simply too shallow and immature to be his wife?

Gustav let out a long breath. "Almschi, I thought you agreed to think of *my* music as *your* music. I'm composing for the benefit of all mankind. This is my calling and you're an indispensable part of that."

His attempt to mollify her while sidestepping her question left Alma trembling in rage.

"Once *I* had a calling! Once I thought I could be someone!" she shouted, not caring if the boaters on the lake heard her shrieking at her husband like a fishwife. "Gustav, you just want to live your life without sharing it with me, not even your books! You up in your hut composing and I'm not even allowed to play piano in case I disturb you. If you wanted to live like a hermit, why did you marry me?"

Gustav grew exasperated, his face etched in sagging lines. "I'm beginning to doubt whether you love me."

Alma swallowed back a string of unspoken curses. Yet even as she raged inwardly, she was shaken by the conviction that she had never felt so inextricably bound up with another human being. Even his disapproval gave her something solid to cling to. His gaze defined her. His solicitude as he softened and embraced her once more, forgiving her for her betrayal.

He took her out in the rowboat, far out into the vast lake so that she could lose herself in the gentle rocking and swaying that was almost like lovemaking. He spoke to her of Nature and God, of immanence and transcendence, of mysticism and the transmigration of souls. Her otherworldly husband who wanted to raise her to his level, and how she coveted this ascension. To look out at the world from his lordly heights.

*If only I could find my inner balance,* Alma wrote in her diary, despairing over how much she distressed both Gustav and herself with her doubts, her aching loneliness. From this moment onward, she resolved not to tell him of her inner battles. Instead, she would pave his way with peace, pleasure, and equanimity. Since she couldn't find her way back to her old self, she would allow Gustav to shape her into a better self.

Alma elected to devote her hours to making a fair copy of Gustav's evolving Fifth Symphony. As the rush of new ideas flooded him, he fell into the habit of neglecting to write out the instrumental parts beyond the first few bars. Over the weeks, Alma pored over the score and heard it rise inside her. She copied it out, filling in the instrumental parts, becoming more and more of a real help to Gustav.

• • •

Rapt with concentration, Alma sat on the stone terrace and transcribed Gustav's most recent draft onto the master score. She had become so proficient at deciphering his frantic, often messy notes that she was now writing in the new parts as fast as Gustav could compose them. What a delight it was to be working in tandem with him — to think she was part of this vast symphony. *No one can say I'm not his colleague. His amanuensis.*

Dipping her fountain pen into the inkpot, Alma was about to fill in a new bar when a cacophony of barking caused her to splatter ink all over the page. Cursing, she realized she would have to copy this sheet over again. Her jaw set in annoyance, she glanced up to see none other than Anna von Mildenburg, her husband's *actual* colleague and former lover. Dressed impeccably in ivory linen and lace, the soprano was as slender as Alma was bloated with pregnancy. The diva was leading a mastiff on a velvet leash.

Not waiting for an invitation, Mildenburg traipsed up to the terrace, where her mutt proceeded to jump on Alma. Shoving the dog away, Alma tucked Gustav's score away in its folder for safekeeping, away from Mildenburg's eagle-sharp eyes.

"What brings you here?" Alma asked, unable to hide her irritation. How dare Mildenburg barge into her and Gustav's summer retreat?

"Not exactly the warmest welcome." Mildenburg tapped her immaculate gloved fingers on the table, as if to mark the contrast to Alma's ink-stained hands. "My dear, I have the most thrilling news! I've purchased the villa next door. We shall be seeing a lot of each other. Gustl will be so delighted."

The skin on Alma's nape bristled. "You mustn't disturb him! I hope you'll keep that dog quiet."

Why couldn't the cursed woman leave them alone? It was bad enough the way Gustav's former paramour fawned over him at the opera.

"So heartless, Alma! I bought this poor creature off a penniless beggar. At least Gustav loves animals. If you don't even have the manners to offer me a cup of coffee, why then I shall have to return in the evening when he's here to receive me. Gustav won't turn me away." But instead of beating a retreat, Mildenburg fixed Alma with a sickly sweet gaze. "I think you and I should have a heart-to-heart about his collaboration with Alfred Roller, which is all down to you and your stepfather. So much expense just for set design! What if this bankrupts the opera? But our Gustav was never good with finances, was he?"

*Our* Gustav? Alma contemplated hurling a potted geranium at Mildenburg's smug face.

"You owe your career to my husband," Alma said coldly. "Don't you dare involve me in your intrigues."

When Gustav emerged from his composing hut several hours later, Alma couldn't bring herself to mention Mildenburg's visit. Let her husband remain in blissful ignorance of the diva next door for as long as possible. With any luck, Mildenburg would grow bored with quiet country living and hop on the next train to Salzburg.

That evening, when Alma and Gustav dined al fresco, the serene murmur of the lapping lake gave her cause to hope. The two of them shared their simple supper while animatedly discussing the final choral movement Gustav had in mind for his symphony.

Meanwhile, a fly began buzzing around his head. Distracted, Gustav kept trying to wave it away, but the creature was so persistent that he finally chanced to swat it so hard that it plummeted to the ground, where it lay twitching and dying. Springing up from his chair, Gustav raised his foot to squash it and put the thing out of its misery. But then his leg froze in midair, as though he were in the throes of a deep moral dilemma.

"There, there, don't despair, my brother," he said, gazing down dolefully. "You, too, possess an immortal soul."

Finally, he managed to put his foot down and crush the insect before sinking back into his chair with a mien of utter dejection, as though tormented by his collusion in the creature's demise.

"Gustav, it was only a fly," Alma pointed out.

"Only a fly?" With sorrowful eyes, her husband shook his head. "Almschi, it was a sentient being!"

172

So his great compassion for animals, which Mildenburg had so pointedly brought up, extended to insects. Alma wondered how he would react if they ever had an ant infestation.

As if on cue, Mildenburg emerged out of the twilight, trailed by her slavering, barking familiar. "Gustl, how good to see you!" she cried, her voice dripping in glee.

Gustav looked from Alma to Mildenburg in bewilderment while Mildenburg mounted their terrace with all the aplomb of a star soprano taking center stage.

"Did your wife not tell you that we're neighbors now, dear Gustl? You must meet Wotan, my new companion. Go on, shake his paw."

With a howl worthy of a Wagnerian baritone, the mastiff leapt up, its huge paws braced in Gustav's lap. Alma looked on in horror as the wretched mutt began to hump her husband's leg. So great was Gustav's revulsion that he knocked over his chair in his escape.

"Augh!" he cried. "Get that beast away from me!"

At least it was reassuring to see that her husband's reverence for the soul of all nature knew some bounds after all. Brandishing a rolled-up copy of the *Neues Wiener Tagblatt,* Alma rushed to Gustav's defense while a red-faced Mildenburg ineffectually shrieked, "Down, Wotan! Naughty boy!"

Elise charged out with a broom, the sight of which sent Wotan cowering behind his mistress.

"Frau von Mildenburg," Alma said. "You must keep that animal off our property at all times. And perhaps it would be more courteous to wait for an invitation before calling on us again."

"I shall be forced to walk home alone then," the soprano said tragically. "In the *dark.*"

"I shall escort you," Gustav said, conquering his aversion of the dog to be a gallant defender of womanhood. He did, however, address Mildenburg with the formal, distancing *Sie,* rebuffing Mildenburg's familiar *Du.*

Careful to keep the leashed dog on the far side of her, Mildenburg took Gustav's arm and threw Alma a smile. So *that* had been Mildenburg's design all along, to get Gustav to walk her home, just the two of them beside the moonlit lake.

"Herr Direktor, please finish your meal," Elise interjected. "*I* shall walk the gracious Frau von Mildenburg home. Do I have the honor, madam?"

With effusive heartiness, Elise took a firm grip of Mildenburg's arm before marching her and her mutt away. Alma nearly laughed aloud to see the indignation on Mildenburg's face.

Gustav pushed away his half-finished plate as though his encounter with Mildenburg's dog had robbed him of his appetite. Reaching across the table, he took Alma's hand.

"Almschi, come inside. I think I'll take a look at *Siegfried*."

Alma looked at him in dismay, fearing that if they sat down to play the opera it would only summon Mildenburg out of the darkness again and she would insist on staying past midnight to sing every aria. But Gustav, it seemed, was determined, and Alma could only follow as he led her to the piano. Pulling her to sit beside him on the bench, he opened the massive bound score of *Siegfried*. Between the title page and the first page, he extracted a score of his own that he had apparently concealed there as a surprise for her. With a flourish, he placed it in her hands. A song drawn from Friedrich Rückert's poem "Liebst du um Schönheit."

"Something very intimate, just for you," Gustav said, caressing her hair.

"A love song." Alma's eyes filled with tears, all the longing and doubt choked up inside her. She was familiar with Clara Schumann's musical setting of this poem, composed more than sixty years ago when Clara had been twenty-two, the same age Alma was now.

"I hid it here five days ago and was waiting for you to find it, Almschi, but it took you too long!"

"Because I've been so busy copying out your symphony," she said.

"Listen." With great tenderness, he began to play and sing.

If you love for beauty, or youth, or riches, don't love me, the poem declared. But if you love for love's sake, love me now and always, and I will love you forevermore. The plaintive beauty of the lyrics sent a rush up Alma's spine.

Then they played and sang the song together, over and over, their four hands on the piano keys, their voices twining in harmony, their love echoing out the open French doors into the gathering night.

Alma was in thrall of her husband, staggered by his genius. *Compared with his endless riches, how insignificant I appear.*

Her pregnancy, it was true, was becoming more and more of a hindrance, especially on their walks together, but her new vocation to write out his scores was profoundly rewarding. Gustav had come to rely on her as indispensable to his creative process. When he finished a new movement or was stymied by a creative block, he fetched her up to his composing hut to ask her advice.

"That choral movement is just too much," she told him. "It's boring, like a hymnal, and the rest of your work is filled with such beauty and energy."

"But Bruckner," he said, crestfallen. "I keep thinking of his chorales."

"Bruckner, but not you," she said gently.

And so he agreed to strip that movement away.

In September, just as they were beginning to make plans to return to Vienna, Gustav's Fifth Symphony was completed. With great solemnity, they climbed arm in arm up the steep path to his hut, where he played all five movements on the piano for her. Alma followed along on the score, her inner ear listening to how the piece would sound with a full orchestra.

The first movement opened with a trumpet solo using the same rhythmic motif as Beethoven's Fifth Symphony, but Gustav's rendition was far darker. He had titled this movement "Funeral March." *Oh, why is my husband so obsessed with death,* Alma wondered fitfully, one hand on her swelling belly.

The stormy vehemence of the second movement then gave way to contemplation with a brief burst of glory before that, too, faded into shadows like the ending of a tragic opera. The third movement was, by contrast, the ebullient scherzo she had critiqued before their marriage. With its alternating waltz and *Ländler* rhythms, it was filled with exhilarating optimism, as if Gustav's lust for life had vanquished his dread of death.

But it was the fourth movement, the adagietto set for strings and harp, so tender and slow, that moved Alma to tears. For this was a love song even more poignant and yearning than "Liebst du um Schönheit." Gustav borrowed a motif from her beloved *Tristan und Isolde*. Most moving of all, he had penciled in lyrics beneath the violin line, a declaration of his love. *How I love you. You, my sun. I cannot tell you with words. I can only pour out my longing to you. And my love, my joy!*

Through her tears, she smiled at him. For a moment, their eyes locked before he continued to play. The adagietto opened seamlessly into the finale, saturated in pastoral bliss, which took the adagietto's main theme and transformed it into an exuberant, happy-ever-after dance. After Gustav played the last note, Alma rushed to embrace him. His arms reached wide enough to hold her and their unborn child.

"It's magnificent!" she cried. "Magnificent!"

They flew outside to dance their own improvised *Ländler*. Circling round and round, Alma caught glimpses through the pines of the deep blue sky.

# 23

||||||||||||||||||||||||||

T he halcyon weather broke with thunderheads rolling down from the mountains, signaling that it was time to pack up and return to Vienna.

Huddled beside her husband on the clattering train, Alma was by now so huge with child that she felt almost ashamed to show herself in public. There was something so undignified, so primitive, about the way her flesh swelled and protruded like overripe fruit fit to burst, all of it beyond her will and control.

At the opera, Gustav began rehearsals for Mozart's little-known work *Zaide.* His life slotted into its old rhythms, everything back to the way it had been before their summer idyll. But for Alma, this could never be — her back throbbed in pain and she was plagued with heartburn. She couldn't even sleep properly, her belly was so enormous, and when she did chance to drift off, nightmares haunted her.

A monstrous green snake thrust itself inside her body through her most intimate parts and took residence inside her. Trying to rip the cursed thing out, Alma tugged at its tail and screamed for Elise, who came running. Grappling and yanking at it violently, Elise finally succeeded in pulling the beast out of her. But then the serpent uncoiled before Alma and taunted her. In its maw, it held all her internal organs. Alma collapsed, hollow and eviscerated.

Trying to shake off the terror of her dreams, Alma prepared the nursery with freshly painted walls and bright curtains, a crib and changing table, a pile of fresh diapers, and tiny clothes and booties. But the baby wouldn't come. Alma was nearly two weeks overdue. Every morning she awakened with a dry mouth and covered in cold sweat, convinced she would be pregnant forever.

At Mama's and Gustav's insistence, she submitted to examination after examination by Dr. Hammerschlag, whose ice-cold fingers poked and prodded her. Hell, Alma imagined, was full of gynecologists.

"The baby has displaced itself in the womb," the doctor pronounced, with a grim, purse-lipped stare as though Alma were a feckless young girl who had brought this upon herself just to inconvenience him. "On account of your overexerting yourself without any thought to your condition."

Mama shook her head despairingly. "Why did you let Gustav drag you up all those mountains, dear? I thought you had more sense."

Mama and the doctor laid the sole blame on her as a matter of course. No one faulted Gustav. He was stainless, eternally absolved.

On the third of November, the contractions came like earthquakes cleaving the ground beneath Alma. As hard as she struggled to claw her way back up, she only tumbled back down into the rent earth. Why had no one warned her that childbirth was a descent into the underworld? Gustav had promised to raise her up to his level, but she sank into the bowels of hell instead.

It was a tearing breech birth so awful that Mama was in tears, holding Alma's hand, begging her not to give up. Even Dr. Hammerschlag had gone pale, as though he feared the worst. As Alma pushed and groaned, she heard Gustav's panicked pacing in the next room. Childbirth was not a thing he could command or direct. It wouldn't adhere to the dictates of his clockwork schedule. She heard him calling to her through the closed door, his voice breaking, but the doctor wouldn't let him in the room. The next contraction split her in two. She thought her screams would shatter the window glass.

And then it was over. Mama smiled at Alma with such pride and affection as she hadn't in a very long while. "Alma, my beautiful girl, now you're a mama, too."

Alma gazed at the tiny wriggling thing that had lived all those months inside her. Those unfocused eyes, as blue as cornflowers. That tiny needy mouth opening for her first wail. The baby overawed her. *Little one, how will*

*I ever be good enough to be your mother?* Alma clutched her newborn daughter to her pounding heart.

Gustav burst in, his eyes full of tears. "Oh, my love, how can any man bear the responsibility of such suffering and keep on begetting children?"

Mama and the doctor withdrew to give them their privacy.

"I was terrified, Almschi," Gustav said, kissing her brow. "What if I had lost you both?"

"It was a breech birth," she said.

He laughed ruefully as he took their baby in his arms. The infant nestled sweetly in his embrace. Just looking at his face, Alma thought that he was born to be a father. He was helplessly in love with their daughter already.

"That's my child," he said, gazing down at her. "Coming out bottom first. Showing the world straight off the part it deserves." He choked up, overcome with emotion, then returned the baby to Alma.

"Maria Anna," Alma whispered to their daughter, named after both their mothers. "Gustav, now we're a family."


Alma's torn, bleeding perineum was full of stitches, necessitating fifteen days of bed rest. Mama, meanwhile, hired the best nanny she could find, a calm and efficient Englishwoman named Lizzie Turner, who cared for the infant while Alma was too weak to do anything but hold her baby and breastfeed, and even that seemed to drain her last strength. She was plagued by excruciating abdominal pain, which Dr. Hammerschlag diagnosed as gallstones. He then put her on a diet even more severe than Gustav's.

Alma felt teary even after she was able to get out of bed and hobble around the apartment. She wept at the sight of Gustav holding Maria and singing her lullabies. He had already given her a nickname, Putzi—dear sweet little one. His heart was an unstoppable font of paternal love. How Alma wished it was as easy for her. She longed to be a good mother, patient and tender, a glowing madonna like her sister, whose letters waxed rapturously about the joys of motherhood. Gretl swore that her new son, named after his father, was the fulfillment of her every desire.

Motherhood, the sacred destiny of all good women! That dumbfounding rush of love that was supposed to come all by itself. But to Alma's despair, she didn't know if what she felt for her daughter was true mother love. Putzi was more beautiful and perfect than she had ever dared hope, that darling girl with her pink cheeks and dark curls. When Alma made herself focus on how very vulnerable the infant was, tidal waves of emotion overwhelmed her. Was this love—or just fear and a woeful sense of her own inadequacy? She discerned none of the bliss Gretl described but felt only weak and broken down, gasping for air as though she were underground.

Breastfeeding was an absolute torment. *I don't want to do this. I can't do this.* Alma struggled to banish such evil thoughts and coo contentedly over her newborn like a good mother should. But Putzi seemed to sense her underlying resentment and retaliated by squalling and rejecting her breast, which sent Gustav, Mama, or Miss Turner running to whisk the baby into their capable arms. Alma felt like an imposter going through the motions—even an infant could see right through her. Putzi knew straight off who her real parent was—Gustav, whose singing could send her to sleep even when the nanny was at her wit's end. It was as if Putzi, like Athena, was sprung from her father's thigh, wholly his. *All I'm here for is to provide milk, like some stupid cow, and I'm not even particularly good at that. Dear God, what is wrong with me?* Alma wondered if she was a proper woman at all. *Gretl is the normal one and I am the sick one.*

And yet, through it all, Alma's devotion to Gustav remained unshaken. She hungered for him, for any sign of affection from him, as never before. *All of me belongs to Gustav.* Her love for him was so all-consuming that everything other than Gustav felt dead to her. But she couldn't possibly tell him this. In her blackest moments, Alma found herself dreaming of how much happier she had been, in love with Gustav and copying his scores, before Putzi had come into the world. If only she hadn't succumbed to him before the wedding. If only she hadn't come into their marriage already pregnant, they might have had months and months of freedom, sensuality, sharing the same bed. *I could have been so much happier.*

How could a decent woman even think such things? Her guilt and shame clung to her like an invisible hair shirt.

One morning in January, when Putzi was ten weeks old, Alma managed to slip out for a few hours to visit the opera. While the nanny lurked in the corridor, prepared to summon Alma if the baby needed to nurse, Alma watched her husband direct the blocking rehearsal of Carl Maria von Weber's *Euryanthe*. How stimulating it was to watch Gustav block out each scene, demonstrating where the singers should move on stage for the most dramatic effect. Every nuance had to be considered. The sight line of the audience, the acoustics, and the electric lighting. Witnessing the rehearsal unfold, Alma began to feel a sense of blessed reprieve blooming in her chest. How good it felt to inhabit her old self again, to once more be that clever, cultured observer, that person who lived for the opera.

Gustav had thought that *Euryanthe* in particular would delight her with its sheer escapism. Drawn from a medieval French romance, it told of a count's wager concerning the fidelity of his betrothed, the eponymous Euryanthe. The victim of wicked conspiracies, this hapless damsel was falsely accused of wantonness, which caused the count to attempt to kill her. But just as he was about to commit the deed, a giant snake entered stage left. What, Alma wondered, would Dr. Freud make of that? Euryanthe sacrificed herself to the serpent in order to save her would-be murderer. Miraculously, she survived. But the count required several more melodramatic scenes of plot reversals before he was fully convinced of her innocence and finally agreed to marry her.

*What a pathetic story line,* Alma fumed.

Fortunately, the grandeur of the music redeemed the work. Mildenburg, who played Euryanthe, was in top form. Her artistry lent a power and poignancy to the role that completely transcended the inane libretto. How vividly she expressed what it was to be a maligned woman.

As much as Alma had come to dislike her as a person, she was spellbound. Mildenburg wasn't a mere diva but a consummate actress. Grudgingly, Alma

181

found herself in agreement with Gustav's assessment that female suffering had never been portrayed with such magnitude as by Anna von Mildenburg. There was no greater tragedian, male or female, on the opera stage. All the critics acknowledged that Mildenburg was Gustav Mahler's greatest protégée. He had nurtured her career while, in turn, her glory reflected back on him. If his post as director of the Vienna Court Opera was his golden crown, Mildenburg was his crown jewel.

As long as Mildenburg was singing, Alma could overlook any personal frictions. But when the singers took a break, her doubts began hammering away. It sickened her to see the camaraderie between Gustav and his star soprano. Mildenburg, his former beloved who refused to give up her career in order to marry him. And yet she spent more time with him — *meaningful* hours wrapped in the golden passion of their music — than Alma, his wife, who had renounced everything for him, even her health. *Gustav, I could have been your protégée!* As the honorary president of the Guild of Composers, her husband took young composers under his wing all the time, such as Arnold Schoenberg, Alex's student and brother-in-law. What if Gustav had been broadminded enough to mentor her, to raise her to his level as a *composer*, rather than treat her as only a wife and helpmeet? What might she have been capable of?

How Mildenburg seemed to gloat, basking in Gustav's attention while he barely even looked Alma's way. *Your sacrifice to him didn't ennoble you, you idiot! It only made you the biggest dupe.*

Mildenburg trilled that she needed some water to soothe her precious throat. Alma stiffened to her fingernails to see her husband letting that *whore* drink from his own glass. Alma's eyes misted red to see him billing and cooing as though he were some besotted pigeon.

Out in the corridor, Putzi shrieked, giving her mother the perfect excuse to bolt and return straight home.

Back in the apartment, Alma locked the door in disgust. After bidding the nanny to set the cradle beside the piano, Alma began to play and sing *Göt-*

*terdämmerung* at the top of her voice, singing to her daughter who gazed up with her huge blue eyes. When the neighbor, in protest, started grinding out military marches on his gramophone, Alma played and sang even louder. She shook in dread of what was truly transpiring between Gustav and Mildenburg, so much that she feared his coming home. What if she smelled that whore's perfume on him?

Shoving *Götterdämmerung* aside, she stormed off to find the forbidden folder of her own music. *Hers!* She began to defiantly play through her compositions. Her piano sonata. Her lieder. *Nothing has reached fruition in me. Neither my beauty, nor my spirit, nor my talent.*

If only Alex was there to work with her, but Gustav would never permit such a thing. *I must recover my own voice, I must, before it's lost forever!* But when she concentrated and listened deep inside, all senses honed, she could hear only his music, those bombastic horns, those tremulous strings. Already, after less than a year of marriage, she had lost her muse. *Once I had a voice, but it's been replaced by his. He wanted to break me and he succeeded.* And now that her husband had robbed her of every last shred of individuality, he was off nuzzling his star soprano, who got to keep her own music—and him, too!

*May he never come home! May he twist his ankle! May he get struck down by a streetcar!*

Alma hated herself. Swooping to lift Putzi from the cradle, she bowed her hot, weeping face to her daughter's infant sweetness.

Lying on her bed with Putzi in her arms, Alma collapsed into a black state that was half sleep, half trance. From her shattered, broken body another self arose and looked down upon her pityingly. This other woman was as glamorous and confident as Mildenburg. And as uncompromising. A woman who wasn't afraid to be selfish, shameless, brazen.

Pity poor Eve who tried to be so good and yet bore the blame for everything. Kill Eve and let Lilith rise, sweet Lilith with her black wings and talons, her coiling serpent's tail. A woman who seized her life, her lust, her desire, her *music* without apology. Lilith, as dark and sultry as the midnight sky, whispered in her ear: *I am a sphinx. I can't be contained. I belong to no one.* A woman, raw and wild, intoxicated with her own power.

Alma jerked awake in a panic to find Gustav shaking her shoulder. Her husband's face was knit in consternation. He had come home for his midday meal only to find the door bolted to him! Of course, Elise had the meal waiting for him on the table and let him in, but what was Alma doing in bed in the middle of the day instead of coming to greet him? Unable to listen to another word of reproach, a torrent of fury lashed out of Alma's mouth as if she were a striking cobra.

"I thought you would be dining tête-à-tête with Mildenburg. Or would that be too indiscreet? Perhaps the sofa in your office would be much more private."

The anger ripping through her voice made Putzi cry. Deft and fleet, Miss Turner tiptoed in to extricate the baby from her weeping, ranting mother.

"Such sordid insinuations!" Gustav cried. "My regard for Anna is strictly professional. Really, this is beneath you, Almschi."

"You take so little interest in what goes on inside me! I've lost all my friends because you won't see anyone! And my music!"

She broke off into jagged weeping.

"Almschi, you made your choice before we were married." Gustav sounded as though he was rapidly losing patience. "And now, when we're blessed with a beautiful daughter, you're bitter that your girlhood dreams weren't fulfilled? If you insist on being so unhappy, that's entirely up to you."

"Oh, God!" she cried. "How can you make such a mockery of my deepest feelings? I'm suffocating."

There was an edge to her despair that cut like a sword through his platitudes. Silenced, he lay beside her on the bed and enfolded her in his arms while she wept. He held her tightly, his face in her hair, as though his embrace could melt away her rage. Banish Lilith and bring back Eve.

# 24

|||||||||||||||||||||||||

Gustav's travel schedule remained as hectic as ever. In late January he was invited to conduct his Fourth Symphony at the Kurhaus in Wiesbaden. During his absence, he wrote Alma once, sometimes twice a day. His letters were filled with a romantic urgency, as though he were courting her all over again.

> *During the adagio, I imagined you gazing at me with your dear blue eyes. Not with that* <u>*worried*</u> *look (I can't bear to see your eyes when they're like that) but with that ineffable sweetness that shines in them when you love me and you* <u>*know*</u> *that I love you as much as you love me.*

Reading this, Alma felt a rush of warmth, as though she were an infatuated girl again. Yet Gustav's time away spelled a welcome reprieve. She allowed herself to relive her girlhood freedoms as much as motherhood and household duties would allow. Returning once more to her favorite books, she not only steeped herself in her beloved Nietzsche but also devoured Maurice Maeterlinck's *Pelléas and Mélisande,* a symbolist drama of forbidden, doomed love. Never mind that Gustav condemned her books as balderdash.

For once, Mama appeared to take her side. "You're no use as a mother if you're miserable. It's *good* for you to read and play piano if it makes you happy, but don't spend too much time alone either. You need to get out and see people. Gustav will have to understand."

Alma's Sunday visits to Mama and Carl's allowed her to spend long lazy afternoons with old friends including Berta Zuckerkandl, Erica Conrat, and Max Burckhard.

When the Easter holidays came, Gustav would have preferred for Alma to remain in the environs of Vienna, but Mama insisted on taking her and Putzi to Abbazia, the lovely resort town on the Istrian coast. On the lido, Alma knelt in the sand and helped little Maria build sandcastles while Mama cuddled Putzi. By and by, Alma recovered in body and mind. Gone were her crying jags and crippling self-doubt. Gretl, Wilhelm, and their baby came along as well. Alma went for long walks on the promenade with her sister, arm in arm, while Gretl twirled her new parasol. How lovely it was to laugh in the sunshine and sip Dalmatian wine, to dine on swordfish and scallops instead of the bland vegetarian fare Gustav favored. To gaze drowsily at the lapping waves and fall asleep over a book. To accompany Mama, Gretl, and the children on carriage rides through the coastal forest of bay laurel trees and take a boat up and down the rocky shore.

Catching her reflection in the mirror one morning, Alma was astonished to notice she hadn't lost her looks after all. She was still the same young woman with the blue eyes and glossy brown hair whom Klimt had longed to paint. Her skin glowed from the spring sunshine and sea air. When Gustav was finally able to join her in Abbazia, they made love for the first time in what felt like an eternity. She kissed and caressed him hungrily, then languorously, taking possession of the voluptuous fullness of her desire until she drove him half-mad with longing for her. Afterward, as they lay spent and naked in the thick linen hotel sheets, she felt as sleek and sated as a purring cat. Pleasure filled her every cell, along with a renewed call to *live* her life instead of watching it pass her by like a funeral procession.

Back in Vienna, Gustav's career ascended to ever more resplendent heights. In June he traveled to Amsterdam to direct his Third Symphony, and then headed down to Switzerland for the Basel Festival, where he would conduct his Second Symphony in the city cathedral.

"Go on, meet him in Basel like he wants," Mama said. "I'll look after Putzi."

"Only for a few days," Alma said, half-dizzy with the sense of freedom since her daughter, now seven months old, was weaned.

Traveling alone to another country! It felt so daring, so sophisticated, so modern. And it was gratifying indeed to see that she could still turn heads. When Alma took her seat in the second-class carriage, the young cadet seated opposite winked at her over the top of his newspaper. Averting her gaze, Alma removed her gloves to reveal her wedding ring and pretended to ignore him while she perused the latest issue of *Ver Sacrum*. It was all she could do to hide her secret smile.

A pity she had nothing stylish to wear and must make do with clothes dating from before her wedding. The clothing allowance in their limited budget all went to Gustav, who needed to look the part of the rising composer and world-famous conductor. He ordered his suits from the best tailors, his shirts from London. Yet her excitement mounted as the train shot through tunnels to pass between glacier-crowned peaks. She thought she had reached the roof of the world.

Stepping out on the platform in Basel, Alma waved her handkerchief at the wiry figure of her husband, who came bounding toward her as though they had been separated for three years instead of three weeks.

"Almschi!" Gustav threw his arms around her. "Wait till you see what's in store! This will be even bigger than Crefeld. Everyone is here, from all over Europe, and they're clamoring to meet *you*."

After dropping off Alma's valise at the hotel, Gustav took her on a walking tour of the old town, the medieval heart of Basel. Such was his eagerness, he was practically jogging. She was obliged to trot to keep pace. They flew by the Renaissance Rathaus with its golden spires, and up and down the narrow twisting lanes that threaded between ancient patrician houses, before they emerged at the square in front of the great cathedral with its twin Gothic towers. Evening rehearsals of the final choir movement were about to begin.

"Erasmus of Rotterdam is buried in the northern transept!" Gustav seemed beside himself. "The great humanist, Almschi. To think that my 'Urlicht' shall be performed at his final resting place! It couldn't be more perfect."

Before Alma could reply, a troupe of top-hatted dignitaries ambushed them.

"Herr Direktor Mahler, this must be your lovely young wife."

Gustav made the introductions while Alma shook hands with the local worthies, who looked as though they were prepared to fling themselves prostrate on the cobblestones, so great was their reverence for Gustav Mahler.

A photographer appeared. "Herr Direktor, would you be so kind as to pose with your wife?"

Alma wanted to shrink away into the darkest alley. She hadn't even had a chance to brush her hair and felt completely disheveled from the long train journey and their dash across town. But in the golden evening light, she took her place at Gustav's side on the cathedral promontory overlooking the foaming blue-green Rhine.

"Herr Direktor, please hold this." The photographer placed a scrolled-up copy of the Second Symphony under Gustav's left arm.

Not one to enjoy smiling for photographs, Gustav squinted and frowned off into the middle distance, looking every inch the moody genius. Alma inwardly cringed at her unfashionable clothes. *Dear God, my hat is so frumpy!* Dropping her gaze in a gesture of feminine modesty, she did her best not to appear taller than her husband.

This festival was a gathering of the greatest living composers in Europe, including Richard Strauss and Frederick Delius. But Gustav Mahler dominated the event, his Second Symphony given pride of place, to be performed in the cathedral, no less. A buzz of intrigue and anticipation seemed to accompany Gustav wherever he went. Alma heard her husband's name on everyone's tongue.

On the evening of the concert, Alma reflected that Gustav's Second Symphony was as fresh and new to her as it was to everyone else assembled here. Though she had studied the score and played it on the piano, she had never before heard it performed. What could be a more magnificent setting for a piece titled Resurrection Symphony than this vast Gothic cathedral, a shimmering galaxy of candle flames beneath that lofty ceiling?

The funereal first movement laid to rest a dead hero. But the longer Alma listened, the more the music seemed redolent with a cynicism that rendered the titular resurrection improbable, even farcical. What could it even mean in this modern world where everything was stripped of its meaning? *Why am I here?* Alma found herself wondering. *What is the point of my suffering and sacrifice if all this will just end in inglorious death? What if my entire existence is some cruel joke?* Such was the despondent pall this music cast on her. It didn't help that the first movement was followed by five minutes of silence—Gustav's attempt to force his audience to confront their darkest fears concerning the mysteries of death and life. Alma wondered if his critics would skewer him for this and accuse him of being unbearably pompous.

The idyllic second movement, in contrast, was redolent with sweet nostalgia for an irretrievable past. Alma caught the briefest glimpse of the girl she had once been, playing her own songs in a Venice hotel while Klimt looked on with admiration and desire. Oh, that kiss that had transfixed her! Then the third movement tore this reverie to shreds with a caustic mockery of youth's broken dreams. It culminated in a death shriek before the orchestra died away. Alma quietly dried her eyes, hoping no one had noticed her tears. This music dragged all her demons into the starkly glaring light.

But she trembled and softened to hear the mezzo soprano open the fourth movement with "Urlicht," so plaintive and naïve, drawn from a folk song filled with the soul's yearning to return to its creator, that primeval light that existed before the dawn of time.

Not even this could prepare her for the majesty of the final movement. Monumental crescendi of percussion and brass signaled the bursting open of graves and the long dead arising for the last judgment. Offstage brass sounded a fanfare from heaven. The nightingale, the bird of death, called out in flute and piccolo, then faded into silence. Very quietly and mysteriously, a choir of more than two hundred voices began to sing: *Rise again! Yes, you shall rise again, my dust.*

This resurrection, when it finally burst out in the first two verses of Friedrich Klopstock's well-known hymn, appeared like a blinding revelation, all sense of punitive judgment now irradiated in pure divine love. The music rendered Alma weightless. It sent her soaring and she arose, suspended in space, lost in staggering, heartbreaking beauty. Nothing on this earth remained but her husband's music that transported everyone around her to the fullness of rapture. Old men wept openly, just as she did, while young couples fell into each other's arms.

Spinning on the podium, Gustav looked at her, and it was all she could do not to tear out of her seat and embrace him, in thrall of his genius that kept seducing her over and over again.

# 25

||||||||||||||||||||||||

After the Basel concert, Alma and Gustav traveled to their summer-house in Maiernigg, where Mama and Putzi awaited them. Here Gustav might at last enjoy a well-deserved rest in the stillness of their lakeside retreat. Except that he seemed incapable of remaining idle for even a day. Loathe to waste his precious time at Maiernigg, he plunged straight into drafting sketches for his Sixth Symphony as though some limitless inner urgency was driving him. But when Gustav wasn't working in his composer's hut, he spent hours playing with Putzi, carrying her around and holding her up to dance and sing. He looked so young to Alma then, as if twenty years had melted off him.

A golden aura seemed to enclose her young family that entire summer. While Mama and Miss Turner looked after Putzi, Alma could join her husband on long hikes up the steep forest paths, just the two of them. Gustav in his oldest clothes and she in a cool white summer dress that shone even brighter in the full blaze of the sun. Unlike the previous summer, Alma was unencumbered by pregnancy and able to savor these walks and the strength in her limbs and her slim body without having to fear any dreadful consequences for her exertions.

Carl photographed her in loosely flowing reform dress as she smiled and held her beautiful, healthy daughter against the backdrop of the hill-ringed lake. She read Rilke's poetry while little Maria played with Putzi.

But the most precious moments were kept secret. Late at night, when the moon shone over the lake like a lover's face, Alma crept up to Gustav's room and slid into her husband's bed. What could be more natural, more freeing?

She broke through his fortress of artistic solitude and called him to embrace the pure eros of being alive in this beautiful world.

That wasn't to say her demons were completely vanquished. Sometimes she was still possessed of an unbearable envy of Gustav's work, his unstoppable fountain of creative inspiration that elevated him to such a high plane that she could only gaze up at him in reverence. And sometimes, in spite of her present happiness, she still yearned with all her soul for the girl she used to be—Alma Maria Schindler, who aspired to compose symphonies and operas. But in the blinding light of midsummer, it was easier to keep the shadows at bay and count her blessings, to revel in her time in the sun.

One August afternoon, Gustav took Alma's hand and led her up to his composing hut.

"I've tried to express you in a musical theme," he said, sitting at the piano and making space for her on the bench beside him. "Whether I've succeeded or not, I don't know."

He began to play an ascending and descending line in a major key—the rest of his work in progress was in A minor. The theme was energetic, sinuous, willful, and tender.

"What do you think, Almscherl?" he asked. "Have I captured your essence?"

She laughed and caressed his cheek. "It sounds like me climbing up the stairs to your room, Gustl."

They shared a long lingering kiss. Then Gustav sprang up and closed the door to his hut. Their arms around each other, they fell to the floor in a tangled embrace.

When they returned to Vienna in September, Alma was expecting their second child. This time she was determined to enjoy her pregnancy. Motherhood no longer terrified her now that she had some clue what to expect, and Mama assured her that this birth would be easier than the first.

But as she settled back into their Vienna routine, a sinking sense of loneliness gnawed at her. Surely she must be allowed to have some excitement in her life beyond being a mere spectator of her husband's career. If she had any say in the matter, she would love to host her own salon of composers, artists, and writers, on par with Berta Zuckerkandl's circle. But Gustav would never stand for such disruption of his solitude and peace. Instead, Alma elected to do the next best thing, inviting Arnold Schoenberg and his wife to dinner. How could Gustav possibly object to sharing his table with the most innovative young composer in Vienna? His accomplishments were even more impressive considering his humble lower-middle-class background and the fact that, apart from his lessons with Alex and a few others, he was self-taught and had never seen the inside of a conservatory. He couldn't even play piano but managed to compose inside his head — the feat of a true genius.

Alma had begged Schoenberg to bring some scores from the song cycle he was working on, the Gurre-Lieder. After dinner, their esteemed guest, only twenty-nine years old and already as bald as an egg, sat beside Gustav on the sofa while Alma played a few of his songs and his wife, Mathilde — Alex's sister! — sang in a haunting contralto. Gustav applauded wildly, his eyes alight with enthusiasm.

How good it was to see her husband like this, so relaxed and expansive. A few carefully chosen guests were good for him, Alma decided, if only to distract him from the tangled politics at the opera. His stagehands were in revolt, demanding better working conditions, complaining that the Herr Direktor had found the funds to build an expensive and controversial new orchestra pit but not to increase their paltry wages. The Schoenbergs' visits helped keep these worries at bay.

Alma befriended Mathilde, also the mother of a little daughter. One morning she visited Mathilde at her home. Her hostess showed her into the music room, its walls hung with Arnold's paintings, art being the twin passion to his music. Alma's eyes riveted on a portrait of Alex, his expression at once soulful and sardonic.

One look at the apartment with its peeling wallpaper and threadbare rugs was enough to reveal how poor the Schoenbergs were. She and Gustav should anonymously purchase some of Arnold's paintings, she decided. Anything to give the Schoenbergs a foothold.

One winter evening the Schoenbergs came to dinner accompanied by a surprise guest—Alex himself. Alma struggled to keep her composure as her former lover chastely kissed her cheeks and offered her a bouquet of white roses for her table before gravely shaking her husband's hand.

During dinner, Alex addressed Gustav with the utmost deference. One hand on her belly where her unborn baby was kicking up a storm, Alma listened and interjected when necessary to keep the conversation flowing.

"I've composed a symphonic poem," Alex told them. "About a mermaid."

For the most fleeting instant, he glanced Alma's way, as if to privately signal that she was the capricious siren who inspired the piece. When she met his brown velvet eyes, she saw no bitterness, only fondness and goodwill. An incredible softness stirred within her, like a long dormant flower coming back into bloom.

"Alex," Alma said later, accompanying him to the door when her guests were saying their good-byes. "I would very much like to resume my lessons with you."

She handed him his hat while her heart beat in hope that she could indeed have all she desired—both Gustav's love and Alex's friendship and musical guidance. Her husband had seemed so kindly disposed toward Alex this evening. Surely now, when Gustav appeared to be approaching the very zenith of fame and success, he could give her the liberty to take the occasional counterpoint lesson. To compose as a *hobby,* a dilettante's diversion. This one boon Gustav could grant her.

"I'll take no money from you, Alma." Alex smiled and used the familiar *Du.* "That would seem like an insult. But I'll gladly visit you from time to time and play piano with you." He gently took his hat from her hand. "That would be a great honor."

A giddy sense of possibility gripped Alma when Alex rang her doorbell two weeks later, his briefcase full of sheet music. She had hoped they might play through his symphonic poem about the mermaid, but instead he opened the score of Schubert's "Die Forelle." When they sat down to play, Alma couldn't help noticing that he perched as far away from her as the piano bench allowed.

It seemed that Alex had selected the most cheerful piece of music he could find, yet "Die Forelle" was fiendishly difficult. Alma welcomed the challenge, anything to distract her from her turbulent feelings about playing with him again after all this time. With full concentration, she threw herself into these swiftly rippling arpeggios intended to portray a trout leaping upstream.

"You've lost none of your technique," Alex said, in a tone of polite amazement, as if he had expected marriage and motherhood to have turned her brain to porridge.

Alma wished he *would* critique her so she might use this stimulus to improve herself. Even his usual sarcasm would be a welcome relief from this patronizing joviality. She had hoped that Alex's mere presence might rekindle her inspiration to compose. But here they sat playing Schubert while Putzi looked on from the nanny's lap and attempted to sing along in her baby jibber-jabber. So much for a tête-à-tête with her former lover. This tableau was so eminently respectable, so sickeningly bourgeois, it could have come from a Biedermeier painting.

Perhaps all the magic of their old collaboration had stemmed from the passion that had once ignited between them, the love and lust that had seemed powerful enough to move worlds. However, it appeared that whatever attraction Alex might have felt for her was now eclipsed by his awe of her husband, which rendered her as sexless chattel. And how could it be otherwise, seeing as she was heavy with child?

So these were to be no formal, professional lessons then, nothing that would help her progress as a composer or resurrect her shattered dreams. It was almost as if Alex had divined the ultimatum Gustav had imposed on her and he didn't want to be guilty of leading another man's wife into the unholy temptation of creative desire. Instead, he was offering to play a bit of Schubert with an accomplished housewife when he had the odd free hour. Still, it was a most generous offer on Alex's part given his hectic schedule.

When he took his leave, Alma made an effort to smile warmly to hide her disappointment. Her most disconcerting thought was this—what if, as her once rapturously fruitful collaboration with Alex attested to, her creative inspiration came from the same murky depths as her passion for him? What if she couldn't write or compose without all these forbidden desires surging to the surface and demanding to be acted upon? Was she depraved enough to betray her husband and seduce Alex just to get her music back? As if Alex would allow himself to be seduced by a pregnant woman.

Alma felt so filthy that she longed to run away to some remote mountain spa and plunge herself into a hot sulfur bath until the stain of her unholy urges could be washed away.

Come June, Alma felt as enormous as the hot-air balloons drifting over Prater Park. But this didn't stop her from going to the Burgtheater to see Gerhart Hauptmann's verse play *Der arme Heinrich*. Drawn from a medieval tale of courtly love, it told of a knight stricken with leprosy who could be healed only by the heart's blood of a virgin who willingly sacrificed herself for his salvation. The haunting cadences left Alma entranced, forcing her to relive the agony of the sacrifice that she had made for love. But from this catharsis, the very thing she had renounced rose phoenixlike, a pure gift. Music emerged in her head, its vibrations thrumming into her fingertips, her very bones.

Even while she and Gustav walked home together after the play, the melody unspooled inside her. *These verses shall be the libretto for my opera.* The German composer Hans Pfitzner had already written an opera based on the tale, but hers would be utterly original. She could hear the overture, the arias, plainer than her husband's voice.

When she went to bed that night, she felt as intoxicated as though she had downed a magnum of champagne. Music filled her dreams, the notes so tangible and real that she could pluck them like jeweled fruits from the Tree of Paradise, singing-ringing rubies and opals that she threaded on spun gold, then wove on a loom of pure sound. *My music. My brainchild. I have created this. I contain this. I hold it all inside me and now it wants to emerge.*

*Now!* Alma jolted awake to feel her waters breaking. A glance at the clock told her it was just before five. Gustav would still be asleep in his separate room. Even Elise didn't rise until six thirty. *Let them sleep.*

After changing into dry clothes, Alma opened the window to gulp down the fresh morning air. The pale blue sky was washed pink with the first hint of sunrise. All the rosebushes in Belvedere Park were in full bloom—she could almost taste their fragrance on her tongue. The birds' dawn chorus filled the stillness, and even then, Alma's music kept washing over her like a waterfall.

She tiptoed to the piano. Her contractions had started, but there was still enough time between them to soft pedal the notes. She must work fast. The contractions were coming on stronger, swelling and subsiding waves in an incoming tide that would soon engulf her. In that clear, free space between the pains, she madly scribbled down her score one note at a time. Gustav slept on—she could hear his snores forming a counterpoint to her high-arching melody as she composed in a blaze of pure white heat. Nothing else existed but this. *Exstase,* she scrawled across the score. Ecstasy.

"Frau Direktor, has your time come?"

Alma wrenched her head to see Elise open the door and peer in at her with a pale, tight face. Alma couldn't speak. She only wanted Elise to close the door and leave her alone.

"Let me awaken the Herr Direktor," Elise said.

Alma shook her head, her tears streaming, but Elise was already trotting down the corridor to rap on Gustav's bedroom door.

While her husband was busy telephoning the doctor, Alma managed to jot down an entire bar before she heard his footsteps approaching the music room, giving her just enough time to hide her unfinished work inside her book of Beethoven sonatas.

"Almschi!" Gustav rushed in, still in his nightshirt and dressing gown. "Never fear, my love. Dr. Hammerschlag is on his way."

She writhed in his embrace, her body jackknifed by a particularly strong contraction. In a frantic attempt to distract her from the pain, Gustav sat her at his desk and began reading aloud from Kant's *Critique of Pure Reason* on the topic of the seeming futility of metaphysics.

"'Why then has nature afflicted our reason with the restless striving for such a path, as if it were one of reason's most important occupations?'" he read with solemn authority, as though quoting a holy text. "'Still more, how little cause have we to place trust in our reason if in one of the most important parts of our desire for knowledge it does not merely forsake us but even entices us with delusions and in the end betrays us!'"

Alma clutched her belly and groaned. In thrall of the contractions, she couldn't understand a word he was saying.

"Pay attention, Almschi!" Gustav cried. "Mental concentration is the only means of conquering pain."

Alma never thought she would be so overjoyed to see Dr. Hammerschlag burst into the room.

Her labor was straightforward and the birth came fast, the baby crowning in a tidal wave of music surging through Alma's brain. A baby girl born at midday on Wednesday, June 15 — the middle of the week, the middle of the month, at the glorious peak of midsummer. A daughter with golden tufts of hair and wide-open blue eyes that seemed to delight in everything around her. Lost in that infant gaze, Alma fell irrevocably in love.

"Isn't she a joy?" she whispered to Gustav, who seemed equally smitten.

*A child formed out of my music, my deepest longing.* They named their new daughter Anna Justine, after Alma's mother and Gustav's sister. But they called her Gucki for her huge wondering eyes.

• • •

Instead of buying Alma flowers to celebrate the new birth, Gustav combed Vienna to purchase her favorite cheeses to satisfy her inexplicable postpartum cravings. Since the birth had been so uncomplicated, Alma hoped she would be back on her feet after a week, but she was struck with a severe case of mastitis that left her bedbound for nearly a month.

Leaving Alma in her mother's care, Gustav set off alone for Maiernigg.

"You know how much I hate to be parted from you, Almschi," he said. "But I can't spare a single day of my summer if I'm ever going to finish my symphony. It's simply a duty."

After Gustav departed, Alma kept her bedroom window wide open day and night, for Vienna lay in the grip of a heat wave, as though the entire city shared her fever.

When not holding the baby or trying to nurse her through the pain, when not trying to comfort Putzi, who was fractious and jealous of the baby and heartbroken that her papa wasn't there, Alma sought consolation in reading a volume of the letters Richard Wagner had exchanged with his lover and amanuensis, Mathilde Wesendonck. Like Alma, Wesendonck had spent countless hours copying successive drafts of her beloved's compositions — his operas *Das Rheingold* and *Die Walküre,* the first two acts of *Siegfried,* and most of *Tristan und Isolde.* But Wesendonck had also continued to write her own poetry, and Wagner, in turn, set five of her poems to music.

While Alma knew she couldn't compare Wesendonck and Wagner's adulterous liaison to her marriage with Gustav, reading their correspondence left her pensive. Why couldn't Gustav soften his stance and give her music even the slightest attention or encouragement? Instead, he rammed Kant down her throat, his favorite philosopher who believed in stark moral absolutes. How would Gustav react if he knew she was composing on the sly? It was almost as though she were having an illicit affair with her own creativity. And now that Gustav was away she would indulge in that affair.

Alma sent her baffled maid to fetch the book of Beethoven sonatas and bring it to her to read in bed. With a sluggish breeze drifting through the lace curtains, Alma looked over the score she had hidden there, composed in a rush during the onset of labor. Not allowed to leave her bed and sit at the piano, she hummed her work under her breath, letting Elise and Mama think that she was chanting a lullaby to the baby in her cradle. Alas, for all the pains she had taken, it sounded like a chaotic jumble of notes that not even Alex at the height of their mentor-student relationship would have taken seriously. Her old teacher Labor would have hurled it out the window.

*Why does it hurt so much to give up composing if I seem so bereft of true talent? Why can't I just put those old dreams aside and be content with what I have?*

Little Gucki woke up crying and Alma eased her from the cradle so she could nurse her at her swollen, fevered breasts. "What will it be like for you?" she asked her newborn, wondering if either of her girls would succeed in accomplishing anything in their own name.

Maybe Gustav would nurture his daughters' potential instead of smothering it, as he had done with hers.

# 26

||||||||||||||||||||||||

August of 1904 was the happiest in Alma's memory, her long-delayed summer idyll saturated in golden light from the moment she stepped off the train in Klagenfurt to be engulfed in her husband's arms. She was so thin from her convalescence that he could lift her off the ground.

"Almschi, you're here at last!" Gustav pressed a bouquet of wildflowers into her hands, then kissed her so passionately, right there on the railway platform, that he caused the upstanding Klagenfurters to tut in disapproval.

When Mama cleared her throat, Gustav finally turned to greet her, the nanny, and the children.

In deference to Alma's still-fragile state of health, Gustav had hired the carriage with the smoothest suspension he could find to convey them to their summerhouse. Cradling baby Gucki in her arms, Alma rode as if seated on a cloud while the Haflinger horses with white-gold manes trotted between the lake and forest. Gustav held Putzi in his lap while he told Alma and her mother of the progress he was making on his symphony.

"I've vowed to finish my Sixth by the end of September," he said merrily. "Or else I fear it shall finish me, ha!"

Alma, her mother, and Miss Turner all laughed, borne aloft on Gustav's high spirits.

When they reached the villa, a surprise awaited Putzi. Gustav had built an enclosed play area where she could dig in the sand to her heart's content with no danger of falling into the lake. Alma sat in the grass and nursed Gucki while watching Putzi and five-year-old Maria playing together. With jubilant cries, the two little girls tossed golden sand in the air.

The celebratory mood continued with the arrival of Ilse and Erica Conrat. As if to atone for leaving Alma behind in Vienna after the baby's birth, Gustav had encouraged her to invite friends to stay.

Those two young women were so stimulating, their companionship a balm to Alma, who still didn't feel strong enough to go rowing or hiking. Instead, the three of them sipped coffee on the stone terrace and discussed poetry, sculpture, and painting. Erica bubbled with enthusiasm about her studies at the university and all the clever people she had met there. With her inexhaustible good cheer, she never failed to draw Alma out of introspection when she felt herself slipping into melancholy after comparing her stasis to the Conrat sisters' progress. While Erica and Ilse took turns holding the baby, Alma prayed that some of their brilliance would rub off on her daughter.

"Imagine little Gucki growing up to be a sculptress like you," she told Ilse.

To celebrate Alma's twenty-fifth birthday, Gustav and the Conrat sisters rowed her across Lake Wörthersee to the genteel resort town of Krumpendorf. While Alma sat at the helm in her white dress with Ilse facing her, Erica and Gustav shared the rowing.

"This feels like a whole opera orchestra," Erica said gaily, as she struggled to keep pace with Gustav. "I tremble for fear of missing a beat."

When they moored the boat and went to take coffee and cake at one of the lakeside hotels, it was like running the gauntlet, with well-heeled tourists and local townsfolk alike rushing to gawp at the famous director and his entourage. Gustav scowled impatiently while Alma kept her eyes fixed straight ahead. Erica kept exclaiming at how wondrous it was, being the center of such attention.

On the journey back across the lake at sunset, Ilse shared the oars with Gustav while Alma chatted with Erica.

"Oh, Alma, how I wish I could paint you!" Erica said. "With the sun setting behind you, your hair's a halo of flame. You look like some beautiful beast of prey."

Alma caught Gustav's eyes and laughed.

Gustav smiled mischievously. "Almschi's my lioness."

That night they sat out on the candlelit terrace. Alma, her mother, and the Conrat sisters sipped Heidsieck champagne while Gustav read aloud from *West-östlicher Divan*, Goethe's lyrical poems inspired by the Persian mystic Hafez.

*Let me praise those living things that choose to die by fire.*

Despite the mildness of the evening, Alma found herself shivering and pulling her shawl around her shoulders.

*If you don't comprehend what it means to die into being,*
*you are but a dull guest on this dark earth.*

At the close of the poem, they all sat in contemplative silence until Gustav began to speak.

"Seen from the eyes of eternity," he said, "there's no difference between a firework that shoots into the air and then vanishes into the lake, and a sun that shines for a billion years. And yet it should be our aim to create works that outlive our short existence and endure for posterity."

"Like Ilse's sculptures," Alma said, feeling once more that awful pang of creative loss, her living death by fire. Her day-in, day-out sacrifice.

"Like your beautiful children, Alma," Ilse said, in a warm rush. "How can carved stone compare to Putzi's living flesh?"

"And Gustav's music," Erica said solemnly.

Gustav began to speak of the wonder he experienced each time he heard one of his compositions performed for the first time, so different from anything he had imagined in his head. At that, he went inside the house. Through the open French doors, they could hear him playing Bach, each note as pristine as the stars blazing in the heavens above. Alma lifted her gaze to those endless constellations. Across the lake, she saw a flaming Catherine wheel fall into the dark water and extinguish itself.

At summer's end, after the Conrat sisters had bidden their fond farewells, Gustav was almost dancing in his excitement to have finally finished his Sixth Symphony after two years of effort and so many creative blocks. His exhilaration proved contagious. Dashing ahead of him into the composing hut, Alma paged through the score. He had composed this work on an un-precedentedly grand scale, using instruments never before heard in a sym-phony—the celesta, cowbells, and even a whip and hammer.

"Wait till you hear it," he said, pulling her down beside him on the piano bench.

The first chords pounded out a grimly determined march, making Alma think of a doomed army heading toward annihilation, but this mood of im-pending destruction was broken by the soaring theme Gustav had composed for her, so tender and lush. A pastoral interlude filled her heart with its lyric beauty, evoking their rural setting with the distant jangle of cowbells. The irregular rhythms of the scherzo movement made her smile at the way they captured Putzi's and Maria's tottering, zigzag dances. But a sense of unease settled like ice in her chest as those childish voices became more and more tragic until they finally died out in a whimper.

*Don't take it to heart,* Alma told herself. *It's just dramatic structure.* A sym-phony without any shadows or tension would be mere kitsch, not compel-ling in the least. Gustav's modus operandi in his previous symphonies was to starkly portray passion, pathos, and darkness, and then transform this gloom into the blinding, light-filled epiphany of spiritual triumph, the victory of pure love. She kept waiting for that final passage into transcendence, her husband's signature of sublime transfiguration, but it never came. The mood only became more harrowing, downright nihilist in its pessimism. The fi-nal movement plunged her into a half-hour-long hallucinogenic nightmare, ending with three blows of the hammer and whip. Gustav struck those notes on the piano keys with such vehemence that Alma recoiled. She felt queasy.

When Gustav turned to her, awaiting her verdict, he looked strangely pale, as if his own music had drained him of his lifeblood.

"It was very powerful," she managed. "Different from all your other work."

Those were the most diplomatic words she could find. Despite the symphony's tender nods toward her and the children, its unbearable bleakness appalled her. It didn't help when Gustav went on to explain that the three blows at the end represented his hero being struck by fate, the final blow destroying him. A chill stole over her, as though her beloved husband had become a stranger.

"How can someone as warmhearted as you compose something so cruel?" Alma asked, shaken to her core.

"It's *music*, Almschi," Gustav said, with an offended air, scrutinizing her over the rims of his glasses. "If it sounds cruel to you, it's because I've thrown in all the viciousness I've suffered in my life. Now let me play you this." He reached for another score. "And please think about *art*, not about cruelty."

Alma knew he had just completed a song cycle he had started years earlier — musical settings of poems by Friedrich Rückert. But when she saw the title, her vision went black. *Kindertotenlieder*. Songs of Dead Children. She pressed her hands to her temples when Gustav began to play and sing. No higher understanding of music and art could shield her from the horror. Rückert, she understood, had written these poems after losing his two young children, those soul-splitting verses dictated by unfathomable grief and loss.

*I often think they've only gone out.*
*They'll be back soon.*
*The day is fine. Never fear!*
*They're only taking the long way back.*

Alma could take no more. In a flood of tears, she tore down the hill to find her own children, ignoring Gustav's exasperated protests that life is a separate thing from art.

• • •

By the time her husband caught up with her, Alma was sitting in the grass with Putzi in her lap and the baby in her arms.

"I could understand your setting such frightful words to music if we had no children," she said haltingly, staring into Gucki's bottomless blue gaze. "Or if we'd lost our children." Her voice broke. She attempted to calm herself so she didn't upset the baby. "I can certainly understand why a grieving man like Rückert *had* to write them. But for *you*, with two beautiful girls, to compose those songs bewailing children who died suddenly even though they appeared in the best of health. Hardly an hour after their parents last hugged and kissed them."

She could say no more, only wipe away her tears before they fell on Gucki's face.

"Inspiration is a mystery, Almschi," Gustav said softly, after a long silence. "I can't control what arises from the depths."

When Alma finally lifted her face to look at him, he appeared so youthful, so vulnerable, so loving. The doting father and husband. Another man entirely from the one who had composed such disturbing music.

"Just because I write about death doesn't mean that any of us will die," he said. "But if it makes you happier, I'll remove the hammer blows."

They returned to Vienna and life carried on, paved in good fortune. Gustav's glory seemed to only increase.

In October he was invited to Cologne to conduct the world premiere of his Fifth Symphony, that blissful ocean of lyricism borne of the first summer of their married love. Gustav was intent on Alma's joining him there for both the rehearsals and performance. With her entire heart, she yearned to do just that. This was the symphony she had most closely collaborated on—she almost felt like its cocreator. Hadn't she copied out the entire score, day by day, filling in the instrumentation and frankly telling Gustav what worked and what didn't?

So great was Alma's zeal to join Gustav in Cologne that she weaned baby Gucki too abruptly. Not only was her little daughter inconsolable, but Alma made herself ill. *Nature is not to be trifled with,* she was forced to concede, struck down once again by mastitis. Dr. Hammerschlag forbade her to travel. When she wrote to Gustav to tell him this unfortunate news, he was utterly distraught.

> *I beg you, Almschi, do all you can to recover. Perhaps you could be well in time for the concert. How awful it would be if I was left on my own for my world premiere. Something like being a guest at one's own funeral. What if the critics hate it?*

Lying in bed with her engorged, infected breasts poulticed with cabbage leaves, Alma felt as though she were in a coffin with the lid nailed down. Concerts in foreign cities seemed as distant and unreachable as the stars in heaven. She plunged into a black pit of despair, for it seemed she was useless as a wife and—judging from Gucki's ceaseless screams as Miss Turner attempted to bottle-feed her—an utter failure as a mother.

Gustav's letters lamented the negative reviews. Through her fever and nausea, Alma read the newspaper clippings he sent. The critics panned her husband's Fifth Symphony as coarse and clumsy. An arrogant improvisation from a composer who never knew what would happen from one bar to the next. *Poor Gustav! What philistines these German critics are!* Their condemnation of the symphony dearest to her heart left her feeling even weaker.

Meanwhile, Gustav rebuked her for being such a poor correspondent.

> *Even if you're too ill to write, you could at least send a postcard, Almschi!*

After the disappointing reception at Cologne, Gustav traveled on to conduct his Second and Fourth Symphonies at the Concertgebouw in Amsterdam, where he received a much warmer response.

By the time Gustav returned from his travels to direct his Third Symphony in the Golden Hall of the Musikverein, Alma was again obliged to stay home. Just when she had recovered her health, both children fell ill, Putzi with a bad cold and Gucki crying around the clock with colic, her shrieks enough to bring down the ceilings.

Alma's sole consolation was that her daughters' demands on her seemed to restore her lost strength. When she finally succeeded in lulling Gucki to sleep in her arms, a rare peace gripped her, a love that blurred all else. Suddenly, her life, which had lost its meaning, appeared to have a clear purpose once more. Her children needed her. *This is why I'm alive—to be a mother to them.* And Gustav? He needed her, too. But he could be so remote, so self-obsessed.

In January, with her children back in good health, Alma could finally attend concerts again. She invited Alex and Arnold and Mathilde Schoenberg to join her in the director's box when Gustav conducted the world premiere of Alex's *Die Seejungfrau* and Schoenberg's *Pelléas and Mélisande*.

Seated at her right hand, Alex seemed beside himself, his lips parted, his breath catching, his eyes soft and adoring. She wondered if she had ever seen him so enraptured. Clearly, he was in love, hopelessly smitten—with Gustav this time around. Alex hardly seemed to take his eyes off her husband the entire evening. So deep was his reverence for Gustav, he didn't presume to speak to him directly but could only blurt out his praise and gratitude to her, Gustav's official intercessor.

"Oh, Alma!" Alex said, taking her hand, his old sarcasm completely blown away. "Please convey my deepest gratitude. To have *him* conduct my work! I feel touched and blessed by his greatness."

That same month also saw the premiere of Gustav's *Kindertotenlieder*. While listening to the performance, Alma attempted to concentrate on the technical details of the production, her ears honed for any missed notes. Anything but think of their daughters when listening to her husband conduct his Songs of Dead Children. She was determined not to let the overwhelming tragedy and grief invade her heart. But she couldn't avoid observing how deeply the audience was effected. Women sobbed into their handker-chiefs — how many babies had they lost? Who but her husband would dare set these songs to music, to allow Mildenburg's shattering soprano to give voice to the unspeakable? The applause was staggering. Alma clapped and cheered with everyone else, but her heart seized in a foreboding that she couldn't shake off. Watching her husband take bow after bow, she couldn't help clenching her teeth. *Gustav, how could you?*

Suite 3

# I AM LOST
# TO THE WORLD

# 27

|||||||||||||||||||||||||

A lma stood on the terrace of their summerhouse at Maiernigg and gazed at the first stars winking from the clear June sky. Having just put her children to bed, she felt restless with the yearning for spiritual freedom. *To be a somebody, not just somebody's wife.*

Here she was, alone with her daughters, left to her own devices while Gustav remained in Vienna to conduct a concert in honor of the shah of Persia's state visit. Yet even in this precious lacuna of solitude, she saw only her husband when she looked out over the lake with its darkling waves. She heard only his voice. His music. How had he come to dominate her entire existence, even in his absence, when he hadn't written in days? *I live only for him.* It was as though she wasn't even a person anymore.

There was so much about him she still didn't understand. Yet she could no longer envision her life without him. He had taken so much away from her that he alone remained her support—the monolith around which her life revolved. So what could she do but devote herself wholly to him? To being a good wife. Virtuous, useful, calm, self-sufficient during his long absences. But that strident voice inside her gave her no peace. *I'm only twenty-five and my life is so dull!* She loved her husband, loved her children. Yet there had to be something more, some spark. Closing her eyes, she allowed her mind to rove off into terra incognita. Into a place where Gustav was not. Where she could unfold, terrifying herself with her own waywardness. Lilith with her talons and wings.

Alma tore into the music room and reached into the forbidden folder of her scores. Sitting at the piano, she began to soft pedal her music, mindful of her daughters sleeping in the next room. *To write a new piece! A nocturne! A sarabande!* But now that she had this solitude and peace to do something for herself rather than for her family, she only drew a blank. Her inner well had been left dry for so long that it refused to yield anything but a puff of dust.

In despair, Alma turned to her diary. Maybe if she found the right words, a new melody might arise in their wake. *If only I were still capable as I once was of putting thoughts to paper.* Would her inner turmoil finally ease if she could give voice to it? Gripping her pencil, she bent over her journal. But no intelligible words emerged. She felt as empty as that page.

Lest this evening be entirely wasted, Alma set to work transcribing a fair copy of Gustav's Sixth Symphony. His bottomless creativity was as vast as an ocean. She was the jetsam bobbing on the waves. She seated herself at the secretary desk, lit the paraffin lamp, then reached to get some fresh paper from the bottom drawer. Unfortunately, the old wooden drawer was warped from the lakeside humidity, so she had to give it a forceful tug to pull it open. This upset the lamp, which toppled to the floor.

With a shriek, Alma leapt back to see the lamp shatter, setting the rug and then the sofa ablaze.

Yelling for Elise and Miss Turner to come down and help, Alma frantically attempted to smother the flames with cushions and blankets. *Dear God, what if I'm to blame for burning my babies alive?* It was as though her buried rage had set the house on fire. She was tempted to fling her own body down into the fire as a living sacrifice if that's what it took to extinguish it —far preferable to living with the guilt of killing her children. *Let me praise those living things that choose to die by fire.* Unbidden, she recalled the verses from Goethe's *West-östlicher Divan* that Gustav had read last summer.

By the time Elise and Miss Turner came dashing to the scene, Alma had managed to put out the flames. Leaving them to sweep up the broken lamp, Alma raced in to her children. After opening the windows to let in the fresh air and release the smoke, she swooped over Gucki's cradle. By some miracle, the baby had managed to sleep through the entire fiasco. But Putzi tumbled out of bed and ran to Alma, lifting her frightened, tear-stained face.

"Mama, it smells bad. Where's Papa? I want my papa!" Putzi's voice broke off into a frightened wail.

"Hush, my darling." Alma seized the girl and hugged her closely, burying her face in her sweet brown curls. "Papa will join us very soon."

Gustav was ablaze with inspiration, immured in his composing hut from early morning to dusk with only a short midday break. One July evening, Alma met her husband wandering down the forest path. He didn't seem to even recognize her—his face was transfixed with visions of that glorious otherworld he lived inside when he was writing a new symphony. But when his eyes finally focused on her, he bounded toward her with all the glee of an infatuated twenty-year-old coming to kiss his sweetheart.

"Almschi!" he cried. "Surely this is our best summer yet! To think I've been here only *four weeks* and I've already finished *three* movements of my new symphony."

"Your Seventh," she said, in hushed reverence.

Alma had heard strains of the music floating down from the woods. *This symphony is fortunate and blessed,* she thought. Boldly modern, yet full of optimism as well as depth and mystery. Not seething with nihilism like the Sixth.

"Gustav, you're unstoppable," she murmured, her voice catching as adoration and envy twined in her throat, wrapping around each other like twin serpents. What a mirror his freely flowing inspiration raised to her stymied compositions, her well of loss.

That night Alma crept upstairs to Gustav's room. The night was so hot and humid, she could almost imagine they were in the tropics.

"My tigress," he said, as she pounced on his bed.

In one rippling rush, her silk dressing gown fell to the floor, leaving her completely nude. In the heat, Gustav was likewise naked, not even a sheet draping his lean, muscled body. Sweat dampened her thighs as she straddled him, her hair whipping over his chest, his hands holding her breasts. Despite the stickiness and torpor and the mosquitoes whining in her ear, she longed for him. Longed to feel truly one with him, his essence plunging into hers, making her complete. Holy and pure. Eve, not Lilith with her burning resentment.

But Gustav could not rise to the occasion. He laughed remorsefully while cradling her face to his pounding heart. "Forgive me, Almscherl. It's just the heat and my sluggish digestion."

Alma sat with her children on the shady lawn. While Gucki slept on a blanket and Putzi colored pictures, Alma opened her journal. Her sweat-soaked dress sagged against her skin as she forced the pencil across the page. Pencil, not ink, so as to better erase her forbidden words. *I long for a husband. For I have none.* Owing to Gustav's loss of libido, they had not made love the entire summer. It was as though Gustav was channeling his entire virility into his music, leaving nothing for her. How long could this go on?

Putting her journal aside, Alma helped Putzi with her drawing. How clever her eldest daughter was with her crayons, and she wasn't even three. Already she was trying to draw their house. So Alma helped her fill in the details. Their happy, fortunate home.

# 28

||||||||||||||||||||||||||

"P utzi's drawing is simply incredible," Gustav said the following March, while Alma packed his suitcase for his trip to Amsterdam.

She made sure to include family photographs and Putzi's artwork, for Gustav had declared he couldn't bear to travel without these mementoes. Putzi, meanwhile, hugged her father's legs as though she would never let him go.

"My little treasure, what an eye you have!" Lifting the girl in his arms, Gustav addressed her with possessive pride, as if he took it for granted that his eldest daughter was heir to his genius.

Putzi's latest picture, which she had accomplished without assistance, was a clearly recognizable portrait of her father at the piano. At the age of three and a half, Putzi seemed to have an understanding of lines, patterns, and representation. Alma had helped her write the word *PAPA* in proud capitals above the image.

The little girl was precocious and self-possessed enough to insist that she accompany her mother to the Hauptbahnhof to see off her father. Putzi was such a handful that Alma was obliged to leave Gucki home with the maid. Gucki, a fussy feeder, was far quieter than her exuberant sister, but her huge blue eyes seemed to take in everything as though she were born to be a silent witness to this turbulent world.

"I'll write every day," Gustav told Alma from the open doorway of the railway car. "*You* write, too, Almschi! No shirking this time."

His last departing kiss was offered not to Alma but Putzi, who clung to his neck with such ferocity that Alma struggled to peel her off him.

Gustav laughed. "Be sure to draw many new pictures for me, my darling girl."

Was it normal to feel this jealous of one's own daughter, Alma wondered, as the train drew out of the station. Surely she should be happy that her husband was such a devoted father. How she had adored her own papa when he was alive! *To the point of rejecting Mama, of thinking her second-rate, a poor substitute.* For the first time in her life, Alma felt ashamed of the way she had treated her mother—now she understood how much it hurt. Her spirits sank as she struggled to console Putzi, who was lost in the depths of a tantrum. When Putzi was like this, no one but Gustav could comfort her.

Gustav's letters home were filled with cheerful allusions to his sensitive bowels.

> *This morning I managed to make a sacrifice to the gods without the aid of aeronautic instruments.*

The Dutch adored him and made much of him, lauding him as the greatest luminary to set foot inside the Concertgebouw in Amsterdam, its astonishing acoustics the perfect showcase for the lush swell of his symphonies.

The Germans proved a much more difficult audience. Their critics seemed to delight in tearing Gustav down, not least because he was a Jew. He was so nervous about the premiere of his Sixth Symphony in Essen, he began to suffer panic attacks and insisted that Alma accompany him to the rehearsals and performance. He made constant alterations to the score, reversing the second and third movements at the last minute.

On the night of the premiere, Alma sat in the guest balcony, her mouth as dry as sand. How slight and vulnerable Gustav appeared on the podium, a wiry bundle of nerves. Gone was his absolute control and assurance that had so dazzled her when she was a starstruck girl of nineteen watching him at the opera. But directing one's own new symphony before a hostile foreign audience was a universe away from conducting someone else's work. Gustav's entire soul was laid bare.

Already thin, he had lost even more weight. How this taxed him—he looked as though he might collapse before his audience of potato-eating industrialists. Alma narrowed her eyes at a woman in a diamond *collier* who yawned extravagantly while her husband snored beside her. When the final movement ended and Gustav turned to take his bows, Alma endeavored to clap loudly enough to drown out the catcalls. Her husband seemed to sway on his feet. His face was etched in deep lines, making him look like an old man. Tears gathered in the corners of her eyes to see him like this. She struggled to push away the foreboding that Gustav had already reached his zenith. That the premiere of this malevolent symphony marked the onset of her family's decline.

Back in the privacy of their hotel room, Alma was struggling to calm Gustav when she noticed an envelope from Alex on the mail tray, addressed to them both. Thinking to distract her husband from his misery, she tore the letter open and found a clipping from *Die Musik*—an article on the American premiere of Gustav's Fifth Symphony in Boston.

"Gustav!" she cried. "Listen to what the *American* critics have to say! 'How everything sings and glows and blooms, as if Schubert had been reborn.' Remember how the Germans scorned your Fifth? The Americans *love* it! Just imagine! Your fame has crossed the ocean."

After the debacle in Essen, their summer exodus to Maiernigg couldn't come quickly enough. Dizzy spells and digestive complaints plagued Gustav, and it was not just his cold reception in Germany that gnawed at him. His critics in Vienna were turning on him, too. The Viennese papers satirized Herr Direktor Mahler as a difficult personality, neurotically obsessed with opera reform and yet even more interested in composing symphonies that nobody wanted to hear.

When Alma and Gustav arrived at their summerhouse, he looked defeated, worn down to bone and sinew. She felt tempted to sweep him into her arms and carry him up the stairs as though he were one of her children. *If I don't look after him, he could quite literally work himself to death.*

Alma found herself fussing over him like a nursemaid. "You need at least two weeks of rest to restore your vitality. No work, Gustl. Just gentle exercise and time with the children. Sit in the sunshine every day."

Her preaching fell upon deaf ears.

Early that next morning, Gustav tore up the path to his composing hut. When he failed to come down for the midday meal, Alma and Elise tiptoed to his hut and left a basket of bread, cheese, butter, jam, fruit, and milk outside his door.

"If he gets any thinner, he'll blow away," Elise whispered, shaking her head.

If Gustav heard their footsteps, they didn't seem to penetrate his creative trance. Alma heard him playing the piano and chanting medieval plainsong.

When he finally stumbled down to join Alma and the children at the dinner table, his hair was sticking out at all angles and his glasses were askew. Fire shone in his eyes. His smile was brighter than a thousand suns.

"I thought you were going to take a few days of *leisure*," Alma said. "Recuperation."

"Almschi, how can I idle away my precious summer like a lazy tourist when the *creator spiritus* itself has laid hold of me? It won't let me go until I've done its bidding."

Putzi burst out of her chair in her joy to see him. She began to prattle on about the new picture Alma had helped her paint that day, but Gustav silenced her with a single reproving glance. Though he insisted the children eat at the table with them, he required that they remain silent in order to allow their parents to converse properly. Two-year-old Gucki simply stared at her father from her high chair, not making a noise, hardly eating either. Alma bent over her in an anxious attempt to coax down another spoonful of semolina.

"Almschi, this will be my most monumental work to date," Gustav said, gesticulating wildly, the candlelight bouncing off his glasses. "Everything

I've done up until now is just a prelude to *this*. Imagine a chorale, but there are no longer human voices, just the sound of the revolving planets and stars. Imagine the universe itself beginning to resound!"

His happiness proved infectious, drawing Putzi out of her sulk. Even Gucki grinned, showing off her milk teeth, and, to Alma's relief, began to eat with a bit more enthusiasm. How rejuvenated Gustav seemed as the sun set in splendor over the placid lake.

While Alma played with the children and supervised Putzi's artwork, Gustav composed like a holy man possessed by a divine vision. His music came drifting down the hill, more glorious by the day, as though it were his soul's anthem taking flight on soft white wings. *Veni Creator Spiritus.* His voice and piano chords wrapped around her and the children like a golden wreath, encircling them in benediction.

Gustav completed his Eighth Symphony in eight weeks. Never before had he been able to compose an entire symphony during a single summer. This was a chorale work on the grandest scale, utterly unconventional in form. The Eighth was divided into two parts. The first was a setting of the ninth-century Pentecost hymn "Veni Creator Spiritus"; the second a cantata drawn from the Chorus Mysticus in the final scene of Goethe's *Faust, Part Two.*

Hearing Gustav sing and play this for her left Alma breathless with joy. *Faust,* her beloved *Faust,* which Papa had given her to read as a child! Her husband's new symphony was a work of colossal majesty.

"Alfred Roller once suggested I write a Mass." Gustav lifted his hands from the piano keys to take hers. "I said, 'No, there's the Nicene Creed.' I just couldn't do it," he told her, her Jewish husband who had ostensibly converted to Catholicism but who rejected its dogma to embrace his own ecstatic mysticism. "But *this,* Almschi, is my Credo."

The two parts of his Eighth were united by the theme of redemption through love—transcendent spiritual love wedded to the embodied eros and ecstasy of the Eternal Feminine.

221

"The Eternal Feminine *carries* us," he said, cupping her face in his hands. "We have arrived. We are at rest. At last we possess that which we could only strive for. Christians speak of heaven's eternal bliss. But *this* bliss is unfolding right here on earth."

He stared at her ardently, as if she were the goddess he had spent a lifetime seeking only to find her right in front of him. His wife and the mother of his children. His adoration washed through her like blessed, blessed rain after a long drought.

Alma twined her arms around him and pulled him to the floor, where they embraced amid the scattered pages of sheet music. For days afterward, she felt as though she were walking on air. As though her skin were covered in gold.

# 29

||||||||||||||||||||||||||

Too soon they were back in Vienna, Gustav once more embroiled in the Court Opera's increasingly contentious web of intrigues. Despite Alma's every admonition to her husband about not overtaxing himself, he shrugged off her concerns.

"Illness isn't the result of overwork," he informed her. "But of a lack of talent!"

Alma could only bear witness to his endless battles with his own limitations. He punished his body mercilessly, rising early then staying up late to direct performance after performance. He would simply not allow his flesh to falter in its service to the creative spirit. However, one morning Alma came by his office and found him asleep at his desk, his head pillowed on a stack of paperwork.

When Gustav wasn't up to his neck at the opera, he was off on tour, directing his own music in Berlin, Munich, Breslau, and Brno. How much longer could his body cope with the strain? Though her husband swore that he hated traveling, he was compelled to tour these far-flung foreign cities to find an audience for his symphonies. The Viennese had precious little forbearance for his ambitions as a composer. But his frequent tours brought him into even deeper conflict with his employer. Prince Montenuovo, who bore ultimate administrative responsibility for the Court Opera, reprimanded Gustav for his absences and accused him of neglecting his duties.

Alma took Mama to the Viennese premiere of Gustav's Sixth Symphony in the Golden Hall of the Musikverein. It was not the Vienna Philharmonic or the Court Opera Orchestra playing his work tonight—Gustav claimed that neither of these orchestras wanted much to do with him lately—but the much less prestigious Konzertverein Orchestra. That this concert was a *local* rather than a world premiere spoke for itself. Gustav knew very well what kind of reception he could expect from the Viennese.

Still, this audience was meant to be friendly. Alma allowed herself a glimmer of hope as she picked out their well-wishers in the crowd. Arnold and Mathilde Schoenberg. Berta Zuckerkandl. The Conrat sisters and their parents. She tried not to stare too long at Alex and his new fiancée—the younger sister of his former love, Melanie Guttmann, who had immigrated to America. Their wedding date was set for June 21, Midsummer Day. *If you had the foresight to wait for him, to trust in his love, he would be marrying* you. What music might she have composed in these past five years if she had refused Gustav's proposal and remained Alex's beloved, his protégée? Alma fought to push away these thoughts, to unclench the tight muscles in her stomach and diaphragm. *Be happy with what you have.*

Just as Gustav lifted his baton to begin the performance, a tumult blared from the uppermost balcony. Alma wrenched her head to see a row of pranksters blowing children's toy trumpets in mockery of her poor husband. A ripple of uneasy laughter spread through the audience. Gustav regarded his hecklers with a thin, icy smile. Then his wiry frame seemed to seize up and freeze. He clutched at his chest, as though struggling to draw breath.

"Oh, God!" Alma seized her mother's hand.

Blessedly, the moment passed. With stoic dignity worthy of an emperor, Gustav turned to his orchestra and the concert went on as though nothing had happened. But before her pulse could return to normal, Alma felt her mother's hand go clammy in hers. Mama's face had gone gray. Her lips were quivering and white.

"Mama, what is it?"

Alma helplessly watched her mother blink and swallow several times before she managed to reply. "Sometimes my chest goes tight and I see black stars."

. . .

Gustav was away again, directing his Third Symphony in Berlin, when Alma took her mother to see Dr. Kovacs, the renowned heart specialist.

"What can a doctor do for me?" Mama fretted, while Alma guided her through the labyrinth of Vienna General Hospital. "Stick me full of needles and tell me I'm too fat, I reckon. Prescribe cold baths and calisthenics."

Alma felt as though she were dragging her reluctant mother down those stark, sterile corridors that reeked of ammonia and carbolic soap. She feared that if she loosened her grip on Mama's arm she would turn tail and flee.

"All he's going to do is examine you. You owe it to little Maria to get this seen to." Alma tried to keep her voice light and breezy to mask her deeper worries.

Once they reached the waiting room, they sat together on a hard wooden bench that reminded Alma of a particularly uncomfortable church pew. In search of diversion, she handed Mama one of the newspapers hanging on a wooden holder. But when her mother opened the pages of *Die Zeit*, she cursed.

Without another word, Mama showed Alma a satirical illustration entitled *A Month with the Director of the Vienna Court Opera*. The image was divided into four cartoons, each of Gustav coming up with an ingenuous new way to shirk his responsibilities at the opera. In the first he was rehearsing his new symphony with an unknown provincial orchestra. In the second he was hunting down a mythical instrument with hitherto unrealized sonorities. In the third he was reading proofs of his new magnum opus. In the fourth he needed time off to recover from his vacation.

With a sigh of disgust, Alma hung *Die Zeit* back up on the rail and pulled down two more papers, one for Mama and one for her, only to discover more scathing commentary on her husband.

With rabbitlike fecundity, Mahler spawns another larger-than-life symphony each year. His Sixth, performed at the Musikverein on January 4, is marked by the most hopeless lack of ideas. Brass! Plenty of brass! An unprecedented amount of brass! Even

225

more brass! Nothing but brass! And that was just the opening movement.

But this was mild compared to the next article that leapt out to grab Alma by the throat.

Not only has Direktor Mahler reaped universal scorn for his dictatorial management of his singers and musicians, treating them the way a lion tamer handles his beasts, but he is also to blame for the deplorable Judaization of our beloved Court Opera.

As if to drive the point home, there followed a vicious caricature of Gustav as a scarecrow looming before the opera house. *Mahler the Jew is driving away our best singers.*

Alma was so stung, she nearly dropped the paper. She knew that the anti-Semitic press had long opposed Gustav's appointment as opera director. But why turn on him with such venom now, a decade after Emperor Franz Joseph had raised him to that lofty post?

Oh, the hypocrisy of the Viennese, with their casual, homespun anti-Semitism that was almost gemütlich in its willingness to make exceptions for a visionary like Gustav Mahler. Hadn't the mayor, Karl Lueger, declared, "*I* decide who's a Jew." Even Mama and Carl, who had absolutely opposed Alma courting Alex because he was a Jew, had warmly embraced Gustav. But it seemed Gustav's personality clashes at the opera and his too-frequent absences had created such a backlash of resentment that he could no longer hide behind the veneer of his Christian conversion. And thus the Viennese press had decided that he was indeed a Jew. One whom they accused of abusing his position of opera director to advance himself, ignoring his duties in order to direct his own symphonies across Europe, as though he were some greedy, itinerant Jewish peddler.

Mama wrested the papers from Alma's hands. "They're vultures, these journalists. Small-minded and ignorant. Pay them no mind."

Alma brushed away her tears. "But why do they *hate* him so?"

For this was nothing less than a hate campaign aimed at her husband. If she read any more of this filth, she thought *she* would have a heart attack.

Mama rested a consoling hand on her shoulder. "Why do they hate Klimt so? They despise anyone who tries to be true to himself. That's what they can't bear. That someone should try to be free."

A young assistant, pale and serious in his starched white uniform, appeared before them. "Frau Moll, Herr Doktor Kovacs is ready to see you."

Mama insisted that Alma accompany her into the examining room. So Alma looked on while the doctor performed his roster of diagnostic rituals on her mother, who appeared indignant at having to sit before a strange man in her underwear.

"Frau Moll," he said. "I'm pleased to say that nothing is fundamentally wrong with your internal organs. But you *must* take this matter seriously or you could well develop a heart condition. You're too adipose and *must* lose at least fifteen kilos." Speaking sternly, as though scolding a child, he then proceeded to lecture Mama about the importance of exercise and a healthy diet. "Walk at least an hour a day, preferably up and down hills, and do deep-knee bends first thing each morning in front of an open window."

Mama narrowed her eyes at Alma, as if to say, *I told you so.*

After seeing Mama home, Alma returned to her apartment to find Miss Turner awaiting her with the latest *Abendzeitung* in hand. "Frau Direktor, I thought you should see this."

Taking the newspaper, Alma blinked at the bold black typeface. *Herr Direktor Mahler to Resign from Vienna Court Opera.*

"So now they're stooping to libel!" Alma ripped the paper in half, hating herself for weeping in front of the nanny.

"Yes, I know what those jackals are writing about me," Gustav said, when he returned from Berlin.

When Alma showed him the latest hatchet piece, he merely glanced over it carelessly, as though it were written about someone else.

Mahler the symphonist has become the enemy of the Court Opera, which he has destroyed.

The article went on to claim that the opera had lost 200,000 crowns due to his mismanagement.

"Lies. All of it." Gustav tossed the paper in his wastebasket. "Likely another one of their bookkeeping errors. They're baying for blood because I'm a Jew. It was all right when the opera was turning a profit, but now that they claim to be losing money they want to pin the blame on me."

*How could he sound so resigned?* Alma thought. *Where is his will to fight?* She clenched her fists while he went back to sorting through the mail that had arrived while he was away. Another letter from the Metropolitan Opera in New York. Heinrich Conried, the general manager, was trying to convince Gustav to become their new principal conductor. Alma's throat closed around the presentiment that their days in Vienna were numbered. Her heart sank to imagine her family driven into exile because of a smear campaign.

"Gustav, you need to *do* something," she said. "Answer your critics!"

He regarded her over the rims of his glasses. "Montenuovo has forbidden me to respond with words. He says I may offer my rebuttal only in deeds. So I'm directing *Die Walküre* this spring. They've loved all my Wagner productions. I hope that this will shut them up. Almschi, don't look so tragic. I'm a public figure. When my suit gets splashed with manure, I brush it off."

She shook her head at him speechlessly. How much longer could he pretend that this was something he could just shrug away?

Leaving her husband to his correspondence, she wandered disconsolately to the nursery, where Miss Turner was reading an English book of Mother Goose rhymes to Putzi and Gucki. Gustav had told her that they all should start learning English. Just in case.

"The north wind doth blow and we shall have snow," Miss Turner read, crisply enunciating each syllable. Seated on either side of her, Putzi and Gucki leaned in to peer over the picture book's bright pages. "And what will the robin do then? Poor thing."

Alma leaned against the doorjamb and shivered.

Even Gustav's new production of *Die Walküre* failed to appease his enemies. "An orgy of darkness," the critics sneered. They denounced it as too modern and even faulted petty details, such as Siegfried's brown wig not making the hero appear suitably Germanic.

Still, Gustav soldiered on, as though grimly determined to show only defiance in the face of his foes. Without asking leave from the opera, he traveled to Rome to direct three concerts. This time Alma accompanied him, eager to escape the toxic hothouse that Vienna had become.

Their journey was beset with ill luck. The train engine broke down three times on the way, causing them to miss their connection. They lost their luggage, even the scores for the pieces Gustav would be conducting. He was obliged to hire a tuxedo for his performances, but they couldn't find one his size. He looked like a boy in his father's clothes, his ensemble held together with safety pins Alma had begged off hotel reception. The whole fiasco might have been comical had Gustav not been so tense and bad tempered, as though bracing himself for the inevitable backlash from the press awaiting them at home.

When they arrived back in Vienna, the headlines assaulted them. The papers demanded her husband's immediate resignation.

Staggering up four flights of stairs with what remained of their luggage, Alma felt queasy and unwell. She might have worried that she was pregnant again except months had passed since they had last shared intimacies. With all the troubles grinding Gustav down, lovemaking seemed the very last thing on his mind.

Before they could reach their apartment door, it sprang open. Out scampered Putzi. "Welcome home, Mama and Papa," their four-year-old said in English, grinning at her own cleverness.

Alma was struck by how beautiful their daughter was with her big blue eyes, lustrous dark hair, and plump healthy cheeks. What a striking woman she would one day be, a genius like her father. How Putzi glowed to see him again, her towering idol.

"What a brilliant girl you are!" Gustav's face brightened for the first time in days as he knelt to embrace her. "Do you want to help your papa open his letters?"

Putzi nodded worshipfully.

"Mind she doesn't cut herself with the letter opener," Alma called out after them, as father and daughter marched off hand in hand to his study, leaving her on the landing with all the luggage.

Miss Turner then appeared, carrying Gucki on her hip. Before Alma could reach to take her youngest in her arms, the nanny stepped back. "I'm so, so sorry."

Gravely, Miss Turner showed Alma Gucki's left hand. Three of the tiny fingers were scalded. "She knocked over my teakettle. It's my fault. I should have taken better care." The nanny's voice was tremulous, as though she feared Alma might fire her on the spot.

Alma cupped her daughter's round little face. More than burned fingers troubled the child. Her skin felt hot and clammy, as though she was running a temperature. Not wasting a second, Alma telephoned the doctor.

"Scarlet fever," Dr. Hammerschlag pronounced, lifting his stethoscope from Gucki's tiny rib cage, now mottled with a bumpy red rash. He opened the child's mouth to reveal the ulcers in her throat and her swollen red tongue. "A particularly virulent strain, I fear. You must send your other daughter away or she'll catch it, too."

*My sweet, precious Gucki.* Her daughter's wide blue eyes were fixed on the ceiling, as though seeing pictures invisible to everyone else. Alma gently turned the child's face to look at her instead. "It's all right, my darling. We'll look after you until you're better. You must be a brave girl for us. When you're well, we'll go to Maiernigg and play in the meadows. We'll swim in the lake—"

"What about Putzi?" Gustav asked, cutting her off. His face was creased, as if he could not comprehend how this horror could visit them on top of all their other woes.

"We'll send her to stay with Mama and Carl," Alma said, swallowing back her anger that her husband seemed more concerned about their healthy daughter than the one who was deathly ill. *My God, what if we lose Gucki?* The girl wasn't even three years old. If the scarlet fever didn't kill her, it could leave her blind or deaf or both.

"I'll take Putzi away at once." Gustav rushed out of the room.

"Your husband is right to be so worried," Dr. Hammerschlag said. "I've seen families with ten children wiped out in a week from the disease."

Because the risk of contagion was so great, Gustav elected to stay at the Hotel Imperial while Alma and Miss Turner cared for Gucki. Acting on the doctor's orders, Alma reluctantly shaved off her daughter's beautiful golden hair.

"It will fall out anyway," Miss Turner said bleakly. "That's what the disease does."

Already a fussy feeder, Gucki struggled to swallow with her ulcerated throat. They could only try to tempt her with smooth, soothing applesauce, buttermilk, barley water, and chicken broth. Morning and night, Alma treated the throat ulcers with a solution of nitrate of silver applied with a camel-hair paintbrush while Miss Turner held Gucki's mouth open and pleaded with her not to gag. Alma sponged her daughter's sore, infected skin and warmed her feet with a hot-water bottle. When the rash finally subsided, the child's skin came off in scales. Even the skin on her tongue peeled off. Alma gave Gucki baths in Epsom salts and massaged her with cooling aloe. The disease was so infectious that all of Gucki's clothing, toys, and bedding would have to be burned.

"When you're well again, we'll buy you new clothes and toys. You'll be better in time for your birthday." Alma tried to speak with conviction, as though her words were a magical incantation that could save her little girl from the brink of death.

Prisoner of the sickroom, Alma was plunged into such loneliness, she could find consolation only in her journal. The thought that she would have to burn these pages as well emboldened her to write the most soul-shaking confessions.

> *Five years of marriage and I am no longer a person. I have lived my husband's life. I've canceled my will and being. Like a tightrope walker, I'm only concerned with keeping my balance. But the scarlet fever has rendered my great sacrifice meaningless. I gave up my music. I put myself aside for husband and family in vain, for I could lose them all overnight.*

What grieved Alma most was how Gustav never seemed to acknowledge the surrender of her existence. What it had cost her. He was too utterly engrossed in *his* work, *his* self-denial, *his* struggle with the opera. In spite of her bearing him two children, he still seemed to regard her as a child. She copied his music for him and even in his absence studied the books he recommended to earn his approval. He praised her for reading Shakespeare in translation but most vehemently disapproved of her reading *A Doll's House* by Ibsen.

Stationed at Gucki's bedside, Alma indulged her rebellious streak, devouring Ibsen's drama about the housewife Nora, as stifled as a mummy in the morass of her bourgeois existence. Patronized, infantilized. Nora, who at the end of the play abandons all security and even her children in the name of freedom.

*My husband's genius has consumed me.* But what if his brilliance was no longer enough to sustain them? What would happen to her family now that Gustav's career seemed teetering on the edge of disaster? Thanks to her tight budgeting, they were finally clear of debt, but they had little in the way of savings. How could Gustav support them on composing alone? Meanwhile, the smear campaign against her husband had reached the point of no return. The most Gustav could do was attempt to negotiate a graceful resignation, one that allowed him to keep his pension and what remained of his dignity intact.

"It's not so simple, Almschi," Gustav told her, his voice rendered strange through the crackling telephone wires. "I can't just step down. I was appointed by imperial decree. Only the emperor can dissolve my contract."

Alma wished she could be holding him instead of the cold, unyielding telephone receiver. To think that during the worst crisis they had weathered thus far she and her husband were reduced to communicating through this contraption.

"But don't give up hope," he said. "There are other possibilities."

Alma understood that he was speaking elliptically for fear that the operator might be listening in, eager to sell any tidbit of gossip to the papers.

"A possibility that allows us to stay in Vienna?" she asked him.

She knew that Gustav's friends in the Vienna Conservatory were angling to offer him the post of director — a most respectable appointment, but one that paid far less than the Vienna Court Opera. Still, it was something. She wished Gustav could just be blunt and spill it out.

"A very solid opportunity," he said.

*That means an offer in writing,* she thought, hope sparking inside her.

"We need never worry about money again," he added.

She closed her eyes and felt a wash of light-headedness sweep over her. *He means New York.* Only the Americans could afford to offer more than the Vienna Court Opera. So that was it. Gucki was seriously ill with scarlet fever, her family torn apart by the forced quarantine. And an anti-Semitic hate campaign was driving them into foreign exile. It had all happened so fast, a vicious downward spiral.

"Be happy," Gustav said, speaking into her silence. "This is good news. Our salvation, Almschi."

She tried to find the words to congratulate him. But despite the evils spewed in the papers, she loved Vienna. Cycling in the Prater. Concerts in the Musikverein. New art at the Secession Museum. Berta Zuckerkandl's salon. The very words *New York* were as daunting as they were glamorous. Could she really start a whole new existence across the ocean in a foreign metropolis, a world away from everything she knew?

In early June, while Gucki was still convalescing, Alma sat at her daughter's bedside and read Gustav's long interview in the *Neues Wiener Tagblatt*. This was one of the few papers that had remained friendly to him. Berta Zuckerkandl's father had founded the paper and Berta was one of the contributing journalists.

*I have not been overthrown,* Gustav announced to Vienna and the world. *I am leaving the Vienna Court Opera of my own accord because I have grown weary of all the lies printed about me in the press.* He made no mention of the post offered to him in New York. Alma understood that this was deliberate —he was still negotiating his salary and terms with the New York Metropolitan Opera.

Alma wished they could talk again on the telephone, but Gustav had left on a hiking expedition in the Alps near Semmering, where he intended to meet up with Anna von Mildenburg and her milquetoast fiancé. Alma had to remain here in the sweltering city until Gucki was well again. Reading about her husband in the newspaper, as though he were a stranger.

# 30

||||||||||||||||||||||||

**O**nly at the end of June did Dr. Hammerschlag declare that Gucki had recovered and that the risk of contagion had passed. Alma wept in relief. Sweet Gucki had survived this living nightmare with her eyesight and hearing undamaged. The child was thin and pale, to be sure, but delicate golden curls sprouted from her shorn head. Her eyes began to gleam in curiosity once more.

"Yes, take her to Maiernigg, by all means," Dr. Hammerschlag said. "The forest air will put the roses back in her cheeks. Make sure she drinks a lot of fresh milk. You're looking rather peaked, too, Frau Direktor. Some sunshine would do you both a world of good."

With the doctor's blessing, Alma packed their trunks. She, Gucki, and Miss Turner boarded the train to Maiernigg, where Gustav would meet them. Mama would come later with Putzi and Maria. Alma felt a tug in her heart to think she hadn't laid eyes on Putzi in almost two months. Mama intended to keep her a few weeks longer, just to be absolutely certain there was no more risk of infection.

And Gustav. It felt like an eternity since Alma and her husband had last been together. Since he had been truly present with her in his heart and mind. She hoped their summer by the lake would restore their harmony. *Please let him finally open up and speak plainly about our future and what choices still remain.*

Alma stepped off the train in Klagenfurt and was engulfed in her husband's arms. She tried to surrender to the sense of weightlessness when he lifted her off her feet. Like Gucki, she had lost weight during their seven weeks of agony. She yearned to lose herself in his kiss, to allow her grinding worries to drop away. *We are together again and all shall be well.*

Gustav released her and took Gucki from Miss Turner. He kissed their child and made much of her until the little girl beamed.

Riding in the carriage to their summerhouse, Alma and Gustav sat side by side with Gucki snuggled between them on the upholstered seat. Their daughter looked as though she couldn't believe her luck to be outdoors in this beautiful world again, healthy and whole, with both her parents stroking her hair and holding her hands.

Gustav could not stop talking about the New York Metropolitan Opera. "Almschi, they've offered me a four-year contract with a salary of 125,000 crowns for a *six-month season!*"

Incredulous, she gaped at him. It was a veritable fortune. The Vienna Court Opera had paid Gustav 36,000 crowns for a ten-month season.

"They're hiring me on the same terms as Enrico Caruso, the most famous tenor in the world!" Gustav was beside himself. "Just think, I shall be directing *him!* The season begins January 1. We'll sail from Cherbourg in December. On the way to Cherbourg, we must stop in Paris and visit Berta Zuckerkandl's sister. She wants to introduce us to Auguste Rodin. He'd like me to model for a bust in bronze, can you imagine?"

Though Gustav was famous throughout Europe, the New York Metropolitan Opera would make him an international star, practically ensuring his lasting fame. Immortalized in bronze by Rodin! Although this good news brought Alma much relief, it still seemed awful that they had to leave their home. Even with all the money Gustav would earn, she worried that everyone would say they were hounded out of Europe by rabid journalists.

"I'll hate to leave Mama behind," she said.

"A *six-month season,* Almschi!" He bounced Gucki in his lap in celebration. "When I'm not conducting in New York, we'll be here in Austria enjoying a six-month holiday. We'll have a foot in both worlds. And I'll have so much time to compose."

• • •

Attempting to overcome her own reservations about New York, Alma allowed Gustav to seduce her with tales of how opulent and cosmopolitan their lives would be.

"You're always complaining about not having any new clothes," he said, after she had put Gucki to bed that night. "Now you can have a whole new wardrobe. Gowns with silk trains." As he spoke, he took her hand and led her upstairs to his bedroom. "The Metropolitan Opera is arranging for us to live in a suite of rooms in the Hotel Majestic overlooking Central Park. You can host a salon as glittering as Berta Zuckerkandl's. We'll have Enrico Caruso as our dinner guest. And if you're worried about your English, there's a very sophisticated community of German-speaking émigrés—"

Alma silenced him with a long, hungry kiss. The only way to purge herself of her anxieties for their future was to pull him down on the bed. It had been too long since they had last made love. She was parched for it. *Oh, God, let me feel something in my body again.* Let the weight of his flesh on hers still the clamor in her mind.

Alma awakened to Gustav's kiss. Early morning sun washed the curtains gold, and she lay naked and supremely rested, the rumpled linens wound around her limbs like twisting serpents. Her husband's face was flushed and soft, his eyes radiant. But he was already dressed, about to walk out the door.

"Here's your dressing gown, Almschi," he said, veiling her body in slippery silk. "Gucki will be up soon and wanting her mama."

Before he could dash off to his composing hut, she wrapped her arms around him and kissed him. Like a cat, she rubbed her face against his chest. Anything to keep them both rooted here, in the world she knew, instead of drifting across the ocean into an alien land that frightened her.

Laughing indulgently, Gustav extricated himself. "Almscherl, I have new music sounding inside my head. I must write it down now or it shall be lost forever."

When he left the room, Alma fell back on the bed with a pang of emptiness.

Through the closed door, she could hear Gustav speaking to Elise. "Today? That can't be. It's too soon."

"Herr Direktor, it's too late to tell them they can't come," Elise said, when Alma, wrapped in her silk dressing gown, came padding down the stairs. "They're taking the early train."

"What's this?" Alma looked from her husband to her maid. She hoped Mildenburg and her fiancé wouldn't be descending upon them.

"A telegram arrived," Gustav said shortly. "Your mother is coming up with Maria and Putzi. Today!"

"Why shouldn't she?" Alma was delighted and didn't understand how Gustav could be so perturbed.

"I thought they would wait another two weeks," he said. "What if Gucki's still contagious?"

"Nonsense," Alma said, losing patience with him. "The doctor gave her the all clear."

Mama and the girls arrived by carriage from the train station in time to join them for supper. While Mama and Maria made more stately progress walking up the path, Putzi raced toward her parents with her arms stretched wide in glee. Alma's heart lifted to see her again, her beautiful firstborn daughter. Every part of the child seemed to blaze with high spirits and good health. Putzi had always been the sturdier child, the more confident child, the one most likely to succeed in forging her trail through life.

At the sight of her sister, Gucki squealed and clapped her hands. Alma hoped that some of Putzi's vitality, her sheer *Lebensfreude,* might rub off on her younger sister and make her as resilient and strong.

Alma expected Putzi to fly straight into her father's embrace. Instead, Putzi threw herself at Alma, clinging to her skirts as though she'd never let her go.

"Mama!" the little girl cried, as Alma hugged her close, inhaling Putzi's clean scent. This was the longest she had ever been separated from either of her children, and it appeared that Putzi had pined for Alma as much as Alma had longed for her.

"Would it have not been more prudent to keep Putzi at the Hohe Warte for a few more weeks?" Gustav asked Mama.

Alma winced, for she'd never heard her husband speaking so sternly to her mother.

"Who am I to question the wisdom of Dr. Hammerschlag?" Mama asked him mildly. "Besides, Putzi missed her mama so much she was inconsolable."

In the following three days, Putzi hardly let Alma out of her sight. Never had her eldest daughter lavished such affection on her, hugging her, chattering to her, picking flowers for her, drawing pictures to make her mama proud.

While Gustav was sequestered in his composing hut, Gucki, Putzi, and Maria held hands and danced in circles across the blooming meadow. Alma watched the little girls twirling and spinning until they tumbled down in the soft grass. She was supposed to keep the children quiet so they didn't disturb Gustav, but she'd had her fill of quiet in the sickroom, had endured enough silence to gag on. It felt like an eternity since she'd last heard her daughters laugh and sing. She reveled in their voices, their out-of-key melodies. *Let no one ever rob my girls of their music.*

Her ebullient Putzi was oddly quiet at breakfast the next morning. Though the day was already warm, the child shivered and didn't touch her fresh bread roll, which Alma had spread with sweet butter and Putzi's favorite apricot preserves.

"At least drink your milk, darling." Alma lifted the china cup with the cow on it to her daughter's mouth.

But the little girl sputtered and choked, milk dribbling down her chin. She burst into tears—not the crying of a tantrum but of a child racked with pain and fear. Alma placed a shaking hand on Putzi's forehead. Her daughter's skin was as hot as a brand.

"What is it?" Mama asked. "Don't tell me Putzi's ill."

Alma's tears blurred her vision. How could this be? Dr. Hammerschlag had sworn there was no danger of contagion. Seated across the table, Gucki looked perfectly healthy, eating her semolina porridge with gusto.

"I'll fetch the doctor," Miss Turner said, leaping into motion.

Since they had no telephone at the summerhouse, the nanny would have to cycle into Klagenfurt to hunt down a physician.

While all this unfolded, Gustav was off in his composing hut, in his world of blissful introspection. *He will be furious,* Alma thought, as she changed Putzi into her flannel nightgown and tucked her under the eiderdown quilt with her little stuffed dachshund, her daughter's favorite toy. *He'll blame this on Mama and me.* She could almost see his face, frozen in horror. *He'll never forgive us.*

Not yet daring to tell him, she tried to coax Putzi to swallow some aspirin powders. Godless though she was, Alma knelt on the rag rug and prayed that this was just a passing spell, perhaps a bout of flu. That when the doctor arrived Putzi's fever would be down and he would scold Alma for wasting his time.

While Alma sat in vigil at her daughter's bedside, the parlor clock chimed the passing hours. By noon, Putzi showed no sign of improvement but only seemed to sink deeper into malaise.

"Speak to me, my darling," Alma begged her, cradling the limp little girl in her arms.

Dark blue eyes as big as galaxies. Long black lashes fluttering like butterfly wings.

"Mama" was all Putzi could croak, and even that seemed a mighty effort.

When another hour had passed, Putzi couldn't speak at all. Could barely swallow. Could only wheeze and cough and choke. This was what it meant to be truly voiceless, as though strangled from within. Peering into her daughter's mouth, Alma saw the thick white film coating the girl's tongue. White, not red. Not the scarlet fever then. Would that make Gustav any less outraged? Putzi's glands were swollen, her throat tender and puffy.

• • •

"Diphtheria," Dr. Blumenthal said, when he arrived in the late afternoon.

Alma shrank to hear the diagnosis, for this was a malady even deadlier than scarlet fever. Gustav was as livid as she had feared, too incensed to even look at her. She had to endure his anger alone now, since Mama had taken the precaution of returning to Vienna with Maria.

"What can be done?" Gustav asked the doctor. "Shall I take her to the hospital in Klagenfurt? On the express train to Vienna?" He conferred with the physician as though Alma wasn't even there.

"She's too weak to move," the doctor said. "We can only hope her condition doesn't get any worse. If it does, she'll die of suffocation."

So passed fourteen days of agony. With Elise caring for Gucki, Alma and Miss Turner took turns watching over Putzi, making sure she could still breathe. They struggled to get her to sip water and weak broth without choking on it. Gustav shut himself up in his study, as though that was the only way he could cope with the possibility of losing his most beloved child. He hardly spoke to Alma, whose thoughts whirled around in a tortured litany. *He thinks this is my fault. Is it my fault?* Was this her punishment for being careless? A bad mother? Hadn't she been filled with resentment when Putzi was just a helpless baby, jealous of the adoration Gustav had heaped on the girl?

Putzi's condition had deteriorated to the point where Dr. Blumenthal said that the only way he could save her from asphyxiation was by performing an emergency tracheotomy to open her throat and windpipe.

Alma's heart no longer beat in orderly fashion but raced sickly out of control while she and Miss Turner worked to turn the kitchen into a makeshift operating room. After Elise had scoured the kitchen table with carbolic soap and boiling water, Alma and Miss Turner sterilized the table, the gauze dressing, and surgical instruments with carbolic acid spray from the apparatus Dr. Blumenthal had provided. At least Miss Turner remained calm and knew what to do. She had trained as a nurse back in England and would be assisting the doctor with the operation.

241

"Be my brave girl," Alma murmured, squeezing Putzi's hand and struggling not to weep while Miss Turner held the linen mask soaked in chloroform to the child's mouth to anaesthetize her.

But before Dr. Blumenthal so much as washed his hands in preparation for the procedure, he escorted Alma out of the room. "This may take all night. Perhaps you should retire to bed, Frau Direktor."

As if she could sleep while he was cutting open her daughter on the kitchen table! What if the chloroform wore off and Putzi felt the scalpel cutting away at her flesh? Alma staggered out the door and vomited into the flowerbed.

It was nine in the evening. Up at the top of the house, light shone in Gustav's study. She even saw his profile in the window, bent over some book. Which one of his weighty tomes of philosophy would he open for solace? Did he notice her below in the gathering shadows, peering up at him like a ghost?

Nature itself turned infernal, the dense air crackling with thunder, the twilit sky a lurid red. Across the lake, a jagged bolt of lightning cleaved a tree. Rain pelted down, saturating her hair, pasting her clothes to her quivering flesh, filling her shoes.

Tearing off down the lakeshore, Alma shrieked and keened. She cursed God and Gustav—had they become one and the same? The cruel lyrics of his *Kindertotenlieder* swelled inside her brain. *In this weather, in this storm, how could I have sent the children out?* Racing around like a demented thing, she screamed and wailed and ripped her skirt in half, but the storm was louder and no one could hear. This was her own private hell.

At five in the morning, Alma slumped beside the cold, unlit tile oven in the parlor. She had changed into dry clothing and wrapped herself in a quilt, but her hair remained damp and disheveled. She bit her lip until she tasted her blood. She wondered if Gustav was sleeping. Before coming back inside the house, she had seen that his light was out. She sucked in her breath to hear the knock on the parlor door. In stepped Miss Turner, who had evidently taken the trouble to put on a fresh apron and shirtwaist so Alma wouldn't see the bloodstains.

"We've finished. You may see her now."

Like a sleepwalker, Alma lurched into the kitchen to see her beautiful daughter with her wide-open blue eyes. Her precious baby with a hole slashed in her throat, into which a metal tube had been inserted to help her breathe. And still she gasped for air. Alma gripped the edge of the table as hard as she could to keep herself from foundering.

"Can she be safely moved to my room?" she asked the doctor. "It's obscene to keep her on the kitchen table."

Alma tucked her daughter into her own bed and sang softly to her while Putzi sucked in air through the tube, struggling for each breath. Was any noise Alma had ever heard more terrifying than that tortured wheeze? Putzi's throat was so swollen from both the diphtheria and the operation that it resembled a bull's neck. Her face was pallid, her little hands waxy and white. Outside the bedroom door, Gustav sobbed and paced, just as he'd done when Alma had labored to bring their daughter into the world four and a half years ago.

Alma ran to wrench the door open. "Gustav, come and take her hand. Let her see her papa—" She broke down and swallowed back the words she couldn't bring herself to say. *Before she goes. Tell her how much you love her before she goes.*

Gustav stood in the doorway. He reeled on the threshold, his face crumpling at the sight of their gasping daughter. His hands covered his ears, as though he couldn't bear to hear Putzi's death rattle.

Alma telegraphed Mama, who came at once, weeping in remorse that she had arrived too late to say good-bye to her granddaughter.

Her arm around her mother's heaving shoulders, Alma showed Mama into her room, where Putzi lay atop the eiderdown. Alma and Miss Turner had washed the body and clothed her in her best white Sunday dress. The hateful tube was gone, and Putzi's slashed throat was mercifully hidden by Alma's lace scarf.

One hand cupped to her mouth, Mama stared at her granddaughter who hadn't lived to see even her fifth birthday. "Oh, Alma, what if Gustav's right and this *is* my fault?"

Alma held her mother as grief racked both their bodies.

Carl, who remained at home with Maria, arranged for the funeral and burial at Grinzing Cemetery, a short distance from the Hohe Warte. Miss Turner ordered the coffin to be delivered from Klagenfurt.

Alma could hardly eat, drink, or get dressed in the morning. She, Gucki, Gustav, and Mama all slept in her husband's room. Alma was terrified of letting any of them out of her sight for fear that they, too, would be snatched from her. They were like birds in a storm, huddled together so the gale wouldn't blow them apart. How could little Gucki, just three years old, comprehend the loss of her sister? Alma slept with Gucki in her arms so she could constantly reassure herself with Gucki's every breath and heartbeat that *this* daughter was alive.

And through it all, Mama went on blaming herself for Putzi's death while Gustav, despite their shared anguish and close proximity, seemed to go on blaming Alma and her mother. As much as Alma tried to cling to him for comfort, a wall of alienation grew between them. He wouldn't accuse her to her face, but his silent reproach hung in the air like smoke.

On the third morning of their encampment in his room, Gustav decided they all needed some fresh air and suggested they walk down to the lakeshore at the bottom of the garden. That much Alma thought she might manage. With Gucki in her arms, she descended the staircase, then stepped out to feel the sunlight and soft breeze on her face. It didn't cheer her in the least, only reminded her that Putzi would never again run and play under that shining sun or show off her pictures of this beautiful landscape. When they reached the lakeshore, Alma felt so unsteady on her feet, she had to set Gucki down. Though Gustav was only feet away, Alma hugged a tree to keep herself upright.

When she heard the noise of people approaching their house, she stiffened, her back to their voices. Let no strangers, however well-meaning, see her this undone. But Mama turned and looked toward the intruders. What she saw made her face constrict. Paralyzed with fear, Alma watched her mother's face turn deathly white. And then she collapsed.

"Mama!" Alma cried, falling at her side. Mama was out cold. In a panic, she looked up at Gustav. "Call the doctor! Get Elise and Miss Turner."

But her husband's eyes were frozen on whatever had caused Mama's sudden seizure. Alma followed his gaze. The men from the carpenter's workshop were delivering the tiny coffin. How could that pathetic wooden box ever contain their beautiful child?

"Gustav, I feel faint," she said. "And something's seriously the matter with Mama."

Even now he wouldn't look at her, only at their daughter's casket. Alma felt so abandoned that it was almost a joy to fall unconscious.

Dr. Blumenthal came to examine Alma and her mother. Mama, he grimly informed them, had suffered a heart attack. They gathered in Mama's room to discuss the doctor's verdict.

"If you're a patient of Dr. Kovacs, you should see him immediately on your return to Vienna, Frau Moll," he said to Mama, as she lay in bed. "As should *you*, Frau Direktor," he added, turning to Alma.

The physician looked so haggard, as though he, for all his professional detachment, had witnessed more tragedy than he could countenance from one family in the space of two and a half weeks.

"You, Frau Direktor," he went on, "are suffering from extreme exhaustion and heart palpitations. I order a complete rest. After the funeral, I suggest you spend a few weeks in a sanatorium. You could take your daughter and nanny with you."

Alma nodded, too worn down to protest that she was only twenty-seven —far too young to languish in some rest home with the elderly and consumptive. After losing Putzi, she felt older than Gustav, older than Mama. She felt ancient, ready to fall in a heap of dusty bare bones.

Gustav, looking on from the doorway, offered no words of solace. But with an attitude of forced jocularity, he said, "Come on, doc, wouldn't you like to examine me, too, as long as you're here?" He spoke as though attempting to lighten the atmosphere and distract them all from their gloom.

Alma held Mama's hand while Gustav unbuttoned his shirt and lay down on the sofa. At first, the doctor seemed to go about his business dismissively, as if he was doing this only to humor her husband. But while he listened to Gustav's heart, his expression turned grave.

"Your heartbeat is arrhythmic, Herr Direktor, probably due to some minor valvular malformation you were born with. Did you not say that heart problems run in your family? I recommend you consult Dr. Kovacs as soon as possible. In the meantime, avoid strenuous exercise."

Alma watched Gustav blink rapidly as he sat up and began to button his shirt, as though trying to wrap his thoughts around what the doctor had just told him. Her temples pounded. She felt as though the entire house were collapsing around them. This diagnosis changed everything. Not only had their young daughter suffered the most gruesome death. Not only had Gustav been harassed into resigning from the Vienna Court Opera. But now it seemed that his very life was in jeopardy. Their life together.

*Now we are truly cast adrift. Cut off at the roots.*

Suite 4

# THE LONELY ONE
# IN AUTUMN

# 31

||||||||||||||||||||||||||

O n a bitter December morning, they left Vienna, the city where Gustav had no future. Alma followed her husband up the ornate portal steps of the Westbahnhof with its arches and pillars, which looked more like an ancient temple than a railway station. Here they would board the train to Paris, the first stage of their journey to New York.

Walking between Gretl and Mama, who carried Gucki, Alma did her best to hold her head up, to play the part of a great man's wife about to embark on the adventure of a lifetime. Could she truly start all over again at the age of twenty-eight? Reinvent herself as everyone in America was said to do? Perhaps the defeated, beaten-down Alma could die and a newer, better self be born.

*Whatever you do, don't cry. Don't make a fool of yourself in public.* It had been hard enough to keep herself from breaking down at their farewell party the night before. Her head throbbed from too much champagne. After her months in the mountain sanatorium at Semmering, sentenced to a strict diet, she had lost so much weight that she could no longer hold her drink. The doctors assured her that her heart was much improved, not that it felt like it. Her heart dragged like an anchor, as if to keep her here in the world she knew.

When they reached the platform, Alma almost reared back at the sight of some two hundred people loitering about, men in their top hats and bowlers, women in their furs. Her spirits lifted at the sight of familiar faces —dear Alex, Erica and Ilse, Arnold and Mathilde, Bertha Zuckerkandl. But her view of her friends was obscured when a wave of people she scarcely recognized thronged around her and Gustav, and shoved bouquets into their arms.

"Frau Direktor Mahler!" A weeping woman glued herself to Alma. "Such a tragedy! Vienna will *never* be the same without our beloved Herr Direktor. It breaks my heart to see you go."

Alma glanced sideways at Gustav, who was likewise ambushed by lachrymose strangers. *Leave him alone,* she wanted to shout. *He hates crowds.*

The mawkish horde made such a din, Alma found it impossible to hear her real friends say their good-byes. Klimt had to peel the woman off of Alma before he could take her hands.

"It's over, Alma," he said, his eyes brimming. "A golden age has ended today. The philistines have won."

In his *Beethoven Frieze,* Klimt had depicted Gustav as a knight in gold armor, the artist as savior of humanity. But those hopes and dreams had withered to dust. When Klimt gave Alma his chaste parting kiss, she wished he would instead kiss her with the full fire of his passion, as he had done nine years ago in Venice. Oh, let him kiss her right here in the middle of this multitude, shocking everyone! At least it would make her feel alive again. Force her husband to notice she was still a woman, not just some ungainly piece of luggage he was dragging halfway around the world. She had become resigned to Gustav's cold shoulder. Back in August, he had forgotten her birthday. She hadn't even received a card from him.

Though Alma sought to cling to Klimt for comfort, the crowd soon drove them apart. But Mama and Gretl rescued her, Mama's stout form forcing a path through the mob, thus allowing Alma and Gustav to board their sleeper carriage. Alma shook in relief, thinking that this would be the end of it.

But no! The seats, table, washbasin, and even the floor were festooned in floral offerings. That overpowering hothouse stink, which reminded Alma only of a high-class funeral, sent bile surging up her gorge. Not content to merely massacre Gustav in the press, the Viennese were now laying both her and her husband to rest in the most ostentatious way possible. How she fumed at the two-faced hypocrisy of the Viennese! No wonder Dr. Freud had become so famous cataloguing myriad complexes and neuroses—look at all the raw material he had in this wretched city! The throng pressed against the windows and open doorway, gawking at her as though in anticipation of seeing her crumple and fall to her knees. Alma steeled herself, not willing to show any sentiment except a glacial smile. But when Gretl hugged her, Alma's tears began to flow. Unstoppable.

"It's so unfair," her sister whispered. "Wilhelm and I are finally back in Vienna and you have to go away. We'll lose each other *again*."

Gretl and Wilhelm were now living on the Hohe Warte, close to Mama and Carl, in a villa also designed by Josef Hoffmann.

When Mama pressed little Gucki into Alma's arms, she truly fell to pieces, afraid she'd break her poor daughter from hugging her too hard.

"Be a good girl for your *Oma*." Alma kissed Gucki, dampening her daughter's cheeks with her tears. "Mama loves you. Papa, too. We'll send you picture postcards. In summer, we'll come back. We'll all be together again and go to the mountains, my darling."

Owing to Alma's fragile constitution, Gustav, Mama, Carl, and Dr. Hammerschlag had deemed it best for little Gucki to stay behind at the Hohe Warte with her grandparents. *Living on the eleventh floor of a foreign hotel with no other children to play with,* Mama had said. *That's no life for a three-year-old.* How was such a young child to make sense of the enormity of the journey before them, that stormy Atlantic crossing in the dark depths of midwinter?

Privately, Alma wondered if Gustav, having blamed her for Putzi's death, didn't trust her to keep Gucki alive in New York. After all, she hadn't been able to save Putzi — what gave her the right to believe that Gucki would be any happier or better off in her care? What if her endless grief and misfortune poisoned Gucki? *Let Mama take her. Let Mama keep her safe.*

"Good-bye, my sweet treasure." Alma drank in the blue heaven of Gucki's eyes before handing her to Mama, who gave Alma one last kiss before stepping off the train.

Flinging thorny yellow roses off the leather seat, Alma sat down opposite her husband. They both faced the window to wave at their supposed

251

well-wishers until the train jerked into motion. As soon as they left their onlookers behind, Gustav slumped against the backrest. He looked every bit as exhausted and emptied out as Alma felt. At the age of forty-seven, his face was more deeply etched with lines than ever before, and she saw the first gray hair at his temples. How this ordeal had aged them both. *These hateful people have wrung us dry.* Neither she nor Gustav spoke. After too many endings, too many partings, neither of them seemed to have any words left for each other.

Twenty-four hours later Alma and Gustav arrived in Paris, where they had arranged to stay two nights at the Hotel Bellevue on the Avenue de l'Opéra in the First Arrondissement, only a short stroll from the Louvre and the Champs-Élysées. This elegant suite with its own piano would have been paradise if they had been visiting under happier circumstances.

They went to the opera to see *Tristan und Isolde,* but Gustav complained of a migraine and they left during the interval, sparing Alma the "Liebestod" scene, which would have forced her to remember the dreams of her youth that now lay in ruins. *Dying for love, dying into love. That flaming rebirth through the transfiguration of love.*

The following morning, Gustav, ever restless, set off on a long walk through the December rain while Alma remained behind. She could simply not force herself to march along beside him through that downpour of needle-sharp rain that was worse than snow, the way it penetrated one's very bones.

Instead, Alma perched on the sofa and watched the carriages rattling up and down the boulevard. A motor car, with its blaring horn, spooked a team of horses. *New York,* she thought, *will be packed with motor cars, with their smell and noise.* Gazing out the seventh-story window, she tried to pretend she was already in her new home looking down at the world with detachment. *Stay aloof so nothing can hurt you anymore.* But her heart came crashing to earth at the sight of a couple walking arm in arm. The young man pulled his sweetheart under an awning and kissed her as though he'd never stop. Alma's eyes misted.

*Marital happiness is a thing as delicate and fragile as a newborn infant,* Mama had told her. *It must be carefully looked after.* One of Mama's reasons for insisting that Gucki remain behind with her was to give Alma and Gustav a chance to rekindle their love. Mama had told her that this year in New York was an opportunity for the two of them to start over again, like newlyweds on their honeymoon, unencumbered by children. On their actual honeymoon, Alma had been pregnant and too sick to enjoy much in the way of uninhibited passion. *Now we have been given a second chance.* Yet here she sat by herself in a beautiful hotel suite while Gustav wandered alone in the rain.

As twitchy as a caged panther, Alma wandered to the piano and attempted to cheer herself up by playing "Winterstürme wichen dem Wonnemond" from *Die Walküre.* She began to sing the hopelessly romantic libretto when a knock at the door sent her hands flying off the keys.

Who could it be? Pausing in front of the mirror, she smoothed her hair before opening the door. A young man with a sensitive face and thick dark wavy locks bowed and held out a slim package wrapped in mauve and silver gift paper.

"Good afternoon, Frau Direktor," he said in Russian-inflected German. "I hope I'm not disturbing you. I discovered by some happy accident that I'm staying in the same hotel as you and the Herr Direktor, and I wanted to pay my respects to you both before you sail to America."

"Herr Gabrilowitsch," Alma said. "What a surprise! Won't you come in? Gustav is out for a walk, but he should be back soon. He'll be delighted to see you."

Ossip Gabrilowitsch, the Russian-born pianist and composer, was a fervent admirer of Gustav and had been a dinner guest at their Vienna apartment in seasons past. His very presence brought back memories of more fortunate days, before her life had seemed so saturated in tragedy. Warmth blossomed inside her breast. She heard herself laugh in pleasure, as she hadn't in months, as she showed her guest in and then telephoned reception to order up tea and cakes for three.

Bowing his head, the young man handed her his gift.

"Should I wait until Gustav comes before I open it?" she asked.

"If you wish, but I chose it especially for you, Frau Direktor, since we seem to share the same taste in literature. Something for you to read on the ship."

Intrigued, Alma peeled off the wrapping paper patterned in sinuous lilies, roses, and vines to find a volume of Rilke's poetry.

"How very thoughtful! I adore Rilke." Her voice rose in glee.

"I'm so pleased."

Ossip Gabrilowitsch was handsome in a wildly bohemian sort of way, with his tousled hair and his crooked cravat that Alma longed to retie for him. Just the sort of dreamy genius she would have flirted with when she was an unmarried girl. While they discussed Rilke, she felt like her old self again, vivacious Alma Schindler with one hand on her hip.

"We've known each other for years, Ossip," she said the next time he addressed her as Frau Direktor. "Shall we dispense with the formalities? Just call me Alma." She used the familiar *Du*, which made the color rise in his face.

Ducking his head, he picked up her copy of *Hedda Gabler* from the side table.

"You're reading Ibsen," he said, with undisguised admiration. "So radical and modern! But I would expect no less from Gustav Mahler's wife."

Now it was Alma's turn to blush. When she had first met Ossip, she had been pregnant with Gucki. But now she was as slim and sleek as an arrow. At least the sanatorium diet had been good for something.

"I, too, am considering immigrating to America," he told her, with an air of quiet confidence while the chambermaid tiptoed in with the silver tray of tea and gateaux. "Europe is in decline, crushed by the weight of its own importance. America is the future."

Alma smiled as she poured fragrant Darjeeling into two impossibly delicate porcelain cups. "So is it true you're going to marry Clara Clemens?" she asked him teasingly, referring to the daughter of the great Mark Twain. Miss Clemens had gained international fame as a concert contralto.

Ossip looked so miserable that Alma regretted her indiscretion. Perhaps he and Miss Clemens had broken off their engagement.

"Ossip, why don't you play one of your compositions while we wait for Gustav," Alma said, swiftly changing the subject. "I adore your piano music."

With a shy smile, he sat at the piano and played his Gavotte in D Minor while Alma sipped her tea and listened, utterly entranced. When Gustav still did not materialize, she and Ossip moved on to four-hand piano playing, reeling off Schubert's "Die Forelle" and then Beethoven's slow, meditative *Moonlight Sonata*. This music always rendered Alma pensive. She prayed her sadness wouldn't spill out and betray her deep unhappiness. Of course, Ossip knew that she and Gustav were mourning their firstborn daughter, but she would rather cut off her head than give this young man any inkling of her terror that Gustav no longer loved her. That she had grown too old and ugly for any man to love. But surely Ossip would deduce for himself that all was not right between her and Gustav. What kind of husband left his wife alone in a hotel room to walk by himself in the rain-soaked streets?

"What an accomplished pianist you are, Alma," the young man said. "You play with a composer's sensitivity."

A tingle ran up her nape. "Before I married, I dreamed of being a composer myself."

Had she truly *said* that? What had come over her?

"Nothing would please me more than hearing your work," Ossip said.

Alma swiveled on the piano bench to meet his dark eyes, so wide and earnest. "I'm not a genius like my husband."

"Let me be the judge of that."

Her head ringing, she darted off to dig her music folder out of her steamer trunk before she lost her courage. If Gustav walked in while she was playing, she would make some excuse and laugh it off. Where was Gustav anyway? This was an exaggeratedly long walk even by his standards. She hoped he wasn't lost. Or worse—what if it was his weak heart? Was this her fault for

255

letting him walk out alone? Forcing these thoughts from her mind, Alma joined Ossip at the piano once more. Far less assured at performing her own music, she nonetheless played and sang three of her songs, including her setting of Rilke's "Bei dir ist es traut." It was difficult to keep her emotions in check. *This is what I lost. My talent might be minor, but this is my voice.*

She arranged her face into a social smile and waited for Ossip to make some diplomatic remark for courtesy's sake. Instead, he smiled at her warmly. "You have a true gift, Alma. A fine feeling for melody."

She shook her head, glancing away. Moisture gathered in the corners of her eyes. *Dear God, please don't let me cry.*

"Play some more for me," he said, as though to save her from her own embarrassment. "Please, Alma." He looked into her eyes until she understood. He was being sincere, not merely polite. He had genuine respect for her as a fellow composer.

Flustered, Alma reached for another one of her songs.

*"Ich wandle unter Blumen und blühe selber mit,"* Alma sang. She wandered among flowers and blossomed with them, unfolding in pure joy.

When she had finished her song, Ossip gazed at her, his eyes soft and shining, reminding her of the way Alex used to look at her when they were lovers. Dusk was falling. It had grown too dark to read her own music. She and Ossip sat side by side on the piano bench, neither of them making a move to switch on the electric lights.

"Alma, I'm afraid I'm falling in love with you." Ossip sounded at once stricken, confused, solemn, and enthralled. "Only my devotion to your husband prevents me from falling at your feet. You are so beautiful." His voice broke.

*Still beautiful after all. Still capable of arousing a man's desire.* Her tears fell like the raindrops running down the windows. His hand found hers. They leaned toward each other, their lips about to touch, when the door sprang open. The electric lights blinded Alma. Ossip released her hand and leapt to his feet.

"Herr Direktor Mahler!" he cried. "How good to see you."

Still hunched on the piano bench, her sheet music on display like evidence of adultery, Alma forced herself to look at her husband. Gustav stood in the doorway, the rain dripping off his overcoat and the black felt fedora he held in his hand. He peered at her and Ossip through his wet, foggy spectacles before taking them off and wiping them with his handkerchief. Her heart pounded sickly. Until Gustav laughed.

No jealous scene followed. No theatrics. Just Gustav disappearing into the bedroom to change into dry clothes and then joining them for the fresh pot of tea Alma ordered. After hurriedly gathering up her music and hiding it away, she busied herself pouring tea and serving cake while Gustav and Ossip discussed shared memories and future prospects.

"I would be lost without my wife," she heard Gustav say.

Her back to the men, Alma drew the curtains on the rain that was turning to sleet.

"Alma sacrificed her youth to me," her husband told Ossip. "No one will ever know how selflessly she offered up her life for me and my work. When I board that ship tomorrow, I'm not leaving home. I'm taking my home with me. My Alma."

She sank into a chair and struggled not to weep. To hear her husband's praise, which she hadn't heard in so long. So Gustav acknowledged her sacrifice after all. Why hadn't he told her so when they were alone together? Why was he instead revealing his naked heart to the young man she had nearly kissed?

"Won't you join us for dinner?" Gustav asked Ossip.

Ossip, red in the face, made his excuses, obsequiously shook Gustav's hand, and shrank out the door.

*Did what happened—what* almost *happened—with Ossip count as adultery?* Alma asked herself, as she and Gustav descended in the elevator to the restaurant below. What would have happened if Gustav hadn't walked in the door when he had? Would she and Ossip have been able to stop at just a kiss?

She terrified herself. Worst of all was the ecstasy that had coursed through her when Ossip told her she was beautiful. *I have become a stranger to myself.*

After they returned from dinner, Gustav took Alma's hand and led her to bed, as though Ossip's desire for her had reawakened his own. So much bewilderment swirled through her head. Was it wrong to revel in this sense of vindication, of triumph, to see the tenderness in his eyes, as though he were stroking her naked body for the very first time? *You gave up your music for him and this is the boon you get in return, for a gift demands a gift.* Four words, as irrevocable as cannon fire, reverberated inside Alma's arching body. *Sex is my power.*

*I may not be a genius, but this is my towering strength.* Her allure as she held him in her thrall. As she made him *see* her. See *her!* Far from being the selfless madonna Gustav had described for Ossip, she had become an insatiable goddess from a savage past. In all other ways, Gustav might dominate her, but in this she was supreme, his queen, her cries rising phoenixlike in the cold night.

# 32

||||||||||||||||||||||||

The next morning, Alma and Gustav took the train to Cherbourg, where they boarded their ship, the *Kaiserin Auguste Viktoria*. On the deck, a brass band played "La Marseillaise." Gustav was in high spirits, a healthy color in his face, she noted with satisfaction. Entering their stateroom with its mahogany furnishings thoughtfully nailed to the floor, they clasped hands and danced, exclaiming at the luxury, the elegance.

"Let us journey forward as victors," she murmured to Gustav, her cheek pressed to his.

Let his appointment at the New York Metropolitan Opera prove the pinnacle of his career, she prayed. The time had come to banish her sadness and play her part as the glamorous young wife of the great conductor and composer who stood on the threshold of international celebrity.

Arm in arm, they explored the ship with its ballroom and library, its salon full of silk-upholstered divans, its smoking room and dining rooms with banquet tables decked in linen and fresh lilies. They joined the other first-class passengers to drink champagne on deck while the sailors ceremoniously lifted anchor and the ship set off through the foamy green waves. Handkerchief in hand, Alma waved good-bye to Europe.

Alas, their eight-day passage was stormy and Gustav was very seasick. Alma fetched him seltzer water and dry toast while he lay rigid in bed, refusing to eat or drink until his queasy spell passed.

"Don't play nursemaid," he admonished her. "Go and enjoy yourself."

With his blessing, Alma danced in the ballroom night after night, floating above the gales in a buzz of cocktails and spirited conversation with the many artists, writers, and musicians from across Europe, all headed for a new life in America. There were so many German and French speakers that her halting English hardly seemed to matter.

"The thing you must understand about New York is that it's swimming in new money," a young socialite told her, the wife of a Frankfurt art dealer. This lady was the picture of sophistication with her silk turban and long amber cigarette holder. "Those plutocrats collect Italian paintings. They import French antiques, marry English nobility. They want to be seen at the opera listening to the most renowned European sopranos. They'll pay anything for that Old World touch to give them legitimacy. That's why they're bringing your husband over!"

On the morning of December 20, Gustav was well enough to join Alma on deck as they sailed into New York Bay. The Statue of Liberty, rising from her island and lifting her torch, left Alma breathless with wonder. Yet even this was eclipsed by the Manhattan skyline. Countless buildings reached higher than the tallest cathedral spires of Old Europe. The New World glimmered like a miracle.

After passing the southern tip of the island of Manhattan, the *Kaiserin Auguste Viktoria* docked at the East River Pier, within view of the Brooklyn Bridge, the largest and most magnificent structure Alma had ever seen.

As first-class passengers, she and Gustav were spared the ordeal of being herded onto the ferry bound for Ellis Island, the fate of those poor immigrants in steerage. Instead, officials gave their papers a cursory inspection before they disembarked. Alma lowered her head and stared at her shoes while Gustav vehemently declared himself German, not Austrian or Bohemian. Her husband, she reflected, was attempting to put as much distance as possible between himself and the perfidious Viennese.

After leaving the ship and passing through the Customs House, a sparkling beaux arts confection resembling a palace, they were free to enter the United States.

"Everything is *new* here," Alma whispered to Gustav. "And so splendid!"

Outside the Customs House, they were hailed by a fifty-year-old man in a top hat and sable-trimmed greatcoat. His gloved hands twirled an ebony walking cane, his spats were immaculate, and he sported a debonair gray moustache. To Alma, he seemed the very picture of an American millionaire. She imagined him flinging open his coat to reveal a flurry of greenbacks falling like confetti. Waving to them, he seemed to exude a uniquely American confidence and openhearted conviviality free from European reserve or snobbery. But nothing prepared Alma for her shock when he greeted them in his native German.

"Herr Direktor Mahler! You look just like your photograph! I'd recognize you anywhere!" He shook Gustav's hand before kissing Alma's cheeks. "Ah, the lovely Frau Direktor Mahler!" He introduced himself as Otto Kahn, the Metropolitan Opera's president and financier. Switching to English, he turned to the tall, slender woman standing slightly behind him. "And this is my beautiful wife, Adelaide!"

"Welcome to New York, Mrs. Mahler," Adelaide said, as soft-spoken as her husband was hearty.

"How do you do," Alma managed, trying not to gape. She had never seen so much mink on one person.

The Kahns ushered Alma and Gustav into their gleaming green Rolls-Royce Silver Ghost limousine while a porter arranged to send their steamer trunks on by a humbler horse-drawn conveyance. Sinking into the green leather seat, Alma could scarcely believe the opulence.

"He's an investment banker," Gustav whispered in her ear.

While the chauffeur drove them up Broadway, Mr. Kahn regaled them with a steady stream of conversation. He was born in Mannheim, he told them, the son of a revolutionary.

"And here I am, the biggest capitalist in New York! But if I earn it, I spend it. I give it away. It's a sin to keep money idle. You know, I'd like to buy a piano for every family in New York. A piano in every apartment would do far more to fight crime than a policeman on every corner.

"Addie and I have donated millions to the Met Opera, and they were still reluctant to let us buy our own box—because we're Jews. At least they don't have pogroms here, eh? I heard the papers gave you a terrible time in Vienna, Herr Direktor—a crying shame. You won't experience that here, this I can promise.

"In fact, I'd like to offer you an even bigger contract than the one you signed. To be precise, I'm offering you Heinrich Conried's job—general director of the Metropolitan Opera. Poor Conried is very ill, you understand. He needs to step down for health reasons. Of course, the salary would be very lucrative."

Alma looked at Gustav, whose eyes seemed to bulge out of his head. They had barely set foot in New York, and he was already being asked to replace the man whose largess had brought them here in the first place. Heinrich Conried, Alma understood, shared a background very similar to Gustav's, born in Silesia to a poor Jewish weaver.

"I'm afraid I can't accept that post," Gustav replied, sounding both shaken and nervous.

Kahn shrugged with equanimity. "My second choice is Giulio Gatti-Casazza from La Scala. He might want to make his own creative changes. But don't worry. As principal conductor, you'll still be in charge of the German repertoire while he'll see to the Italian repertoire. German and Italian opera, that's what our patrons pay for. The Vanderbilts, Astors, Carnegies, and Rockefellers. You'll meet them all!"

They drove past the Metropolitan Opera on Thirty-Ninth and Broadway, an imposing structure if not as grand and gorgeous as the Court Opera in Vienna. Gustav looked tempted to leap out of the automobile straight into his new workplace, but the Rolls-Royce kept moving.

As they progressed through Midtown, Alma looked out at the people crowding the sidewalks, who appeared considerably more down-at-the-heels than the Vanderbilts and Rockefellers. Even through the closed windows, she could hear the babel of languages. Yiddish and Italian. She saw women in heavy boots with thick woolen kerchiefs tied to their heads as if they had just tramped down from the Russian steppes. She lost count of all the black and Oriental faces she saw. New York literally heaved with immigrants, as if all the world had been squeezed into one noisy, hectic city. *All these dislocated people, driven from their homes, desperate for a better life.* Her stomach flipped to think that she and Gustav were just two more of them, albeit much more comfortably provided for.

Mrs. Kahn, meanwhile, attempted to converse with Alma in English, speaking so softly and swiftly that she could understand only the odd word. *Charity. Museum. Art. Children.* A pang rose inside Alma to think how little Gucki would have craned her head to peer up at those buildings rising like canyon walls to dwarf the bustling streets. How Gucki would have delighted in the Christmas decorations on the shop fronts, the strings of bunting and colored lights. New York made Vienna seem so small, so provincial and quaint. Vienna was history. This was the modern world in all its glory.

"New York streets are laid out in a grid, so if you can count, you can find your way around," Kahn said. "Frau Direktor, you'll be able to travel all over the city in our new subway system while your husband's at work. No need to hire a cab. How's that for modern living?"

The farther they traveled uptown, the more elegant the department stores, concert halls, theatres, and town houses appeared. When they arrived in the Upper West Side, the chauffeur opened the door. Alma stepped out in front of the Hotel Majestic, rising twelve stories into that crisp winter sky. This wasn't a dream—she and Gustav would truly be living here. Residential hotels were the ideal accommodation for visiting artists and musicians. Their suite, so the Kahns promised, was as commodious as an apartment and lacked only a kitchen. Food could be ordered up from the restaurant below. The hotel staff would see to their cleaning and laundry, which spared Alma from having to hire servants.

After they bade farewell to the Kahns, the concierge escorted them through the marble lobby with its crystal chandeliers and into the elevator of brass and frosted glass. *The eleventh floor!* Never had Alma risen to such heights in any building anywhere in the world. Her heart raced, and she could still feel the ocean's swell in her unsteady legs.

Just when she thought the vertigo might overpower her, they stepped out into a corridor blazing with electric light. The concierge showed them into their suite, where their luggage already awaited them by some miracle. Taking Gustav's hand, Alma rushed through the parlor and dining room with their walnut furniture, marble fireplace, and built-in bookcases and cabinets of solid oak.

"Look, Gustav! *Two* pianos!"

She darted to the large leaded windows that looked out on the snowy expanse of Central Park. Far below, figures skated on a frozen lake while a brass band played Christmas carols. Beyond the park rose the splendor of the Upper East Side, where the Rockefellers and Carnegies lived.

"Oh, Gustav, this is like living in a mansion in the sky!" She threw her arms around her husband, who hadn't yet removed his coat or hat. "Everything they say about America is true," she murmured, loosening the winter scarf tied around his neck. "Here we can start all over again."

"I'm glad you like it, Almschi." He kissed her before extricating himself from her embrace and retying his scarf.

"Gustav, you're *not* leaving already," she said, her spirits sinking as he headed for the door. "We've only just arrived."

But he was as jumpy as though he had downed ten cups of strong Viennese coffee, frantic in his urgency. "Almschi, I'm expected to direct my debut performance on New Year's Day after only *nine days of rehearsal,* and I don't even know what opera they've chosen! I'll be back for dinner!"

At that, he dashed off to the subway.

Much to their relief, they discovered that Gustav's debut performance would be *Tristan und Isolde,* an opera he knew inside out, having directed it so many times before. When he wasn't rehearsing at the Met, he spent most of the day in bed to spare his heart, following his doctor's orders. He even took his meals in bed — his own separate bed in his own separate room. Her once-active husband who used to sprint like an athlete, never sitting still if he could help it.

Christmas Eve in New York, their first without their daughters, was more hellish than anything Alma could have imagined. Gustav didn't want to be reminded of the holiday and refused to suffer as much as a wreath over the mantelpiece. Instead, there being no rehearsals that day, he worked in bed, buried in his scores. Alma huddled on the window seat and looked out over Central Park. Families were everywhere. Skating, tobogganing, gliding along in horse-drawn sleighs. She shoved open the casement, allowing frigid air to flood the room, just to hear the distant voices of happy children. That drove a blade through her heart. Slamming the casement back down, she sobbed. Gustav, if he even heard her through his closed door, didn't come to her. How she wished she had Mama or Gretl to pour out her heart to. *Anyone.*

Little Gucki's absence, far from freeing her and Gustav to enjoy a second honeymoon, made them both miserable. Without their only surviving child, what was left to bind them together as husband and wife? What revenant of love or desire remained? Their lovemaking in Paris already seemed a lifetime ago. Alma shrank inside to think that Gustav still blamed her for Putzi's death, which had left them indelibly estranged, each of them locked inside their separate grief. If they could only *talk* about Putzi, remember her together. But Gustav couldn't even tolerate hearing their dead daughter's name.

Now Gucki, left behind in Vienna, seemed lost to them as well. What Alma would have given to have her near. To shower her in kisses and presents. She would buy Gucki her first pair of ice skates, and they would go skating together in Central Park, Gucki's little mittened hand in hers. Even Gustav would burst out of his cave when he heard their daughter's laughter. Beautiful Anna Justine with her eyes like the sky.

Dusk fell and Alma was still frozen on the window seat. The coldness between her and Gustav left her paralyzed. But she jerked to hear the knock on the door.

Having no servant to make excuses and send the intruder away, Alma dragged herself up and dried her eyes before cracking the door three inches and peering out. She had a terrible cold, that's what she'd say. That was why her nose and eyes were swollen and red. No, she hadn't been crying. But the sight of the smiling middle-aged man with his waxed moustache left her mute. He held out an ornate tin box of gingerbread.

"Do I have the honor of addressing Frau Direktor Mahler?"

To her astonishment, he spoke not only German but Viennese German. For one blinding second, she could believe she was back home and that somewhere across the room Gucki was clapping her hands, anticipating unwrapping the gifts beneath the tree.

"Maurice Baumfeld is my name," the visitor told her, shaking her hand. "Director of the Irving Place Theatre and a great admirer of your husband, I might add. I've come to wish you both a merry Christmas and a warm welcome to New York."

When Alma attempted to smile graciously, she thought her face would break in two. There was no hiding her unhappiness from Herr Baumfeld.

"Forgive me, but I see it's not very merry for you, is it?" His face knit in concern. "In a foreign place, so far from home. Well, no need to be lonely, madam. You and the Herr Direktor must come and share dinner with me and my family. I'll wait while the two of you get ready. Don't look so bashful, Frau Direktor. I insist! It would be a crime to leave you two alone on Christmas Eve."

Trembling in gratitude, Alma ran to fetch Gustav.

"We can't possibly say no," she said, dragging him out of bed as though he were her child. "It would be beastly to refuse such kindness."

So Alma and Gustav found themselves in a handsomely furnished brownstone several blocks away. Though the Baumfelds were Jewish, they, like the assimilated Jews back home, celebrated Christmas in true Austrian style, with all the trappings except Midnight Mass. Their seven children sang "Stille Nacht" while their mother lit the white candles on the tree. Alma played carols on the piano, taking requests from the children who thronged around. She struggled not to weep all over the three-year-old girl who kept tugging on her skirt and telling her she was pretty. An older child brought her a cup of mulled wine. Soon enough, she and the other adults, apart from Gustav, became agreeably tipsy.

Then Frau Baumfeld summoned them to the holly-bedecked table, where they ate roast goose stuffed with apples and served with red cabbage and roast potatoes. Back in Vienna, Mama was probably serving an identical meal. Alma pictured her mother's table with Gucki, Maria, Carl, Gretl, Wilhelm, and their little boy gathered around. Mama had probably tied a red velvet ribbon in Gucki's silky golden hair. But the Baumfelds were so convivial and their children so endearing, they managed to draw Alma out of her homesick introspection. Likewise, Gustav seemed more relaxed than she had seen him since they had first set foot in New York. What a gift it was to see him smile while he listened indulgently to the Baumfelds' little boy chattering about his pet turtle, who was also named Gustav.

Alma thought back to their lovemaking in Paris. She began to wonder if there was a chance she was carrying a new life inside her to redeem Putzi's death. Maybe this time she would bear a son — would that make Gustav love her again? She bit her lip and made herself laugh and smile along with everyone else.

Later, after the children had opened their presents and finally trudged reluctantly to bed, the Baumfelds served coffee and liqueurs. Herr Baumfeld told them of his dreams of a German-language theatre company. He made it sound possible to live a full artistic life in New York without necessarily mastering English — an idea that gave Alma considerable hope, considering her own struggles with the new language.

Before long, Baumfeld's theatre troupe burst in. A perfect hostess, Frau Baumfeld opened several bottles of champagne. *An effort the lady could have spared herself,* Alma thought. The actors and actresses were already in their cups, their language louche enough to make even Alma blush. She hoped the children upstairs wouldn't hear.

Jolly as ever, Herr Baumfeld introduced her and Gustav to his company. The most inebriated among them, a blonde with a plunging neckline and too much kohl around her eyes, lurched toward them and offered her hand for Gustav to kiss. Her fingernails were painted as red as sin.

"*Enchanté*, Herr Direktor," she slurred. "My name is Pauline, but everyone calls me Putzi."

Alma watched Gustav go white around the mouth before he reared away as though fleeing a leper. Murmuring excuses, she stumbled in his wake as he shot out of the house. On the icy sidewalk, he gasped and doubled over. Alma's stomach pitched in panic. Was he having a heart attack? When she reached for his arm, he drew himself up and rubbed his eyes. The Baumfelds' maid, meanwhile, stepped out to hand them their coats and hats. Alma stammered her thanks.

Fortunately, the Hotel Majestic was close enough so Alma and Gustav could walk home, dodging the revelers and the families headed for church. But wherever Alma looked, from one lamplit window to another, she saw her dead daughter staring back at her. The last look Putzi had given her before Alma had left her on the makeshift operating table at Maiernigg.

Feathery snowflakes drifted down, touching their faces, reminding Alma all too cruelly of her first walk with Gustav six years ago. When he had been so fervently in love with her, abandoning all reason and restraint. *You know, it won't be easy to marry a man like me.* Alma reached for his hand and squeezed, but Gustav only blinked and looked straight ahead. She saw that his eyes shone with the tears he could not allow himself to shed on these cold, windy streets. She shivered and shook. All the excitement and promise New York offered could do nothing to heal their grief.

On December 26, Gustav was back at the Met, leaving Alma alone for most of the day. And yet he needed her. Who else was there to listen to his apprehensions about his looming debut? Gustav was appalled at the Met Opera's shoddy staging. Though his soloists were among the best in the world and the auditorium was luxurious, the dressing rooms were cramped and there was very limited space for rehearsals. The scenery and props had to be stored beneath the stage.

"Almschi, they hired me to raise the Met to European standards, but that will take years!" He paced the floor until Alma wondered if the downstairs neighbors would complain. "What I wouldn't give to bring Roller over here! Now I understand why Kahn offered me Conried's job. Conried's a megalomaniac *and* he has syphilis! All I need. A syphilitic boss."

On New Year's Day, his opening night, Gustav was so nervous that as they entered the elevator he stepped on Alma's evening gown, ripping off her train and most of the back of her skirt. Half-undressed, she was obliged to flee back to their suite and frantically stitch her gown back together. Meanwhile, Gustav was a bundle of convulsing nerves on two skinny legs.

"Go!" she told him. "Otherwise you'll be late. This will take me ages."

But he gripped her bare shoulder and kissed the top of her head more tenderly than he had touched her since Paris. "They'll have to wait. I can't go without you, Almschi. Facing the Astors and Vanderbilts alone? What if the reviewers eviscerate me?"

He sounded like a man fighting not only to save his career but also his entire existence. Perhaps, for Gustav, they were one and the same.

The telephone rang shrilly. It was Conried, predictably racked with apprehension as to why his star conductor was late.

"Don't shout at me!" Gustav shouted into the receiver. "Anyway, it's your fault—why did you put us in a hotel so far from the opera? If you want to be helpful, send an automobile to drive us down!" He had never sounded more Bohemian, as though he had never left his native village of Kalischt. In spite of herself, Alma laughed. She caught his eye until he cracked a smile and laughed, too.

"It's finished," she said, holding up her mended gown. "Lace me back in, would you? And watch where you put your clumsy feet, Gustl!"

The interior of the Metropolitan Opera was a jewel case of white, red, and gold with a magnificently painted ceiling. It seated 3,635, or so Gustav had told her, and every one of those seats was full. The auditorium echoed with impatient murmurs.

Mr. Kahn was gracious enough to show Alma up to the director's box, where she joined Mrs. Kahn and Conried, who looked as though he might die of apoplexy if the performance was delayed another second. Conried did indeed look ill, Alma observed, as she shook his plump, pasty hand. She strove to mask her discomfort over touching a person who was slowly dying of syphilis. The disease had left him half-crippled.

To distract herself, she looked out over the audience where New York's elite were assembled. Debutantes and socialites glittered like galaxies in their diamond tiaras and *colliers*. Alma sat down abruptly, the better to hide her torn skirt that she had so hastily stitched back together.

A hush fell over the auditorium as the lights dimmed.

*"Finally!"* Conried muttered.

Alma leaned forward to see her husband mount the podium, his tuxedo tails flapping. Her jaw relaxed to see him move with such agility, as though he had never been diagnosed with a heart condition. But when he turned to face his cheering audience, his face was guarded, almost severe. She knit her hands together to think how nervous he must be, directing his American debut after only nine days of rehearsal. Back in Vienna, he would have spent months preparing for such a production.

The curtains opened to reveal the slapdash backdrop of ocean waves and the clumsily rigged stage ship. Gustav was right—in terms of staging, the Met was no better than some provincial opera in the Tyrolean hinterland. But when he lifted his baton and the orchestra began the overture, the lush swelling notes swept her away. The acoustics were superb, as was his cast. The Swedish-born soprano Olive Fremstad was singing the role of Isolde for the first time. The beauty of her voice eclipsed even Mildenburg's back in Vienna. Heinrich Knote had come over from Munich to play a smoldering Tristan. He was the perfect heldentenor—slim, youthful, and expressive, his rich voice seducing every lady in the audience.

But Alma's eyes kept returning to the true star of the evening—her husband. The others, too, she noticed, kept their opera glasses trained on him. Gustav was mesmerizing, his movements economical and precise. He rode the orchestra with the assurance of a master equestrian. At one moment, he curbed its luxuriance so as to better showcase his vocalists, allowing them to be heard with ease. At another, he gave the orchestra its head so it could race forward with brio into dramatic crescendos. This lean yet muscular interpretation heightened both the suspense and the sensuality. Never had the libretto sounded this lucid, and Fremstad shone in this spotlight, her diction flawless.

"I've never heard *Tristan* like this," Kahn said, in the interval. "It sounds like something entirely new."

Conried appeared ecstatic. "This is how Wagner *should* sound! Frau Direktor, your husband is a genius."

The "Liebestod" scene was more sublime than Alma had ever heard it, moving her to tears, her silk gown nearly melting off her flesh. It was as though Gustav were making love to her through his exquisite music.

When the opera reached its dramatic close, she was lifted out of herself in rapture. Blind to that audience of millionaires and jewel-encrusted grande dames, she leapt to her feet and applauded madly. Then she saw that everyone else had also risen to give her husband a standing ovation. The thundering clapping and cheers threatened to bring down that painted ceiling.

Turning on the podium, still gripping his baton, Gustav looked dazed, as though flabbergasted that his debut had been such a success. *Truly, this is one of his greatest triumphs,* Alma thought. In one stroke, her husband's brilliance had entirely changed their fortunes.

# 33

||||||||||||||||||||||||||

S uch a fantastical city New York was, a living fairy tale. Electric lighting all up and down Broadway, turning night into day. *We should be so happy here.* There were good days, such as their luncheon party at Conried's apartment, furnished as though it were an Old World castle with heavy Gothic chandeliers set with gaudy colored lightbulbs. There was even a full suit of medieval armor lit from within by a red light. Alma had never seen such hilarious kitsch, but Conried took his décor very seriously so she was obliged to keep a straight face. Only when she and Gustav left the building and emerged on the sidewalk could they dissolve into helpless laughter.

The newspapers sang Gustav's praises, hailing him as one of the greatest conductors New York had ever known. Yet, despite the acclaim heaped upon him, he didn't seem happy. Instead, he remained fixated on his heart condition. Nervous, quick-tempered, and irritable.

Alma lived for Mama's letters assuring her that Gucki was healthy and well. For the photographs of Gucki playing with Maria. Of Gucki perched at the piano Alma had once thought of as her ultimate refuge. In all the photographs, Gucki looked so serious, her huge eyes dominating her round little face. What would it be like to reunite with her daughter when she and Gustav finally returned to Vienna in May, Alma wondered. Would Gucki still know her mother? Or would she regard Alma as a stranger?

After a sleepless night, Alma rose from her chilly bed. Wrapping herself in her dressing gown, she padded in slippered feet to the door of the suite, unlocked it, then wandered down the hall until she came to the communal stairwell with its long leaded windows facing east. Sitting on one of the steps, she hugged her knees to her chest and stared out at the night sky starred with electric lights. Here she would wait for dawn, her ears pricked for any human noise welling up from below to puncture her ghastly bubble of loneliness and isolation.

It was February and they had been in New York for two months. For all its glamor, the city still felt alien and strange. Winter here was harsher and colder than anything Alma had experienced in Austria. The blizzards terrified her with their winds that seemed strong enough to blast out the window glass. And now a further complication presented itself. Tentatively, she laid a palm on her belly. *It's time to tell Gustav. Don't delay it any longer. It's not going to go away.* She hadn't had her period since late November and was feeling faint in the mornings, though not as violently sick as during her previous pregnancies.

She would tell Gustav this morning before he left for rehearsal. Why was she so afraid? He loved children. *He loves them more than he loves you.* Dissolving into tears, she held her hands to her face. How could they possibly fit an infant into this new life of theirs, straddling two continents, when they hadn't even managed to make room to include Gucki? Alma worried that he would be angry at her for ruining his carefully laid plans, just as he had managed to salvage his career from the ashes. Would this baby prove the death blow to their marriage, obliging Alma to stay behind in Vienna with Mama and Gucki while Gustav spent next year alone in New York, living like a monk? Or worse, *not* living like a monk and falling in love with one of his beautiful sopranos? The most forbidden thought pulsed inside Alma: *Do I even want this child?*

If only she had a friend to talk to. But even Frau Baumfeld, as kind as she was, was not the sort of intimate confidante to whom Alma could pour out her anguish.

The first light of day, red with promise, bathed Alma's face. *Go tell him! Be brave!* Grabbing hold of the bannister, she pulled herself to her feet and swayed as the blood rushed to her head. Gustav would be awake. She would have to call down to order his breakfast. Before he left for the Met she *would* tell him.

273

Key in hand, she let herself back into the suite to find her husband already dressed and on his way out the door.

"Gustav," she said, laying both her hands on his shoulders. Absent-minded though he was, he must have noticed something wasn't right. Surely he would ask her why she had been wandering around the hallway in her dressing gown. "Gustav, I must speak to you."

"Later," he said, kissing her distractedly. "I have an early meeting with Conried. If I can't convince him to let me ship over Roller's stage backdrops from Vienna, I swear I'll tear out my hair. They brought me over here, so they should at *least* allow me to stage an opera properly!"

Left alone once again, Alma played piano until she thought her fingers would turn to stone. One more day passed and then another, and still she didn't tell him. She felt too raw, too vulnerable, and the moment was never right. There was always some more important matter pressing him. Another reception to attend where she was obliged to play the charming wife of the great man, hiding her loneliness and desperation behind a big smile and a flutter of her painted fan.

One morning she awakened to cramps. A bright rush of clumpy blood stained her sheets. The contractions ripping through her felt exactly like childbirth except this was no birth. Just another death. *You can't even keep a child alive inside your own body.*

A noise ripped out of her, an animal wail, too tortured for even Gustav to ignore. He came running to find her doubled over on the floor, her blood pooling beneath her. While she gazed up at him through her tears, he looked at her as though she were a sphinx. Some creature he couldn't understand at all.

"You didn't even tell me you were expecting, Alma. Why hide it from me? Didn't you want the baby?"

Was he accusing her of deliberately aborting their child? Alma felt her heart go completely black.

• • •

Gustav telephoned Dr. Fraenkel, yet another Viennese émigré. While the doctor worked to still her hemorrhage, Alma squeezed her eyes shut. She wanted to disappear from the earth. Afterward, Dr. Fraenkel dosed her with strychnine. She lay alone in her room, her hands clasped rigidly over her emptied womb. The drug stiffened her to the tips of her toes. She saw Putzi cradling the dead unborn baby. *Why did you let him die, Mama?*

"I can't understand why she kept it hidden from me," she heard Gustav telling the doctor in the next room. "Had I only known, I wouldn't have expected her to stay out so late at the opera. What am I going to tell her mother?"

"Herr Direktor," said Fraenkel, "your wife is *nervenkrank*. She's suffered a complete mental and physical breakdown. I order four weeks of bedrest."

*Nervenkrank.* Sick in her nerves. Just like Gretl, who had wanted to shoot herself the summer before she married Wilhelm. *It runs in our family.* Alma imagined Gustav writing this in a letter to Mama and Carl. She felt as though she were one of Dr. Freud's innumerable female patients, destroyed by hysteria, the particular curse of her sex. This the sum of all her loss. At least now she had an excuse, an explanation for all this inner turmoil. She could simply surrender. Collapse into the bottomless well of grief.

275

# 34

||||||||||||||||||||||||

I love Gustav very much, so don't take this the wrong way," Mama said. "But if you are indeed *nervenkrank,* he made you that way. You weren't like this before you married him. Just look at you, Alma, all skin and bones!"

Mother and daughter swayed in the carriage as it trundled up the rutted road. Though it was May and the sun blazed in the South Tyrolean sky, the High Puster Valley lay swathed in snow. Lifting her eyes to the jagged Dolomite peaks, Alma contemplated her mother's words. She hugged Gucki, who snuggled in her lap. How her little girl had grown! Next month Gucki would turn four.

"Gucki will come with us to New York next season," Alma said, stroking her daughter's golden curls. "Otherwise, *I* won't go."

"That's the spirit, my dear," Mama said. "Of course, you're his wife and you must be loyal. But you also need to look after yourself. Besides, you must be strong for Gustav. He needs you. Without you, he'd fall apart."

Mama's words brought to mind their journey back from New York to Cuxhaven, where they had arrived in Germany on May 2. By then, Alma had recovered sufficiently from her miscarriage to take charge of their luggage as they went through customs. Gustav had wanted to help, but his hectic season in New York and his guest productions in Boston had left him utterly depleted. He looked so old and feeble that the customs agent had intervened. *Your father needn't trouble himself, Fräulein. You can settle everything with me.* Unfortunately, Gustav had heard him.

"You're not just his wife," Mama said. "You're his everything."

*Not that I feel like that,* Alma thought. But it was true that Gustav seemed unable to navigate life's practicalities without her. Here she was in this remote alpine valley, in search of another summerhouse so Gustav could have the peace and privacy to compose again and heal his shattered nerves. Returning to Maiernigg, where Putzi had died, was unthinkable, so they had sold their lakeside villa and now urgently needed to find a new retreat. The more remote, the better as far as Gustav was concerned. While Alma went house hunting, he was conducting in Prague.

*I greatly enjoyed the graham bread that Justine gave me for the journey,* he had written in his most recent letter. *It seems to have the desired effect on my digestion. Please order me another loaf for Sunday evening. I should be back in Vienna by half past seven. I wonder what we'll manage to find for the summer? I leave it entirely up to you, Almscherl.*

The steaming horses labored uphill until the farmhouse came into view. Trenkerhof, as it was called, appeared significantly more rustic than the villa in Maiernigg. A massive old farmhouse with snow mantling the carved wooden eaves. Nestled high on the mountainside, it commanded sweeping views of the valley. What spoke most strongly in its favor was that it was isolated enough from the surrounding farmsteads to give Gustav the solitude and silence he so craved.

Käthe Trenker met them at the gate, her face chapped and ruddy from the mountain wind. Speaking in her heavy dialect, she gave Alma, Mama, and Gucki a tour of the rambling old house with its steep staircases, timber beams, and thick walls. It was primitive to be sure. No electricity. Just tiled ovens for warmth and plenty of candle sconces and paraffin lamps for light.

"I can cook for you, *meine Herrschaften,*" Käthe said. She and her brother, who ran the farm, lived in a separate wing of the house. "All summer we have fresh milk, butter, farmer's cheese, and eggs. In autumn, apples and pears from the orchards. And you, little Fräulein," she said, beaming down at Gucki, "will have barn cats and kittens to play with!"

"I would like to rent this for the summer," Alma said, warming to Käthe's earthy pragmatism. "June through the end of September. Only I must ask if you can hire a carpenter to build a hut at some distance from the main

277

house and barns. My husband requires a composing hut. Of course, we'll pay you for this."

Käthe raised her eyebrows as if she had never heard such an eccentric request in all her life. But then she nodded and said it would be done as soon as the snow had melted.

"Mameli, come!" Seizing her hand, Gucki tugged Alma up the wooden stairs to a cozy little chamber with flowers painted on the tile oven. "*My* room!"

The child leapt on the bed built into a niche in the pine-paneled wall.


On June 10 the Mahlers moved into Trenkerhof. Käthe Trenker's eyes threatened to fall out of her head at the sight of the three pianos they brought with them—one for Gustav's newly built composing hut and two for the main house. After taking a tour of the eleven rooms, Gustav chose the two largest and lightest ones for himself with an air of good cheer, as though completely unaware of his own egotism. Not wasting a moment, he plunged into working on *Das Lied von der Erde,* The Song of the Earth, symphonic settings of eighth-century Chinese lyric poetry by Qian Qi and several other Tang dynasty poets. His first new composition in two years.

Alma hoped that this burst of creativity might signal the return to their happy family summers before they lost Putzi. That the pure mountain air would restore Gustav's serenity and cure him of the hypochondria that had plagued him in New York. Alas, the gorgeous alpine setting seemed to only make it worse. Awakening every morning to the sight of those towering mountains the doctor had forbidden him to climb was torture for Gustav. How was a man who so loved hiking to make his peace with a sedentary existence?

"I feel like an addict deprived of my morphine," he told Alma over a spartan lunch of graham bread, apples, dried fruit, and decaffeinated Kaffee HAG. He stared wistfully at those gleaming peaks.

Her husband's dietary regime was a cause of considerable contention between him and Käthe. He was appalled when Käthe served him farm-fresh butter instead of his favorite butter in the familiar factory wrap. Even more disturbing for Gustav was her semolina pudding made with fresh milk from her cows. Käthe, in turn, was exasperated by his insistence on eating apples out of season. Alma had to order them from Australia. Alma often found herself caught in the middle of Gustav and Käthe's disputes.

"You're always taking *her* side," he fumed. "I suppose you want me to address her as the Honorable Fräulein Käthe now."

"Maybe the esteemed Herr Direktor should find another doctor," Käthe told Alma when they were alone. "One who tells him to calm down, shut his mouth, and go for a quiet stroll."

Before they lost Putzi, their summers in the mountains had been their reprieve, their blessed refuge, but this summer, demons seemed to chase Gustav. Continually anxious about his heart, he carried a pedometer in his pocket to count his steps. He obsessively measured his pulse. No excursion or distraction seemed to lift his gloom. Even the solace of his composing was weighted with foreboding. Though *Das Lied von der Erde* was, technically speaking, his ninth symphony, he had a terror of calling it that.

"Beethoven's Ninth Symphony was his last and then he died," he told Alma.

It seemed the only person who could truly make him happy that summer was Gucki. How he delighted in their daughter's drawings. Her portrait of stout Käthe at the stove stirring her semolina pudding sent Gustav into gales of laughter until he had to wipe the tears from his eyes.

"One day our Gucki's work will hang in a gallery, Almscherl."

The steady stream of guests and old friends who had missed Alma while she was in New York provided a welcome diversion. Mama and Carl came with little Maria. Then Gretl and Wilhelm and their son.

One afternoon in August, much to her surprise, Alma opened the door to find Alex's sister, Mathilde Schoenberg, on the doorstep. Even in this remote valley, Alma had heard the news that Mathilde had abandoned her husband

and two children to run off with the artist Richard Gerstl, a thing that Alma found both shocking and, if she was truly honest with herself, exciting. To be so bold and brave and careless, like a heroine in an opera. Why was it always *painters* that discontented wives fell in love with, Alma began to wonder.

But Mathilde's face was blanched, and her eyes swollen and red as though she hadn't slept in days. The two of them went to sit in the meadow behind the barn, where Gustav couldn't hear them, and Mathilde poured out her confession there.

"I'm going back to Arnold," she said, weeping into her hands. "*If* he takes me back. Richard's threatened to kill himself if I leave, but how can I live without my children?"

"Arnold adores you," Alma said, her arm around her friend's shoulder. "Of course, he'll take you back. Your children need their mother. As for Richard, he's a grown man."

How hypocritical she sounded, dispensing this advice as though she herself had never been tempted to go astray. Alma quivered to recall the euphoria that had exploded inside her when Ossip Gabrilowitsch had almost kissed her in Paris. But Mathilde's dilemma brought home the harsh consequences of adultery, particularly for the straying wife. What if Arnold *didn't* take Mathilde back? What if he wouldn't let her see her own children? Mathilde would be left homeless, trapped in a failing affair with an overwrought lover who was threatening to blow out his brains. Men like Klimt could have affairs as a badge of bohemian freedom, but there was no way Mathilde could come out of this without an awful stain that would haunt her for the rest of her life.

"At least you and Gustav are happy together," Mathilde said, drying her eyes. "He worships you."

Alma tried to smile. *It's the other way around,* she wished she were brave enough to say. *I worship him.* Despite everything, she lived in awe of Gustav. For if she didn't, she'd be forced to confront her most forbidden emotions, the awful fear that she had made the wrong choice. That she would have been far happier with Alex.

• • •

In September Gustav took the train to Prague to begin rehearsals of the world premiere of his Seventh Symphony, which would be performed at the International Exhibition held in honor of Emperor Franz Joseph's seventy-eighth birthday. Alma stayed behind and saw to the packing and the removal of their belongings back to Vienna before they set off again for New York in November.

At Gustav's insistence, Alma joined him in Prague to attend the final rehearsal. Her train was delayed, so she arrived during the final movement. For Alma's benefit, Gustav asked his musicians to play through the entire twenty-minute rondo finale one more time.

The orchestra was rehearsing in a pavilion hall where waiters scurried from table to table with napkins and silverware in preparation for the gala dinner that evening. Gustav had the temerity to ask them to set up a table for her in the middle of the central aisle. Why was Gustav making such a show of her, placing her right in front of the stage? Instead of a gesture of respect, it felt humiliating. The waiters rolled their eyes at her behind her husband's back.

The rehearsal had evidently gone at least an hour over time. Disheveled from the train, Alma felt as worn out as Gustav's musicians, her nerves stretched to their breaking point, her concentration shot. For now she had to prepare for their journey back to New York and find a suitable nanny to replace Lizzie Turner, who had returned to England. A governess equally fluent in German and English would be ideal.

Instead of focusing on the music, Alma's mind kept roving back to Vienna, where Gucki was, staying with Mama once again. The little girl had a sore throat. Mama had assured her it was a trifling thing, not a serious illness, but Alma couldn't keep herself from worrying. How swiftly Putzi had succumbed when she and her mother thought there was no danger.

After the finale had finished, Gustav joined her at the table. He was so worried that this birthday celebration for the emperor was the worst possible venue to premiere such a long and challenging symphony. He was petrified the critics would tear apart his Seventh the way they had done with his Sixth.

"Almschi, look at these tables and linen napkins! All they want to do is stuff themselves with schnitzel and listen to Strauss waltzes!"

This time Alma simply couldn't find the right words or reassurances. She was hungry and tired, and her mask slipped. Not the adoring wife and helpmeet who worshipped him but a twenty-nine-year-old woman who felt the tatters of her youth slipping away all too quickly. Lilith roiled inside her, seething with resentment for her husband who either ignored her, patronized her, or positioned her on some lofty pedestal not of her choosing. All depending on *his* mood. His level of neediness. His fixation with death and solitude and his career above all else had worn her to the quick. If only she were still that twenty-two-year-old girl he had married, that young woman overflowing with emotional intensity. Where had it all gone? She felt her eyes glaze over just to hear his torrent of words—all about himself. *I can't go on like this. What does he want from me?* Why couldn't he be this earnest and attentive when she needed him?

"Don't you like it, Almschi?"

"Of course, I like it," she said, aware of the orchestra members and music journalists hovering around them. Gawking and eavesdropping. She felt like a zoo animal on display. "You're a genius." She feared her words sounded as wooden as the planks beneath her aching feet.

Out of the corner of her eye, Alma noticed one young journalist studying her with an expression of undisguised contempt. She could almost read his thoughts. *She's a monster, a philistine! She doesn't even understand his music.*

# 35

||||||||||||||||||||||||||

Snow drifted down, crystaline and perfect, outside the windows of the Savoy Hotel on Fifth Avenue and Fifty-Ninth Street. In their ninth-floor suite, Alma and Gustav hosted their New Year's Eve soiree with none other than the world's greatest tenor, Enrico Caruso, who lived on the tenth floor.

Caruso, thirty-six and achingly handsome, put a record on the gramophone and led Alma in a tango, teaching her the steps of the exotic Argentinian dance that was all the rage. She felt so passionate and alive, her new evening gown of scarlet silk appliqued with serpentine embroideries in metallic thread flickering like flames in the candlelight. Though she supposed that both her gown and this dance were far too flamboyant for an expectant mother—she was three months gone and not yet showing—she surrendered to the extravagant moves, almost swooning in the tenor's arms when he dipped her low enough for her coiffure to graze the floor before he swung her back up again. Laughing in pleasure, she kicked her heels high while her guests looked on. The venerable Polish coloratura soprano Marcella Sembrich. The renowned sinologist Friedrich Hirth. And Ossip Gabrilowitsch, who was also staying at the Savoy.

Ossip's eyes burned into Alma, raising the blood to her cheeks. It was almost too thrilling—dancing the tango with a dashing Italian while being ogled by a smoldering young Russian. She wondered if Gustav even noticed. At least her husband knew she was pregnant this time around.

Then, at the very climax of their tango, four-and-a-half-year-old Gucki, who was supposed to be in bed, upstaged Caruso when she jumped out from her hiding place, a stack of opera scores that rose higher than her head. In her white flannel nightgown, the little girl whirled and twirled across the parquet floor, mimicking the tango's moves while everyone laughed.

"Brava!" Caruso cried, lifting her up and planting a kiss on her cheek before passing her to Alma. "Isadora Duncan herself couldn't be more graceful."

"She loves to be the center of attention," Gustav said drily. "Just like her mother."

Alma smarted and carried her daughter back to bed. She had given their new nanny, Lizzie Turner's younger sister, Maud, the night off. Twenty-two-year-old Maud was undoubtedly off celebrating with the other young nannies and governesses residing in the Savoy.

After Alma had finally succeeded in coaxing Gucki to sleep, cuddled up under the quilts with her stuffed rabbit, she rejoined the party. There was a swirling mélange of conversation in German and Italian. Though she and Gustav lived half the year in New York, they moved in circles that were as solidly European as the world they had left behind.

Gustav's second season at the Met had been fraught with conflict. The new director, Giulio Gatti-Casazza, had brought over his own star conductor, Arturo Toscanini, who had insisted on directing this season's premiere of *Tristan und Isolde,* stealing the limelight from Gustav, who had spent months painstakingly staging and rehearsing the opera. Though Gustav was contractually bound to finish this season at the Met, he did not intend to return the following year. Instead, he'd signed a contract with the New York Philharmonic. Three weeks ago he had conducted the North American premiere of his Second Symphony at Carnegie Hall. Though poorly publicized and attended, it had been rapturously received. The orchestra had given Gustav a standing ovation.

"To your success, my friend!" Caruso lifted his glass to Gustav. "I much prefer you to that Milanese peacock! Why, Toscanini is so vain, he puts all the female divas to shame." Caruso playfully kissed Marcella Sembrich's hand.

Much to Alma's relief, Gustav seemed more confident about his health lately. He took Gucki for walks through snowy Central Park and sometimes walked to work.

"Let Gatti-Casazza do his worst," Gustav said. "Meanwhile, I'll take all the money the Met pays me so I can spend the summer composing in peace."

He *will be in the mountains composing,* Alma thought. *While* I'll *be at Mama's, having the baby.* The child was due in June. They had given up their Vienna apartment in the Auenbruggergasse, and their furniture was in storage. She was already dreading the eight-day Atlantic crossing and hoped it wouldn't be too rough.

"To your music, Herr Direktor!" Ossip raised his glass.

They gathered around the grand piano to hear Gustav play from his newly completed *Das Lied von der Erde* while Sembrich sang. Alma, despite her many uncertainties, thought her heart would break from her love of Gustav and his artistry. These Chinese poems he had set to music were true songs of the *earth,* as opposed to his early symphonies of heavenly transcendence. The lyrics were a bittersweet ode to the transience of mortal existence coupled with the sensual ecstasy of being alive. The second movement, "Der Einsame im Herbst," The Lonely One in Autumn, gave particular voice to her deepest yearning.

"I've never heard anything so beautiful and sad," Alma said, when the music had ended. "You can't separate its sadness from its beauty."

"Just like life itself," Gustav said. "When I was young, I used to romanticize death. But now, when I can taste my own mortality, I've never been less certain of any kind of afterlife. What if this is all there is?"

Alma stared at him, her throat thick with emotion to hear him speak so frankly of his deepest fears. How she wished they were alone together. She would wrap her arms around him and hold him. His openhearted tenderness would be heaven enough for her. But she stepped into the background once more while Friedrich Hirth proceeded to unroll a Chinese scroll painting on the dining table.

"Herr Direktor, I brought this as an homage to your *Das Lied von der Erde,*" Hirth said. "A visual tableau of the poetry of impermanence."

Alma leaned close to examine this exquisite artwork. A silver river wound like a liquid dragon through green hills. The river rolled past peasants toiling in their rice paddies. Past fishermen mending their nets. Past artisans firing

285

their pots. Past wandering monks with their begging bowls and merchants returning from their expeditions. Past a teahouse high on a bluff where mandarins were taking their refreshments while a courtesan played music on some exotic instrument. Human beings, from the lowliest to the most exalted, lived out their short, measured lives while that river flowed into eternity.

The image filled Alma with an unspeakable melancholy, a sense of emptiness devouring her from within. *How vain and foolish our little lives are.* Ossip looked up from the scroll, his eyes soft. She lowered her head so no one could see her blush. Ossip had hardly said a word to her all night, but his every glance spoke volumes. *He's still in love with me.* The memory of their encounter in Paris sent her pulse tripping.

Hirth rolled up his priceless scroll just as the clock chimed midnight.

"Happy 1909!" Alma called out to her guests. "May it be filled with happiness!"

"The Year of the Rooster!" Hirth cried.

They ran to the windows to see the sky explode with fireworks and then exchanged New Year's kisses. Caruso kissed Alma a bit longer and more greedily than he should have—he was Neapolitan, after all. But it was Ossip's much more bashful kiss that sent an electric charge through her. She had to laugh and push him away lest she betray her deep hunger and need.

His face bright red, Ossip sat at the piano. "I dedicate this to our beautiful hostess."

He played Brahms's Intermezzo in A Minor, one of her favorites. Alma closed her eyes, allowing the music to carry her away to a place beyond sadness.

Afterward, her guests said their good-byes. Gustav excused himself and went to bed. But Ossip lingered. Left alone together, he and Alma sat on the window seat and watched the falling snow.

"They say there will be a blizzard tomorrow," Ossip said.

Alma shivered. "American weather terrifies me. Blizzards and tornadoes and hurricanes! Vienna was never so extreme. But you're Russian. You're not afraid of winter storms."

286

His eyes moved over her face. "I think it's more than the weather that frightens you, Alma. I thought you were going to start crying when you looked at that Chinese painting. The only time you came alive tonight was when you were dancing with Caruso." Ossip sounded palpably jealous, which made her smile in spite of herself.

"That's not true," she said. "I was very, very happy when you played Brahms for me."

"I'm so glad. I just wish I had the power to make you happy for longer than the duration of one piano movement."

She swallowed, floundering.

"I think we must be brave enough," he said, "to seize whatever chance of joy life brings us." He stared into her eyes with unmasked love.

Alma quivered. The best thing would be to cut him off now before he said too much. Before either of them transgressed the bounds of propriety. She rose shakily to her feet while he remained seated, gazing up at her.

"Alma, I tried to forget you. It's not right what I feel for you. I idolize your husband, but I . . ."

It seemed he couldn't go on speaking. Instead, he kissed her hand. And then the inside of her wrist. Alma's knees went weak.

"If I respected your husband any less, I would elope with you." His young face was incandescent.

Had Gustav ever looked at her like that? *I married the wrong man. Ossip would support my composing.* She imagined the two of them clasping hands and leaping out the ninth-story window. Instead of falling to their deaths, they would float through the snowy sky above this enchanted city with its constellations of electric lights. But the reality that she was three months pregnant brought her crashing back to earth.

"No." Alma drew away, crossing her arms in front of herself. "I could never do that to my husband."

Ossip rose from the window seat. "May I at least offer you my love from afar? My fealty? You the lady in the tower and I your knight errant?" His eyes shone.

She breathed in his smell of tobacco and sandalwood. With his intelligence and intensity, his sheer devotion, this man was irresistible. Her thoughts roved back to the Chinese painting and her own constrained and truncated life. *What if this is all there is?* She couldn't say for certain if she moved toward Ossip or he toward her. But their kiss engulfed her, that slow-burning consummation of their almost kiss in Paris. Never had Alma thought that a kiss could be as powerfully erotic as lovemaking itself, inflaming every part of her body, saturating her in bliss. She thought she would fall gasping over the edge of ecstasy. Finally, she tore herself away.

"Goodnight, Ossip," she said, breathing as hard as if she had raced up nine flights of stairs.

"I love you, Alma Maria."

Alma walked him to the door. After one last breathless kiss, he wrenched himself away and stole out. Alma locked the door behind him, then leaned against the solid oak and swayed, savoring the aftermath of their kisses still burning on her mouth. The taste of him on her tongue. She tiptoed to her room. *All night I shall dream I'm sleeping in Ossip's arms.*

She stifled a shriek to see Gustav sitting on her bed, his face haggard. "Do you care to explain your infidelity?"

He seemed to regard her as though she were Jezebel incarnate, quaking before him in her scarlet dress.

"I wasn't unfaithful," she said, shocking herself with the force of her anger that rose stronger than shame. *If you hadn't left me feeling so lonely and unloved, this never would have happened.*

"I overheard your entire conversation. Do you think I'm stupid? He wanted to run away with you."

"But I told him no!" Her voice rose and cracked. "I told him my place is with you."

"You kissed him! I can see it on your face. That glow like you had when you were a girl."

When Gustav was angry, he frightened her. Those throbbing zigzag veins like lightning bolts on his temples. He had become the wrathful Zeus.

She covered her face and wept. "Of course, I kissed him. It's New Year's Eve! Would you deprive me of his friendship?"

"If you call that *friendship,* you're as big a child as Gucki." With that parting remark, Gustav walked out of the room.

Alma couldn't sleep that night, could only huddle at the window and watch the falling snow blanket the expanse of Central Park. *So white and pure. Unsullied.* Unlike the passions inside her fractured heart.

# 36

||||||||||||||||||||||||||

I n February 1909, Gustav's appointment with the New York Philharmonic
was officially announced. He had a committee of women to thank for the
ease by which he could make this transition just as his relationship with the
Metropolitan Opera had turned sour. Mrs. Minnie Untermyer and Mrs.
Mary Seney Sheldon had raised more than $100,000 to fund a newly formed
Philharmonic worthy of Gustav's vision and genius.

These ladies invited Alma as their guest of honor to a gala luncheon at
the New York Women's Club, an immense structure designed in the style
of an Italian palazzo with marble floors, arched loggias and balconies, high-
beamed ceilings and massive chandeliers. There was even a ladies-only swimming pool and gymnasium in the annex. When Alma stepped into the grand
entrance, Mrs. Seney Sheldon greeted her with air kisses and showed her to
her seat at the head table. These women were so elegant, flawlessly coiffured
as only rich American ladies could be, not a strand out of place. Alma felt
positively shabby in her best tweed suit and crepe-de-chine blouse. Even her
pearls felt drab compared to their diamonds and gold. While the waiter filled
their crystal glasses with punch au kirsch, Alma endeavored to speak her best
English while she answered the ladies' questions about her husband. Of her
own thwarted musical dreams she didn't dare speak.

As kind and hospitable as these ladies were, Alma had to admit she was
intimidated. What a debt Gustav owed them. What if he, with his quirks
and stubborn egotism, managed to alienate them—who would come to
their rescue then?

Alma's halting attempt at small talk was interrupted when a latecomer galloped in with a ricochet of boot heels on the marble floor. A petite woman in an ill-fitting coat and a skirt that appeared the worse for wear.

"Howdy, ladies!" she called out. "Sorry I'm late. My dang bicycle had a flat tire."

Had this transpired in Vienna, such a person would be most unceremoniously shown to the door or at the very least snubbed. But the rich society ladies rushed from their places to swarm around this woman, greeting her with much acclaim. Following their example, Alma went to shake her hand.

"Mrs. Alma Mahler, this is our other guest of honor," Mrs. Untermyer said. "Miss Natalie Curtis. She's an ethnomusicologist and lived for years with the Hopi Indians in Arizona. She's written two books on Indian culture, and she's also a composer."

Alma felt a rush in her head halfway between envy and blinding awe. Meanwhile, Miss Curtis pumped Alma's hand enthusiastically. She was, Alma noted, not even wearing gloves. Her mousy hair was windblown and scraped back in a careless bun.

"Frau Direktor Mahler, what a pleasure to meet you," Miss Curtis said, in flawless German. "I'm a huge fan of your husband. I studied piano in Bayreuth with his great admirer, the late Anton Seidl. My Hopi name is Tawi-Mana, by the way. That means Song Maid."

Alma's mouth opened as wide as a fishbowl. *How truly democratic America is!* The wealthiest and most glittering ladies in New York bowed down in humble respect before Miss Curtis's brilliance and originality.

"You lived with Indians?" Alma asked in English, out of consideration for the other ladies. "In Arizona?" She could scarcely imagine such a thing.

Mrs. Seney Sheldon laughed affectionately. "Not only did our dear Miss Curtis camp in the desert for six years, she brought an Apache chief to a party at President Roosevelt's home in Oyster Bay. She and the chief cornered Mr. Roosevelt to discuss tribal land rights."

Alma stared at Miss Curtis in abject wonder. In Austria there were New Women like the Conrat sisters who studied at the university and pursued a life in the arts, but never had Alma imagined that a woman could be *this* free, *this* intrepid, *this* bold. *Only in America.* Although Alma was officially here on Gustav's behalf to sing his praises to his wealthy patrons, she found herself entranced by Miss Curtis's every word. Four years older than Alma, Natalie Curtis came from an established New York family who were friends with the Roosevelts. She had studied at the National Conservatory of Music of America to become a concert pianist, but at the age of twenty-five, she visited Arizona and fell in love with the Hopi culture. And thus she had dedicated her career to helping preserve Hopi music, recording it on wax cylinders.

"Do you know that the Bureau of Indian Affairs forbade these people to speak their own language and sing their own songs?" Miss Curtis asked, her brown eyes flashing in righteous anger.

Alma shook her head. To be honest, she'd never given much thought to the world outside Europe and New York.

"So Miss Curtis browbeat Mr. Roosevelt into changing that law, too," Mrs. Seney Sheldon said, in a tone of frank amazement.

"Now I'm studying black folk songs," Miss Curtis said. "The music of former slaves. I want to see black people performing in Carnegie Hall. Just like your husband, Mrs. Mahler."

Alma wondered how Gustav would react to that.

"Mrs. Untermyer told me you are also a composer," she said, hoping Miss Curtis wouldn't hear the plaintiveness in her voice.

"Why, yes, ma'am, I certainly am. Shall I play you something, Mrs. Mahler?"

Though they were in the midst of their luncheon with the white-gloved ladies delicately picking away at their quail on toast, Miss Curtis swept herself off to the piano to play a piece of haunting beauty. Alma had never heard anything like it anywhere—it sounded as radically innovative as anything Arnold Schoenberg had composed. Why wasn't Natalie Curtis's music being performed in Carnegie Hall? *Perhaps, with these ladies' intercession, it will be.*

"It's drawn from an Indian theme," Miss Curtis said, when she returned to the table to polish off her quail, which she ate with her hands. "A Pueblo corn-grinding song."

She was so confident, so assured, so absolutely convinced that her vocation could make a difference in the world. *She doesn't need to flirt with men at parties just to feel alive.* Alma wished she could yank off her own skin and step inside Miss Curtis's. *This is what a woman might accomplish if she believes in herself. What I might have achieved had I only been brave enough to stand strong without a man.*

"We white people have it all wrong," Miss Curtis told Alma. "We spend half our lives acquiring things, then spend the other half taking care of those things. But what good are *things* if we don't have a chance to truly live?"

Alma could only nod in agreement. The gulf between what she had and what she yearned for had never seemed greater. This August she would turn thirty. *When, if ever, am I going to truly come alive?*

"A chief once told me that white people's faces are lined with the tracks of hunted animals," Miss Curtis said, while mopping up her plate with her bread roll.

Alma shifted uncomfortably in her chair and thought of Gustav's drawn and furious face when he had accused her of infidelity. Those furrows in his face that only deepened with each passing year of their marriage.

"Mrs. Mahler, are you feeling all right?" Miss Curtis's eyebrows lifted in concern. "You've gone awfully pale."

Alma felt a twinge in her belly, which she rested her hand on, the universal sign language of pregnancy—that mysterious and terrifying frontier into which the adventurous Miss Curtis had never set foot.

At half past four, Alma returned to the Savoy, where Gucki was drawing pictures and Miss Turner the Younger, as Gustav liked to call her, was knitting for the new baby. The sight of those little booties made Alma wrench away. The twinge in her womb had turned into cramps. She thought she would split in two.

Not even bothering to unpin her hat, Alma collapsed on her bed and lay on her side, hugging her knees to her belly. *No, no, no.* Surely this couldn't be happening to her again. And yet she felt the gush between her legs that she knew to be blood. Would Gustav blame her for this, too? *What's wrong with me?* It was as though her flesh had risen up in sullen defiance, rejecting her husband's seed. *I'm no longer capable of having babies. Only ghosts.* Alma bit the corner of the pillow to keep herself from screaming while Maud Turner and poor frightened Gucki hovered in the doorway.

This time Dr. Fraenkel gave Alma laudanum, which she found far more amenable than strychnine. Leaving the broken vessel of her body behind, her spirit roved free over the red Arizona desert where Miss Curtis sat recording Pueblo women singing as they ground their maize. That sound faded, and Alma's own music surged through her brain like a tidal wave. She was unmarried and free. She could do anything. Clad in a virginal white dress, she performed her lieder at Carnegie Hall while the ladies from the New York Women's Club cheered her on. Except it wasn't enough for her to be single like Miss Curtis. *I want it all. My music, love, sex, and children. What I want doesn't exist.*

But after the laudanum had worn off, she reflected how Mrs. Seney Sheldon and Mrs. Untermyer were married with children *and* they were fiercely ambitious. They were giants, shaping the cultural landscape of America's leading metropolis with their new Philharmonic. They held her husband's professional future in their white-gloved hands. And they held up a mirror to her weakness. To how she had given away every last scrap of her power.

After a thorough and excruciating examination, Dr. Fraenkel proclaimed that there was nothing physically wrong with Alma that prevented her from carrying a pregnancy to term.

"I suspect the origins of your wife's recurring spontaneous abortions lie in hysteria," the doctor proclaimed to Gustav in the next room while Alma lay in bed and grimaced at the ceiling. She thought her shame would completely obliterate her.

In terms of physical health, Alma recovered soon enough. But she felt like an empty shell on two legs. Despair stuck to her like pitch. The utter hopelessness. No one had ever warned her that grief is cumulative. That loss after loss—first Putzi and then two miscarriages—would snowball into an impossible weight that would crush her. Smash her bones to splinters. Any little thing could set her off in floods of tears. The sight of a pregnant woman with that beautiful glow on her face. Or if Gustav smiled or spoke warmly to Maud, who was blameless of any indecency.

Unlike Putzi's death, the miscarriages were invisible losses, which made them all the harder to bear. No funeral cortege or mourning garb marked her as bereaved so that others might be extra gentle with her. No, Gustav expected her to carry out her duties as before, attending his performances and guarding his precious privacy. Dashing outside to bribe some organ grinder to go away lest the noise disturb her husband. It had become too much. She could no longer keep up the façade of holding it all together. For just as he had refused to talk about Putzi's death, he never spoke to her about her miscarriages. Yet his unspoken blame thickened the air between them. He seemed to think that these failures of hers—spontaneous abortions!— were something appalling that must be hidden away like her blood-soaked nightgown.

But Natalie Curtis was kindness itself, stopping by to visit every afternoon with cakes and cornbread she had baked herself. The blessed woman didn't seem the least bit fazed by Alma's despondency.

"Don't blame yourself, Alma," she said. "Half the married ladies I know have had at least one miscarriage. Probably your own mother, too."

Her eyes filling, Alma nodded, remembering when Mama had confessed about losing a baby before becoming pregnant with Maria. Natalie's solicitude was as fortifying as her golden cornbread spread with thick sweet butter and honey. At long last, Alma had a true friend in this country. A confidante like no other.

To distract Alma from her grief, Natalie played Hopi music and her own compositions on the piano. Then one day, when Gustav was out, Alma played four of her songs for Natalie. The two of them sang in harmony.

"Why did you stop composing? These are good enough to be performed at Carnegie Hall."

"My husband required it," Alma said under her breath, her voice barely louder than a whisper.

Natalie seemed absolutely livid. "If any man tried to take my music away from me, why I'd—" She glanced at Gucki watching them from the open doorway and stopped short. "I can't say what I'd do in front of an impressionable child because it involves too many cuss words. But honestly, Alma, what's stopping you? What can he do if you just compose anyway? Chop off your hands?"

Alma could only laugh drily and change the subject. What could a free spirit like Natalie understand of marital sacrifice? Of Gustav's coldness?

After Natalie left, Alma went to Gustav's desk to read his volume of Novalis's poetry. *I will find one perfect poem and set it to music. Just one song.* Perhaps this would keep her from tipping off the edge of despair. Instead, she came across an unfinished letter written in her husband's hand. She would have ignored it had she not seen her own name. It was addressed to her stepfather.

> *Alma is very well. About her present state she has doubtlessly written to you herself. She has been relieved of her burden. But this time she actually regrets it.*

For a long moment, she couldn't breathe. Black stars swam before her eyes. His words sank in slowly, as insidious as poison. How could he even think she had been glad to miscarry? How could he misread her and blame her so? To think he could be this heartless. Was he blind and deaf to her inner torment? Not even Natalie's compassion could ease this pain.

Alma crumpled at her husband's desk and began to write a letter. *Mama, help me. I can't go on.*

# 37

||||||||||||||||||||||||

I t was simply no good that Gustav Mahler's wife should be seen to suffer from frequent bouts of nervous debilitation. Mama sailed to New York to take charge of the household until it was time for Alma and her family to return to Europe. At least Alma didn't have to explain her grief to her mother, who knew firsthand what an awful thing a miscarriage is.

"You must devote the summer to your recovery," Mama said. "But try to forgive Gustav for his blunderings. What do men understand of such things?"

A rest cure was in order, but Alma had to bide her time. First, they stopped in Paris, where Gustav, at Carl's behest, sat ten fitful, fidgeting days for Auguste Rodin, who sculpted his bust in bronze—comparing Gustav's visage to Mozart's, no less. Then it was off to Trenkerhof in the High Puster Valley. Only after installing her husband in their summer home and making certain everything was in order could Alma board the train to the sanatorium. Gustav escorted her, for by now her nerves were so shattered that he didn't seem to trust her to make the journey alone. She wept in open daylight and could scarcely sleep.

After the four-hour rail journey, they arrived at Löweneck, a thermal spa nestled in the Alps just west of Trento. Mama had arranged for Alma to spend four weeks here. What better place for a nerve-sick woman to revive her spirits? Empress Elisabeth had taken the waters here, as had the king of Belgium. This elegant clinic was enclosed by fifteen hectares of parkland graced with Caucasian spruces, gingkoes, and North American maple trees. Gucki and Miss Turner would be staying here as well. Gustav, after all, needed his solitude to work unburdened by domestic responsibilities.

"Be a good girl and do as the doctors say," he told Alma, in what sounded like forced good cheer. They stood before the white spa hotel with its geranium-bedecked wrought-iron balconies. "Absolutely no coffee or alcohol. You must follow the regime for at least two weeks before you'll see any benefit."

Her husband seemed to believe that if only she adhered to a life as ascetic as his own all her ills would simply melt away. Through her tears, she searched his eyes for some spark of warmth to melt through the icy wall that had reared up between them. But even when he kissed her good-bye, she felt he wasn't truly present with her. Perhaps her nerve sickness had left him at wit's end and he no longer knew what to do with her. His eyes were distant and distracted, as though he heard not her voice but the notes of a new symphony bubbling up inside him. He seemed itching to be away from this sanatorium and back in his composing hut.

"I'll write to you every day, Almscherl," he promised. After hugging and kissing their daughter, he rushed to catch his train.

Alma submitted to the diet of lettuce and buttermilk. Rising at dawn, she dressed in the regulation linen shift before walking barefoot for an hour through the gardens while the grass was still chilly and wet with dew. She performed calisthenics. Afterward, still in her shift, she repaired to the baths where the *Bademeister* hosed her with hot and cold water. She drank liters of the *Heilwasser* with its high arsenic and iron content that the doctors swore was therapeutic. In the afternoon, she spent time with her daughter and admired Gucki's drawings. Five-year-old Gucki was still innocent enough to believe that a girl's talent mattered in this world.

The days with their fixed routines were bearable, but evenings after dinner were an agony. That was when Alma's darkest thoughts came home to roost like a murder of sooty crows. Left on her own without distraction, she could only brood on Gustav's seeming indifference to her pain. All her wasted creative potential. *I gave up my music for this?*

Standing listlessly on her balcony, Alma looked down at the fashionable people gathered in the garden below. In their evening dress, they glittered beneath the Chinese lanterns. Their laughter and gaiety sank knives into her heart. To see those carefree Viennese and Milanese, one might think this so-called rest cure was a lark, an excuse for bored countesses to flirt with young bankers. To enjoy a *Liebelei,* a lighthearted flirtation or even a full-blown love affair. Alma had never felt more sexless. Unloved and unlovable. As dried up as a dead leaf. After discovering Gustav's letter to Carl about her supposed abortions, she had taken to locking her husband out of her bedroom. *Another miscarriage would kill me.* Yet, despite all this, she would have fallen straight into Gustav's arms if only he could show her that he still cherished her.

None of her doctors seemed capable of understanding her discontent. On the surface, Gustav was as dutiful a husband as any woman could ask for. True to his word, he wrote to her every day, but his letters discussed abstract topics in his schoolmasterly tone, as though she were not his wife but his backward pupil. About her current malaise he had written:

> *The meaning, my dear Almschi, of all that has happened to you, of all that has been laid on you, is a necessity for the growth of the soul and the forging of the personality.*

As if he believed that she, at the age of nearly thirty, still did not possess a fully formed personality, much less a soul. He sat in judgment of her like an Old Testament patriarch.

> *Why such a sad letter today, Almschi? You complain of being lonely, but Gucki is with you and Miss Turner. You're surrounded by people. Just think of my solitary existence here, day in and day out.*

Even at this, her lowest ebb, he penned her letter after letter devoid of any sense of intimacy or tenderness. They could have been written by anyone.

• • •

Only when Alma stopped replying did Gustav become worried enough to announce that he was coming to visit.

When he stepped off the train, she failed to recognize him. He had gone to the barber but had been too absorbed in his newspaper to pay attention to what the barber was doing. As a result, his beautiful black hair that she so loved was shorn as close as a convict's. His strange appearance frightened their daughter, who burst into tears. To prove he was still her papa, Gustav sang to Gucki and covered her in kisses.

Bad haircut notwithstanding, Gustav seemed jovial and relaxed. "Almschi, I've had a most productive few weeks. I finished editing *Das Lied von der Erde* and found a publisher for the Eighth Symphony. Except I couldn't manage to start work on anything new."

As it transpired, he refused to even set foot in his composing hut until Alma returned.

"It's simply no good, Almschi, without you there to stand guard. The farm apprentices keep leaping over my fence and banging on the windows if I try to work in there. They even let the baby pigs and goats loose outside my hut. Can you imagine trying to compose in that racket?"

Of Alma's own emotional state, he made no inquiry. Indeed, his outburst left her feeling as though her weeks at the sanatorium were a selfish indulgence. He needed her to get on with his work, and if this need wasn't exactly the love and attention she so craved, at least it was better than his former chilliness.

Since the spa didn't seem to be doing her much good and since Gucki had developed diarrhea from the ghastly diet, Alma packed her things. She, Gucki, and Miss Turner accompanied Gustav on the train to their summer home.

The first morning Alma was back at Trenkerhof, Gustav joyfully retreated to his composing hut. As though her very presence filled him with inspiration and optimism, he made swift progress on his new Ninth Symphony. His composing, in turn, seemed to rejuvenate him and lend him renewed physical confidence. They went on hikes together once more, up those meadows thick with monkshood and lady's mantle. Alma in her broad-brimmed hat, her walking stick in hand to negotiate the steeply twisting stony trails. Gustav with his woolen jacket slung over his walking cane that he carried jauntily over his shoulder. He glowed with an almost boyish animation.

"Almschi, I'm going to include a tuba fart in my *Ländler* movement. My secret revenge on those boneheaded farmhands!"

She laughed while trying to ignore the pang inside — her unhealed loneliness and hurt. Her longing for him to open his eyes and truly *see* her. *At least here at his side I have a purpose,* she tried to console herself. *A vocation of sorts.* The custodian of her husband's artistic solitude.

# 38

||||||||||||||||||||||||||

In autumn it was back to America, where Gustav would embark on his first season as director of the New York Philharmonic. The Atlantic crossing was exceptionally stormy. While her seasick husband locked himself in his cabin, Alma tended their seasick daughter. Yet as ill as Gustav had been on the ship, when they arrived in New York on October 20, he plunged straight into rehearsals of Beethoven's *Eroica,* which was to premiere on November 4.

To live in New York was to live life twice as fast as in the Old World. The stately Viennese waltz was swept aside for the frenetic, syncopated rhythms of ragtime. Alma worried how Gustav's workload would affect his heart, though he insisted he was up to the challenge. For wasn't having his own orchestra a dream come true?

While Gustav was rehearsing, Alma cut newspaper clippings of the reviews singing his praises. New York throbbed with excitement about the Philharmonic and Gustav Mahler, Europe's most prestigious conductor. She smiled at the poetic justice that even after Toscanini had connived to drive her husband away from the Metropolitan Opera Gustav effortlessly outshone his rival. The critics crowed how Gustav's brilliance would elevate the Philharmonic to dizzying heights. At last, New York would have an orchestra to rival the renowned Boston Symphony.

Such was her husband's celebrity that Alma couldn't even walk across the Savoy lobby without being accosted by at least one breathless admirer of Gustav's. A timid lady even begged Alma for her autograph. Every day brought a flood of cards and letters from their American friends and acquaintances. To be foreign in this country was not just to be other but also exotic and exalted. Sought after. Each afternoon, Alma sorted through the pile of invitations to parties and receptions, trying to select the ones that would be the most enchanting or the most impolitic to refuse.

The president of the New York Philharmonic invited them to dinner. This being America, the president was a woman — Gustav's great patron, Mrs. Mary Seney Sheldon.

Arriving at their hostess's Murray Hill mansion, Alma and Gustav ascended the oval staircase to the *piano nobile,* the noble floor, with its grand dining room. Walls of veined Cipollino marble imported from Switzerland were set off with mosaics of dolphins and nereids. Instead of a chandelier, three great lamps with alabaster shades hung from antique brass chains. On one end of the room was a fireplace big enough to roast an ox in. On the other end was a bow-shaped minstrels' gallery where a brass quintet played — Gustav raised his eyebrows at this bit of American ostentation. The ceiling boasted a fresco of Ulysses defying Circe.

Dinner parties started early in America. Alma was shown to her seat at precisely seven fifteen. When a liveried manservant came to fill the Waterford crystal goblets, he poured lemon cordial instead of wine. A woman of good Methodist stock, Mrs. Seney Sheldon shunned alcohol.

"Let's lift our glasses to Mr. Mahler," their hostess said, shimmering in her sapphire blue gown and diamond *collier.* "Who has promised to build the greatest orchestra America has ever known!"

*No more Herr Direktor then,* Alma thought, glancing surreptitiously at her husband to gauge his reaction. Just plain Mr. Mahler. No differently addressed than a cab driver or shopkeeper.

So many eminent guests were present, Alma didn't know where to look. Seated across from her was Sara Delano Roosevelt, a cousin of the former president's, and farther down the table were her son, Franklin, and his wife, Eleanor, who was deep in conversation with Natalie Curtis. How Alma wished she was sitting close enough to join their discussion. Instead, she exchanged small talk with her host, Mr. George Rumsey Sheldon, a banker.

304

It was fortunate that Otto Kahn was sitting beside Alma and entertained her with pithy asides in German.

"Sheldon's a bigwig in the Republican Party," Kahn whispered. "That's why the Roosevelts are so cozy with him. He helped get their cousin elected."

"Mrs. Mahler, you and your husband must visit the family estate in Oyster Bay," Sara Roosevelt said. "We would love to show you around."

"It would be a great honor to meet the former president," Alma said, delighted at the prospect.

"I'm afraid Teddy's off in Africa at the moment," the lady said. "Big-game hunting, don't you know."

Everyone turned at the sound of Mrs. Seney Sheldon tapping on her water glass. "Ladies and gentlemen, Mr. Mahler will now discuss his upcoming program for our beloved Philharmonic." Mrs. Seney Sheldon spoke of the orchestra with a possessive pride that was almost maternal. Alma understood that their hostess traced her ancestry back to the American Revolution. The daughter of a great philanthropist who had founded Methodist Hospital in Brooklyn, Mrs. Seney Sheldon seemed intent on leaving behind her own legacy of enduring cultural significance.

All eyes were on Gustav, who rose from his chair to address the twenty-odd guests seated at the table. Alma watched him explain how the forty-seven concerts he would direct that season would be divided into four categories. A Beethoven cycle. Subscription concerts for their dedicated supporters. Popular concerts on Sunday afternoons to draw in larger crowds. And a series of ambitious "historical" concerts, highlighting the work of obscure and seldom-performed eighteenth-century composers such as Händel. The repertoire would be wide-ranging, featuring everything from Schubert and Tchaikovsky to startlingly modern works, including Richard Strauss's *Till Eulenspiegels lustige Streiche.*

"I will be introducing new composers never before performed in New York, such as Claude Debussy," Gustav said. "The purpose of the Philharmonic is not just to entertain but also to educate."

Alma covertly scanned the polite but mildly skeptical faces. Everyone present possessed a degree of intellectual sophistication—nearly every man at the table had studied at either Harvard or Yale. It looked as though they didn't believe they required further edification.

"But Mr. Mahler," one of the bankers said. "What if the public doesn't want to pay good money to listen to some unknown oratorio by an obscure composer? If we lose too much money, this project will fail."

"Part of our purpose is to take artistic risks," Mrs. Seney Sheldon said, coming to Gustav's rescue. "New York has never seen anything like this."

"Mr. Mahler, what's your opinion of American music?" Natalie asked. "Some European composers, such as your Claude Debussy, have been influenced by ragtime. Would you ever consider including *our* music in your repertoire?"

Had Gustav ever dreamed he would be interrogated by a female ethnomusicologist, Alma wondered. Natalie's challenge was so passionate and earnest, it reminded Alma of when she herself had confronted Gustav all those years ago at Berta Zuckerkandl's party, demanding to know why the Herr Direktor had given Alex's ballet such short shrift. With her, Gustav had been disarmingly erudite and charming. But obliged to reply to Natalie in English, Gustav was at his most stilted.

"My dear Miss Curtis, I do not think this Negro idiom you call ragtime is something for Carnegie Hall. All cultures must take their time to evolve. It took Northern Europe a thousand years to evolve from barbarism to civilization. So I think it is fair to say that your ragtime has not evolved to the degree of European classical music even though some composers, such as Debussy and Satie, have experimented with primitive African influences."

Natalie's face turned as stony as the marble walls. It looked as though she was on the brink of some stinging reply but, out of respect for Mrs. Seney Sheldon, decided to hold her tongue. Alma, her face burning, stared at the uneaten beef Wellington on her plate. The only one to break the icy silence that followed was Otto Kahn.

"My wife and I think ragtime is just swell, don't we, Addie? We even dance the cakewalk on occasion. Are you calling us *primitive,* Gustav?" Kahn laughed warmly, as though to wash away any lingering hostility. "No, of course, you didn't really mean that. You're just understandably partial to the great music of Europe that you know best, which we're all going to enjoy during this concert season. To Mrs. Seney Sheldon and Gustav Mahler!" He raised his glass of lemonade. "To the New York Philharmonic!"

After dinner, the men adjourned to the smoking room while the ladies gathered in the salon, another American peculiarity. While the maid served Chinese tea in hand-painted porcelain cups, the ladies' eyes slid uncomfortably past Alma as though they could not quite get over her husband's faux pas. Natalie, in particular, looked as grim as an executioner.

"Alma Maria, would you care to join me in the garden for a cigarette?" she asked.

"I don't smoke," said Alma.

Natalie, however, was already propelling her out the French doors into the moonlit garden dripping in ivy. Her friend did not, in fact, light a cigarette, but from within her embroidered silk purse produced a hip flask. "I think we could both do with a shot of something stronger than lemonade. You first."

Alma regarded the leather-bound flask with some trepidation before raising it to her lips. It burned all the way down her gullet and brought tears to her eyes.

"Arizona firewater," Natalie said, with some satisfaction. "Out West I used it for disinfecting rattlesnake bites." She took a long slug before hiding it in her purse again. "Now don't get me wrong, Alma. I'm awfully fond of you and I wish your husband all the best, but he has to remember that this isn't the Old World anymore. He has to play to the audience, not talk down to them. Mrs. Seney Sheldon raised money from the Rockefellers, Morgans, and Carnegies for this orchestra. Her donors don't want to be lectured on the inferiority of the American way."

Alma endeavored to speak in Gustav's defense but was only just recovering

307

her powers of speech from the Arizona firewater. "In Vienna my husband had absolute authority over his repertoire. Not even the emperor told him what to do."

But she stopped herself from trying to explain that Gustav aimed to raise both the Philharmonic and his American audience to his level—just as he had attempted to raise *her* to his level. As Natalie had so bluntly pointed out, Americans did not take kindly to being belittled and patronized.

Natalie was so daring and resourceful. To think she had once been audacious enough to grab the ear of President Roosevelt and make him change the law to help the Indians whose rights she championed. By comparison, Alma felt like a drudge. A limp rag, wringing her hands and meekly defending her husband. What must it be like to feel strong? A force to be reckoned with? *To speak my mind without fear.*

"Just tell him to watch his step," Natalie said, in a gentler tone. "He doesn't want to fall out of favor with Mrs. Seney Sheldon."

"Will I see you at the Women's Club?" Alma asked, following her friend back into the salon. "You must come to the Savoy for tea. I've missed our chats."

Natalie had been terribly busy this winter, and Alma hadn't seen nearly as much of her as she wished.

"I'll keep tomorrow free just for you, Alma. But then I'm going away." Natalie cracked a grin. "You can tell Mr. Mahler I'm off to Virginia to study black music."

Mrs. Seney Sheldon's dinner party was over by nine fifteen. *No wonder Americans are so productive,* Alma reflected. Their social life consisted of dry parties that ended early enough to insure everyone could be in bed by ten.

Gustav, however, was in a foul mood during the cab ride back to the Savoy. "Of all the indignities," he said. "Having to explain myself to a committee of women."

"Be careful, Gustav. Women are *powerful* in this country. You must take them seriously." Alma spoke softly and her voice shook.

But when had Gustav ever encountered women like Mary Seney Sheldon and Natalie Curtis? Back in Vienna, not even Berta Zuckerkandl had wielded that kind of influence. Mrs. Seney Sheldon and Mrs. Untermyer were living proof that even married women with children could be ambitious without apology in this country. Yet Gustav only seemed to view them as an aberration. *And this is precisely why he demanded I give up composing,* Alma thought, with a sickening lurch. Not because she wasn't talented but because he regarded ambition and independence as unacceptable for any female. He would never recognize women as truly talented except for the female singers who were his protégées and served to showcase his brilliance.

*But I was never an aberration,* she thought, fighting back her tears as she looked out the cab window at the darkened city streets. *Never abnormal. It's my life that's an aberration.* It had been so much easier to resign herself to her allotted role in Austria because there it was every woman's lot, with a few rare exceptions—spinsters like Ilse Conrat who were pitied as the third sex. But the women of New York had revealed to her how shackled she was. How she longed to break free, but she didn't know how. She feared she would only keep coming up against Gustav's brick wall.

A pall descended on her, like a black curtain blowing over her face.

# 39

‖‖‖‖‖‖‖‖‖‖‖‖‖‖‖‖‖‖‖‖

A lma, you don't look well," Mama whispered. "You're not expecting again, are you?"

Alma forced a smile and shook her head. She and her mother sat with Sophie Clemenceau in her private balcony in the Théâtre du Châtelet in Paris, where Gustav was directing the French premiere of his Second Symphony. This was meant to be a moment of triumph for him. Yesterday Sophie Clemenceau had hosted a luncheon in Gustav's honor with none other than Claude Debussy, whose music Gustav had championed in New York. But the French composer had been cold and aloof to both him and Alma.

Training her opera glasses on Debussy, Alma watched him yawn and dig out his pocket watch as though he could hardly wait for the concert to be over. As for the rest of the audience, Gustav's soaring symphony of transfiguration appeared mere background music for the real drama at hand. Everyone seemed to be gawking at the Countess Greffulhe, who at the age of nearly fifty was still Paris's reigning beauty. Her diamond tiara scintillating in her lustrous dark curls, she appeared to be having a steamy tête-à-tête with the handsome young Don Perosi, a Vatican envoy and composer of sacred music. Their faces were so close, they almost appeared to be kissing. A titter arose at the sheer scandal of it all. Had Gustav any clue of what was transpiring behind his back, he would have thrown down his baton in despair.

But even the countess and her priest were upstaged when Debussy walked out in the middle of the second movement.

"Mahler—*quel malheur!*" Debussy said, in a voice that could be heard through the concert hall. "Too Schubertian. Too Slavic. Too Viennese."

He might as well have said *too Jewish*.

Alma saw Gustav's back stiffen. Still, he carried on conducting, as though struggling to pretend that he hadn't just been humiliated and condemned by France's foremost composer.

Gustav was in a bitter mood when they traveled on to Rome, where he would direct three concerts with the orchestra of the Accademia di Santa Cecilia, one of the oldest musical institutions in Europe. Unfortunately, the best players had left for a concert tour of South America, leaving only the second-rate musicians behind.

Alma watched Gustav and the orchestra rehearse his own Bach Suite in the circular Augusteo Concert Hall, newly built on the ancient site of Emperor Augustus's mausoleum. The building's graceful art nouveau curves and magnificent acoustics merely served to underline the orchestra's incompetence—it sounded as if everyone was playing in a different key. She had never heard a professional orchestra perform so poorly.

Though still April, it was sweltering. The musician's faces glistened with sweat. Gustav's was boiling red—a thing that made Alma brace herself. If he was renowned for being a severe taskmaster with his musicians, he rarely lost his self-control. But he was doing so now. Italian-German dictionary in hand, he railed at them, his insults echoing like gunfire. *Stupidita! Indolenza!* She trembled, as though those words were aimed at her. But the musicians, rather than being suitably chastened, stalked away in contempt, leaving Gustav and Alma alone in the auditorium. She could hardly look at her husband, hardly knew what to say that wouldn't bring his wrath down on her. *How are you going to direct three concerts with these people now that you've made them your enemies?*

As Alma could have predicted, the two subsequent performances were abysmal, the worst Gustav had ever conducted in his entire career. This time it was more than a few audience members who walked out. To Alma's alarm, Gustav canceled the third concert altogether.

"But you can't just break your contract," she said. "If they hear about this in Vienna, it will be all over the papers. Your critics will make a meal of this! Gustav, can't you see this through? Just *one* more concert. Maybe be kind and try to win them over?" She addressed him as if she were as bold and confident as Natalie Curtis.

She and Gustav were, after all, living from one temporary contract to the next. They no longer possessed a home but divided their peripatetic existence between hotels and their rented summerhouse. What if Gustav, with his impossibly high standards, burned all his bridges and alienated everyone? What if he made himself deathly ill from his own rage?

"Alma, how can you even *presume* to tell me what to do?" he demanded, his anger enough to scorch her. "Do you have any idea what it's like to scratch out a living directing one bad orchestra after the other?"

He laid into her as though he held her responsible for the burden of supporting a family and all its associated travails.

She wept helplessly. "Why do you have to be so hard on people? Maybe they're not stupid or indolent. Maybe they're just afraid of you."

He turned away and announced they would be taking the first train to Vienna in the morning. Hadn't she better sort out the tickets and telegram her mother with their arrival time?

It was mercilessly hot even at night. After tossing for hours in her Roman hotel bed, Alma had finally fallen asleep. She dreamed of coolness and reprieve. A silver waterfall gushing down a fern grotto, the liquid collecting in a rippling green pool. Pure water lapping over her feet and ankles.

Something hot and sticky seized hold of her and shoved her thighs apart. Hands clutched at her breasts. She awoke with a start to find Gustav on top of her, attempting to make love to her — if it could even be called that. She felt no love from him at all. No tenderness. Just this businesslike grappling and thrusting as though she were some anonymous whore he was using to service his urges. When he was finished, she shoved him off of her, pulled the bedsheet over her head, and howled like a beaten dog.

"Almschi, why are you behaving like this? I'm your *husband*. We have to be up anyway. The train leaves in an hour."

Two days later Alma was back at the Hohe Warte. She locked herself in her girlhood bedroom and refused to come out.

Her mad sister Gretl was the sane one now, reasonable and calm in her crisply ironed white dress. She carried in a tray of food adorned with a small vase of fragrant white lilacs. White — the color meant to calm the hysterical. It was past three o'clock in the afternoon, and Alma was still lying in her old bed where she had once dreamed of becoming a somebody. A composer.

"It's only a bit of nervous exhaustion," Gretl said, setting down the tray at Alma's bedside. "From all that travel and then coming back to Vienna and seeing those nasty articles about Gustav."

As Alma had foreseen, the Viennese newspapers had gleefully printed columns and columns of garbled dreck concerning Gustav's concerts in Rome. MAHLER'S CAREER IN SHAMBLES the headlines had screamed.

"You just need another rest cure," her sister said. "Then you'll feel fresh and happy again. But now you should eat something."

Gretl planted herself on a chair as though she intended to perch there until Alma did as she was told. Alma regarded the steaming plate of chicken paprikash. Once it had been her favorite dish. Mama had served it the first time Gustav stayed for dinner eight and a half years ago. But Alma could no longer stomach the thought of shoving it down her throat.

"At least have the bread roll," said Gretl. "Shall I butter it for you?"

Ignoring her sister, Alma paged through the photo album Mama had left on her bedside table. No doubt her mother had thought these pictures Carl had taken last summer at Trenkerhof would bring back happy memories. On the first page was a family portrait. Gustav filled the center foreground. Though he was a slight man, he seemed to take up as much space as a mountain. His image was sharp and clear, brilliant sunlight shining on his white summer cap and his shirtsleeves. He looked relaxed and at peace with the world. It was one of the few pictures that showed him smiling. Beside him stood Gucki. Three-quarters of their daughter's face and upper torso were visible in the photograph. She squinted into the sun and looked as though she was trying to smile. In the background, nearly entirely obscured by her husband, was Alma. Only the brim of her straw hat, the blurred outline of her cheek, and part of one arm could be made out. Certainly not her face. Her stepfather's photograph had literally relegated her to her husband's shadow. *I don't exist anymore.*

"No point in going back to Löweneck if it didn't do you any good." Gretl pried the photo album from Alma and handed her half of the buttered bread roll. "But I *swear* by Wildbad Sanatorium in Tobelbad! They don't just starve you and hose you—they have the most divine hot mineral baths. *New* therapies, too. It's run by a very forward-thinking naturopathic doctor. So many clever people go there. You'll be surrounded by artists and intellectuals. Mama's arranged for you to stay a full six weeks. And Carl made Gustav promise not to take you away too early like he did last time."

Alma smiled wanly and bit into the bread roll. Gretl rewarded her with a blinding smile. Bounding from her chair, she bounced on the edge of Alma's bed.

"You'll be *amazed*," her sister said, "at what six weeks of rest and therapy can do!"

# 40

||||||||||||||||||||||||||

**W**hat is the point of any of this? Alma heaved herself out of bed with the ringing of the sanatorium's wake-up bell. The sun had barely risen, but it was time for the morning hike. *Some rest cure.*

She felt like a faulty piece of machinery. Every spring she broke down, the consequence of her husband's intense spirit driving her on until she could take no more. And then she, accompanied by her daughter and the nanny, entered a clinic where the doctors attempted to solder her back together so she could resume her duties. At least until the following spring when she fell apart again. But what if she couldn't be fixed this time? What if she simply couldn't go on with her life as it was? In trying to be the woman Gustav wanted her to be, she had only destroyed herself. *I no longer have a self. I am nothing.*

Gustav remained as tone deaf as ever to her anguish. She had nearly ripped his last letter to pieces.

> *Such a sad little epistle, Almschi! It truly makes me depressed to learn that you're still angry about Rome. Yes, I remember being irritable and annoyed because you were doing your utmost to persuade me to stay and carry on. I simply didn't understand you. Perhaps meanwhile you've come to see things differently. In any case, I shall never put up with anything like those rehearsals and concerts again.*

Alma yanked her loose shift over her head and shuffled out for her morning walk. Hiking barefoot up and down the steep Styrian hills, through forest and meadow in every weather, was the hallmark of Wildbad Sanatorium's

315

philosophy. As she plodded down the stairs and out the door, Alma kept her head down, not wanting to be drawn into discussion as to why the wife of the great Gustav Mahler was here being treated for hysteria.

She scarcely understood why Gretl had enthused about this place. As far as Alma was concerned, the regime was nearly identical to what she had experienced at Löweneck. She had to wear the same kind of hideous sack, resign herself to the same buttermilk and lettuce diet. Only the hot mineral baths were different.

When Alma had returned from her walk, she lowered herself with clenched teeth into the simmering outdoor tub. This sanatorium believed in doing nearly everything outdoors. The healing stimulation of Nature, the doctors called it. Gretl had loved the baths, but Alma felt as though she were being boiled to death in a cannibal's cooking pot.

At long last the *Bademeister* told her it was time to get out. Still in her shift, Alma clambered over the rim of the tub, inhaled one breath of the crisp, pine-scented air. And then she fainted.

When Alma came to, she found herself on one of the outdoor beds used for sun baths. Her wet shift was covered in a warm wool blanket and Herr Doktor Lahmann, the head of the clinic, smiled down at her with what resembled paternal benevolence. He measured her pulse and told her to rest until her blood pressure had returned to normal. Alma nodded like an obedient child, all the while wishing he would just leave her alone. Why couldn't they simply leave her be?

"Frau Direktor Mahler," the doctor said. "I'm very concerned about you. You seem so melancholy and withdrawn. Sadness and loneliness feed on each other. It would be much better if you could socialize with the other cure guests."

*Cure guests!* She nearly snorted at the absurd euphemism for the patients being treated for hysteria and nerve sickness.

"Every cure guest's needs are different," he said. "For you, Frau Direktor, I prescribe dancing."

"Dancing," she echoed, her voice as flat as the felt slippers they let her wear when she wasn't forced to go barefoot.

"You can wear a pretty dress if you like," the doctor said, as though reading her mind.

The therapeutic dancing commenced at two o'clock in the solarium. One of the more musically gifted cure guests was stationed at the upright piano and played waltzes by Franz Lehár. Alma, clad in the gauzy linen-and-lace tea dress she had packed in case Gustav or Mama came to visit, halted on the threshold. Who would they make her dance with? Some wheezing old man with halitosis?

Seeing her hesitate, Dr. Lahmann came to take her ceremoniously by the hand and lead her up to a tall, slender youth of almost unbearable beauty. She tried not to blush or gape. With his dark hair and moustache, he was handsome enough to play Walther von Stolzing in Wagner's *Die Meistersinger von Nürnberg*. While the doctor made the introductions, the young man gave her a courtly bow, enhancing the illusion that Alma could leave the wretched realities of her life behind and escape into the fantasy of a romantic opera.

"Frau Direktor Alma Maria Mahler, may I introduce you to Herr Walter Gropius," the doctor said, before stepping away.

A frisson passed through Alma from the moment this young man took her hand and wrapped his arm around her waist. What was such a healthy, cheerful-looking person even doing here, she wondered. Flirting with him simply wouldn't do. Surely a young man like him would see her as a needy, neurotic matron. He was only doing her a kindness by agreeing to dance with her. She tried to stay cool and detached, but he was so very charming.

"Dancing makes a nice change from boiling in the baths," he said, with a laugh, inviting her to laugh along. His accent revealed him to be German.

"You're a long way from home, Herr Gropius," she said, as they glided across the parquet floor. He was so tall, she had to tilt her head just to look at him. "Tell me about yourself."

"I'm an architect."

So he wasn't just good-looking but also accomplished. She learned that he was from Berlin and that his doctor had sent him here to be treated for a persistent chill. He had recently established his own very successful partnership with another rising young architect. And he had just turned twenty-seven. In August Alma would be thirty-one.

"My partner and I have designed a shoe factory," Gropius said, his manner genial and uncomplicated. Not self-important in the least. "And before you laugh, Frau Direktor, let me tell you that it will be the most modern and avant-garde shoe factory you can imagine. Clean, simple lines. Walls of glass windows instead of oppressive brick. Why shouldn't the working class enjoy space, air, and light?"

His youthful idealism was beguiling. She smiled into his eyes, the darkest shade of hazel. This young man was simply too perfect. She glanced across the room to see Dr. Lahmann beaming in approval.

"Herr Gropius, if I commissioned you to build a house for me, what would it be like?" Alma pretended for a moment to be a woman of means. Unmarried and independent.

"A truly organic building, free of untruth or ornamentation or any hint of kitsch." Gropius lifted his eyes in exasperation at the elaborately molded ceiling with its cherubs and floral garlands. "Everything bold and free."

"And the people who live in your houses—will they also be bold and free?" she asked him teasingly.

"That's my dream, Frau Direktor—that architecture can change the world. I want to design apartments that are simple, functional, and affordable. Every working-class family should be able to own a home."

They began conversing about a modern utopia and the emancipated men and women who would live in it. She told him of her connections to the architects of the Vienna Secession.

318

"I was a close friend of Josef Maria Olbrich's while he still lived in Vienna," she said, blushing slightly to remember how Olbrich had wooed her —it seemed like another lifetime. Two years ago, her old admirer had died of leukemia. "But the New Yorkers are the cutting edge!" she went on, not wanting to dwell on melancholy thoughts. "Their skyscrapers are the new cathedrals."

She described what it had been like to live on the eleventh floor and then told him of all the exciting freethinkers she had met in America. Of Natalie Curtis and Hopi music.

Gropius seemed entranced. "You must lead a very cosmopolitan life, Frau Direktor, being married to such a famous man."

Her jaw clenched. "I don't want to talk about my husband."

"If the truth be told, neither do I," he said, his face softening. "I would much rather talk about *you*."

Alma's skin went as hot as though she were up to her neck in the bubbling thermal springs. Gropius was the first man in eight years to see her as her own person, not as an appendage of Gustav Mahler. Even Ossip's infatuation had been held in check by his awe for her husband. She suddenly felt shy and uncertain.

"My father was an artist," she said. "Emil Schindler."

"I know and admire his paintings. He was the greatest Austrian landscape artist. But what about *you?*" He looked at her entreatingly.

"I . . ." Alma closed her eyes. "I dreamed of being a composer. I still have a folder full of music."

"After the dancing hour finishes, I would love to hear it." He nodded toward the piano in the corner.

She stared into his eyes and thought she would weep in amazement. This young architect, nearly four years her junior, was falling in love with her. *And if I'm not very careful, I shall fall hopelessly in love with him.*

Alma went to get her secret folder of songs that she carried with her everywhere, the way some women carry prayer books or photographs of old lovers. Arranging her music on the piano, she played and sang her songs for Gropius.

*This is harmless,* she assured herself. *Gustav will never find out. Never trouble himself about what I get up to at a sanatorium, of all places.* Here in this rural spa, she felt suspended in time and space. In this sheltered lacuna, she could finally wriggle out of the straightjacket of being the wife of an exalted genius. She could simply be. Be herself, the Alma she once was. Passionate and questing. *Oh, to live. To truly live.*

After she had finished playing, Gropius took her hand. "Your music is so full of sensual beauty. You're a true artist. A freethinker like me. A New Woman."

She was speechless, any words she could think to say drowned out by the tidal pounding in her head. This was a dream. She would wake up and return to cold reality any second. *Well, then, let me enjoy this dream while it lasts.*

"Will you call me Walter?" he asked, using the familiar *Du*. "I want to hear you say my name."

"Walter," she murmured, as he leaned forward to caress her cheek.

"And may I call you Alma?"

She nodded, offering her mouth to his kiss.

When Alma joined Miss Turner and Gucki in the garden later that day, she took her daughter in her lap and covered her in kisses. "Show your mama what beautiful pictures you've drawn today, sweetheart. You'll grow up to be a great artist like your grandfather."

"Frau Direktor, you look so well," Miss Turner said. "This cure seems to be just what you needed."

This was just a *Liebelei,* an infatuation. This was *healthy.* The next morning Alma embarked on her barefoot hike with more verve than ever before. Walter walked at her side, his face flushed with the secret mirth they shared. When they were out of view of the other cure guests, they held hands. Laughing, they raced across a meadow sparkling with dew. Walter gave her a head start before sprinting after her. When he caught her around the waist, she whooped with both shock and pleasure. They tumbled into the damp grass together.

"What did Dr. Lahmann call his medical philosophy again?" Walter asked, tracing her brow with a harebell blossom. "The healing stimulation of Nature?"

They shared a sweet, lingering kiss that made her tremble. The hard and brittle places inside her softened and became as pliant as dough. This young man was indeed her medicine, the magical elixir that restored her youth. For the first time since New York, she was happy. Grateful to be alive. Until Walter had given her the kiss of life, she had been a walking corpse.

*You raised me from the dead,* Alma was about to tell him. But when she opened her mouth to speak, his tongue twined with hers. Gently lifting the small of her back, he arched her body to his. A tingling burning filled her entire being. *I've forgotten what it was to feel like this. To be cherished and held.*

At least her ugly shift served a purpose. She hitched it effortlessly to her waist and pulled her lover inside her. *My lover!* The ecstasy that flooded her was so powerful, she had to cover her mouth to keep from crying out and betraying their secret.

More than just a *Liebelei* then. Alma had to admit she was falling deeply in love. The heightened sense of being alive again after so many months of numbness made her reckless, daring to write the unthinkable to her husband. To ask the unaskable.

> *Gustav, do you even love me anymore? I haven't felt your tenderness in so long.*

He replied from Munich, where he was rehearsing his Eighth Symphony with a monumental choir and orchestra that totaled more than one thousand musicians. The performance, which would take place in September, would surely be the crowning glory of his career.

*Almschi, you silly sausage, why trouble your head with such nonsense? I've never been fonder of you than I am now. How could you think otherwise?*

When she neglected to reply, he berated her.

*How should one react to such a woman-child who can't even answer my letters?*

And when she still didn't write, his tone turned from complacency to consternation.

*After your last sad letter and then your silence, I must ask if you're concealing something from me. I keep sensing something between the lines.*

Lest he grow too suspicious, Alma sent him Gucki's latest drawings along with a letter that praised their daughter's progress on the piano, which she practiced every evening to the cure guests' delight.

*Our little Gucki's a prodigy, just like her brilliant papa!*

Late that evening, Alma and Walter stole away to sit beside a stream while the moon arched above the swaying trees. In the sapphire hush of night, Alma finally found the courage to pour out her despair, to speak of the deep wounds of marriage that she hadn't been able to confess to anyone else, even her mother or sister.

"He seems to think I'm some lesser being. Not a fully developed person. Eight years of having an ascetic schoolmaster for a husband! You gave me more passion and pleasure in *one night* than he gave me in our entire marriage."

Walter wiped away her tears. "Your husband is of the old generation who thought wives were there to serve and suffer. Come away with me, Alma. We can live a free life. Two free souls together. It's simply wrong that you should be his spiritual slave."

The future he painted for them was intoxicating. She wanted to distill his words into a bottle and imbibe a little of that potion every day for the rest of her life.

During the dancing hour, Alma endeavored to veil her love from the other cure guests, which was no easy thing. If Walter so much as looked at her, she sparkled and warmed. Waltzing in his arms, she felt like Alma Schindler in days of old, twenty-one and so full of hope and potential, breathlessly discussing art, architecture, music, and literature. Walter listened as though she were the most beautiful and cultured woman he had ever met.

"When you smile at me like that, it drives me mad," he whispered. "I want to make love to you right here in the middle of the dance floor."

She attempted to remain demure. "Young man, you'll have to wait until after I put Gucki to bed. Then I shall tiptoe to your room."

They danced as close to each other as they dared. Her cheek brushing his chest, she felt his body heat rising through his collarless linen shirt.

"I'll build us a house," he whispered. "With walls of glass so we won't have to hide."

How luscious it was to indulge in the fantasy that their romance could stretch on forever. That she wouldn't be obliged to return to her husband after her six-week cure was over. She quickly pushed all thought of Gustav from her mind.

"I will compose while you design your beautiful buildings," she said.

"Will you write a song for me?"

"I will! A hymn to Eros!"

His eyes softened even more. It was so hard not to kiss him.

"Alma," he said, laughing. "Here we are dancing and the music has stopped."

"I didn't even notice." She glanced around the emptied room before turning to him mischievously. "We *are* the music, my love."

The thought that they were alone emboldened her to twine her arms around his neck and pull him close. But his face went pale, and he stepped away from her as a nurse marched in.

"Frau Direktor, you have a visitor."

Alma spun in panic. Had Gustav come unannounced? It seemed impossible, with him so busy rehearsing his Eighth Symphony in Munich. But it was Mama, her face set in deep, grave lines.

"Hello, Alma. Won't you introduce me to your new friend?"

"Herr Gropius is an architect," Alma said, flushed and stammering. "He studied in Berlin with one of Papa's friends," she added, as if that would mollify her mother.

"What an honor to meet you, Herr Gropius," Mama said, with cool politesse. "Would you give me a moment alone with my daughter, please?"

His face bright red, Walter retreated.

"I wasn't expecting you, Mama." Alma pressed her fingers to her throbbing temples.

"Well, *that* was obvious!" Mama folded her arms in front of her chest. "Gustav asked me to see if you were all right. He's worried because your letters were sounding strange. *Now* I understand why. At least I have to commend your taste. Herr Gropius is a very good-looking young person."

A viselike grip closed around Alma's brow. She thought her brain would be crushed to pulp. "Will you tell Gustav?" Collapsing on a bench, she began to sob. *It's hopeless. My life is hopeless.*

"Alma, don't!" Mama's voice cracked. She sat beside her and hugged her. "I mean to *help* you. Now listen to me."

Dazed, Alma sat up straight and looked at her mother.

"Darling, I know marriage is sometimes very hard. Gustav is a good man but a difficult husband. I know you've been miserable for quite some time —I'm not blind." Mama was in tears herself. "Carl and I made a terrible mistake. We should have let you study at the conservatory. We should have let you marry your Alex. *He* would have made you happy."

Mama's admission sent Alma's thoughts spinning in a dizzying rush. Was

324

it so transparent that her marriage was a failure? Her mother spoke as if it weighed heavily on her heart that both Alma and Gretl had spent their married lives in and out of sanatoriums and she held herself responsible. As though she wanted to help salvage what she could of her daughters' dignity and happiness.

"Men make the rules," Mama said, holding Alma close. "And we break them so we don't go mad. Sometimes a wife must grant herself certain liberties if she's to go on in her marriage."

The look her mother gave her was so complicit that Alma wanted to pinch herself. Mama was giving her *permission* to be unfaithful? Then she remembered the liberties Mama herself may have taken — her rumored affair with Papa's trusted colleague, Julius Victor Berger, who might have been Gretl's natural father. And then the affair with Carl, Papa's protégé.

"Now tell me honestly, do you truly love this Herr Gropius? Does he truly care for you?"

Alma spoke from the depths of her tangled emotions. "He made me live again when I thought I was dead."

"There must be no scandal, Alma. Divorce would be unthinkable for a woman in your position. We have Gucki to consider, and Gustav's heart condition. He's so much older than you." Never had her mother's words sounded so stark and clear. "You must have something to live for when Gustav's no longer with us. You and Herr Gropius are still young. If his love is genuine, he can wait until you're free. Just like Carl waited for me."

Mama's pragmatism dumbfounded Alma. So it was possible to have it all, to remain respectably wed to Gustav and have a discreet affair with Walter. Then, when she was a widow, after a suitable period of mourning, she and Walter could marry and live in his dream house with its walls of glass, with nothing to conceal. Everyone's good name would be preserved intact.

And if Mama's proposal seemed cold-blooded, Alma had to concede that it was the only solution that wouldn't ruin her. She simply couldn't go on in her marriage as it was. But if she ran away with Walter, she would be in exactly the same predicament as Mathilde Schoenberg was the previous summer. If Gustav repudiated her, she would lose everything. Lose Gucki. Lose all she had worked for in her eight years of marriage. Those hundreds of pages of Gustav's scores she had copied and transcribed for him. If Walter tired of her, she would be left with nothing but disgrace, shunned from respectable society.

"Mama," Alma said, moving on to more immediate concerns. "I don't want to have a child that isn't Gustav's. Will you go with me to the doctor in Graz? I want to be fitted for a Dutch cap, but I'm afraid he'll say no." She had heard too many stories of how doctors humiliated women who asked for contraceptive devices.

Her mother nodded. "Yes, that's most sensible. You can be frank with Gustav about this, at least. After those miscarriages, he'll have to understand."

After Mama had a long conversation with Walter, making certain that he was a decent young man from a good family, she agreed to become their ally, the sworn guardian of their secret. With Mama accompanying her to browbeat the doctor into compliance, Alma visited a gynecologist in nearby Graz and returned to the sanatorium with her new Dutch cap.

"I want to have your child," she whispered to Walter, when she crept into his bed. "But not *yet*."

Pouncing on him, she tugged off his pajamas, then gazed down at his long muscled body washed golden in the lamplight. Walter Gropius, the most beautiful man she had ever loved.

"You are my Apollo," she murmured, caressing every inch of his flesh with her tongue. "My shining Eros. I want to devour you."

He groaned and pulled her into his embrace, kissing her until she thought he would steal her breath away. Secure in the knowledge that she wouldn't be punished for her sin by pregnancy or miscarriage, she gave herself to him with exquisite surrender. She abandoned every inhibition, every rule of how a respectable woman must behave. Not Gustav Mahler's wife anymore but herself, her deep original self that she thought she had lost.

In the aftermath of their lovemaking, reality intruded once more. Nestling her head on Walter's chest, she told him her news. "My husband sent a cable from Munich. He's coming to visit for two days."

Walter drew her up so that they lay face-to-face. He appeared absolutely stricken with jealousy of a man he hadn't even met. "You're not going to sleep with him, are you?"

She couldn't keep herself from smiling at his possessiveness. "He'll probably be too distracted by his rehearsals to bother."

To calm her nerves and soothe Walter's anxieties, Alma made love to him all night before the day of Gustav's arrival. It was the most urgently charged lovemaking she had ever experienced, as though their entire future was at stake and Walter wanted to love every single trace of Gustav out of her. In the morning, when she washed, her skin felt flushed in the afterglow of bliss. But that only made her more jittery. If Gustav was canny enough to sense from her letters that something was not quite right, how would she manage to dissemble when they met face-to-face?

Alma watched her husband emerge from the car that had fetched him from the station. After the way he had behaved to her in Rome, she had expected to feel aversion at the very sight of him. But he appeared like a completely different man, almost plaintive. It was he who seemed nervous, raking his hand self-consciously through his hair.

"Look, Almschi! No bad haircut this time!" Gustav stepped toward her, as though about to embrace her, but he stopped short, looking her up and down as though he no longer recognized her. "For a while, your letters left me so depressed, but now I understand."

Alma closed her eyes and braced herself. *He knows.* He'd had to take only one look at her to see that she had betrayed him. Then she opened her eyes to feel his fingers stroking her hair.

"I haven't seen you looking this fresh and healthy in years, Almscherl. Whatever therapies you've been taking here have done you a power of good."

· · ·

Alma strolled with her husband and daughter through the meadows and woods. Though she had thought it impossible, she felt a stirring of renewed affection for Gustav. For all his genius, he was a driven and lonely man. During his Munich rehearsals, he had been conducting so furiously, he managed to pull a muscle in his upper arm. After his visit here, he would be going to their summer home at Trenkerhof, where she would join him in two weeks when her cure was complete.

"But you'll be alone up there for your fiftieth birthday," Alma said, taking his hand. "Won't you at least invite Justine?"

Gustav shook his head. "You know how I hate having a fuss made about my birthday. My real celebration will be when you and Gucki join me, and we can live as a family again. But I absolutely forbid you to break off your cure early for my sake, Almscherl. Stay here for as long as you can. You're on the road to recovery, but if you suffer another relapse, make sure that you're still being cared for."

Alma kept her head down so Gustav wouldn't see her blush.

Suite 5

# MY STORM SONG

# 41

||||||||||||||||||||||||||

I n mid-July Alma left the sanatorium to rejoin Gustav at Trenkerhof. They danced a *Ländler* in the meadow outside the farmhouse while Gucki skipped circles around them. Gustav twirled Alma round and round until she was laughing and dizzy, clutching his shoulders so she wouldn't fall. *What a mystery love is!* To think it had taken an adulterous liaison to restore their marriage. She effervesced with a vitality and joy that Gustav seemed to find irresistible.

As far as her husband was concerned, their life had been restored to its proper order. In Alma's absence, he had struggled with the most basic matters of day-to-day living, unable to find his socks without her help. While Alma and Gucki wandered through the fields and picked wildflowers, Gustav was happily ensconced in his composing hut. He had just started work on his Tenth Symphony. Smiling to herself, Alma listened to his distant piano notes mingling with the birdsong and chiming cowbells.

She felt as though she were floating above the earth, living in a cloud of euphoria, even in Walter's absence. *Blindsided by love.* By both her reveries of her wild nights with Walter and the present reality of her measured days with Gustav. Her heart brimmed for them both. Did that make her a bad woman, immoral and duplicitous? But she overflowed with optimism and bliss. *I am in love with two men, both of them geniuses.* A virile young lover who was destined for great things. And a titan at the height of his powers. Gustav, with his towering soul—her man-child who couldn't function without her. Could she truly love them both at once?

*Yes, it's possible to be happy. Yes, there's such a thing as perfect joy.* This love triangle had been her bridge back to life. Suddenly, she was restored to the world, enamored of this earthly existence with all its complications and contradictions, this divine immanence of sunlight on grass and her daughter's laughter and prancing little feet. Walter had resurrected her. Gustav remained unsuspecting and supremely pleased with the result. Everyone had benefitted. Walter's love allowed her to go on serving Gustav without resentment.

Of course, she had sworn Walter to secrecy. He remained at the sanatorium and sent her searing letters via general delivery.

*Alma, your passion is so intense, it shakes me like an earthquake. I'm falling to pieces for you. When can we see each other again?*

They would meet for a secret tryst some day. Mama would help them find a way. *We must be patient and tread carefully,* Alma had written to Walter. She discovered he'd had previous affairs with married women, so he knew the risks involved. As much as she ached for him, she had no intention of ruining her family with some careless indiscretion.

Later, during Gucki's afternoon nap, Alma would cycle to the village to see if there was a new letter from Walter waiting for her at the post office. And mail her latest outpouring to him.

*You float before me like a figure of light—a most beautiful youth. I want your beauty to melt inside me.*

Gucki at her heels, Alma entered the farmhouse with her arms full of wildflowers. She found Gustav seated at the grand piano, his face drawn deathly white. It looked as though he could hardly sit upright. The china tray where Käthe left the mail lay shattered at his feet.

Alma dropped the flowers and ran to him. "Gustav, what is it? Your heart?"

"Can you explain *this?*" He thrust a letter at her—an envelope addressed to Herr Direktor Mahler, Trenkerhof, Alt Schluderbach, Tyrol. Recognizing Walter's handwriting, Alma thought her heart would explode.

"Gucki," she said. "Go to Miss Turner. Now!"

"Read the letter, Alma." Gustav's voice was so cold, as if he had disowned her.

Though the envelope was addressed to her husband, she saw to her horror that the letter within was written to her.

> *Beloved Alma,*
>
> *You have driven me to madness. All I can think of is you, the way you gave yourself to me as no other woman could. I cannot forget the vision of you naked in my bed, your hair spilling over my pillow, your exquisite voluptuousness.*
>
> *Beloved, you must end my torment. If you truly care for me, as you swore you did, you will leave your husband and begin a new life with me. You know you don't love him. Your heart is mine. I am coming to Trenkerhof to ask for your hand. You can't stop me, Alma. I beg you to make up your mind and choose what is right.*
>
> *Your Walter*

Alma tore the letter in half. Fleeing Gustav's stony eyes, she rushed to the kitchen and tossed the cursed missive into the stove.

Käthe looked up from the dough she was kneading. "Are you all right, Frau Direktor?"

Alma shook her head. Her tears scalded her. Walter knew very well that he was supposed to write her via general delivery, not send any letters directly to the house, certainly not addressed to her husband! Yet it seemed he had deliberately betrayed her to force her hand. Had he intended to so infuriate Gustav that he would boot her out the door and leave her no choice but to go crawling back to Walter? She wanted to pack her bags and run away from both men.

*"Alma."* Gustav stalked into the kitchen, prompting Käthe to slink out the back door. "I'm still waiting for an explanation," he said, in that chilly, controlled rage that he had perfected in their eight years of marriage. "So *this* was what you were hiding from me." He looked at her as though she were more wretched than the dirt on his shoes. "Did he seduce you? Or did you start flirting with him?"

When Alma held her hands over her face and refused to answer, Gustav took her by the shoulders.

"Was it just one night?" he demanded. "Or did you carry on the entire six weeks?"

Alma shrieked and shoved Gustav away. It was too late for her to burst into tears and beg his forgiveness. Too late to fall to her knees and beseech him to raise her up, raise her to his level. She was the djinn that had escaped the bottle and could not be forced back inside no matter how her husband tried to shame her. Trapped and cornered, she turned on him, turned into a fury, her rage rising to meet his, fire to his ice.

"To hell with you, Gustav! For *eight years* I longed for nothing but your love! But you just overlooked me. You never even saw me. Everything I did was for you—it all revolved around *you*. I gave up my music, all the things I loved. It was always up to me to make the sacrifices. You treated me like a servant. You treated me like a *whore*, Gustav, climbing on top of me in Rome when I wasn't even conscious. Can you even remember the last time we actually made *love?*"

He went pale and backed away, holding out his hands as if to ward himself, but she closed the distance between them and shook his shoulders so that once and for all he was compelled to *see* her.

"You blamed me for Putzi's death. You were *horrible* to me after the miscarriages. You ignored my birthdays. I didn't even get a proper wedding. I gave and I gave until there was nothing left and I thought I would die. Then I met a young man who saw me as a person. Who *made love* to me! To *me!* I was dying for tenderness, Gustav! Dying!"

334

Exhausted by the force of her confession, she collapsed against the kitchen wall. She braced herself for his reprisal, his denunciation, his schoolmasterly lecture on the immaturity of her soul. Instead, he seemed to reel, as if it had never before entered his mind that he could lose her. That she could leave him.

"Don't you love me, Almschi?" His eyes glittered with tears.

"Do you love *me*?" she asked him, leaning against the wall to hold herself upright. "You have to love me for who I am. Not for who you would have me be. I destroyed myself trying to be the woman you wanted me to be. That woman is dead."

*Eve is dead. You killed her with your cold neglect.* Lilith rose to take her place. Lilith with her scorching anger, her savage wings. Gustav wept and kissed her hands until she held him, rocking him in her arms and weeping with him. Lilith with her raw, open heart.

Nothing between them could ever be the same. Gustav seemed to be frozen in a state of shock, so terrified Alma would abandon him that he couldn't bear to let her out of his sight. She had to wait until he was in the bath before she could pen a frantic note to Walter and beg Käthe to mail it for her.

> *How dare you expose me in this way? Do you want my husband to lose all trust, all faith in me? Do not under any circumstances come to Trenkerhof!*

Late that night, a sickening crash awakened Alma from her fitful sleep. Scrambling out of bed, she found her husband collapsed on the floor.

"Oh, Gustav. It's your heart."

Kneeling beside his body, she pressed her hand to his neck to feel his pulse. She helped him to his bed, wrapped him in blankets, gave him his medicine, sponged his brow and chest. She cradled him to her breast.

"Almschi," he said, in a choking voice. "I want to make you happy. Please tell me it's not too late."

When he gazed into her eyes, she felt borne up on a love so infinite that it staggered her. *How is it that Gustav and I seem to float between heaven and hell and back again?*

A week passed before Gustav could return to his composing hut and attempt to work. Taking advantage of this reprieve, Alma cycled off to the village in an attempt to clear her head—and see if there were any letters from Walter at the post office. She had reached the bridge over the River Rienz when a figure stepped in her path. The shock nearly sent her tumbling off her bicycle.

"Alma!"

Walter, his beautiful face eclipsing the sun. He kissed her with all the stored-up longing of their two-week separation. She kissed him back, her body burning for his, before she came to her senses and pushed him away.

"Walter, I told you not to come. I forbade it."

"But I was so worried about you now that your husband knows about us."

"Thanks to *you!*" she hissed.

Walter reached for her again, but she wriggled out of his grasp, tearing her sleeve. She cycled back to Trenkerhof as fast as she could. *Please let Gustav be in his composing hut,* she hoped and prayed. She wanted to flee inside the house and pretend this meeting with Walter simply hadn't happened. But Gustav was sitting in the garden, as though anxiously awaiting her return.

"Almschi, what happened?" He looked deeply disturbed. "Your blouse is torn."

There was no point in lying. "Walter was hiding under the bridge. I swear I told him not to come!"

Gustav went white. Then his mouth firmed in resolve. "I'll fetch him for you."

"Gustav, no!"

But he had already set off in his impossibly fast march that she had never been able to keep up with.

• • •

At sunset Alma looked out her bedroom window to see the two men walking up the lane. Gustav led the way while Walter trailed in his wake. What had they been discussing for so long?

She reared away from the window and slumped on the edge of her bed, her shaking hands clamped between her knees. This was purgatory. Why had Walter insisted on coming, destroying her fragile peace with Gustav?

Her door opened and her husband walked in. She hadn't seen him looking so devastated since they lost Putzi.

"Gropius has asked me for your hand," he said gravely. "I told him the decision is yours. He's downstairs waiting for your answer."

Deaf to her protests, Gustav took her arm and led her down to the salon, where Walter stood at attention, as tall and straight as a fir tree. Gustav left them alone.

"Walter, this is madness," she whispered. "I begged you to wait."

"Alma, hear me out," he said boldly. "The time for deception is over. You have to make up your mind. I've already made my choice." He seized her and kissed her until she kissed him back, her body softening in his embrace. "I can give you a long happy future. You think you're doing your husband a kindness by staying with him? Can't you see how tortured he is now that he knows you're in love with me? Don't ask me to wait until the poor man is dead before I can love you in the open."

"Hush! He'll hear you!"

The ceiling creaked with Gustav's footfalls as he paced upstairs. There followed a silence that filled Alma with dread. Leaving Walter, she flew up to Gustav's study. Seated at his desk, her husband was reading the Old Testament by the light of two guttering candles that threw ghostly shadows against the wooden walls.

Gustav looked up at her and spoke in his most controlled voice. "Alma, the time has come to make your choice. Whatever you decide will be right. And final."

He closed the Bible, took her right hand, and pressed her palm on the leather cover. Alma quailed. So it was down to this. If she chose Walter, it would be no bid for freedom, no thrilling existence as a New Woman. She would merely pass from one man's possession into another's. *Make your choice?* She wanted to scream that this was no choice. *I love both men. I will be owned by neither of them.*

"I'll give him my decision," she told Gustav. "Now let me go."

He slowly released her hand. A hollow ringing filled her ears as she walked down the stairs to the salon. When she stepped toward Walter, he seemed to radiate hope and assurance, opening his arms wide. She entered his embrace and kissed him until he pulled away.

"Well?" he asked breathlessly. "Are you mine?"

She smiled tenderly and traced the perfect curve of his lips. *Oh, to have a child with him. My beautiful young lover who raised me from the dead.*

"I can't leave him, Walter," she said quietly. "It would kill him. You know he has a heart condition." *The love Gustav and I share is so unfathomable, I couldn't leave him even if he were hale and hearty.*

"But you love me!"

"I love you," she whispered, wanting him more than she ever had. "But we must wait. If you want to be with me, we will find a way. But no more surprise visits, or else I'll have nothing more to do with you."

*Whatever you decide will be right. And final. I have decided that from this moment onward I shall be my own woman.*

Not giving Walter a chance to argue, Alma called Gustav down. Her husband lit a lantern and escorted her lover back to the main road. Walter could still catch the late train to Graz. The silent house creaked and settled, and Alma's breath misted the window as she watched the departing lantern until the night swallowed its light. *Men make the rules and we break them so we don't go mad.*

When Gustav returned, they fell into each other's arms. His face was transfigured, an ecstasy of love that Alma had been yearning for all their married life.

# 42

||||||||||||||||||||||||||

"H ow could I be so blind that I nearly lost you, Almschi?" Gustav held her
as though he were terrified she might vanish. As though she would bolt
out the door after her departed lover. His confrontation with Walter had
shaken him to his depths.

It tore Alma's heart to see him like this. "Come, love," she whispered,
leading him to her bed.

But when she sought to offer him the ultimate proof of her devotion,
Gustav couldn't rise to the occasion no matter how she tried to inflame him.
He wept in shame and misgiving, as if he understood only too well what had
drawn her to a younger man.

Alma awakened in the morning to find him gone. There was only his
note on her pillow.

*I am possessed of dark spirits. Come and exorcise them. Here I lie
prostrate and await you. May I still hope for salvation or am I
damned?*

Her heart seizing, Alma dashed to his composing hut. She found him
sobbing facedown on the floor, the draft pages of his Tenth Symphony scattered around him.

"Gustl." She held his head to her breast. "Darling, we can begin again.
We can be *happy.*"

But could they? Once Alma had borne on her shoulders all the unspoken pain of their marriage, that load that had finally toppled her. Now that

she had thrown off that yoke it appeared her former nerve sickness had descended on Gustav.

"Play from your new symphony. Please, darling."

She guided him to the piano. Through every crisis, his music had been his refuge. Gathering the pages of his Tenth off the floor, she sought to arrange them in their proper order. But she shook to read the words he had scrawled across the score.

*To live for you, to die for you, Almschi.*
*The devil is dancing with me.*

After much prevarication, Gustav arranged to consult Dr. Sigmund Freud in Leiden, Holland.

What had distressed her husband most, Alma wondered, after seeing him off at the station. Encountering Walter, his rival? Or confronting the raw, wild, untamable side of her, the wife he thought he knew? The thought that *she* had unhinged him left her paralyzed. Yet there was no going back to the woman she used to be. What had happened to her this summer was nothing short of an awakening. Now Gustav would have to overcome his shock of living with a woman who was no longer asleep.

In Gustav's absence, Alma missed Walter more than ever despite having sent him on his way. His letters still reached her via general delivery. In her confusion and despair, she couldn't keep herself from pouring out her yearning to him. *In my heart, I am with you so intensely, you must surely feel it,* she wrote. *I long for the day when we can live in the open, with nothing to separate us but sleep.*

Though Alma wrote to Walter, at night she dreamed only of Gustav. Her husband was lost and she had to find him. After a long search, she came to a cottage in an overgrown garden. When she entered the dwelling, she discovered a narrow elevator that took her many stories high. *I will ascend to your heights at last, my love.* She emerged in an apartment where she had never been before, flooded with dazzling light. There was her husband's grand piano but no sign of Gustav. She called out his name until he appeared from another room. "Almschi!" he cried. "My madly beloved Almschi!" His play of expressions — from earnest to angry to indifferent to adoring — was clearer than it had ever been.

When Gustav arrived back from Holland, he seemed electrified, as if he, too, had suddenly been jolted out of an eight-year slumber. The two of them set off on a long walk to discuss the many revelations he had gleaned from his four-hour session with Dr. Freud.

"Normally, psychoanalysis takes years," Gustav told her. "But Freud found the seed of my troubles in one afternoon. The problem isn't that I'm too old for you, as I feared. Freud said my age is part of what attracted you. You lost your father when you were only thirteen, just on the cusp of adolescence. You idolized him and unconsciously sought an older man to replace him."

These words gave Alma pause. She stooped to pick an alpine aster and twirl it in her fingers. Yes, Papa was the colossus around which her childhood had revolved, and she had never recovered from the loss of him.

"It's true," she said, tucking the delicate purple flower into the buttonhole of Gustav's waistcoat. "I wanted a man who was wiser than I was. Someone brilliant and accomplished. A man I could look up to. But what made you choose me, Gustav?"

Why, she wondered, hadn't he married the kind of woman his friends would have considered worthy of him. Someone closer to his own age and not the least bit flirtatious. Someone who loved solitude as much as he, who could happily share his ascetic existence.

Gustav seemed evasive, almost embarrassed. Looking away from her, he squinted into the blinding sun, reminding Alma of her dream of finding him in that light-filled room.

"Freud told me I have a mother fixation—a Holy Mary complex. I hated and feared my father, but I loved my mother above all else. Freud says that I look for her in every woman. She was careworn and ill. She limped and suffered under my father's temper. He beat her, Almschi." Gustav took off his spectacles and rubbed his eyes. "Freud said that unconsciously I wanted you to suffer as she had. To turn you into her."

Alma stiffened, twisting away from him.

"Then when you did suffer—from childbirth and the miscarriages—I was frightened and couldn't face it. It only reminded me of how Mama died and abandoned me."

"The summer you finished the Sixth Symphony," Alma said. "Do you remember how you told me that if I was suddenly disfigured by some disease like smallpox—if I was too ugly for any other man to look at—then at last you could show me how you loved me?" Her stomach turned at the bitter memory. *Old wounds ache.*

"But I finally understand how and why I wronged you." Gustav took her hands. His face was flushed in love, as though the clock had turned back nine years and she was still Alma Schindler, the girl he had lost his heart to. "All I want is to make you happy. To win back your love. Freud was right. You're not just my wife. I've been utterly dependent on you all these years. You're the center of my universe. My light."

They embraced, his heart beating its irregular rhythm against hers.

*"She loves me,"* he whispered in her ear. "These words are my life's essence. If I can no longer speak them, I'm dead."

Finding a secluded spot in the high meadow, they lay together in the grass. Alma soon discovered that Freud had helped Gustav recover more than repressed memories. Never before had he made love with her like this, with such tender urgency, loving the hurt away until every part of her glowed. *Yes, there's such a thing as absolute rapture.* As in her dream of the elevator, they ascended to the very heights.

· · ·

The following weeks were like the honeymoon they never had. Every night they slept in each other's arms. Gustav wrote love poetry for Alma.

*Breath of my life,*
*My lyre-play,*
*My storm song,*
*You wondrous being!*

Yet nothing prepared Alma for the thunderbolt of returning from a walk with Gucki to hear the music ringing from Gustav's composing hut. Not his new symphony. Not *his* music at all. But hers. Nearly nine years after he had forbidden her to compose without even having taken a serious look at her work, he was playing her songs.

At first, she froze, petrified. Then she quaked, torn between anger and shame. How had he even laid his hands on her music folder that she'd taken such pains to conceal from him? It felt like a violation. An act of treason against their newfound love. Her music was the most profound, most vulnerable part of herself. The mirror of her soul. Its loss was her deepest wound.

Alma stormed off to the hut. But when Gustav saw her in the open doorway, he smiled at her with such joy that she couldn't say a word.

"Almschi, what have I done?" he asked, drawing her down beside him on the piano bench. "These songs are good. They're excellent!"

She could not overcome the sheer unreality of seeing her song "Laue Sommernacht" on her husband's piano. Of hearing him play and sing it for her with such feeling.

*Upon a mild summer night, beneath a starless sky*
*in the wide woods, we were searching in the dark*
*and we found each other.*

*We found each other*
*in the wide woods, in the starless night.*
*Our entire life we only groped along,*
*only seeking, until you, my love,*
*shone in your darkness!*

Alma kept shaking her head, still not trusting that the forced silence of her music had ended. *I was a girl when I wrote this. My poor forgotten music.*

"It's so atmospheric," Gustav said. "You approach the text with such sensitivity. Love shimmers in every note. It reveals your essence, Almschi."

"Don't patronize me!" After all they had been through, Gustav's condescension would be more than she could bear. How poor and half-formed her work was compared to his.

"I'm not." He wrapped his arms around her. "It's true your songs could benefit from polishing to bring them to fruition, but you have a *gift*. You make such bold tonal experiments." He began to leaf through her other scores. "Some of this reminds me of Schoenberg's early work. Let me play this one."

He selected her song "Ich wandle unter Blumen."

"Let *me* play it," Alma said, with an upsurge of possessiveness.

Miracle of miracles, she was playing her music for Gustav in his composing hut during his precious summer vacation when he should have been working on his Tenth Symphony.

"I wandered among flowers," she sang, "and blossomed with them."

To think that this was the same song she had played eleven years ago, at the age of nineteen, in the Venice hotel the day Klimt had given her her first kiss. All the promise and possibility of her lost youth came flooding back.

"Exquisite," Gustav said. "So full of longing. Let's hear another one, Almschi."

"But why now?" she asked him, struggling not to cry. "After *nine years?*" Why had he put both of them through all this suffering?

"Because I was wrong. God, how blind and selfish I was."

Had he truly gained such insight from a single visit with Freud, Alma wondered. It seemed almost too good to be true. *Can I trust this?*

"I'll never forgive myself," he said, "until you start composing again. This one is sublime." He reached for her song "Die stille Stadt." "Let's choose five lieder to work on. We'll have them published, along with my Eighth."

"You're serious?" Alma thought the walls of the composing hut would start to spin.

"Once you let Alex be your mentor. Now won't you give me a chance, Almschi?" She heard a plaintive catch in his voice, as though he were haunted by both his past mistakes and the fear that he had lost her love and might never win it back. "I want to devote the rest of our life together to encouraging your work."

They held each other, both of them in tears.

*Veni Creator Spiritus.* The creative spirit swelled inside Alma as it hadn't since she was a girl. In his schoolmasterly way, Gustav was just as strict about her composing as he had been about her giving up her music nine years earlier. He insisted that she work on her songs for hours each day. When he was off in his composing hut, she sat at the piano in the main house and revised her lieder. The five songs Alma had chosen to polish and perfect were "Laue Sommernacht," "In meines Vaters Garten," "Bei dir ist es traut," "Die stille Stadt," and "Ich wandle unter Blumen."

*My life's most ardent desire has become clear again,* she wrote to Walter. *To compose! I can scarcely believe such happiness can exist!*

*Why can't I give up Walter?* Alma asked herself with a guilty twinge, now that Gustav was taking such pains to prove his love for her. Surely any decent woman would put an end to this clandestine correspondence. Yet, for all her joy and excitement to have Gustav supporting her music at last, a lingering fear remained. What if Gustav's benevolence was short-lived? How could she go on if he reverted to his old ways? Like a woman who had nearly drowned once before, Alma refused to let go of Walter, her secret lifeline.

After this summer's storm, no man could ever possess her again. Lilith blazed inside her, unrepentant. Fueled by her forbidden fire, Alma began to write new songs, including a setting of Richard Dehmel's poem "Ansturm." This was her ode to the tempest that had shaken her marriage and left a completely new existence in its wake. Her love song and apologia to Gustav.

*O don't be angry with me if my desire*
*bursts darkly out of its bounds;*
*I fear it may consume us*
*unless it gets out into the light.*

*You know of my inner surgings,*
*and when the tides crash on the shore,*
*stranding high over your peace,*
*you tremble, but not in rage.*

# 43

||||||||||||||||||||||||

I n September, while Gustav was in Munich for the final rehearsals of his Eighth Symphony, Alma and Gucki stayed with Mama in Vienna. On this golden afternoon, Miss Turner took Gucki and ten-year-old Maria to the amusement park on Prater Island. With Carl and the children out of the house, Mama invited Walter Gropius to tea.

Seeing her lover for the first time since they had parted in July left Alma so jittery she could scarcely hold her teacup without spilling on herself. Walter had to only look into her eyes to reawaken her longing for him. Her desire continued to burst darkly out of its bounds. As for Mama, she had taken a shine to Walter and he to her. It was Mama's explicit benediction that had enabled their affair to go on.

"One thing is certain," Mama said, as Walter stirred sugar into his tea. "There must be no scandal. Nothing to bring shame on Gustav—that's out of the question. So what to do? You love my daughter. You and Alma must be strong and disciplined. And patient. I firmly believe the love you two share will outlast everything else. You have a very beautiful goal before you."

Walter nodded reverently. Mama rose from the table, patted his shoulder, and then left him and Alma alone. When she closed the door behind her with a gentle click, Alma and Walter sprang into each other's arms.

"How can we bear to wait?" Walter gripped her tightly. "Do you still love me as much as before?"

"Can't you tell from my letters?" Alma kissed him until she ached. She wanted to make love with him here and now—right on her mother's velvet sofa. Of course, she would do no such thing. "I love you every bit as much as I did in Tobelbad."

"Except you've changed since Tobelbad." He traced every curve of her face. "You look so happy. Complete."

"I'm *composing* again!" She sought to infect him with her glee. "My life has a *purpose*."

Walter appeared downcast. "Sometimes I fear your love for me is just a diversion. You used me to win back your husband."

"You begrudge me my husband's affection?" Alma frowned and pulled away. "Do you expect me to live for passion alone, like Anna Karenina? I have a family to think of. Besides, aren't you very young to burden yourself with a wife and another man's child? I fear if I clung to you too tightly, you'd run away."

"Take me seriously." He wrapped his arms around her once more, pulling her body to his.

"I do." She kissed him long and hard. "Why else would I be meeting you here? Risking so much? Why else would Mama be helping us?"

"I'm burning for you," he whispered into her hair. "Burning, Alma."

They fell on the sofa and kissed until Alma thought their combined yearning would set them both on fire.

"Your husband knows, doesn't he?" Walter asked her later, when they had to pull themselves apart for fear of going too far in Mama's pristine parlor with Carl's paintings staring down at them from every wall. "You and he have an understanding, is that what it is? As long as you remain discreet, as long as you don't leave him, he'll look the other way?"

The thought that Gustav knew stunned Alma. "Perhaps he does know," she said quietly, staring down at her hands in her lap. "Perhaps his soul is bigger than yours or mine could ever be."

She jerked at the sound of Mama's brisk knock on the door. "Alma, the children are back."

"Yes, Mama," she called, before pressing her face to Walter's heart. "We must say good-bye for now."

"Will I see you again before you leave for New York?" He clung to her.

"Are you coming to Munich for Gustav's concert?"

He nodded. "I'm staying at the Hotel Regina."

"I'll try to meet you in back of the hotel, but only to *talk*. Trust me?" She kissed him before letting him go.

On the train to Munich the next morning, Alma mulled over Walter's words. How much *did* Gustav know or suspect? When Miss Turner got up to stretch her legs and Gucki and Maria were happily chattering to each other, Alma turned to her mother.

"Did Papa know about you and Carl?" she asked. For now she understood that the dark rumors of her mother's past affairs were true.

Mama's face went bright pink. "Yes," she said, looking out of the window with an air of contemplation. "It was never discussed, you understand. But he knew and accepted it. At least Carl was his friend and student, someone he loved and trusted." Mama blushed again, as though lost in memories of her tangled past.

Back in those days, Mama would have been exactly the same age as Alma was now. A woman with a genius husband, a younger lover, and two daughters. How had her mother managed to keep up the appearance of utter bourgeois respectability? Was it hypocrisy on Mama's part, as Alma had suspected in her younger days? Or was it a deep emotional honesty? Her mother, more than anyone, knew what it meant to love two men.

"Love and marriage," Mama said, still staring out the window. "It's so much more complicated than people realize."

Alma remembered herself just before her thirteenth birthday. She stood with her father on the island of Sylt only weeks before he died of appendicitis. All these years later, she could still see his face, his play of moods. Love, sadness, and peace had seemed to exude from him simultaneously. Never had she felt so close to him, beside him on the seashore in late August while he taught her to see the world with a painter's vision. To recognize all the gradations of color. Every subtle shade and tone. After Papa opened Alma's eyes, nothing could ever be black-and-white again.

• • •

When Gustav met them at Munich Hauptbahnhof, Alma was troubled to see how thin he looked, a feverish brightness in his eyes. "Gustl, are you ill? Have you been working too hard? If only I'd been here to look after you."

"It's only a sore throat. Nothing to be alarmed about. Eh, Gucki?" As if to prove he was fit for duty, Gustav lifted their six-year-old daughter in the air until she giggled helplessly, as besotted with her father as Alma had once been with hers.

Gustav had reserved a suite for them at the Grand Hotel Continental. He opened the door with a flourish. There were pink roses awaiting Mama and Gucki in their rooms, and scarlet roses in his and Alma's room.

"It smells like paradise," Alma said, as she danced around with him. "The Garden of Eden."

Gustav led her to the desk where something far more precious than roses awaited her: the newly published score of his Eighth Symphony, opened to the dedication page.

*For my beloved wife, Alma Maria*

"Gustav!" Alma turned to kiss him.

"There's something more," he said. "Look, Almschi."

Beside his massive score was a much slimmer one bearing the same title page design — a dreamy Jugendstil illustration of a laurel-crowned maiden playing a lyre.

*Five Songs by Alma Maria Schindler-Mahler*
*for Voice & Piano*

Alma was so elated, she thought she would float off over the rooftops of Munich. *I am a real composer,* she thought, with a shiver of triumph.

"Gustav, I have you to thank. For everything."

They tumbled down on the bed and held each other, his tenderness enveloping both of them in a golden cloud. For this was the crux of the mystery of their shared awakening. Gustav loved her, truly *loved* her. Loved Lilith more than he had ever cared for Eve. They were happier together than they had ever been. Men say they want Eve, say they want Holy Mary, while secretly it's Lilith they crave. They follow her deep into the labyrinth. Lilith with her wings and searing kisses. Her wild edge and dark undercurrent. This, her freedom in body and mind, that drove her to compose again. All that passion and creative stirring welled up from the same forbidden place, that velvet blackness between her thighs, the ecstasy that seized her in their lovemaking, carrying her and Gustav to heaven.

Nearly insensible with anticipation, Alma sat in the director's box with Mama and Gucki. Her daughter was bouncing on her seat in excitement — this was the first time Gucki had been allowed to attend one of her papa's evening concerts.

The Neue Musik-Festhalle was a starkly modern edifice of glass, steel, and concrete built to commemorate the 750th anniversary of the founding of Munich. Every one of the three thousand seats was occupied. In honor of this momentous occasion, Alma was wearing the diamond tiara Gustav had given her for her birthday two weeks ago.

Dignitaries, critics, and intellectuals had poured in from every corner of Europe to attend this premiere of Gustav's Eighth Symphony. Sophie Clemenceau and the composer Camille Saint-Saëns had come from Paris. Richard Wagner's son, Siegfried, was here, not to mention Richard Strauss. Alex had come from Vienna, as had Berta Zuckerkandl, Anna von Mildenburg, Alfred Roller, and Justine and Arnold Rosé. The writers Arthur Schnitzler and Thomas Mann were also in attendance.

And there, across the auditorium, was Walter staring back at Alma until she flushed and had to hide her face in her program. Yesterday they had met for a fleeting stroll, the two of them stammering to each other with the awkwardness of infatuated children. Deeper intimacies she couldn't risk. All of Munich was talking about her husband. Any false step of hers would be noted and gossiped about until she died of infamy.

Though Gustav had yet to appear, all eyes were on the stage. Never had Alma seen such a vast assembly of musicians. An orchestra of 170 was arranged in ascending tiers rising toward the organ gallery. Eight solo vocalists were positioned behind them. Three choirs totalling 850 singers, including 350 young children, squeezed into the remaining space to the left and right of the orchestra. Little wonder Gustav had exhausted himself with the rehearsals.

An electric charge passed through the auditorium when Gustav entered through a side door. The audience rose to their feet when they saw him climb the high podium. When he faced the crowd, there was a stupendous silence that was an even deeper homage than the standing ovation that followed. Through it all Gustav stood motionless. A monolith.

Only when it was quiet again, so quiet that Alma could hear her heartbeat, did Gustav turn and signal the choirs to stand. He lifted his baton, paused, then brought it down, unleashing a thunderous organ chord. One bar later, the five hundred voices of the double adult choir sang "Veni Creator Spiritus." Alma leaned forward to see her husband transform those waves of sound into fountains of light.

This segued fluidly into the second part of the symphony—the final scene of Goethe's *Faust, Part Two.* Ancient Latin church music gave way to secular German poetry, Gustav's mystical vision uniting the two disparate parts into a transcendent whole. Goethe's Faust sold his soul to the devil. Yet in this climactic scene, he gained redemption through the agency of the Feminine Divine.

"Virgin, Mother, Queen," Faust sang in his guise of Doctor Marianus. "Goddess, be gracious."

"Look up!" the choir sang.

Slowly and quietly, the Chorus Mysticus began, almost in a hush, taking its time to build inexorably into a long crescendo before mounting into a heart-stopping triple-forte climax that had the audience literally leaping from their seats.

*All that passes*
*Is merely a parable;*
*The unrealized*
*Is now fulfilled;*
*The ineffable*
*Is now made manifest.*
*The Eternal Feminine*
*Draws us onward.*

After the last resounding chord faded away, a few seconds' silence passed before the standing ovation that stretched on for twenty minutes. Facing his audience, Gustav appeared as overawed by their response as they were by his masterpiece. This, his greatest triumph, the crowning apex of his career. Alma cheered and clapped until she lost sensation in her hands. Then she hugged Gucki and Mama. Her husband's most challenging and innovative symphony had been rapturously received and understood by this most eminent public. His detractors would be silenced under this avalanche of acclaim.

Alma and Gustav held each other in the cab back to the hotel.

"It was magnificent!" she told him. "Magnificent! No one in that audience will ever hear another concert like this again."

They arrived back at the Grand Hotel Continental to be swept into a gala reception. Alma sipped champagne with old friends while Gustav's countless admirers offered him their tribute. Siegfried Wagner shook his hand. Thomas Mann nearly fell flat on his face while paying his respects. Justine, overcome with emotion and sisterly pride, threw her arms around her brother and wept in joy. All trace of Gustav's sore throat had vanished. He seemed young, healthy, jolly.

"This is his day of glory," Alex said. "Tonight he's proved that he's Austria's greatest living composer. No one can doubt that anymore. There are even rumors that the Vienna Court Opera wants him back as their director."

Alma shook her head derisively. "After the way they humiliated him, I doubt he'd even consider it."

"Maybe he won't need to conduct at all anymore," Berta Zuckerkandl said. "Now perhaps he can live on his own music alone."

Alma tried to imagine her and Gustav's future together without his having to conduct other people's work as his main source of income. *We can live in the country and devote the rest of our lives to composing.*

"Gustav dedicated this symphony to *you,* I see," Berta Zuckerkandl said, paging through the score that Alma had brought down to show her friends. "Anyone in the audience could understand why. My dear, I've never seen you more beautiful. You look like a queen with diamonds in your hair."

As Berta spoke, Alex regarded Alma with his soft dark eyes, as though he had never stopped loving her. At a loss, Alma offered him a copy of her *Five Songs.*

"I know it's a small thing compared to Gustav's work," she said. "But I signed it for you. A tribute to my great teacher."

When she met Alex's gaze, she felt twenty-one again. Was it love, her boundaryless love, that was the bridge between past and present? That gathered her former and future lives and selves into something whole and complete?

At midnight, Gustav bade his well-wishers farewell. Arm in arm, he and Alma stepped inside the gilded elevator. *Just like in my dream,* she thought. *Except now we rise together.*

Suite 6

# ECSTASY

# 44

||||||||||||||||||||||||||||

I n October it was time to return to New York. A week before their departure, Gustav traveled to Berlin to visit old friends. Alma arranged to make
her own way to Paris, where she and Gustav would meet up before continuing their journey together.

And thus her last forbidden adventure slotted into place with clockwork
precision. Having booked one sleeping berth for herself and a separate one
for Miss Turner and Gucki, Alma boarded the Orient Express in Vienna at
noon. When the train stopped in Munich, Walter boarded and crept into her
couchette. They made love voraciously, as though for the last time. How much
longer could she expect a twenty-seven-year-old man to wait for her? Some
force possessed her and she was no longer a wife and mother. No longer any
one thing, elemental and wild. Utterly free. The laws of feminine propriety
had nothing to do with her.

"Leave him," Walter begged her. "It's what you really want. Let's just run
away together."

Alma silenced him with kisses, lapping his flesh with her tongue as though
she were a mother cat, until he surrendered to her. To this stolen moment in
time, this dizzying rush of desire made all the sweeter by its impermanence.
This wood-paneled sleeping compartment was their sanctuary. Outside the
window, the world rushed past in a blur of darkened, harvest-shorn fields
and slumbering towns. Alma and Walter made love until their sweat ran
together and they lay panting and exhausted in each other's arms, their flesh
welded into one body. She inhaled the musk of his skin as the train rocked
them to sleep.

The following afternoon, the Orient Express arrived at the Gare de Lyon in Paris. Alma held her daughter's hand while disembarking and directing the porters handling her family's luggage. If Miss Turner had any clue as to what her mistress had been up to on the train, she managed to conceal it under a heroic mantle of British reserve.

Alma and Gustav spent one night in Paris before traveling on to Cherbourg and boarding their ship, the *Kaiser Wilhelm II*. Though summer was long past, the sun shone in clemency. The ocean was as smooth as glass, mirroring the heavens. This Atlantic crossing was the calmest her family had ever experienced, the first time Gustav had been able to enjoy the voyage without being holed up in his cabin with seasickness.

In possession of the new camera that Mama and Carl had given her for her birthday, Alma photographed her husband and daughter on the ship's deck. Gustav beamed at her and squinted into that dazzling light, his hands resting protectively on Gucki's shoulders.

*How can I be both women?* Alma asked herself. The resourceful adulteress who had contrived this last rendezvous with her lover *and* the serene wife walking on her husband's arm, her soul lifting to be united with him again, who adored him as the center of her existence? How dare she think she could have it all—an adoring husband, a beautiful daughter, a lover, *and* her music? Why didn't the weight of her sin crush her to pieces?

Alma had never felt closer to Gustav than she did that season in New York. Her husband was a changed man, ever attentive to her and Gucki despite his long hours with the Philharmonic. Like courting lovers, he and Alma walked arm in arm through Central Park. Heads bent together, they discussed their future. The decades they still had before them.

"I'll carry on with the Philharmonic again next year," Gustav said. "After that, we'll have enough saved to retire to the country."

They had purchased land at Breitenstein, high up near the Semmering pass, where Gustav loved to hike. In the summer they would hire an architect to design their new home.

"We'll plant a garden and an orchard, and grow our own food," Gustav said.

"We'll call it Villa Mahler," said Alma.

As they spoke their dreams aloud, their future home seemed to take shape and form before their eyes.


Gustav's second season with the Philharmonic was far more successful than the first. He had compromised with Mrs. Seney Sheldon's committee to create a more popular repertoire that included American composers as well as his standard roster of French, Italian, and German work. His touring schedule took him to Pittsburgh, Cleveland, and various locations in upstate New York.

In early December Alma went up on the train to meet Gustav in Buffalo, where he was directing Beethoven's *Pastoral* Symphony. The two of them stole away on a day trip to Niagara Falls, that popular honeymoon destination. The wild grandeur was like nothing they had ever seen in Europe. The American Falls, over a thousand feet wide, plunged 176 feet into the Niagara River. Farther down were the Bridal Veil Falls and, separated by Goat Island, the Horseshoe Falls on the Canadian side.

The winter day was as cold as it was bright, brilliant sun gleaming on the snow. Every tree glistened with ice and frost. Though the river was frozen in places, the sheer volume of water coming over the falls gushed down in a roar. The plummeting water and rising mist created fantastical ice formations. Miniature icebergs bobbed in the foaming river.

Alma clasped Gustav's hands when they stepped inside the elevator and descended to the viewing platform beneath the American Falls.

"It's like a cathedral," she said.

A cathedral of towering ice filled with the thunder of falling water beneath the high, frozen roof. The strength of the greenish light coming through hurt their eyes. Holding each other for warmth, they spent hours under and near the falls.

That evening, with the boom of Niagara still sounding in her ears, Alma watched Gustav conduct Beethoven.

"Finally, a proper fortissimo," he told her afterward.

Not wanting to spend too much time away from Gucki, Alma returned to Manhattan the following morning. On the train journey back through that frozen landscape, she read Gustav's most beloved novel, *The Brothers Karamazov* by Dostoyevsky. She sent Gustav a telegram when she arrived back at the Savoy.

*Splendid journey with Alyosha.*

He telegraphed his reply the next day.

*My journey with Almiosha even more splendid.*

Gustav returned from his tour and Alma prepared for Christmas. She ordered a tree and dozens of candles and bought presents for her family. On the afternoon of December 24, she sent her husband and daughter out for a walk so she could wrap their gifts. Though Gustav didn't particularly care for Christmas, Alma had never lost the childlike thrill of expectancy. The delight of giving and receiving.

This year their suite boasted a large corner sitting room with a sweeping view of Central Park. Glancing out the window, Alma saw Gustav and Gucki engaged in a snowball fight. For a six-year-old, Gucki's aim was astonishingly good—she landed a snowball in her father's face. Alma observed him cleaning the snow off his spectacles. She could almost hear their laughter rising through the wintery air.

• • •

Later, after Gucki had her bath and changed into her new dress of green tartan silk, Alma was about to start lighting the candles on the tree. With an air of ceremony, Gustav took the matches from her hand. He and Gucki escorted her out of the room.

"It's a *surprise*," Gucki said solemnly.

Smiling to herself at their conspiracy, Alma retreated to her room to read Mama's latest letter. Her mother planned to join them in New York in March and then they could all sail home together. Alma looked up from the letter when Gucki appeared again.

"Papa wants your good tablecloth," the child announced, with a most mysterious air.

Somewhat amazed, Alma opened the linen closet and handed the lace-and-linen cloth to her daughter, who bore it away. A short while later, Gucki returned, this time holding her father's hand. "Follow us, Mama."

Alma accompanied them into the festive room. All the candles were lit and a fire crackled in the hearth. "It's beautiful," she said.

"Mama, *look!*" Gucki turned her around and pointed.

There, on the dining table, was a mound covered with the white table-cloth and pink roses. Alma froze. Something awful climbed up her throat, for it looked exactly like a funeral shroud. But then she blinked and forced that horrific image away. Smiling and clapping her hands, she drew back the roses and cloth to reveal the gifts Gustav had bought for her — the first time he had gone to the trouble of surprising her on Christmas. Her heart over-flowed to behold his offering of love. He had given her a bottle of perfume, a thing that she loved and he detested. Another box held a gift certificate for a diamond solitaire of her choosing. His largess left her speechless.

Gucki cradled the perfume bottle as though it were the grail. "Let me smell it, Mama."

Alma anointed her daughter's wrists with the scent of tuberose. "Now open one of your presents, Guckerl."

She hoped her daughter would enjoy her new ice skates. That Gustav would approve of the tweed traveling suit she had custom-made for him by the best tailor she could find.

They spent their Christmas Eve as a family with no guests to intrude on the enchantment. Gustav played excerpts from *Das Lied von der Erde,* which Alma so adored. Gucki, the young prodigy, performed a piece by Mozart that she had learned by heart. How earnest and intelligent their daughter appeared, seated on the piano stool, her little feet not touching the floor. The candlelight gleamed on her glossy fair hair cut in a bob.

"She has your profile," Alma whispered to Gustav. "She's a genius, just like you."

The three of them sat together on the window seat overlooking Central Park, a milk-white shimmer with illuminated skyscrapers rising like castles in the distance. At the stroke of midnight, all the church bells in the city rang as one. Every boat and ship in the Hudson River blasted its fog horn. A moment of such fragile beauty. Alma held her husband and daughter, and wept without even understanding why.

All the while, Alma had been revising her old songs and writing new ones. She was working at the piano one January afternoon when the telephone rang. The concierge announced that a visitor was on her way up—none other than Frances Alda, the renowned soprano.

"What a pleasure," Alma said, opening the door to the flame-haired beauty.

After taking her guest's mink coat, she invited her into the parlor. The lady was the epitome of elegance, clad in a linen-and-wool suit with a daringly short skirt that revealed her booted ankles. She recently had married Giulio Gatti-Casazza, director of the Metropolitan Opera, and she was one of the Met's brightest stars.

"I saw you in *La bohème* last month," Alma said. "You were magnificent! You must be here to see my husband. Let me get him—he's in his study."

"Mrs. Mahler, it's *you* I've come to see," the lady said warmly. She opened a slim briefcase. "Our mutual friend, Natalie Curtis, thought I would be interested in this." With a flourish, she held up the score of Alma's own *Five*

*Songs.* "I've read through your lieder, Mrs. Mahler, and with your permission, I'd like to choose one to perform on March 3 in Carnegie Hall." The New Zealand–born soprano spoke with such a strong antipodean accent that Alma wondered whether she had understood her correctly. "My personal favorite is 'Laue Sommernacht.'"

Alma thought she might faint. So her published songs weren't just a vanity project. A celebrated opera singer had discovered her work. "This is a great honor, Mrs. Gatti-Casazza."

"Miss Alda, actually. I've kept my own name. Of course, my husband would prefer me to sing as Madame Gatti-Casazza like a good Italian wife. But I worked so hard to establish my stage persona as Frances Alda." She smiled. "But I think you know what it means to be married to a famous man, Mrs. Mahler. Shall we go through your song? You can accompany me on piano and tell me if I'm interpreting it correctly."

When Alma sat at the piano and Miss Alda began to sing, Gustav emerged from his study. He appeared absolutely entranced.

"Mrs. Gatti-Casazza," he said, shaking her hand. "What a surprise."

"The good lady wants to perform one of my songs," Alma said, not caring if she gushed like a schoolgirl.

"*One* of your songs? Why not all five?" Ever the enterprising impresario, Gustav appealed to Miss Alda.

"I'm afraid the repertoire is already set," the soprano said. "As much as I love Mrs. Mahler's songs, I have room for only one."

Gustav glanced at the score on the piano. "Let's hear you sing 'Laue Sommernacht' then."

Shivers ran up and down Alma's back while she played and listened to Miss Alda's heartbreakingly beautiful voice singing her song.

"Is this how you want it to sound?" Gustav asked Alma.

She was too euphoric to think straight. Here it unfolded, her dearest dream come true. Her work was going to be performed in Carnegie Hall. Out of all the songs by all the composers in all the world, the great Frances Alda had chosen one of hers.

# 45

IIIIIIIIIIIIIIIIIIIIIIIII

Alma and Gustav lived in harmony. Walter's secret letters had dwindled, and she was content to let it rest. Everything was as it should be. Her lover's infatuation had run its course, and the affair itself had served to purge her of her demons, allowing her to love her husband with a wide-open heart.

Such happy winter days, walking with Gustav and Gucki through Central Park. Meeting Natalie Curtis at the Women's Club for lunch and sharing her good news that Frances Alda would be singing one of her lieder. Miss Alda sent her piano accompanist to the Savoy to consult Alma's artistic direction. He played her piece for her to make sure he had the tempi right. *This is how it feels to be a professional composer!* When she wasn't working on her own music, Alma continued giving piano lessons to Gucki.

One morning in February, Gustav awakened with a fever and an inflamed throat. Though he didn't seem to think it was anything serious, Alma took the precaution of telephoning Dr. Fraenkel. She looked on while the doctor took her husband's pulse and temperature, and peered down his throat.

"Tonsillitis," Dr. Fraenkel said solemnly. "I'd advise you to bow out of tomorrow evening's concert."

"I couldn't possibly!" Gustav sounded offended by the very notion. "I'm conducting the world premiere of Busoni's *Berceuse élégiaque.*"

Gustav had come down with tonsillitis in the past and had always shaken it off. Apart from a septic throat just before Christmas, he had enjoyed excellent health this winter. Still, Alma was sobered to see how concerned Dr. Fraenkel was.

"Maybe you should do as he says," she told Gustav, after the doctor had left. "Stay home until you feel better."

Gustav shrugged. "I've conducted with a fever before. But I'll rest in bed until it's time for the performance if that makes you happy, Almschi."

The following evening, Alma made sure her husband was warmly dressed. She bundled him in blankets for the cab ride to Carnegie Hall. Dr. Fraenkel came along and joined Alma in the director's box, where they watched Gustav conduct with his usual vigor, his thin body whipping like that of a jockey on a racehorse. Alma breathed in relief to see that everything seemed to be going well.

During the intermission, she and Dr. Fraenkel rushed down to check on Gustav in his office backstage. The doctor had brought aspirin powders, and Alma carried a bottle of Gustav's favorite seltzer water and a fresh lemon. They found him slumped in his chair, as though conducting the first half of the concert had drained the life from him. Alma's throat tightened, but then Gustav looked up at her and smiled.

"I have a headache" was as much as he would admit.

However, he gratefully accepted the aspirin and seltzer water that Alma infused with fresh lemon juice. In his customary fashion, he appeared to pull himself together, as though his health was a matter of personal willpower.

Gustav conducted the second half with fiery brilliance, tilting between passion and vehemence. Half god and half demon. His forty-eighth concert in three months, and he was giving it his all, as though this performance would be his last. An ice-cold presentiment seized Alma. Dr. Fraenkel gripped her hand, as if exactly the same thought had occurred to him.

When all three of them returned to the Savoy, Dr. Fraenkel examined Gustav once more.

"The fever's gone," the doctor said in astonishment.

Alma's heart leapt. So it was nothing, after all.

"I told you so," Gustav said cheerfully. "I conducted myself back to health. So much angst over a sore throat!"

In a matter of days, Gustav's throat inflammation was gone. He was giving Gucki piggyback rides through their suite. Not long afterward, his fever returned, but it was mild and gave him no cause for alarm. Then it worsened only to recede again before returning with a vengeance. At night the fever ebbed, then mounted again during the day. Gustav kept vacillating between illness and moments of respite when he swore he was on the mend. These ups and downs kept Alma on a knife-edge.

One morning he collapsed, as he had done at Trenkerhof last summer. Alma held his head in her lap and pressed cool, damp towels to his chest while Miss Turner phoned the doctor.

"Almschi, I'm not right, am I?"

Gustav's face, deathly pale, glistened with cold sweat. His breathing was shallow and weak. His beautiful slender fingers had gone stiff, curling inward at the tips, as though some poison were paralyzing him. Alma kissed his fingertips, as if her love had the power to cure him.

"You'll have to telephone Mrs. Seney Sheldon," he told her. "She'll need to find another conductor."

Gustav's resignation terrified Alma. She had never seen him this broken.

Dr. Fraenkel arranged for a specialist from Mount Sinai Hospital to come out.

Alma sat at Gustav's bedside and held his hand while the specialist inserted the biggest needle and syringe she had ever seen into her husband's arm. The doctor and his assistant needed to withdraw blood to prepare a diagnostic culture. She had to look away, but Gustav endured his ordeal with stoic fortitude. The procedure was so laborious that afterward the bed, bedroom floor, and bathroom were spattered with his blood.

"We'll take these samples back to the laboratory," the specialist said, when he was finished. "We should have the results in five days." But his drawn countenance gave Alma little cause for hope.

"Almschi, look on the bright side," Gustav said, when the specialist and his assistant had left. "My fever's gone down. Maybe there's actually something to that old technique of bleeding patients to make them well again."

Even as he lay in the bed linens spattered with his own blood, he was trying to inject humor into their tragedy. If they didn't laugh, they would never stop crying. The room looked like a murder scene.

Alma wrapped him in his dressing gown and helped him to the sofa in the sitting room while the hotel maid cleaned away the bloodstains and made up his bed with fresh sheets and blankets.

"You should eat something, Gustl," Alma said. She ordered up an omelet and tea from the restaurant downstairs, and fed him as though he were her child, putting every little bite in his mouth.

"When I'm well again, we'll have to go on like this," he said. "You feeding me. It's so nice."

Little Gucki stared at them, her huge eyes spilling tears. Just seeing the frightened look on the child's face made Alma fear that she, too, would begin to weep. How could that poor little girl make sense of what was happening to their family?

"Don't cry, Guckerl." Gustav kissed their daughter's forehead. "Your mama's looking after me."

Miss Turner, who looked as though she were also trying her best not to cry, said she would take Gucki ice-skating.

"If she falls, catch her," Gustav said. "I catch you every time you fall, don't I, Gucki?"

*How could I have ever betrayed this beautiful man?* Alma asked herself.

After Miss Turner and Gucki had left, and the maid had departed, Alma read to Gustav from his beloved Dostoyevsky. But he still had enough strength to reach forward and take the book from her hand.

"Almschi, you're still so young and beautiful. You'll be in great demand when I'm gone."

Her eyes filled. "Gustav, don't."

But in the same humorous voice as before, he began to list her potential

367

suitors. "Max Burckhard has loved you since you were a girl. Klimt is still single. Alex never stopped loving you. And I daresay, Dr. Fraenkel's quite infatuated with you, in case you haven't noticed. Who shall it be?"

It seemed he made a point of deliberately excluding Walter Gropius from his list.

"No one." Alma kissed him. "Don't speak of it."

"Burckhard is banal. Klimt is a rake. Alex, alas, is married. Fraenkel's not artistic enough to suit you. It will be better if I do hold on and stay with you, after all."

Alma had to laugh and cry at the same time. In the white winter light, she lay beside him on the sofa and embraced him. She held his hands to her breasts and loved him as fiercely, as tenderly, as his weakened body allowed.

"My madly beloved Almschi," he said. "Breath of my life."

*What blooms between us is ecstasy.* Together they had endured every storm. *Our love,* she thought, *is nothing less than divine.* A bliss without repose that blurred the edges of life and death.


"Viridans streptococci," Dr. Fraenkel announced. He had come to personally deliver the results of the blood test.

Alma, seated at Gustav's bedside, exchanged a blank look with her husband. It seemed he was as clueless as she as to what that diagnosis even meant. But it was impossible to ignore how devastated Dr. Fraenkel appeared.

"My friend, you have a serious bacterial infection," Fraenkel told Gustav. "You were born with a heart valve defect, which is itself a cause for concern. The streptococci have now settled in the heart tissue. The result is a slowly progressing inflammation of the inner lining of the heart—endocarditis. Compromised heart function has led to poor circulation—hence the clubbing in your fingers."

"What can be done?" Gustav asked, with clear-eyed practicality.

"You might try Collargol injections," Fraenkel said. "But if you're well enough to travel, I suggest you go to Paris to consult André Chantemesse. He's one of the world's leading bacteriologists."

Black spots swam before Alma's eyes. Her skin went clammy. No doctor in all America was qualified to treat her husband's disease? She sensed there was an awful truth that Dr. Fraenkel was trying to hide.

When she saw him to the door and handed him his hat and coat, Fraenkel hovered over her in paternal concern—or was it more than that? Was there any substance to Gustav's jest that their house doctor was in love with her? He gazed at her with a possessive air, as if the tragic inevitability of her husband's illness would one day make her his own. The thought made her want to spew. Fraenkel already knew her most intimate parts from tending her after her miscarriages. She wanted to shriek in his face. *Stop looking at me like that, as though my husband were already dead.*

"Alma," he said, clutching his hat to his heart. "You need to prepare for the worst."

Alma looked after Gustav day and night, hardly leaving his side. Mama was on her way over to join them and they would all sail back together. Maybe the Parisian specialist could cure Gustav. As long as hope remained, Alma would clutch at it with her last strength.

Their friends, the Baumfelds, had thoughtfully sent over invalid's food for Gustav, including a tureen of soup that Alma now warmed over a spirit stove. When she carried the soup into Gustav's room, he looked up at her expectantly. "Isn't your concert tonight?"

In the wake of his illness, she had nearly forgotten that Frances Alda would be singing "Laue Sommernacht" at Carnegie Hall. Miss Alda had sent her two tickets. This was the moment Alma had longed for her entire life, and yet it seemed obscene to leave Gustav alone.

"I insist you go," he said. "Miss Turner and Gucki will keep me company. I only wish with all my heart that I could be with you and share your moment of glory, Almscherl."

When Alma entered Carnegie Hall, she found Natalie Curtis awaiting her in the lobby. Messy hair, scuffed boots, and all.

"Do you think I'd miss this?" her friend asked, kissing Alma's cheek.

They sat together in the gallery with a bird's-eye view of the stage. Alma had wanted to hide in the back row, but Natalie drew her forward. Even her friend's enthusiasm couldn't quell Alma's nerves. It seemed almost embarrassing to see her own name in the program. What would people say about her? Her song was such a little thing compared to Gustav's massive body of work. He was the genius and she the half-formed dilettante. And what did her music even mean to her if she lost him? What if she was to blame for what might prove to be his fatal illness? *You're a whore. Your affair made him ill. He knew, knew all along. Knew what you got up to on the Orient Express night train to Paris.*

"Alma, why on earth are you crying?" Natalie gave her arm a squeeze. "I know your husband's not well, but wouldn't he want you to be happy tonight? I think we need to toast your success."

Natalie discreetly passed Alma her hip flask of Arizona firewater.

The curtain swept open. The crowd fell silent at the sight of Frances Alda, unbearably beautiful with her red hair and slanting green eyes, her creamy shoulders rising from her sea-green gown. Alma listened to the concert with her heart in her throat, her own song being performed last in the repertoire. Then the moment arrived. Alda's exquisite soprano gave voice to "Laue Sommernacht." Her soulful interpretation rendered the piece as worthy as any song written by anyone. Every note was incandescent with yearning. Alma was in tears, but they were no longer tears of shame. *I did this. I am a composer. All that striving has come to fruition.* Was this how Gustav felt when he directed his own work? Her heart broke for him. If only he could be here to hear Frances Alda sing.

*Upon a mild summer night, beneath a starless sky*
*in the wide woods, we were searching in the dark*
*and we found each other.*

Alma grabbed Natalie's hand in disbelief when her song was encored. The sense of delirium that possessed her was unlike anything she had experienced since the day she went into labor with Gucki and thought she had an entire opera pouring out of her. The applause made her quake, especially when Frances Alda lifted her arm to direct the audience's attention to Alma in the gallery. Her heart raced. She felt dizzy. It seemed impossible that all these people were cheering not for Gustav but for her.

Alma hurried back to the Savoy to find Gustav awaiting her return with the keenest suspense.

"Almschi, how did it go? Tell me everything."

He held out his arms. She kicked off her shoes and nestled beside him on the bed.

"Gustl, they encored my song!"

He looked so joyful, the color returning to his face. "Thank God for that! Almschi, I swear I've never been in such a state of excitement for my own work. I'm so proud of you."

# 46

〡〡〡〡〡〡〡〡〡〡〡〡〡〡〡〡〡〡〡〡〡

M ama arrived in New York to help look after Gustav while Alma packed and prepared for her family's passage back to Europe.

On April 8, the day of their departure, porters were waiting with a stretcher for Gustav. He waved it aside, leaning instead on Alma's arm as she helped him to the elevator. The Savoy's enormous lobby was empty. The hotel manager had cleared everyone out to spare Gustav the humiliation of being gawked at in his weakened state. At the side entrance, Mrs. Untermyer from the Philharmonic committee was waiting with her car to drive them to their ship.

Once they had settled him inside the car, Gustav craned his head to peer out the window at the skyscrapers. "Our last view of New York, Almschi." Gustav held her hand. "Take a good look."

Clinging to her grandmother, Gucki looked frightened and sad. Miss Turner hid her face in her handkerchief.

When they boarded the ship, they found their cabin filled with flowers from friends and people they didn't even know. Gustav cracked a smile. "Who knew we were so popular, Almschi?"

But by the time they lifted anchor, he was already asleep in his narrow bed.

"I hope the passage is calm," Alma whispered to Mama. "He gets so seasick."

Her eyeballs felt like sandpaper. It hurt just to look at her husband's unconscious body, his face as white as the pillow. His emaciated hands lay folded on the blanket. It wrung her out to see him so weak, this man who had once been consumed by fire.

• • •

Alma and Mama took turns nursing Gustav—he would let no one else near. Almost every day, he insisted on getting out of bed to prove he was still alive. Alma and her mother dressed him in his tweed traveling suit and helped him onto the sequestered area of the deck that the captain had screened off for Gustav's privacy. When the ocean was calm, he propped himself up, supported by the rail and his walking stick wedged between the deck boards. Despite his every effort to remain valiant, his eyes were listless and dull, his mouth clamped in a grimace of pain.

When they anchored in Cherbourg, Carl was there to meet them. Together they took the train to Paris, arriving at the Hôtel Elysées at five in the morning. After settling Gustav in bed, Alma collapsed. The journey and her mounting fears had worn her to tatters. She hurt down to her bones.

Two hours later, she awakened to find Gustav on his feet. She lifted herself groggily on one elbow to see him telephone reception to order up breakfast. Before she could quite take it all in, he opened the balcony doors and stepped out into the April sunlight. *Is this a dream?*

"Almschi, it's a beautiful day," he called to her. "Let's order an automobile and go to the Bois de Boulogne."

She jolted out of bed. Yesterday she and Mama had to carry him from the ship to the train, but she rushed to his side to find him fully dressed. He had even shaved. She drew her fingers across his cheek in amazement.

"Gustl, it's a miracle."

"I knew I would be well again the moment I set foot in Europe. New York winters are too cold for me, Almschi. As soon as I recover my strength, let's go to Egypt. We'll see nothing but blue sky."

Crying out in joy, Alma called Gucki into the room to see her papa walking around like a cured man. Mama and Carl dashed in. All of them laughed and wept in relief. It seemed that Gustav was truly saved. Over breakfast, he spoke of the future concerts he envisioned.

"I always wanted to direct *Der Barbier von Bagdad*."

In a festive mood, the entire family squeezed into a chauffeured automobile. Gustav was in raptures over the beauty of this spring morning with the magnolias in full blossom. Narcissi and primroses bloomed in the window boxes. The trees in the Bois du Boulogne were flush with soft new leaves, and in their dappled shade, children chased hoops while gallants cantered along on their warmbloods.

Alma lost herself in the wonder of all this resurgent life after nearly two months of bearing helpless witness to her husband's decline. She reached for Gustav's hand only to discover his flesh had gone stone cold. His face was as white as bone.

They rushed Gustav back to the hotel and summoned Dr. Chantemesse, but the most the world-renowned bacteriologist could do was send Gustav to a nursing home in the Rue du Pont where he ordered more blood tests, only to rhapsodize about the flourishing state of Monsieur Mahler's streptococci.

"I've never seen them in such a marvelous state of development!" He invited Alma to peer into the microscope. "Just like seaweed!"

"What a useless man," Mama muttered, as soon as Dr. Chantemesse was out of earshot.

In desperation, Alma sprinted to the post office to telegraph Dr. Chvostek, the most respected doctor in Vienna, and beg him to come to Paris. Remarkably, Chvostek arrived the following day. After examining Gustav, he urged Alma to take her husband on the next express train to Vienna, where he could be cared for in the Sanatorium Loew.

Hearing the news, Gustav smiled for the first time that day. "Home to Vienna. What a relief."

Vienna, the city that had spit him out like a broken tooth.

Gustav was so weak, he had to be delivered to the Gare de Lyon by ambulance, then slid onto the train on a stretcher. Alma winced at the sight of the orderlies trying to manipulate the stretcher down the narrow corridor without accidentally tipping Gustav on the floor.

The Orient Express night train from Paris to Vienna—here she was, retracing her journey of forbidden love with Walter, this time with her mortally ill husband. It was too awful. Again, the thought reared in her head that she had killed Gustav with her infidelity. *You ungrateful whore. You Jezebel. You destroyed this great man.* How could she face the world again? She would be forever reviled. Blood on her hands.

Alma sat up through the night and watched over Gustav while he slept. Whenever they drew into a station, Carl and Dr. Chvostek stood guard to ward off the hordes of journalists. Gustav's progress toward Vienna resembled that of a dying monarch's. Every newspaper in Germany and Austria demanded quotes on the Herr Direktor's condition.

As the train rattled through the darkness, Gustav opened his eyes and looked up at Alma as she gazed down at him.

"Ah, you're there," he said. "My angel."

She stroked his beautiful black hair. "Sleep, Gustl. You need your rest."

But he appeared wide awake. More lucid than he had been in days.

"How many funeral marches did I write into my symphonies, Almschi?" He laughed, then sobered. "I don't want any music at my funeral. No religious oration. No pomp. Just a plain headstone with MAHLER carved on it. Anyone who comes looking for me will know who I was. The rest don't need to know."

Alma was struck dumb to hear him speak of himself in the past tense.

"I want to be buried with Putzi in Grinzing Cemetery." His voice broke.

Alma cradled him while they wept together. The rising sun now illuminated the window shade. In its fragile pink light, she lay beside him on the berth and stared into his eyes.

"Gustl, I can see straight into your soul." *Your beautiful soul.*

"I forbid you to wear black to mourn me or hide yourself away when I'm gone. See your friends. Go to concerts and plays. I want you to *live,* Almschi. Life is precious."

Her heart split open. She could no longer imagine facing her life without him.

Gustav's room at the Sanatorium Loew overflowed with wreaths and bouquets. A basket of lilies arrived from the New York Philharmonic. But Gustav seemed oblivious to these offerings. He grew more disoriented by the day. Justine came, distraught beyond measure to see her beloved brother barely hanging on to life. He didn't recognize his own sister.

Leaving Gucki in Mama's care, Alma slept in the room next to Gustav's. She was terrified of letting him out of her sight. As long as he breathed, he still lived. He was still hers. Even now, in his confused state, her presence seemed to mean something to him.

"My Almschi," he said, over and over.

When Mama brought Gucki to see him, Gustav found the strength and clarity to take their daughter in his arms. "Be a good girl, my child."

On his fifth day in Sanatorium Loew, Gustav began to fight for each breath. The doctors gave him oxygen. Afterward, he lay dazed, propped on his pillows and conducting with one finger. As Alma watched him, he turned to her and smiled radiantly, as though he had just glimpsed a world of such beauty that she couldn't even imagine.

"Mozart," he said, with huge, shining eyes.

A few hours later, he fell into a coma.

The doctors let Carl sit with Gustav until the very end but forced Alma to leave, even to vacate the room beside her dying husband. She simply could not understand how they could be so callous as to drive her away. Was it because they feared a woman's hysteria and grief? Dr. Chvostek put her into a hired cab and sent her home to her mother, as though she were no older than Gucki. Wrenched from her husband's side, Alma felt as though she had been flung out of a train in a foreign country. *I have no place on earth.*

Gustav died the following night at 11:05 p.m. in the midst of a thunderstorm. He was fifty years old. Sleepless with anguish, Alma fell ill with a fever that turned into pneumonia. Sick in body and soul, she kept twisting in bed to gaze at Gustav's photograph on her bedside table. Never had the words "till death do us part" seemed so brutal. *How can it be that I'm separated from you forever?*

She was too ill to attend his funeral. Even if she had been well, her stomach turned at the very notion of watching her husband being shoved into a grave. How could that radiant man be a corpse inside a coffin? *Gustav, you are light. Pure light.*

While she stared at his photograph, his Second Symphony of transfiguration and transcendence played inside her head. His soul had broken free of his wasted body even as hers remained imprisoned in her flesh. The death mask Carl had made of Gustav watched over her from its place of honor on her bookcase. Fighting her weakness, she wrenched herself up from her sickbed. Taking the death mask in her hands, she kissed its lips.

In her grief, she could hardly eat or drink.

"Keep this up, and you'll soon be where your husband is," Dr. Chvostek said.

That only made Alma smile. She imagined stepping through the veil to find Gustav and Putzi waiting for her. How could she resist such longing and temptation?

After the doctor left, she drifted off to sleep. Hours later, she awakened from a dream of Gustav's Second Symphony to see a small figure wreathed in the late afternoon sunlight. Shining hair and eyes as wide as heaven. The figure seemed to be made entirely of radiance. Was it an angel come to take her away? She cupped a white peony in her little hands.

"Mama," Gucki said, offering the flower.

Her daughter, the only thread keeping her in this world. The beautiful little girl whom she had so sadly neglected during Gustav's illness. Alma drew back the covers and made room for her child. Burying her face in Gucki's hair, she smelled her clean skin. Anna Justine, angel of life, calling her mother back from the void.

Alma's convalescence was long and slow. But Gucki and music were her door back into the world of the living. For Gustav's soul lived on in his symphonies, and Gucki likewise craved the comfort of her father's music. Forcing herself out of her sickbed, Alma dressed and dragged her weakened body to the piano where she had composed her first lieder. And there she took her place beside her seven-year-old daughter. Alma played and played. Sometimes she and Gucki played together. Other times, her daughter sang. Alma and Gucki made music all day long. They took their meals at the piano. Alma played through Gustav's symphonies and song cycles until at last she had finished his entire monumental repertoire.

Then there was only her music left. Her songs. She played them over and over, scarcely believing that she had written them. Gucki sang the lyrics in her pure, high voice. The voice of innocence.

On a warm July afternoon, Alma played piano with the windows open, the curtains fluttering as wide as wings. Gucki's and Maria's voices drifted in from the garden. Alma smiled to hear her daughter laughing and playing again as a child should. Glancing up from her score, Alma saw Mama in the doorway.

"Alma, you have a visitor."

She shook her head. "I'm not seeing anyone. Take their card. I'll write them a note."

In the past seven weeks, Alma had been deluged with condolences. Her mail, opened and unopened, piled as high as a snowdrift. Dr. Fraenkel wanted to come to Vienna and whisk her away on a trip to Corfu. She rooted her fingers stubbornly on the piano keys.

Mama merely stepped aside, revealing the tall figure behind her. Walter.

Alma opened and closed her mouth, then rose shakily from the piano bench. Was it truly him, come all the way from Berlin? Mama closed the door behind her while Walter slowly crossed the room. Moving with a lion's grace, he was just as handsome and elegant as she remembered. He took her hands and they searched each other's eyes.

"I'm so sorry for your loss," they said in unison. Walter was mourning his father's death.

"I wasn't expecting you," Alma said. "I didn't know if you would come."

Their correspondence had been sporadic at best.

"I wanted to wait a decent interval after your husband's funeral." Walter bowed his head.

Alma nodded, her eyes filling. Walter pulled her into his arms. For a long while they held each other in silence, both of them too choked to speak.

"Now we've known each other for more than a year," Walter said.

As a widow, Alma could lift her face to his and kiss him without betrayal. Lean into his embrace. Gustav had wanted her to go on living. *Life is precious.* Yet she and Walter hadn't seen each other in eight months and they were both bereaved. To think that this was their first meeting since their night of love on the Orient Express back in October. Alma felt like a completely different person from the miserable wife who had fallen so desperately in love with Walter at Tobelbad the previous summer.

"It's been hard for you," he said. "I can see how you've suffered, looking after him until the end."

Alma couldn't keep herself from crying. "I never realized how much he needed me. He was such a noble soul. Even when he was dying, that man's love was like nothing I ever—" She swallowed back her words. How could she be telling this to Walter? But she wanted him to understand the heaven and hell she had gone through this past year. She yearned for his empathy. Let him hear her truth and love her, scars and all.

"What do you mean his *love?*" Walter took a step back. "You weren't intimate with him, were you?"

The very question left Alma floored. "He was my husband."

Walter expelled a sharp breath. "So when did you become his wife again? I thought he was impotent."

Alma closed her eyes, unable to get over her incredulity. Had Walter truly been that naïve? "I was *always* his wife. Of course, I loved him. I gave him everything."

Walter rubbed his eyes as though he could no longer bear to look at her. "So you can't be faithful to anyone then? Not to him and not to me."

Alma reeled as though he had punched her. "How dare you? You had no

379

qualms about loving another man's wife, but now you lecture *me* on being faithful?"

"You were never mine! Only his. Your love letters to me were full of Gustav. His health. His music. His praise of your music. You're still his." He waved his hand at the stack of Gustav's scores beside the piano. At Rodin's bronze bust of Gustav on the sideboard.

"Walter, please." Alma reached for his hands and spoke from the depths of her heart. "I *love* you. Let me love you."

"I wonder," he said coldly, "if you can truly love any man."

Stung, she fought down the urge to slap him. "And you?" she asked him. "Do you love me?"

"I honestly don't know anymore." His eyes were flinty as he pulled free from her grasp. "You're a different woman than I thought you were. I think it's best if I go."

Shaking in anger and hurt, Alma grabbed him by the lapels and forced him to look her in the eye. "After all the risks I've taken for you, all the torture we *both* caused Gustav, you want to just walk away."

His eyes slid past hers. "I need to think things through, Alma."

She let him go. Watched him stumble away. He nearly bashed his head on her mother's hanging lamp on his way out of the room. When he was gone, her lungs deflated. Too numb for tears, she sank onto the piano bench. *First I had two men. And now I have none.* She stared blankly at her music.

Did Walter's abhorrence prove that she was an awful woman? Not only had she destroyed Gustav with her betrayal, she was a heartless monster incapable of real love. That parting look Walter had given her, as though she were pure filth. A cesspool that unsuspecting men could drown in. So vile that no man would ever be able to love her once he knew how truly depraved she was inside.

Alma began to play her song "Ansturm." Her voice cracking in pain, she sang, giving herself to the crescendos. For the first time in her life, she stood entirely alone. Beholden to no one. Not to a husband. Or to a lover. Or to Mama and Carl. *Even if I am a bad woman, I'm my own bad woman.* Alma played her song defiantly to its end.

*Gustav loved me, truly loved me, for exactly who I am.* If a soul as profound and wise as he could love her so deeply, then surely there must be something about her that was loveable. She cupped her hands over her face and sobbed, stirred to her depths. Love surged inside her. For her departed husband. For her living daughter. For this precious life.

*What if there are no good women or bad women?* she asked herself. What if pure and impure, faithful and loose, madonna and whore were simply poisons used to reduce a healthy woman to a gibbering, nerve-sick wreck? *Men make the rules and we break them so we don't go mad.* And what if she were not just one color or hue, dark or light, but the whole spectrum? As in Goethe's *Faust,* the Eternal Feminine was not just the Holy Virgin but also the Magna Peccatrix, the great sinner. Golden Lilith bloomed inside her. Every facet of womanhood, sacred and profane, from the heights to the depths. What if every woman, her included, embodied all of it? The paradox and totality.

The time had come to face life again with wide-open eyes. Playing her music, Alma saw her future open before her. *I will leave my mother's house.* Even though Carl thought it unseemly for the Widow Mahler to rent her own apartment, Alma resolved to do just that. Tomorrow she would begin making enquiries to find a new home for her daughter and herself. *At the age of nearly thirty-two, I am finally my own woman.*

Alma began to play a song she had written as a girl, her setting of Otto Julius Bierbaum's poem "Ekstase." Ecstasy. *For you, Gustl.* For her husband who had returned to the ineffable. In death, in life, Gustav would always be a part of her. Always.

*God, your heavens are now revealed to me,*
*And your wonders lie before me*
*Like meadows in May, shimmering beneath the sun.*

*You are the sun, my god, and I am with you.*
*I see myself ascending into paradise.*
*Your light surges within me like a chorale.*

*Then I, the wanderer, open my arms wide*
*And fade into the light like the night*
*Surrendering into the red burst of dawn.*

Alma rose from the piano and stepped outside into the sunlight for the first time in seven weeks. *Today I know the eternal source of all strength.* Kneeling beside Gucki on the green grass, Alma hugged her daughter. *It is in nature, in the earth, in the people I love.* She would go on living with her head lifted high but with her feet on the ground where they belonged.

*There are so many different lives and selves within one woman's life,* Alma reflected. As a girl, she had dreamed of living for her music, of composing operas and symphonies. Then, for nine years, she was the wife and muse of a great man. Now she was a widow with a half-orphaned daughter to raise by herself. How many more incarnations were still in store for her? She was on her own, as unfettered and free as a woman could be, even as her grief cracked her wide open.

What new life might emerge? What new woman?

# HISTORICAL
# AFTERWORD

|||||||||||||||||||||||

Readers will be interested to know that after Mahler's death in 1911 Alma went on to publish two more collections of lieder: *Four Songs for Voice and Piano* in 1915 and *Five Songs for Voice and Piano* in 1924. Three additional songs were discovered posthumously, two of which were published in 2000. Beyond these seventeen surviving lieder, nothing else remains or has been found. We do know that, according to her early diaries, Alma composed or drafted more than a hundred songs, various instrumental pieces, and the beginning of an opera. These "lost" works may have been destroyed in World War II after Alma fled Austria and left most of her belongings behind, *or* she may have destroyed them herself. We will never know what posterity might have lost.

Her surviving songs are now regularly performed and recorded, and are available on CD and YouTube. Susanne Rode-Breymann's *Die Komponistin Alma Mahler-Werfel,* Sally Macarthur's "The Power of Sound, the Power of Sex: Alma Schindler-Mahler's *Ansturm*" in *Feminist Aesthetics in Music,* and Diane W. Follet's luminous essay "Redeeming Alma: The Songs of Alma Mahler" were crucial texts in my portrayal of Alma as a composer. The exhibition "The Better Half—Jewish Women Artists Before 1938" at the Jewish Museum of Vienna was pivotal for my portrayal of the sculptor Ilse Conrat and the prevailing and crushing misogyny that all creative women in early twentieth-century Vienna were up against.

Mahler's death left Alma a very well-to-do widow. Shortly after we leave her in the novel, she made good on her aspiration for an independent life, finding an apartment for herself and her daughter. In 1912 she began a head-long, turbulent affair with the young Oskar Kokoschka. The artist immortalized their passion in his iconic painting *The Bride of the Wind*. But when Kokoschka's behavior became rather too alarming (he was obsessed with her dead husband and liked to dress in Alma's clothing and sign his letters with her name), she broke off with him and reconciled with Walter Gropius. Alma and Gropius married in 1915 and had a daughter, Manon, but Gropius's lingering jealousies of Alma's former love interests cast a shadow on their marriage. In 1917 Alma fell in love with the young poet Franz Werfel, and in 1918, she gave birth to a son, Martin, who died in infancy. After divorcing Gropius in 1920, Alma helped nurture Werfel's career as he went on to become a best-selling novelist. They married in 1929. In 1938, only weeks before the Nazi Anschluss, they fled Austria (Werfel was Jewish) and later dramatically escaped Vichy France by hiking over the mountains into Spain, where they eventually reached Lisbon and sailed to the United States. They lived in Los Angeles, where Werfel worked as a novelist and Hollywood scriptwriter.

After Werfel's death in 1945, Alma moved to New York, where she championed Gustav Mahler's posthumous reputation and was an inspiration to the young Leonard Bernstein. She died in New York in 1964 and is buried in Grinzing Cemetery, Vienna, with her daughter Manon Gropius, who died of polio at the age of eighteen.

Anna Justine Mahler, known by her childhood nickname Gucki in the novel, was Alma's only child to outlive her. Unlike her mother, Anna succeeded in fully realizing her artistic dreams, becoming a celebrated twentieth-century sculptor. Her bronze bust of Gustav Mahler is housed in the Concertgebouw in Amsterdam, one of her late father's most beloved concert venues.

Alma's sister Gretl was permanently institutionalized for her mental illness in the autumn of 1911. She died in an asylum in 1940, possibly the victim of a Nazi-run euthanasia program.

• • •

Trying to capture Alma's essence in one novel proved to be an extraordinary challenge—she was truly a larger-than-life woman.

This is a work of fiction, but the major events and characters in the novel are based on fact, including Alma's friendship with the ethnomusicologist and activist Natalie Curtis. In the interest of streamlining the narrative, I have conflated some parties and concerts. For example, Alma did go to see the Vienna premiere of Mahler's First Symphony but not with Zemlinsky. However, she and Zemlinsky went to many other concerts together. My two main research bibles were *Alma Mahler-Werfel: Diaries 1898–1902*, selected and translated by Antony Beaumont, and *Gustav Mahler: Letters to His Wife*, edited by Henry-Louis de la Grange and Günther Weiss. I also drew on Alma's memoir, *Gustav Mahler: Memories and Letters*, edited by Donald Mitchell and Knud Martner.

The biography I found most illuminating was Susanne Rode-Breymann's *Alma Mahler-Werfel: Muse, Gattin, Witwe*. As coeditor of the German edition of Alma's diaries and a professor of music, Dr. Rode-Breymann has unparalleled insights into Alma's life and work. The most fair and balanced of the English-language biographies, in my opinion, is Susanne Keegan's *The Bride of the Wind: The Life of Alma Mahler*. Jens Malte Fischer's monumental *Gustav Mahler* was key to my portrayal of Mahler.

Biographers have differed dramatically in their readings of Alma Mahler's life and their interpretations of her character. She was a complex, transgressive, ambitious, and often perplexing woman full of unending contradictions. In the popular imagination, Alma Mahler-Gropius-Werfel is the mercurial femme fatale with the three genius husbands, not to mention her artistic lovers on the side. The cliché of Alma as the voracious, man-eating, hysterically self-dramatizing seductress leaves a hollow impression. There certainly had to be more to Alma than that to explain why such a brilliant and sensitive man as Mahler loved her so profoundly.

The deeper I delved into Alma's story, the more complex and compelling her character revealed itself to be. Shortly before her marriage to Mahler, the twenty-two-year-old Alma Maria Schindler wrote in her diary, "I have two souls: I know it." Born in an era that struggled to recognize women as full-fledged human beings, Alma experienced a fundamental split in her psyche —the rift between being a distinct creative individual and being an object of male desire. The suppression of her true self in order to give up her own music at Mahler's behest and become the woman he wanted her to be was unsustainable and inhuman. Eventually, the authentic Alma erupted out of this false persona.

What emerged was a free-spoken woman far ahead of her time, who rejected the shackles of condoned feminine behavior and insisted on her independence and her sexual and creative freedom. Like unconventional women throughout history, Alma faced a backlash of misinterpretation and outright condemnation.

But Susanne Freund's 2007 documentary, *Big Alma*, and the more recent German-language biographies, such as Susanne Rode-Breymann's work, reflect a much more nuanced view of Alma. Haide Tenner's *Ich möchte so lange leben, als ich Ihnen dankbar sein kann*, about the five-decades-long correspondence and friendship between Alma Mahler and Arnold Schoenberg, reveals a lesser-known side of Alma, namely that she was a devoted patron of other artists. She provided Schoenberg and his family with much needed moral and financial support. Arnold Schoenberg's daughter, Nuria Schoenberg Nono, quoted in Tenner's book, remembers Alma as a dear and loyal family friend, and is saddened by the tarnished image that some biographers have attached to her. Some people, Schoenberg Nono told Tenner, just want Alma to be bad.

Alma was not only a composer and a patron, but also what in German is called a *Lebenskünstlerin*, or life artist—she pioneered new ways of being as a woman and this in itself was a work of art.

A symphony of gratitude goes out to my editor, Nicole Angeloro, whose insight and expertise are such an inspiration to me, and to my agent, Jennifer Weltz, for believing in this book from the beginning. As always, I remain indebted to David Hough for his copyediting and fact-checking brilliance. Arias of praise go out to the entire team at Houghton Mifflin Harcourt.

I wish to declare my endless love and gratitude to my husband, Jos Van Loo, for sharing my love for the music of both Mahlers and accompanying me to countless concerts, three research trips to Vienna, and a pilgrimage to Alma and Gustav's summer homes in Maiernigg, Austria, and Dobbiaco, Italy.

I would be a much poorer writer without the sisterhood and support of my writers group. Huge hugs and thanks to Cath Staincliffe, Sue Stern, Olivia Piekarski, Anjum Malik, and Livi Michael for sharing Alma's journey with me. I also wish to express my gratitude to Jenna Blum, M. J. Rose, Kris Waldherr, and C. W. Gortner for reading *Ecstasy* in manuscript.

Lastly, I would like to fondly thank all my readers for supporting me book after book. You, dear reader, are the reason I write!